ABOUT THE AUTHOR

Cathryn Hein is the best-selling author of eleven rural romance and romantic adventure novels, a Romance Writers of Australia Romantic Book of the Year finalist with *Santa and the Saddler*, and a regular Australian Romance Reader Awards finalist.

A South Australian country girl by birth, Cathryn loves nothing more than a rugged rural hero who's as good with his heart as he is with his hands, which is probably why she writes them! Her romances are warm and emotional, and feature themes that don't flinch from the tougher side of life but are often happily tempered by the antics of naughty animals. Her aim is to make you smile, sigh, and perhaps sniffle a little, but most of all feel wonderful.

Cathryn currently lives in New South Wales at the base of the Blue Mountains with her partner of many years, Jim. When she's not writing, she plays golf (ineptly), cooks (well), and in football season barracks (rowdily) for her beloved Sydney Swans AFL team.

To discover more about Cathryn and her books, visit cathrynhein.com

Facebook: facebook.com/cathrynhein
Twitter: @CathrynHein

Also by Cathryn Hein

Rural Romance
The Country Girl (coming 2018)
Chrissy and the Burroughs Boy (coming 2017)
Wayward Heart
Santa and the Saddler
April's Rainbow
Summer and the Groomsman
The Falls
Rocking Horse Hill
Heartland
Heart of the Valley
The Horseman's Promise

Romantic Adventure
The French Prize

Heart

OF THE VALLEY

CATHRYN HEIN

First published 2012

This edition published by Cathryn Hein 2016

ISBN 9780994467485

Heart of the Valley is a work of fiction. All names, people, places, businesses, events or incidences, are fictitious and a product of the author's imagination. Any similarities to actual people, living or dead, or actual places or events are entirely coincidental.

Cover Art by Kellie Dennis at Book Cover by Design www.bookcoverbydesign.co.uk

For Jim

ONE

BROOKE CANTERED INTO THE RING, heart pumping. The brightly coloured bunting separating the Ardellan Agricultural and Horticultural Society's showjumping rings flapped and whirred in the early autumn breeze. A brief squeal sounded over the tannoy as the announcer turned on his microphone. Brooke placed her hand on Poddy's dark bay neck and stroked his tense muscles, circling at the canter as she settled him.

'Next in the final round of our feature showjumping event, the Carlyle Transport Stakes, we have Brooke Kingston from Pitcorthie in the Upper Hunter Valley, riding K D Poseidon.'

A smattering of applause sounded from the showground's historic iron-laced grandstand. Brooke halted in front of the ground jury's box and saluted. Poddy shuffled with impatience, head shaking at the hold on his mouth. The bell rang, signalling the start of their forty-five-second countdown—the maximum time permitted before commencing their round. Acknowledgement complete, Brooke eased Poddy into another canter, shortening his stride until he bounced along like a rubber ball, power concentrated on his hocks, a coil of energy wound tight.

As they approached the start flags she leaned forward to whisper into his twirling, black-tipped ears. 'Let's blow 'em away, Pod.'

The words out, she released her hold.

Poddy exploded through the gates, sailing over the first fence, landing cleanly, hunting for the next. Brooke braced her legs, using them to wheel his body into the sharp turn and racing him towards the second obstacle. He lined it up, calculating ahead, his muscles already stretching in anticipation of her aid to lengthen his stride. Bounding over, they hurtled to the next fence, a straight upright, and took it at an angle, cutting the corner and saving valuable time.

A multicoloured oxer followed, then a rustic gate. Poddy's hoof rattled the timber but Brooke barely heard it, her mind on the approaching combination—another upright succeeded two short strides later by a parallel bar. Poddy tossed his head, fighting as she reined him in. Stride set, she lowered her weight, driving him forward. Up they rose, then down, two compact strides and up again. Excitement trilling through her veins, she gave him his head and urged him home.

They took the final triple bar at a gallop, tearing through the finish flags and out of the ring, almost barrelling over a fat pony as Brooke fought to pull up. High on adrenaline and laughing from the sheer thrill of the jump-off, she cantered back to the ring edge, joyfully slapping Poddy's sweaty neck.

She pulled up alongside Andrew Chiang, who was lounging in his saddle with a deceptively sleepy look on his face. Tanned from a long Australian summer, his Chinese-Australian skin glowed golden and lustrous, the colour set off by a black bespoke riding coat cut to make the most of his lean figure. His long, slim but muscled legs, encased in pristine white breeches, dangled free of the stirrups, the buffed surface of his long, black, hand-crafted leather boots as glossy as Poddy's coat. Only his helmet, a bulbous monstrosity they were all forced to wear at events, spoiled the picture of privileged glamour.

Andrew's long-nosed dapple grey regarded them with equally

sleepy eyes before returning to his doze. Like Poddy, Sir Barnaby—or Barney, as he was fondly known—had seen it all before.

Brooke poked her tongue out and grinned. 'Beat that, Chiang-man.'

He raised his eyebrows and tilted his head, the unsecured strap of his helmet swinging. 'You call that fast?'

Poddy snorted and shook his mane as though insulted. He jigged on the spot, nostrils flaring and wet neck shining like polished timber, still high on the fever of the jump-off.

She rolled her eyes. 'You won't do better.'

'Want a bet?'

She eyed him, heart still pounding, breath still coming short. He had that look on his face, the mischievous one that had dragged her into trouble more times than she could remember.

Oh, well, nothing like living dangerously. 'What's the prize?'

He licked his lips, theatrically preparing them for a sloppy kiss. 'You. Tonight. On top of the Ferris wheel.'

She shook her head, smothering her laughter, knowing the come-on was faked. They'd known each other since they were ten, when Pony Club and children's games ruled their lives. Kissing Andrew would be like kissing one of her brothers. 'How about dinner instead?'

'Wuss.' He wiped his mouth on the back of his hand and fastened his helmet strap. 'All right. Pub or takeaway?'

She screwed up her nose, thinking. The pub would make a nice change but leaving the horses made her anxious. If it was only Poddy she wouldn't worry—nothing upset the old campaigner—but Sisyphus had a bad habit of living up to his Sod nickname, and her needy other mount, Odysseus—Oddy for short—fretted when left alone for too long.

'Takeaway. I saw a Thai place on the way in to town.'

He gathered his reins. 'You're on.'

Like a machine switched into action, Sir Barnaby immediately perked up. His eyes widened and his ears twirled, alert for his master's commands. Overconfident as always, Andrew threw her a cheeky wink. 'Better get your purse out, Brooke, because when the Barnstormer and I hit the track, you won't be able to see us for dust. You're going down.'

'Not a chance, Chiang-man. Not a chance,' she called to his back as Andrew and Barney trotted off to the warm-up area. Grinning, she slid off Poddy and, chatting nonsense to the horse as she worked, ran the stirrups up the leathers and loosened the girth, before reaching for the lightweight fleece rug with navy-blue and gold trim she'd left near the bunting. The wind held too much of an edge to leave Poddy standing sweated up and without cover.

Show noise filtered across the grounds. The varying calls of live-stock, screams from the stomach-tumbling rides, squeals and babbles of hyper-excited children. Lively sounds of people enjoying a sunshiny day, and very different to the previous year when it had rained so hard they'd practically had to bog-snorkel around the grounds. There'd been one plus that year, though: using her superior driving skills to extract a humiliated Andrew's four-wheel drive from the mud had provided Brooke with crowing rights for months.

Task complete, she unfastened the brass buttons of her riding coat, a dark-navy, feather-light wool-blend jacket with a nipped-in waist that gave her slim, colt-legged and boyish figure flattering curves. The coat was a present from her fashion-conscious mother, who insisted Brooke look her best in the ring. 'Even if you lose, you should still look like a winner' was Ariel Kingston's motto, and one she stuck to with preened perfection. But no amount of expensive tailoring or hairstyling could change Brooke's casual attitude to her appearance. To her mother's eternal frustration, Brooke remained at heart a scruff, albeit a well-dressed one.

She undid the straps of her helmet and tugged it from her head, dragging strands of golden-brown hair from the loose bun she'd hastily fixed that morning. She brushed them off her face, the sweat on her forehead turning cool in the breeze, and wished she'd remem-bered to bring a drink. Or, better still, asked her mother or her best friend Chloe to strap. But Chloe was stuck in Scone styling a bridal party's hair and her mother was at Rosehill Gardens for Ladies Day, the opening event of the Sydney Carnival. Brooke's racehorse-trainer father and brothers needed her mother far more than she did. Ariel Kingston's owner-schmoozing ability was as legendary as her poise and elegance.

As Brooke observed the other competitors and waited for Andrew's round, she nattered to Poddy, the bay's ears twitching as she caressed his nose and blew adoring kisses, telling him what a champion he was. While she loved all her horses, Poddy remained her darling. Her father had given her the prestigiously pedigreed but achingly slow ex-racehorse as an eighteenth birthday present and at first she'd been dismayed. The animal was greener than spring grass, three years old and still maturing, but he possessed the temperament of a gentleman and she'd always relished a challenge. It had taken six years of hard work, frustration and joy to bring him to the standard he was now. And it'd been worth every second.

The steward called Andrew up. He cantered past, holding his big silvery mount beautifully collected, the horse's pace as easy as a rocking horse. He threw Brooke another wink and a cheeky grin before floating gracefully into the ring like Pegasus. The announcer called the combination, the last pairing in the jump-off. Brooke and Poddy still held the lead but only by three quarters of a second and Sir Barnaby was perfectly capable of beating their time. He had before. On multiple occasions.

Brooke tickled Poddy's chin, his black velvety muzzle silken against her fingertips. 'But he won't this time, will he, Pod-baby?'

Her body tensed as Andrew raised his whip hand to his helmet and saluted the ground jury. For comfort, she tangled her fingers in Poddy's mane, grip tightening as Andrew wound Barney up for the first fence. With a subtle leg aid and quiet slackening of his hold, Andrew sent Barney catapulting through the starting gate.

He cleared the first, second and third obstacles with ease, cutting corners and jumping at an angle as Poddy had done. The bigger horse's stride was longer than Poddy's but that made his turns less tight. Brooke's breath caught as Barney gave the oxer a solid rap, only for the pole to bounce back into the cup and stay put. Her fingers dug harder into Poddy's neck as Andrew and the horse easily cleared the gate and made a lightning-fast turn towards the combination.

Barney soared over the upright, a good four inches clear, but his speed carried him too far into the gap. Sensing the danger, Andrew tightened his grip, trying to rein the horse in and shorten his stride. Brooke held her breath, hope rising as Barney took off too close to the second element. Muscles bulging in his rump and as courageous as ever, the horse hauled himself up, his dark-grey forelegs tucked to his chest. His front hoofs cleared the front bar but a single trailing back hoof caught the rail and this time it didn't bounce back into the cup. With a rattle and thud it fell to the ground.

Though they galloped for the final triple bar, Andrew's wry smile showed he knew he'd lost.

'You can buy a bottle of wine with that dinner,' Brooke called as he cantered past.

He wheeled back, grinning despite his loss, and slopped his tongue over his lips. 'Kiss for the loser then?'

She laughed, shaking her head, joining him in the walk back to the float area, Barney blowing hard, his grey coat charcoal from sweat. 'And what would your lovely Mel have to say about that?'

'Nothing. We broke up.'

Brooke stared at up Andrew. 'You didn't? When?'

'Last week.'

'How come you never said anything?'

He shrugged and she cast him a sympathetic look. Sometimes these things were hard to talk about. Brooke had only broken up with her boyfriend of nineteen months eight weeks before. She knew how it felt, how it *still* felt if she dwelt on it too hard. Yet Jackson was never going to last, not after he took that job at the mine and their interests began to diverge so much. It hurt at the time but she could appreciate now that the affection they'd shared in the past wasn't strong enough to keep them going into the future, whereas Andrew and Mel had seemed perfect for each other. Both outwardly warm and laidback, but possessing cores of steely ambition. And they looked stunning together, too. Effortlessly graceful with their sinuous, athletic bodies and expensive clothes. Even their bluntly cut, glossy black hairstyles matched.

She reached up and placed a comforting hand on his knee. 'I'm sorry.'

He covered her hand with his own and squeezed. 'Don't be. It was never going to work out.'

'Why not? I thought you really liked her.'

'Nah, my heart belongs to you, remember?'

'And mine belongs to Poddy so you're wasting your time.' Brooke kissed Poddy's cheek for emphasis, laughing as Andrew clutched his hands over his heart and pretended deep hurt.

They parted ways, Andrew riding back to the stables and Brooke heading for her Ford truck and matching dark-blue gooseneck horse trailer, her transport and accommodation for the two days of the show. The gold Kingston Lodge Racing logo, with its fancy writing and streaming-maned horse's head, glittered brightly on the side.

Unlike most competitors, who housed their horses in the show-ground's ageing stalls and enjoyed raucous nights of bed-hopping and boozing in the town's hotels and motels, Brooke preferred to keep her horses in the gooseneck's custom-designed portable yards. Their night-time snorts, stamps and snuffles helped her sleep, and the gooseneck's facilities, while cramped, were more than adequate for her needs.

Oddy whickered in delight at her approach. She fondly caressed his ears while unhooking the gate to Poddy's yard and leading him inside. True to form, Sod ignored her, concentrating instead on tearing hunks of lucerne from his haynet. Having competed in two classes in the morning—for a second and a fourth placing—the horse was finished for the day and enjoying a well-earned rest.

'Hey, cranky-pants,' she said, ducking into his yard to pinch his bucket of water. Sod eyed her warily as she approached, relaxing and letting her rub his chin when she made no move to strip his rug.

Unlike his stablemates, who both possessed gorgeous natures, Sod had the temperament of a crotchety old man. He bit when upset, bucked when grumpy, shied at the slightest thing and farted loudly at inappropriate times, but he also jumped like a kangaroo, turned as fast as a polo pony and could be as affectionate as a puppy when the mood took him. Of the three horses, Sod would be the one to take Brooke places. Provided he augmented his prodigious talent with some manners.

With Poddy untacked, his coat rubbed dry and a fresh haynet hung, Brooke gave him a last kiss on his perfect white star and left him to prepare Oddy for his class. The cheery chestnut kept rubbing against her as she tacked him up, as though unable to believe she was paying him attention. For the thousandth time she marvelled at his sweetness. He was a lovely creature, although she sometimes wished he harboured a fraction more spirit. In the showjumping game, horses needed to be as competitive as their riders.

No matter their personality, she adored her three boys. Other horses waited at home—her father's spelling racehorses and a couple of youngsters she was bringing on—but Poseidon, Odysseus and Sisyphus were her lights. They filled her heart. She couldn't imagine life without them.

Once Brooke had Oddy groomed, tacked up and booted, she led him out to the warm-up area where Andrew waited with his second string horse, Amazing Jake, for the designer to open the course for walking.

He squinted into the afternoon sun. 'Looks tight.'

Brooke nodded, eyeing the designer who was measuring the third element of a treble with a tape measure. 'But no problem for the Oddster.'

'That sook.' Andrew tugged on Jake's ear. 'Jake'll walk all over him.'

'You want another bet?'

'Yeah, why not.' Andrew rubbed his chin, espresso-coloured eyes narrowing wickedly. Recognising the look, Brooke braced herself. 'How about this time, if I win, you kiss me.'

She made a face and then stopped, staring at him. A knot formed in her belly. He smiled but something in his expression—the crinkle of his eyes or the not-quite steadiness of his mouth—told her he was serious.

This wasn't the first time she'd seen that look. Twice in the last month she'd noticed it. The first occurred on a sweltering evening at Willowgrove, Andrew's luxurious property on the southern side of Scone, when he'd invited her up for a swim in his pool. Instead of her usual modest black one-piece, to help beat the heat she'd donned a silver designer bikini, another of her mother's gifts. As she hauled herself from the water, refreshed after the swim, Andrew's face had stilled. For five squirming seconds he stared at her so intensely she was sure the bikini had become transparent. Embarrassed, she plunged back into the pool and swam to the opposite end only to find on emerging he had his head stuck in the bar fridge and was paying her no attention at all.

The second happened only last Thursday night in the pub carpark after their habitual post-work catch up with Chloe. On the way out, Brooke had spied Jackson with his new girlfriend and though she was over him, her heart had still ached at the happiness in his eyes. Happiness that had been sadly absent during their last weeks together. Noticing, Andrew had walked her to her car, not talking, just staying close, there in case she wanted to talk or cry or yell. They'd leaned against the car and stared up at a night sky cascading with stars. She'd felt his gaze and glanced across. That same intense, hungry expression had skittered across his face and then vanished, making her wonder if she'd seen it at all. But she had, and then, as now, it made her insides tighten and nervous prickles race up her spine.

'Look, Andrew, I—'

The announcer cut over Brooke's words as he declared the course open for competitors.

Andrew handed her Jake's reins, his uncertainty disappearing, replaced once more with his confident swagger. He fixed the buttons of his jacket and tightened his tie. 'Go on. Live a little.' And with that he sauntered into the ring.

Brooke couldn't stop watching him as he walked the course. She and Andrew had been friends for years and other than an experimental kiss when they were twelve, not once had he made a pass at her—not one that she took seriously. He was an irrepressible flirt and made endless cracks about them getting together, but she'd always thought them jokes. Now, she wasn't so sure.

She stroked the thin white streak at the tip of Oddy's nose. She'd never been attracted to Andrew, despite his many qualities. He simply wasn't her type. She liked tall, hardy men with wide shoulders and strong, solid arms that closed around you and kept you safe from the world. Men with sun-kissed hair, stubbly jaws, dirt under their nails and crow's feet around their eyes, who made her insides jangle and her heart gallop with just one look. Not metrosexuals who'd make her feel like she was kissing a relative.

He returned, shaking his head. 'Terrible course. Jake'll be fine, but Oddy . . .' He sucked in air between his teeth. 'Going to be tough for him.'

Brooke threw him the horses' reins. 'We'll see about that. Oh, and that bet? You're on. But if you lose, you have to streak the length of the stables. Twice.'

As she knew he would, Andrew didn't even blink. The man had no shame. 'I always knew you wanted to see me naked.'

'You're forgetting I've already seen your dangly bits. At Pony Club camp, remember? You lost a bet with Darren Spalding and had to jump the grade five showjumping course in the buff.'

He grinned and wiggled his eyebrows. 'Must have impressed if you can still recall that.'

Feigning disgust, she tossed up her arms in an 'I give up' gesture and headed off to walk the course, laughing when he called after her, 'I've grown a whole lot bigger since then.'

Andrew hadn't been joking about the course. It was tight, and although a lower grade with smaller jumps, it was much twistier than the morning's track and would take careful riding. No room for any slips in concentration or she and Oddy would have a rail down, and in this event, with so many other experienced riders competing, a single rail would see them out of the jump-off.

Brooke took her time warming up Oddy, keeping him settled and well collected, cantering small figure eights and flying changes of his leading leg in the dusty warm-up arena. Satisfied with his responsiveness, she cantered him over the practice jumps, patting his neck and praising him when he cleared them without a rattle.

In a fluke of timing, she'd drawn the slot before Andrew, which meant no opportunity to see how Jake performed. Oddy and Jake were of a comparable type, both quivery thoroughbreds with similar-length strides. If Jake struggled around any of the turns, or experienced difficulty with the fence spacings, Oddy was likely to fare the same. This time, however, with Oddy going first, Andrew had the advantage.

As Brooke headed for the ring, butterflies launched in her stomach. She didn't normally suffer from nerves, not in these lower classes, but Andrew's bet put her on edge. Stupid, really, when she had every faith she and Oddy could win.

The steward called her number and she cantered through the gate, one hand stroking Oddy's neck. She bent forward to whisper to him, the horse's ears twitching back to listen. 'Come on, Odd-job, let's show them what you're made of.'

With a salute to the judges, she cantered another tight circle and directed Oddy through the start.

Seventy seconds later she cantered through the finish flags with her head lowered. The horse had motored around the course as smoothly as a Lamborghini, clearing each fence as though it were a thirty-centimetre-high cavaletti. All except for the last. Eager for the line, Oddy took off too early and dragged the top rail. Not his fault. He was an inexperienced horse and she should have kept him reined in. Although inside she cringed at the error, she made a show of slapping his neck and telling him how well he'd done.

'Get ready to pucker up,' teased Andrew as he rode past.

Brooke trotted back to the edge of the ring, butterflies still rampant in her stomach. She'd never reneged on one of Andrew's bets and she wasn't about to start, but the thought of kissing him made her feel flushed and strange. Not excited strange. More weird, fearful strange, as if this one bet could change everything between them.

He went clear, expression exultant when he halted Jake alongside her. 'So, I'll see you at the gooseneck about seven then?'

She pointed a finger at him. 'Don't forget you're buying dinner. And wine.'

He leaned over to nudge her. 'Sexy bloke like me, you shouldn't need any Dutch courage.'

She rolled her eyes. 'Despite what you might think, Chiang-man, you're not God's gift to women.'

'You'll think differently later.'

Making a grossed-out noise, Brooke whirled Oddy around and rode off.

———

Brooke leaned against the sink, winding and unwinding a long strand of her freshly washed hair around her finger, gnawing her lip as she stared at the gooseneck's door. Instead of tying her hair back in a ponytail as she usually did, she'd left it out, its natural soft waves curling locks around her face and shoulders, a curtain she could hide behind should the need arise. Steam from the trailer's tiny shower thickened the air, kinking her hair further and making the cramped kitchenette seem more claustrophobic than ever. She glanced at her watch again. She still had ten minutes to kill before Andrew's arrival, and if they were anything like the last sixty, they'd be long ones.

Forcing herself to relax, she sat at the corner banquette and, with her chin resting on one hand, picked up one of the knives she'd laid out earlier and dangled the blade like a pendulum from her finger-tips. The thick stainless-steel hilt flickered in the light, reflecting the pale faux-timber panelling of the gooseneck's living area.

Many of the best times of Brooke's life had been spent in this small space. Fun nights with Andrew and Chloe gathered around the table after long days competing, drinking wine, playing poker or Monopoly, laughing at stupid jokes and making even stupider bets with one another. Even in the days when she'd been driven every-where by her grandparents the gooseneck rattled with laughter. This was also the space where at sixteen she'd first fallen in love, when Thomas Edwards ignored Chloe's dazzling looks and impressive cleavage, leaned against the shower door, thrust his hands deep into his pockets and smiled crookedly at her with eyes so summer-sky azure they'd made her float right out of her seat.

And now she was going to kiss Andrew here.

She dropped the knife and stared at the table top, tracing a finger over one of the many scratches on its dark-blue surface, resurrecting the memory of that other time they'd kissed. She could still recall the sweet innocence of it, the strange feeling of reaching some momen-tous point in her young life. How the touch of their mouths signalled the end of childhood and the onset of adolescence.

She closed her eyes and remembered the look on Andrew's face, the delight it held, and the way, when they'd parted, he'd entwined his fingers in hers and asked if that meant they were now boyfriend and girlfriend. Unsure if he was being serious, and rattled by the feel-ings his kiss had evoked, she'd blushed and said no. Andrew had pulled away, his expression full of hurt, and for a few days she'd thought that one kiss had killed all that was special between them. Then he'd bounced back as though it had never happened, and their friendship had carried on as it always had, filled with jokes, bets, rivalry and laughter. Until now.

She glanced at her watch again. The hands had barely moved. Even the second hand strained to make its way past the numbers. She wiped her fingers across her forehead, cursing the moisture there, then slumped back with her arms crossed and her mouth pursed. Two seconds later her knee began to jig.

Unable to stand the wait any longer, she slid from the banquette, yanked open the door and clomped down the step to seek the comfort of her boys, each rugged up and bedded down in his portable yard for the night. She fussed over them, straightening rugs, checking water buckets, examining legs for signs of soreness. Tired after his day, Sod let her play with his ears and velvety muzzle without trying to nip. Not to be left out, Oddy leaned over the rail and nudged her arm and she scratched him affectionately between his ears, smiling when the horse lowered his head and revelled in the attention.

She smelled Andrew before she saw him, delicious curry aromas sweeping into her nostrils and making her stomach rumble despite her tension. Giving each of the horses a kiss and a pat, she ducked under the rail to meet him.

'Is that the delivery boy I detect?'

He held up two bags. 'Curry puffs and spring rolls followed by Massaman and jungle curries with steamed rice, and all washed down with a bottle of New Zealand sauvignon blanc. Happy?'

She held the gooseneck's door open and waved him inside. 'Sounds good.'

They settled either side of the banquette and began piling food onto plates. Andrew cracked the seal on the wine and poured her an oversized glass, pushing it towards her with a glint in his eye that only made her anxiety swell.

She leant back with her arms crossed. 'Will you stop looking at me like that? You're putting me off my dinner.'

'Like what?'

'That "you just wait" look.'

He leaned forward, laughter in his expression. 'You mean like this.' He tilted his head and gave her a sultry pout, moistening his lips as he did so. He dropped his voice to sex-dripping huskiness and followed it with an even more exaggerated pout. 'Come on, baby. You know you want me.'

The sight was so comical Brooke couldn't help but laugh. Smiling, Andrew picked up his fork and pointed it at her. 'The trouble with you, Brooke, is you take things far too seriously.'

She opened her mouth to argue and quickly shut it again, conceding that, in this instance, the accusation was probably well founded. She'd taken one of his jokes and contrived it into something fateful, yet she couldn't wipe the impression that he'd been serious when he made the bet. No matter how she tried to dismiss it, she hadn't imagined that look, or the disquiet it instilled.

He waved at the food. 'Come on, tuck in before it gets cold.'

It took a full glass of wine, half a curry and a great deal of horse talk and competitor gossip before she relaxed. Andrew ordered her to sit and let him sort out the dishes. Content to relinquish responsibility, she watched him idly as he dumped the leftovers in the bin and collected plates for washing.

He was wearing clean jeans and a dark-red, fine wool jumper that hung loose on his lean frame. An image appeared in her mind, of Andrew gambolling naked around the showjumping ring, arms held curled in front, tossing his head and snorting as he pranced and hurdled the low fences. They were both only seventeen, young, over-hormoned and still growing into their skins, yet she felt no desire then, and she felt none now. No spark existed. It never would.

He startled her out of her reverie. 'What are you thinking about?'

She blinked and shifted uncomfortably, alarmed she'd somehow made her thoughts obvious. 'Just Oddy. I shouldn't have let him have his head like that.'

He rinsed another plate and left it on the drainer. 'Is that really what you were thinking about?'

She swallowed, not knowing how to answer, and fingered the stem of her plastic wine glass. 'No.'

He wiped his hands on a tea towel and turned to her, leaning his hip against the bench. 'Care to share?'

She shook her head. 'Not really.'

'You were thinking about kissing me, weren't you?'

'Not exactly.' She raised the glass and took a long slug, her nerves ringing.

He tossed the tea towel aside and held out his hand. 'Come here.'

'Andrew, I don't think this is a good idea.'

His expression narrowed, congealing the already thick atmosphere. 'A bet's a bet, Brooke.'

'I know but—'

He grabbed her hand and hauled her up. 'No buts.'

His grip held firm, as if he feared her escape. Heat pulsed from his palm, as intense as the yearning in his eyes. The wine evaporated from Brooke's bloodstream, leaving her coldly sober and desperately unsure.

'Andrew . . .'

He scraped the hair away from her face and cupped her jaw. 'Shh. Don't spoil it.'

She closed her eyes. How could this be happening? This was Andrew, her friend. They weren't meant to be doing this.

His breath grazed her lips, delicately spiced. 'I can't wait any more. I've waited too long already.'

He traced a finger down her cheek and her eyes fluttered open. Andrew's gaze hung on hers. His mouth parted in expectation, and she realised he wore the same blissful expression he'd had when they were children, kissing for the first time.

Carefully, he lowered his head.

His mouth caressed hers sweetly, with care and tenderness, exploring the soft flesh of her lips. As he deepened the kiss, his hands drifted to her neck and shoulders, dragging her closer, squeezing her against him until his erection pressed into her groin. Alarm clanged through her brain, urging her to pull away, but Andrew clutched her tight, a moan rumbling in his throat.

Panicked, she braced her arms against his chest and pushed hard.

He stumbled backwards into the bench, wincing as he connected with its rigid edge.

She shook her head, trembling. 'This isn't right.'

Expression pleading, he held out a hand, a gesture out of character for the overconfident Andrew she knew. When she didn't respond he let it drop. Blinking, he stared at the cupboard above her head.

The curry-tainted air condensed further. Brooke wanted to throw open the door and race into the night, but the look on Andrew's face shod her feet in lead.

'Do you have any idea how long I've wanted to do that for?' he asked eventually.

Her heart spasmed. How could she not have seen this? How could she not have realised his jokes hid truths? Her throat was so choked she could barely whisper. 'I'm sorry.'

He let out a harsh breath. 'Yeah. Me too.'

She hung her head, overwhelmed with guilt that she'd hurt him. 'I don't—'

He cut off her words with a hand over her mouth. Eyes huge, he shook his head. 'Don't say it, Brooke.' Their gazes met, his full of hurt, hers overflowing with sympathy. He dropped his palm and leaned forward to plant a gentle kiss on her forehead. 'I have to go. I'll see you tomorrow.'

As soon as he departed she slipped out into the night to cry into Poddy's mane, mourning a friendship she knew would never be the same again.

———

With three mounts, Brooke had a full schedule the following day, and though their paths crossed frequently, she never seemed to find time to stop and talk to Andrew. She felt his scrutiny, but whenever she looked his way he turned aside as if the very sight of her hurt him.

Sensing something was up, the other competitors cast meaningful glances at one another and murmured behind their hands. Brooke ignored them, concentrating instead on the horses, but her mind refused to settle. Poddy and Oddy behaved impeccably, neither putting a foot wrong in their classes, but Sod, ever alert for inattention, put on a bucking display in the warm-up area so vigorous and inventive it would have made a bronco blush. Brooke ended up on her backside with a mouthful of dust, her white breeches streaked with dirt and humiliation flushing her face, while Sod careered gleefully around the ground kicking up his heels like a naughty teenager, refusing to be caught.

By the time she'd packed the gooseneck for home her movements were sluggish with exhaustion and despondency. In all the years she'd competed, this was the worst show she'd experienced. All she wanted was Kingston Downs, a hot bath to ease her aches and red wine to help her forget.

Wearily, she led the horses into the gooseneck and secured their gates, before lifting the tailgate and locking it in place.

'Brooke?'

She let out a breath, preparing herself, before turning and leaning against the cold door with her hands held tight behind lest she be tempted to touch him. 'Hey.'

As though suffering the same fear, Andrew kept his fists thrust into his jeans pockets. His gold complexion seemed paler than normal, its sheen dull. Tiredness shadowed the skin under his eyes. 'I saw your fall. You okay?'

'Yeah. Just a lovely purple bum cheek to match the bite marks on my arms.'

He smiled a little. 'You need to watch him. He knows when you're upset.'

'I'm not upset, I'm just . . .' She waved a useless hand. She didn't know what she was.

'Upset. Yeah, I know.' He sucked in a breath, vulnerability etched on his face. 'I'm really sorry.'

Her heart squeezed. Tears began to form and sting. This was all so wrong. 'You're my friend. I don't want things to change.'

'But I do. Surely you knew that?' When she didn't answer he shook his head. 'Don't you get it? I love you. I didn't mean for it to happen but it did.'

She closed her eyes and sagged against the float. He loved her. He'd come out and said it and made it even worse.

'Brooke, honey. Don't.' In a stride he had her wrapped in his arms, her face pressed against his chest as his heartbeat raced in her ear. He stroked her hair, soothing. 'It'll be all right. We'll work it out. I promise.'

She sniffed, feeling pathetic but comforted. 'Are you sure?'

'Yeah. I'm the Chiang-man. The best, remember?'

She laughed and he let her go. Sniffing, she wiped his jumper where she'd left tiny teardrops. 'Yeah, you're the best.'

'Just not the best for you.' From inside the float came the rattle of restless horses. Placing warm hands on her shoulders, he twirled her around and pushed her toward the truck cabin. 'Time for you to get going.' He stood by the door while she organised herself, no mischievous glint in his brown eyes, just sorrow. When the diesel engine cranked to life he rested his fingers on the window edge. 'Drive carefully, and if you need me, call. I only have a few things to sort out here and I'll be on the road behind you.'

She covered his hand with hers. 'We'll talk later in the week, okay?'

He smiled and winked, almost back to normal. 'You can bet on it.'

But his humour was a facade. As she manoeuvred onto the exit road, she checked the side mirror. Andrew stood watching her, hands thrust into pockets, shoulders slumped. A washed-out replica of the vibrant man she knew and loved. Hollowness lodged in her heart and stayed.

Every kilometre she covered on the three-hour journey home

seemed paved with guilt. It hung in her chest and anchored her bones, gritted her eyes and sweated her palms. By the time she reached the turnoff to Pitcorthie, eight kilometres from Kingston Downs, she felt shredded with exhaustion.

But home approached, and soon she'd be free to wallow in its comfort. No matter what went on in her life, she could always rely on Kingston Downs to make her happy. Home, her boys and the constancy of the Hunter Valley's magnificent landscape. A girl didn't need much more.

She smiled to herself. It'd be all right. They'd make it all right. Relaxed for the first time since she left the showgrounds, she glanced down for the radio volume knob, hoping for some cheery music, before returning her focus to the road.

The stray bullock burst into her vision like a creature from a nightmare. It stood in the middle of the road, dumb face turned toward her headlights, thick grey body as huge and unmoving as a granite boulder.

She didn't have time to think. She simply acted. She hauled on the wheel, jerking it to the left, her foot slamming the brake. Too late, the truck's headlights illuminated the concrete culvert and deep dips of the dry creek. Tyres locked, she pulled the opposite way but momentum hurtled her forward. The left tyre hit the concrete and exploded. The front listed, skidding the truck over the edge. Panicking, she yanked the wheel, released the brake and stomped on the accelerator, but the truck only kept tipping, forced forward by speed and the weight of the trailer behind. A terrifying screech pierced her ears.

'No. No. No!'

But she'd lost control of the vehicle. The wheel spun crazily in her hand, wrenching muscles. The truck pitched, crashing into the deep drain and dragging the trailer with it. Airbags exploded around Brooke's head and side, trapping her in place.

Somewhere in the darkness, an animal began to scream.

TWO

THE THICK SYDNEY traffic moved like a trail of brightly coloured slumberous beetles in the weak July sun. Brooke clenched her fists around the steering wheel in frustration, and resigned herself to peak-hour hell. How stupid to think she could cut across town at this hour of the morning and sneak in a quick hello at Kingston Lodge before her father and eldest brother Angus disappeared to barrier trials at Warwick Farm. Now she was too late to catch them and would instead arrive early at her parents' Bondi Junction house, and while she adored her mother, lately things had been tense between them. She let out a ragged breath. Who was she kidding? Since the accident things had been tense with all her family, and were getting worse.

As the exit to Anzac Parade neared, she contemplated heading to Randwick and the stables anyway, but quickly dismissed the idea. She'd only run into Mark, and she'd had enough of her brother's smug inquiries. One more comment about her 'little problem' and she'd be likely to thump him. Mark wasn't her favourite at the best of times—they'd never been close, not even as children—but she borderline hated him at the moment. A feeling Brooke suspected was quite mutual. Although why he should hold her failing so against her she couldn't fathom.

She couldn't drive the float any more. Not since the accident. She hadn't told anyone, not even Andrew or Chloe, about the nightmares, of her hands covered in Oddy's blood, his rasped cries of agony shattering her insides like smashing crystal. Even four months after the accident she still heard him. That noise like no other. Of pain, of panic. Then worse, the gradual quietening as his blood flooded the side of the gooseneck, soaking her clothes, staining her skin forever like a dark-scarlet tattoo.

No one knew the extent of her distress and she wasn't about to reveal it. Certainly not to her family and definitely not to that shrink Mark suggested Brooke visit last time they'd spoken. She'd make it through this on her own. All she needed was time, the sanctuary of Kingston Downs, and her horses.

She slid off the eastern distributor and wove her way through the streets, finally reversing her dark-blue LandCruiser into a parking space only a few houses away from her parents' terrace. Theirs was a modest house—two storeys and a converted attic, with a tiny courtyard. A small home for three energetic children to grow up in, but they'd always regarded the stables and the farm as their playgrounds. Bondi Junction was where they ate, slept and were forced to do homework, and by the time Brooke reached her teens, she barely considered it home. That title belonged to Kingston Downs, where, in the days before her pop's arthritis forced Brooke's grandparents to warmer climes, they had farmed and coddled the yard's spelling racehorses and embraced her delightedly against their warm hearts.

Her mother answered her knock, wafting a perfume of turpentine, and for once looking less than immaculate in a paint-splotched T-shirt and jeans, her glossy dark brunette hair caught up in a loosening knot. She wore no makeup, and her skin radiated good health and a rigorous beauty regime. For a woman who'd turned fifty less than a year ago, she had the appearance of one much younger, with only a few fine lines around her mouth and eyes betraying the progress of time. Her soft brown eyes, so like Brooke's, widened before she broke into a delighted smile.

'Brookie!' Slender arms wrapped around Brooke as her mother squeezed her tight and planted a firm kiss on her cheek. 'You're early. I wasn't expecting you for another hour at least.' Ariel released her to look at her properly, tut-tutting and shaking her head in mock dismay as she took in Brooke's clothes—a too-loose pair of jeans with mud around the cuffs, grubby boots, a horsehair-covered windcheater, and hair tied up even more messily than her mother's.

'I had hopes of beating the traffic and calling in to the yard to catch Dad.'

Her mother's perfect eyebrows shot up. 'At peak hour?'

Brooke shrugged and gave a wry look. 'Sod made me late.' Not to mention furious. The rotten horse had thrown one of his temper tantrums while being led to his day paddock and had escaped to the farthest reaches of Kingston Downs where he'd pranced about in the early-morning darkness, nose haughtily in the air, refusing to be caught. Brooke was so angry with him it took a good hour of the three-and-a-half-hour trip to Sydney and a full playing of her favourite band's latest album for her to calm down.

'Ahh,' replied her mother, understanding. She stood aside to let Brooke inside. 'Still no improvement?'

'He's getting better. Today was just a bad day.'

Ariel touched Brooke's shoulder as she deposited her overnight bag on the polished timber floor. 'And you?'

Brooke kept her expression carefully neutral. 'Fine.'

'Are you—'

'I'm fine, Mum. Honest.'

Brooke forced herself to act bright, although the urge to walk straight back out the door was huge. Her mother, like everyone else, was only being kind, although it was this overwhelming kindness causing the rattiness between them. Brooke hated it. The weakness it implied made her teeth grind.

Needing calm, she surreptitiously pressed the middle finger of her right hand into the crease of her left inner wrist and counted to three as she rubbed. She'd learned the anxiety treatment technique from an acupressure site on the internet and found it sometimes helped.

'So what are you working on?'

Ariel shook her head, as protective as always about what the family referred to as 'Mum's little hobby'. 'Nothing important.'

'Come on. Show me.' Brooke nudged her playfully. 'Go on. You know you want to.'

Ariel released an exasperated sigh. 'Oh, all right.' She held up a finger. 'But you're not to laugh.'

Brooke slapped two hands over her heart. 'I promise I won't.'

She followed her mother into the kitchen, past walls covered lovingly in photographs of family and horses. The Kingstons at the races, at the stables and the farm. The three children as babies, crawling on grandparents, horses and dogs. Brooke's father, Christopher, with his first Group One winner and the horse that made his name, Gallant Raider. Brooke aged seven on her hairy black pony Rascal, grin bursting across her face as a show judge wrapped a blue ribbon around the pony's chubby neck.

Noticing a new picture, she paused to inspect it. The candid image caught them all in the courtyard at Kingston Lodge. Brooke stood with her eldest brother, Angus, both slender, leggy, brown-haired and brown-eyed like their mother. His hand was on her hair, ruffling it even messier as she tried to tickle his stomach. Beside them, but slightly apart, amused but not laughing as they were, stood her other brother, Mark, dressed as he almost invariably was in a suit, tie perfectly knotted, hair cut brutally short to disguise his natural wayward curls. Their parents were also laughing, but not at Brooke and Angus. Their eyes were focused on each other, soft with adoration.

'Who took this?' she called out to her mother, who'd walked on. 'I don't remember it.'

Ariel returned to her side. 'Dennis,' she said, referring to their farrier. 'It was back in March, before your—' She halted and cast Brooke a sympathetic look, 'accident' hanging unsaid and gallows-like between them. 'When you came down for your father's birthday. Dennis had bought a new camera and was testing it out, and snapped this. We thought he was only photographing the horses but apparently he was madly snapping away at everything. It's good, isn't it?'

Brooke nodded, her pleasure in the photograph ruined. The inference that they'd been happy then, as opposed to now, post-accident, made her insides feel like lead.

Sensing her anguish, her mother touched her hand. 'Come on. Let's inspect my latest creation. But remember, no laughing.'

Sucking in a breath, once more feigning brightness, she nodded and continued her journey to the rear of the house, past the kitchen and open dining area, immaculate and tastefully decorated. Her mother favoured natural tones and textures. The walls were off-white, the furniture pale timber, the kitchen appliances burnished stainless steel. Colour came from strategically placed vases and knick-knacks—a delicate bronze figurine in the centre of the dining table, a red and gold Murano glass serving platter bought on a holiday to Venice, a glossy-leaved potted ficus in the corner, and a pair of Ariel's landscapes on the far dining-room wall. The effect was modern, light and, despite the pale tones, warm.

Brooke stepped through a set of stained-timber French doors and onto the covered deck that comprised half the terrace's tiny backyard. A canvas the size of three A4 sheets balanced on a timber easel, washed by light streaming through the deck's strip of Laserlite roofing. Nearby stood a timber and scrolled-iron stool and matching table, upon which a large wooden box lay open. Tubes of paint in various stages of use were clustered inside, while the lid held a rag and a palette knife. Brooke sniffed appreciatively, conjuring a long-forgotten scent of childhood. A time when her mother was less involved in the yard and had more leisure to indulge her hobby.

As Ariel hovered, Brooke stood in front of the easel and studied the painting, a frown on her face as she contemplated the thick brushstrokes and built-up paint. She took a step back, the frown fading as she saw what her mother had done. A colourful crowd, restless and excited, stood impatiently on the lawn at Royal Randwick. The people were indistinct, without faces and with abstract bodies, but their tension radiated from the canvas, almost melting the cleverly slathered layers of paint. She could sense the crane of their necks, the tight clutch of their race books, their excited chatter. In front, cantering past, were several glossy brown slicks of horses, daubs of colour crouched on their backs. It was the most alive painting Brooke had ever seen. A condensation of drama. Thoroughbred racing made real in art.

She turned to her mother in amazement. 'It's incredible.'

'You like it?'

'Like it?' Brooke shook her head. 'You don't *like* paintings like this, Mum. You fall in love with them.' She stared back at the scene, mesmerised. 'It makes me feel like I'm there, on race day. I can almost hear the crowd.'

She looked up. A bright pink flush of pleasure rose up Ariel's neck and cheeks. Her mother's lips were forced together as though holding in a sob, and her normally dewy milk-chocolate eyes appeared dewier than ever.

Her mother took a shaky breath. 'Thank you. That's quite the nicest thing you could say.'

'I could say it because it's true.' Brooke stared back at the painting, still astonished it came from her mother's hand. 'You've never done anything like this before. You used to always paint landscapes. Gum trees and things.'

'I'm trying something different,' said Ariel as she began packing up her paints. 'I was feeling a bit jaded and an artist friend suggested I do something more animated. As I don't know anything more animated than the races, that's what I thought I'd try.' She nodded at the canvas. 'This is the sixth in the series.'

'Can I see the others?'

'Maybe later.' Paints organised, she closed the lid of the box and held it out to Brooke. 'Here, you take this and I'll bring the rest. It's time we made ourselves glamorous. I've a big day planned. Lots of lovely girlie indulgences.'

Brooke wanted to groan at the thought of what she'd have to endure but her mother's mood was too buoyant to spoil, and Ariel was right. A day indulging in silly girlie things and pampering might be just what she needed.

But by lunchtime, Brooke wondered how she'd ever countenanced such a thought. Three solid hours at the hairdresser's was too much for anyone, especially when the hairdresser made such a point of criticising Chloe's work. As far as Brooke was concerned, Chloe was the best hairdresser there was, and no purse-lipped, nose-pierced scissor-wielder would ever convince her otherwise. Lucky they'd served glasses of champagne or she'd never have made it through the ordeal. Now she sat in one of the most exclusive restaurants in Sydney, with a postcard view of the glittering harbour, wishing she could scrape her newly manicured fingernails down her newly made-up face before setting to destroy her oh-so-perfect new chin-length bob. She felt like a fraud and more than a little freaky, no matter how many times her mother beamed at her and told her how gorgeous she looked.

As for lunch, the food was proving impossible to enjoy because it seemed each time she put a fork to her mouth another besuited businessman stopped by their table to chat to Ariel and wallow in her charm, all under the pretence of asking about their horses. Brooke wondered why her mother didn't tell the lot of them to bugger off and ring the yard instead. She would have.

'I don't know how you do it,' Brooke grumbled as an admittedly good-looking, silver-haired banker type said goodbye, a giddy smile on his face. Ariel had not only rattled off the names and performances of the owner's horses, but remembered his wife and child's names too. The entire conversation achieved with perfect grace, as though nothing pleased her more than to chat with such a delightful man.

Ariel dabbed at her mouth with her napkin even though she'd barely touched her meal. 'It's my job.'

'You do it well.' And Brooke meant it. Her mother was an expert at placating even the most obnoxious of owners.

Ariel eyed her. 'You could too, you know.'

'It's not me, Mum. I don't have the patience or the skill. Give me a difficult horse any day, but an owner?' She feigned a shudder. 'No thanks. Besides, I'm happy on the farm.'

'But are you, Brookie? Are you really?'

At her use of 'Brookie', an alarm clanged in Brooke's head. That was twice she'd used it—first on her arrival at the terrace and now. Her family only ever used that nickname when bad news was on the horizon. Dropping her hands under the table, she shifted her finger to her inner wrist and pressed.

One, two, three.

'You all need to stop worrying. I'm fine.'

And she was. Mostly.

For a long, uncomfortable moment her mother focused sharp eyes on her daughter. Though Brooke tried to remain nonchalant, anxiety buzzed her insides. But then Ariel smiled tightly, picked up her cutlery and began pushing food around her plate, leaving Brooke to observe her anxiously, wondering what she suspected.

God knew how much of herself Brooke had exposed. Too much if the 'Brookie' was anything to go by.

Returning her hands to the table, Brooke placed her own cutlery carefully together and pressed at her mouth with the napkin, using the linen curtain to set her face to inscrutability. She dropped it by her plate and leaned forward, determined to act normal. To prove how well she was coping.

'So what have you planned for us this afternoon?'

Ariel gave up pushing food around, set her cutlery down and edged her plate away. 'It's a surprise.'

Brooke's mask slipped a little. Any more pampering and she'd scream. 'What sort of surprise?'

Ariel patted her hand. 'A nice one. Do you want dessert or coffee?'

Brooke shook her head. Between the champagne and nibbles at the hairdresser's and the rich restaurant food, she'd already had far too much. And she wanted air. She could still feel 'Brookie' prickling between them, itching her skin and making her fingers twitch with the urge to scratch herself raw until the memory of it faded.

Fortunately the 'surprise' her mother had organised made her forget soon enough. At first she was dismayed to discover Ariel had booked her a long session with one of the city's top stylists, but either the stylist had been well briefed or she was a mind-reader. The clothes she chose were in colours Brooke liked and in styles that didn't make her feel like one of those wannabe heiress types who the gossip mags so liked to tease for their 'wardrobe malfunctions'. Even Brooke was surprised at how much she enjoyed the session, though where she'd wear most of the clothes, she had no idea. She rarely attended the races these days and her social life in the Valley amounted to not much more than outdoor barbecues and her usual Thursday night drinks at the Pitcorthie pub with Chloe and Andrew. But Ariel insisted this was her special treat, and despite Brooke's protests, forced the bags of clothes into her arms.

After a quick stop at a local greengrocer, they returned home, chatting about friends, relatives, the yard, and other trivial matters as they prepared dinner. The subject of Brooke's horses remained care-fully avoided, and though she thought it a little odd—the topic typi-cally hovered at the forefront of their conversations—sheer relief helped offset her qualms. Plus the day had been too lovely to spoil with upsetting talk.

The first to arrive from the yard was Mark. He strode into the kitchen, looking, as he always did, like a stockbroker. Of the Kingston men, he was the shortest, but his body was honed from hours spent in the home gym he'd installed in his Coogee apartment, and his blue-grey suit emphasised the width of his hard-worked shoulders. His white collar sat perfect, as did his contrasting blue tie, held neatly in place with a University of Sydney tie clip. To Brooke's surprise he'd let his hair grow a little, taming the natural curls with gel so it sat up in trendy dark spikes. It made her immediately wonder if her brother had unlaced a bit. Maybe he'd found a girlfriend?

Mark smiled and gave her a dutiful dry-lipped kiss, but like everything about it him, it contained no warmth. 'Good day?'

'Great, thanks. And you?'

He shrugged, hands dug into his trouser pockets. 'Same as always. Money coming in, money going out.' He tossed her a look. 'Too much of it in some places.'

Brooke's jaw turned rigid. Mark was the family's business manager and the cost of running Kingston Downs was his favourite bugbear, especially now they were only using it for long-term spelling. But he tended to forget how much income the hay crop generated, and while Brooke might not be performing her duties as well as she once had, she was hardly an expensive employee.

'Mark,' Ariel warned softly, and to Brooke's astonishment he said no more. Usually once he started, her brother didn't let go, quizzing her about the diesel or fertiliser bill, or questioning the necessity of soil tests—whatever issue he'd decided needed attention. Constant nags that never failed to raise Brooke's hackles and did nothing to improve their thorny relationship.

Half an hour later, Angus turned up, bottle of red wine in hand and a huge grin on his face. Tall and rangy like his father, his navy wool jumper with its gold Kingston Lodge Racing logo reeking of horses, he enveloped Brooke in an angular but warm embrace.

'How's my favourite sister?'

She poked him in the ribs. 'Your only sister.'

Showing no respect for her new hairstyle, Angus ruffled her head. 'Still my favourite.' He peered at her closely, nose half-screwed up. 'Is that makeup you're wearing?'

Brooke held her palms against the blunt ends of her bob and bounced the cut while striking a pouty pose. 'Yes, and I've even *product* in my hair.'

'You look like a girl.'

'Probably because she is,' said Ariel, closing the oven door after stirring the casserole and coming over to kiss Angus. 'And a gorgeous one at that.'

'Gorgeous? Brooke?'

Brooke smacked him lightly in the chest. 'I can be when I choose.'

'The trouble is,' replied Angus, 'is that you never choose.'

Brooke shrugged. 'No much call for it on the farm.'

For a tense moment, Angus, Mark and Ariel all exchanged a look before Ariel clapped her hands and began to shoo the boys into the lounge to wait for their father, following them out to set the plates on the table.

Hushed words flowed from the lounge. Frowning, Brooke picked quietly through the cutlery drawer, trying to keep the rattle to a minimum so she could listen in. The conversation didn't sound friendly. Rather, it sounded like people trying to express their anger, but quietly. She stopped and placed the cutlery on the bench, and pressed her finger to her wrist, willing away her tension while telling herself nothing was wrong. She was just being over-sensitive.

She turned to face the lounge as the murmurs ceased. Her mother appeared grim-mouthed at the door before spying Brooke and hastily setting a pleasant smile on her face.

'Is everything all right?' Brooke asked.

Though her mother's smile remained, it didn't reach her eyes. 'Just the boys arguing over nothing, as usual. Now, I think we deserve a glass of wine after our big day, don't you?'

Brooke almost said no. She wasn't being oversensitive. Something wasn't right. It hadn't been all day, and the unrelenting buzz of anxiety warned her she needed to keep her wits, but as she opened her mouth to refuse the front door banged. In seconds, her father had her in his lanky embrace.

'How's my girl?' he said, planting a fat kiss on her cheek before holding her at arm's-length. 'Well, aren't you looking glamorous?' He winked at Ariel. 'Give your mother a run for her money. Did you have a good day?'

'Yeah, it was great.'

'Well, that's good then. So how are things at the farm?'

Ariel handed them each a glass of wine and disappeared into the lounge with her own glass and two bottles of Corona, leaving them to chat. As Brooke told her father about what she'd been doing, which, to be fair, in the dead of winter wasn't much, her tension eased. His gentle manner and air of solidity, characteristics that made him so good with horses, calmed her far better than any alcohol could.

'And how's Poddy?'

At the mention of Poddy Brooke's throat thickened. She ducked her head to hide her sadness. 'He's okay.'

Her father stroked her hair in comfort. 'It hurts, I know.'

But he didn't know. No one did. Every time she looked at Poddy the guilt almost floored her.

'I found a friend for him,' she said, pulling herself together. 'A Shetland mare.' She smiled a little as she thought of the fat, shaggy-maned pony. 'I think they're in love. Poddy follows her around like a puppy, but he's so much happier now he's not being bullied by the others.'

Christopher Kingston smiled, transforming his face. He wasn't handsome like Ariel was beautiful. Years of early mornings, hard work and outdoor life had left him weather-beaten, with a face full of crags and broken capillaries. Neither did he possess Ariel's slender elegance, but he was fit and looked healthy for his fifty-four years, and carried himself with the calm confidence of a successful man content with his place in the world.

Bar Andrew and Chloe, he was also the only person Brooke could tolerate talking about the accident.

'I'm glad. For you both. Is Sod still playing up?'

'A bit. Not as bad as he was but he still won't float.'

'He needs time to forget what happened. Like you.'

Brooke shook her head. 'I won't ever forget.'

'No. But it'll get easier. You'll see. And a break from there will do you good.'

She frowned. What break? She was only in town overnight and then under sufferance. She loathed leaving Poddy alone. If it weren't for Chloe's promise to look after things she wouldn't even be here. But any questioning about what he meant was stymied by the oven timer ringing and the return of her mother and brothers to the kitchen.

Ariel refused help; instead she ordered Brooke and her brothers to sit at the dining table while she and their father dished up. Brooke settled in her usual seat alongside Angus, casting surreptitious glances at her brothers. Both wore subdued expressions, as though steadying themselves for something distasteful.

Her finger crept to her wrist. Digging her finger in, she counted to three and hauled in a breath. 'Okay, what's up?'

Angus and Mark shared a look, Angus giving his head an almost imperceptible shake, before focusing on her. 'Nothing.'

'Don't give me that.'

His mouth turned grim. 'We'll talk about it later, okay?'

Panic welled in her chest. She let go of her wrist. The pressure point wasn't working. Nothing was working. Everything was *wrong*. 'No. I want to talk about it now.'

'Later, Brookie,' said her father, leaning across to place the salad bowl on the table. He touched her shoulder. 'It's fine.'

But it wasn't fine, not when her brothers looked like that and not with 'Brookie' crawling over her skin like a million ants. Her hand fluttered to her throat. What the hell was going on?

One by one the plates were laid. Her parents took their seats. Angus's red wine was poured. The salad bowl handed around. Seasoning and dressing passed. Ariel's Middle Eastern-style chicken casserole wafted scents of tomato and saffron in Brooke's nose, but did nothing to encourage her appetite. She poked at the food while her family attempted stilted conversation and threw looks her way.

Though no one seemed keen on their dinner, the men acted

overly keen to help clear up. Leaving Brooke and her mother at the table they congregated in the kitchen, clattering plates noisily.

She stared at Ariel. 'It's bad news, isn't it?'

Her mother leaned across the table for her hand. 'Not bad news, Brookie.'

Brooke jerked it out of reach. She didn't want false comfort. She just wanted the truth. 'Don't lie, Mum. Anytime anyone calls me Brookie, it's bad.'

Ariel looked toward the kitchen. One by one, the men stopped what they were doing and filed back to the table. Solemn-faced, they settled, Angus with his arm draped along the back of Brooke's chair and his fingers lightly touching her back.

Ariel looked at Christopher and then at Brooke. 'You know how worried about you we are, don't you?'

Brooke remained silent, her jaw clenched tightly shut.

Mark filled the gap. 'And I'm sure you also appreciate that your little issue with transporting horses has caused the yard logistical problems, and we've had to make adjustments. Very expensive adjustments.' He spoke soberly, but Brooke heard a hint of relish in his voice and her loathing for him deepened. 'But it's been four months now and the time has come for you to face facts. You can't do the job you're paid for and it's affecting the business. It's time you moved to Sydney, got sorted and made yourself useful. After all, you're not going to make any sort of business out of showjumping. You can't even drive to events.'

'Cut it, Mark.' Her father settled his sympathetic gaze on her. 'It's only temporary, love.'

'It might not be,' interrupted Mark. 'There's interest there. Serious interest.'

Brooke fought the tide of cold dread creeping up her body towards her brain. She blinked, trying to clear the approaching fog and stave off the pounding that grew louder in her head with every frightened beat of her heart. She had to stay rational. In focus. She had to fight this.

'What interest? What are you talking about?'

'We've had an enquiry about the farm. From a solicitor acting on behalf of someone looking for property in the area.'

'No.' She shook her head, air compressing in her lungs, making it hard to breathe. 'No.'

'You can move back here,' said her mother. 'Bring Sod with you, and together we'll make you and him better. You went through a terrible trauma, Brookie. You know it's affected you badly and you're not yourself. You need to heal and you can't do that on your own.'

'There's nothing wrong with me. I told you, I'm fine.'

'Been driving the float lately, Brooke?' asked Mark.

'You can go and get —'

Angus grabbed her shoulder, keeping her in place. 'Don't.'

'Brooke, love,' said Christopher, 'we're not doing this to hurt you. You've been hurt enough. But we all feel this is for the best.'

'Whose best? Yours?' She stabbed a finger at her father, then redirected it toward Mark. 'His? Because it's certainly not for mine.'

'Brookie.' Ariel reached out, her eyes wet with distress, but it was nothing compared to the distress Brooke felt. This was her life they were ruining. How could they not see that?

Brooke hauled in breaths, trying to calm herself. She dug her finger into her wrist, silently repeating her mantra – the only thing she had left to cling to now even her father had set her adrift.

One, two, three. One, two, three. One, two, three.

'I'm fine. Yes, I have a problem with towing the float but I'm working on it. Other than that, I'm perfectly normal. I appreciate your kindness, but honestly, I'm fine.'

Ariel shook her head. 'I don't think you are, Brookie.'

'Stop calling me Brookie. It's driving me insane!'

Mark rolled his eyes. 'Oh for God's sake, calm down. It's not the end of the bloody world.'

Hatred shot like quicksilver through her veins. She cast a death stare at her brother while her parents shared a look.

Her father spread out his hands. 'I'm sorry, love, but it's all arranged.'

Every millilitre of blood in her brain shot south. She faced her father, swaying slightly as her head emptied. 'What do you mean?'

'He means,' said Mark, 'that we've already employed a manager to take over.'

'So unemploy him.' She stared at each of them. 'Pick up the phone and call whoever it is and tell them the job's off.'

No one made a move. Stubborn silence roared.

She slapped her palms on the table. 'You can't make me leave!'

'You'll have to,' said Mark. 'The cottage is part of the deal.'

She shook her head, tears flooding her cheeks. 'You can't do this. Kingston Downs is my home.' She pointed to her chest. '*My home!*' She turned to Angus, her ally, and clawed at his shirt. 'You can't let them do this to me. Tell them, Angus. Please. Tell them they can't do this.'

'I'm sorry. I really am.'

And with those simple words, her heart broke.

THREE

THE MOMENT LACHIE spied the timber post-and-rail fence delineating the roadside boundary of Kingston Downs his heart began to beat faster. Keeping one eye on the road, he surveyed the passing landscape, admiring the lush paddocks and immaculate fences, so different to Delamere, his parents' property west of Forbes in the Jemalong Irrigation District, four and a half hours away. A short distance on, he slowed as he saw the curved, dark brick entrance with its blue and gold Kingston Lodge Racing sign.

He flicked the indicator and turned into the drive. As the ute straightened, he took one hand off the wheel and brushed it down his thigh. Stupid to be nervous, but despite his eagerness for the job, he was. The place looked so upmarket it made him feel inadequate, like a mongrel invading a pedigree show.

The expensive timber and coated-wire fence continued either side of the drive and into the distance, enclosing laneways, small paddocks and rows of shrubby windbreaks. In the paddock to the right, two winter-coated horses grazed on verdant, hock-high pasture. Hearing the crunch of tyres on the graded gravel road, they jerked their heads up to eye his red Toyota Hilux, ears pricked as they stared. He wondered how much they were worth. Probably more than he'd earn in his lifetime. Even with their thick coats and dropped bellies they looked like prime horseflesh, all noble-headed and strong-boned and possessing the look-at-me quality of champions.

He flicked a look at the Jack Russell terrier sitting next to him on the passenger seat. The dog's little black eyes glittered bright with anticipation. 'What do you reckon, Billyboy? Pretty flash, huh?'

Interpreting Lachie's words as permission to leave his perch, Billy released one of his trademark sharp yips and scrabbled over Lachie's legs to rest his paws on the door and stare out the window.

With a smile, Lachie wound down the window to let Billy sniff the air. A blast of cold hit them both, pinning Billy's black and tan ears back and making him squint. Neither of them cared. Excitement was enough to keep them warm.

Lachie tickled Billy under the chin as the dog's clever gaze raked the surrounds, and his little white body quivered with wound-up energy. So much to explore, so many things to sniff, chase and yap at. A veritable dog funhouse.

And Billy needed a bit of fun. They both did.

He veered right, following the drive past an outdoor dressage arena surrounded by a low white rail, its sand surface smooth and raked of tracks. Beside it, another arena, this time enclosed by a tall timber post-and-rail fence and containing multi-coloured showjumping fences arranged at various heights and angles. On the other side of the drive, fronted by a broad expanse of yard and as perfect as everything else at Kingston Downs, stood a large blue Colorbond barn with six horse enclosures, each with its own shelter, running down the side. Only one horse was in residence, a heavily rugged animal that followed his progress with its ears pricked and nostrils flared.

Further ahead, overlooking a scraggly-looking lawn and mulched garden beds filled with shrubs, stood Lachie's new home. Under the bright late-winter sun the timber cottage appeared even prettier than the first time he saw it. Its panelled walls glowed white, the window frames dark blue, and he could easily imagine himself kicking back on the front verandah with a cold beer on a hot day.

He couldn't remember much of the interior from his first visit except that it was a weird combination of mess and Scandinavian style, like a saddlery crossed with an IKEA store. Tack and riding gear were strewn from one end of the two-bedroom cottage to the other, perfuming the air with leather, neatsfoot oil and saddle soap. Photographs of horses and grinning people he didn't recognise perched on every cleanly designed birch-coloured shelf, while the walls showcased what looked, to his inexpert eye, like some excellent landscape paintings. 'The decor's thanks to my grandmother. Nan loves anything modern,' Mark Kingston had said by way of explanation when he spied Lachie's confused expression. 'The mess is courtesy of Brooke.' Neither he nor Mark felt comfortable invading Brooke's space, especially in her absence, and they'd rushed the inspection. Not that it mattered. Lachie would've taken the job even if the place were a rat-infested hovel.

His fingers tightened on the wheel. Christ, he hoped Brooke had gone as Mark promised. The last thing he wanted was the boss's spoilt brat of a sister watching his every move. He knew the sort. He'd encountered enough of them at university. Stuck-up little rich girls, with private-school accents and designer clothes, who smiled at him with perfect teeth and promise in their eyes. Girls he knew from hard experience it was safer to avoid.

A dark-blue older-model LandCruiser was parked in the wide gravel space between the house and an ageing but sturdy-looking machinery shed containing a John Deere tractor and a range of haymaking equipment. He halted alongside it, experiencing a foolish flush of relief that he'd taken out a loan and bought a new car to replace his old Holden ute. The dented beast had served him well but its tired engine had become unreliable, and the new Hilux looked more professional. Something, he suspected, that mattered in a place where billionaires bought and sold properties and horses on whims.

He opened the door, Billy hurtling out and racing around in ecstatic yappy circles before scampering to the nearest fence post to sniff and cock his leg.

'Billy!' Immediately the dog returned to his side. Lachie bent and touched his head in approval. A month ago the dog wouldn't have paid a scrap of attention. Billy's former owner, Lachie's late grandmother, had been too wrapped up battling kidney disease, further complicated by diabetes, to teach him obedience. Having—for the second time in his life—told his father to shove it, Lachie had moved in with her while he scouted for a professional position, and had itched to train the dog. But between working his guts out for a local farmer and tending his grandmother, plus all the other household chores, he hadn't had the time. At least the young terrier, despite his hyperactivity, had given her affection and joy in her last days.

A screen door banged. Lachlan looked up to see a rangy, dark haired man a bit older than him descend the steps.

'Jesus,' he said, eyes widening as he looked Lachie up and down. 'Mark said you were a fair lump of a lad but I wasn't expecting a giant.' He held out his hand. 'I take it you're Lachlan Cambridge. I'm Angus, Mark's brother. Sorry he couldn't be here. Some drama with a syndicate.' He grinned. 'Nothing unusual there, which is why I try to keep away from that side of things.'

Lachie shook his hand, returning the smile, and appreciating Angus's firm grip and the deep lines around his eyes, the sign of a man who laughed often. 'Everyone calls me Lachie,' he said. He glanced up at the sky, vibrant blue despite the cold wind. 'Great day for it.'

'Yeah, although a change is on its way. It's supposed to be miserable for the rest of the week.' Angus cast an amused glance at Billy. The terrier sat with his legs flopped to one side and his head cocked as though listening in. 'Clever-looking dog.'

Lachie scooped the Jack Russell up and ruffled his head. 'This little rat is Billy.'

'He'll have fun around here.' Angus scratched the dog's ears.

'Plenty of mice and bits of hoof to chew on, although keep him away from Brooke's horse Sod. He's liable to get stomped on.'

At the mention of Brooke an alarm went off in Lachie's head. Mark had said his sister was moving herself and her horses to Sydney, intimating she needed to be closer to family, hence the property requiring a new manager. A plausible-enough explanation, which was why Lachie had ignored his gut when he toured the house the first time. It wasn't the home of someone preparing to leave.

Carefully, he placed Billy on the ground, taking a moment to gather himself. 'Brooke's still here, is she?'

Angus's grimace gave him the answer.

'Don't worry, you won't have to live with her.' Angus pointed past the barn and yards to where the drive split and ran parallel to the main road. A simple whitewashed stone building with a blue Color-bond roof and guttering sat at the base of a rise. 'She's moved into the old dairy.'

'Okay,' said Lachie. It wasn't, but it was too late to back out now. He was here and there wasn't a chance in hell he'd return to Forbes and his old job. Or go crawling back to Delamere. Not yet, anyway.

Angus nodded in understanding. 'It'll be all right. Brooke knows the deal even if she doesn't like it. Besides, if Mum and Mark get their way she won't be here for much longer. Come on, I'll give you a hand with your gear.'

Used to moving around, Lachie had packed light. It didn't take him and Angus long to load up. Angus held the cottage door open with his foot to let him enter first.

'Stay,' Lachie ordered when Billy tried to follow them inside.

'It's all right. He can come in if you want. Brooke allowed her collie inside when he was alive. Used to shed hair everywhere but she didn't care. She loved that dog. She loves all her animals.' Angus stared across the yard, and it was clear his attention had slipped elsewhere. 'Too much sometimes.'

Lachie suppressed a sigh. Why was it both Kingston brothers couldn't stop talking about their sister? Mark had been no different, although his tone held none of the affection Angus's possessed when discussing Brooke. Mark made her sound like an uppity cow who needed toeing into line, whereas Angus seemed to feel sorry for her. Whatever she was, he'd have to deal with her. Something Lachie wasn't looking forward to one bit.

The house had changed from his last visit. While the decor remained the same, with its incongruous pale colours and contemporary fixtures, all the photos had disappeared. Also gone was the horse paraphernalia. No saddlery hung over the backs of the kitchen chairs, no bridles from doorknobs. Not even a hair-covered brush, mud-splattered boot or scuffed helmet sullied the scrubbed birch surface of the kitchen table. Now the cottage looked more like an IKEA catalogue than ever, and he couldn't help thinking how sterile it felt.

'You don't have much gear,' Angus remarked when they'd dumped his bags in the main bedroom, also fitted with pale birch furniture.

Lachie shrugged. 'Since the house came fully furnished I figured I only really needed clothes, a few books and my laptop.' That wasn't entirely true, but Angus didn't need to know that was pretty much all he owned. Except for Tamsyn's ring, which he still couldn't bring himself to sell, and the Toyota, which mostly belonged to the bank. Four years of uni had sucked most of his savings, even with the part-time work he'd picked up, and money had been tight at Delamere, especially once Lachie had convinced his brother Nick to go to uni. Still, he wasn't about to complain. If missing out on a few luxuries meant Nick had a future, then it was worth it.

His heart clenched a little as he thought of his poor mum, now with both her boys living away from the district, but when Lachie told her about Mark's job offer she'd urged him to go. Minette didn't want him wasting his degree or his life, not after all he'd achieved. He'd nearly done that once already, when his teenage impetuosity saw him storm from home. She wouldn't let him do it as a man.

Sad as it was, Lachie's grandmother's death had freed him, and given it'd take one hell of a father–son reconciliation to get Lachie back at Delamere, a return to the farm was off the agenda. At least in the months since Lachie had been living with his grandmother, his mother had known a bit of peace instead of suffering through the endless arguments he and his father couldn't stop themselves from having. Lachie loathed seeing her eyes reddened, wide and liquid, her lip trembling with worry, yet his father always knew which chain to yank when it came to his son's temper. Lachie prided himself on his steady nature but Harry Cambridge had a way of making a volcano erupt in his gut. He wouldn't put his mother through that again.

'You had a look around with Mark, didn't you?' asked Angus as they returned to the kitchen, breaking Lachie from his thoughts.

'Only a brief one. Mark didn't have much time.'

The corner of Angus's mouth twitched a wry smile. 'Probably too scared he'd run into Brooke.' Catching Lachie's look, he explained, 'They don't get on.'

Lachie kept his mouth shut. Involving himself in a Kingston family feud wasn't on his agenda. Ever. He had enough trouble dealing with his own.

'I don't know where she is,' continued Angus over his shoulder as he pushed open the screen door. 'Brooke should be the one to show you around. She's the one who's been running the place, after all. Never mind. You'll just have to put up with me as tour guide. Come on, I'll show you the stables.' Angus took off in long strides towards the barn.

Lachie followed, shoving his hands in his pockets and hunching against the icy wind while Billy trailed with his nose to the ground and his black-tipped tail waving like a metronome.

'She's probably up at Andrew Chiang's,' said Angus as he caught up. 'Those two are as thick as thieves. Been that way since they were kids. Everyone expects they'll announce their engagement one of these days but Brooke insists she's not interested.' Angus grinned. 'Be the only girl round here who isn't.'

Lachie had no idea who he was on about. 'Can't say I know him.'

'You probably don't, but you'd know of his family's company, Herbal Heaven.'

Lachie's eyebrows shot up. That was one company he'd definitely heard of. They were one of the biggest brands in Australia's multi-billion-dollar alternative-medicine industry.

Angus nodded towards the rugged horse in the yard. 'That's Sod, one of Brooke's showjumpers. Complete nutjob, so best to keep out of his way.'

Lachie followed Angus into the barn through a side door, whistling for Billy, who was sniffing dangerously close to Sod's yard. Despite the shed's swept concrete slab, a large grated drain running down the centre and not an animal in sight, the smell of woodchips, manure and horse dominated the air. Four vacant stables, two on each side, occupied one end of the shed. A pristine tack room, with a front wall of steel grille, its heavy-locked door gaping open, took the right-hand centre space. The interior walls were lined with timber, and every one of its hooks and saddle mounts contained a piece of equestrian equipment. Stacked on the floor beneath were square plastic tubs, each labelled: 'bandages', 'leads', 'boots', 'brushes', 'hoof care' and so on. Alongside the tack room was a feed locker with huge galvanised-steel bins and a floor you could eat off. Two high-stacked, powder-coated metal shelves stretched up the side wall, one filled with supplements and veterinary supplies, the other with neatly folded horse rugs.

'Impressive, isn't it?' said Angus. 'Brooke's a total grub around the house but she keeps this place spotless.'

Lachie peered in to one of the stables. A dense bed of woodchips covered the floor. It looked so comfortable he could imagine sleeping on it himself. 'Much better than the place I worked at before uni, that's for sure.'

'That was out Orange way, wasn't it?'

'Yeah. Only a small stable, but Noel trained the odd winner.' He also drank and gambled too much but that was a whole other story. Anyway, Lachie was grateful for the time he'd worked there. If it weren't for his stint at Noel's and the experience it gave him with horses, he probably wouldn't have this job.

He left the stable and inspected the feed-locker shelves, picking up worm pastes, liniments and wound treatments.

'Mark told you that you don't have to worry about the horses' veterinary care, didn't he?' asked Angus.

Lachie nodded. It was one of the first things he checked when Mark phoned him about the position. While he had enough confidence to run the farm side of things, taking care of thoroughbreds worth hundreds of thousands—possibly millions—of dollars made him break out in a sweat.

'But we still expect you to keep an eye on them. Won't take much effort. There are only half a dozen here now and with the exception of Pompey Girl, who'll be coming back into work in the spring, they're all long-termers. Just give them the once-over a couple of times a day to make sure they're happy and healthy, and if you spot a problem contact us straightaway. If you're uncertain, ask Brooke, and if for one second you think it could be serious, phone the vet. The number's by the phone along with all our contact numbers.'

'Thanks. Hopefully I won't need it.'

He left the feed locker and headed to the other end of the shed. Parked to one side, looking more like a luxury motorhome than horse transport, stood a dark-blue high-cab horse truck. Its tyres shone with black, its paintwork unscratched. Even the aluminium fittings sparkled with newness. Opposite, also dark blue but bearing the ravages of use, was a smaller aluminium float. Both trailers sported the gold Kingston Lodge Racing logo.

Lachie pointed at the truck. 'That's what I'll be driving?'

'Occasionally perhaps, when we transfer more than two horses, but it's more likely you'll be using the float and Brooke's new Land-Cruiser.' He slapped his palm against the truck's side. 'You should check it out later. It's a cracking set-up. Dad picked it. He thought it'd be better for Brooke than another gooseneck. Although God knows when she'll get her act together enough to use it. The way things are going Mark will probably have the truck sold first.'

Lachie gave Angus a sharp look, alerted by the exasperation in his voice. Something was going on here, although he had no idea what. He tried to think of a way to probe but before he could, Angus ushered him out of the shed.

'Come on, I'll show you around the rest of the place.'

They took the Hilux, driving down lanes bordered with more timber and coated-wire fences. Not a twist of barbed wire or ringlock fencing existed on the property, and not a fence post stood crooked nor a wire unstrained. Even the gates hung even. It wasn't a huge farm, only a hundred and forty hectares, but Lachlan knew a property in this area even that small wouldn't sell for less than seven figures.

Horses dotted the paddocks, enjoying the lush grass. Whatever his assumptions about Mark and Angus's sister, he couldn't deny she'd taken great care of the property. The pastures were a vivid green, showing no sign of disease or nutrient deficiency. As he drove, Angus talked about each of the horses, describing their careers and the reasons they were out of work. Some Lachlan had heard of, while the names of others rang no bell.

Towards the river, on the fertile alluvial flats, the small paddocks gave way to unfenced lucerne stands and plantings of forage oats. Angus indicated for Lachie to pull up and they stepped out to walk through the plants, Angus explaining the farm's management as he went. 'We renovate the stands on rotation, switching between lucerne hay production, silage, and oaten hay, which we sell. This one's nearing the end of its life, but it'll be up to you to choose when to replace it and what with.' He pointed further along the river flat, towards another bright green stand. 'That one only went in last year. A new semi-winter active variety called Abacus that's performed well in local trials. Brooke seems to be pretty happy with it.'

Aware of the variety, Lachlan nodded. He'd tried to convince his father to sow a paddock at Delamere with it but the old man deemed the older and cheaper varieties good enough, despite their lower yields and poorer disease resistance.

They walked the flats, Angus quizzing Lachie on his haymaking knowledge and nodding his approval when Lachie acquitted himself well. Having escaped Delamere at eighteen, Lachie wasn't an expert by any means, but he'd absorbed enough from his father to get by. And in the five years between leaving home and going to uni, between myriad unskilled casual jobs, he'd worked a few haymaking seasons for other famers—although when it came to some of the cowboy operations he'd endured, it was more a case of learning how *not* to do things.

The crops inspected, they drove back towards the paddocks. At a gate halfway along the lane, Angus asked him to stop. Lachlan followed him out of the ute, Billy close on his heels. Leaning over the gate, Angus stuck his fingers in his mouth and whistled. A dark head immediately poked up, ears pricked and nostrils wide. In a second the horse was trotting towards them.

Not until he came closer did Lachie notice the tiny round pony cantering alongside, its black forelock so thick and long it was a wonder the animal could see where it was going.

Grinning, Angus turned to him. 'Say hello to Venus and Poseidon. Venus is the pony, although she has grand ideas of being a racehorse.'

Lachlan laughed as the black-and-white Shetland belted ahead of its lovely-looking equine mate, bucking and snorting like a red-blooded stallion.

Despite Venus's best efforts, her stumpy legs proved no match for the flowing stride of the big dark bay. Arriving first, the horse stopped at the fence and blew air on Angus's face before nuzzling him with affection. 'This is the love of Brooke's life, Poddy.' Angus ruffled Poddy's forelock. 'And he's a big sook.'

Lachlan held out his fingers for the animal to sniff and caught sight of the horse's closed eyelid and sunken eye socket. 'What happened to his eye?'

'Poor bugger lost it in the accident. Brooke keeps him away from
the others because they pick on him, especially Sod. She bought
Venus to keep him company.'

'What accident?'

'Brooke's accident.' Angus stared at him and clocking Lachie's
blank look raised his eyes to the sky. 'Mark didn't tell you, did he?' He
rubbed his hand through his hair, making it stand up on end. 'Fuck.'

For the second time since his arrival, Lachie's nerves hummed
with alarm. He should have known this job was too good to be true. 'I
don't know anything about an accident,' he said carefully.

With a sigh, Angus crossed his arms and leaned against the rail,
shaking his head. 'Sometimes my brother's such a prick.' He cleared
his throat and focused on Lachie. 'But that's not your problem. Look,
the reason you have this job is because Brooke had an accident
towing the gooseneck with three of her horses on board. One was
killed, Poddy here lost his right eye and fractured his tarsal bone, and
Sod—he's the horse back at the yard—is a wreck. Unfortunately, so's
Brooke.'

Lachie didn't like where this was heading. To keep calm he
stroked Poddy's cheek but the horse sensed his anxiety and moved
away to nudge at Angus. Venus took his place, bunting her woolly
head against Lachie's hand for attention. He tangled his fingers in her
thick forelock and rubbed.

'So what's her problem?'

'She's developed a phobia about floating the horses. According to
her it's just temporary and she'll get over it, but it's been four months
now and she still can't tow anything. Not even Venus here. It
wouldn't matter, only it's caused issues for the yard. We can only
send long-termers here now because it's such a pain getting the horses
back to Sydney. Everything else goes to a contract spelling property
near Londonderry, which costs money, obviously. It's driving Mark
mad that this place is being underutilised.' He rubbed at his head
again, as though revealing all this made him uncomfortable. 'Mum's
worried sick about Brooke, understandably, and wants her home

where she can get help. Mark feigns concern but I know he thinks Brooke should either pull her weight or get herself a proper job instead of leeching off the business. Between the two of them, they convinced Dad she'd be better off in Sydney. So now you're on the payroll and poor bloody Brooke's been given her marching orders.'

'Which she refuses to obey.'

'Yeah.' He stroked Poddy's nose. 'Don't blame her, either. She loves this place. It's her home. And despite what my idiot brother thinks, she does a good job of running it.'

Lachlan whistled for Billy and picked him up, needing the comfort of his wriggly body. Brooke might be a spoilt brat but no one deserved to be booted out of the place they loved.

When Mark had phoned him telling him he had a job available and he couldn't think of anyone more qualified for it, Lachie leapt at the chance. Not for a single moment did he consider the vacancy might have been the result of a family argument. All he saw was a job that provided him with the means to support himself and Nick while his brother completed his science and teaching degree. A chance to put his own degree to use and hone his skills, ready for the day when his obstinate father finally came to his senses and gave him the run of Delamere.

'So she's not exactly happy about my presence.'

Angus tossed him an apologetic look. 'No.'

Lachie pursed his lips and nodded. 'I'll try to keep out of her way.' Although how he was supposed to do that on a property this small he didn't know, and given the circumstances she'd likely spend all day spying on him, double-checking his work.

'Look, I'm sure she'll be all right once she gets used to it. Anyway, as I said, if Mark and Mum get their way she won't be here for much longer.'

Billy squirmed in his arms. He placed him back down. Immediately the terrier tore into the grass, nose down, tail up and wagging furiously as he chased whatever had caught his attention. Lachie let him be. He had ground rules to sort out.

'Just so I'm clear, I don't answer to her.'

Angus grinned. 'Jesus, no. And don't let her think you do, either. No, you talk to Mark or me and if neither of us is available, contact Dad. But given Mark pays your wages he's technically your boss. Just keep in mind he doesn't know that much about farming or managing this place. The person who knows the most about it is Brooke. She's been running around Kingston Downs since she was in nappies. Much to Mum's annoyance.'

Lachie frowned. He was sure Mark had told him Kingston Downs originally belonged to his grandparents. 'So this was your parents' property?'

'No, my grandparents', but Brooke spent every weekend and every holiday here she could. Moved in permanently the moment she finished school and took over management four years ago when Nan and Pop retired to Port Douglas.' He pushed off from the rail. 'Come on. She should be back from wherever she went by now.'

They hopped back into the car. As he drove, Lachie stared through the windscreen wondering what the hell he'd caught himself up in. He'd been here barely an hour and already he felt snagged in the Kingstons' undertow.

Annoyance settled its fat backside on his mood. He was irritated with himself for not sensing any problem before, but Mark had acted as if nothing was wrong and he'd stupidly believed him. So much for their friendship, although friendship was probably stretching it. If the truth be known, they'd been not much more than rugby teammates at university. Mark wasn't the sort of man to develop close friendships. A good bloke and not a bad five-eighth when he was on form, but stand-offish.

'Don't worry, you'll like her. Everyone does,' Angus said, interrupting his thoughts. 'She's good fun.'

Somehow, Lachie didn't think that'd be the case for him, but he said nothing. Silence, he'd learned, was usually the best response in these situations.

Angus glanced at him and back at the road. 'Mark mentioned you play rugby.'

'Don't mind a game, but I doubt I'll have time for it. Seems like there's plenty to keep me busy here.'

'You never know. The Pitcorthie team's always short, so even if you could only manage a game every few weeks, they'd be happy to sign you up. Ask Nate at the pub if you're keen.'

He pulled up next to the yards. The dark-brown horse was gone from its enclosure. As they stepped out of the ute, a slim girl in checked, suede-seated riding breeches and a dark-blue jumper with hay caught in the knit led a saddled and heavily booted Sod from the barn. She stopped and regarded them warily, messy bob swinging around her heart-shaped face. The horse raised a hoof and pawed at the ground before bunting her in the head with its nose.

One glance and Lachlan knew he'd imagined her perfectly. No question, Brooke Kingston possessed the look he knew too well. Blemish-free skin, shiny, perfectly cut—albeit untidy—hair, and the haughty bearing of a person who considered herself better than him. She stared back with eyes the colour and clarity of aged cognac, which widened, as everyone's did, when they took in his size. Lachie stood 195 centimetres in his socks, with shoulders like an axeman and legs muscled from hard work and sport. People stared, women especially, and normally he took it in his stride, but something about Brooke Kingston's gaze, the way her lips parted as she slowly raked the length of his body, made him tense. It reminded him of Tamsyn, and look where that landed him. Dumped and broken-hearted, that's where.

Angus kissed her cheek. 'Hey, Brooke.'

'I wasn't expecting you until tomorrow.'

'I thought Mark called.'

She shook her head, a sudden expression of distress flicking across her features before flattening to thin-lipped composure.

Angus gave her shoulder a squeeze. 'It'll be all right, I promise,' he said softly before turning aside to introduce Lachie. 'This is Lachlan Cambridge.'

He held his hand out. 'Nice to meet you.'

As she reached forward to shake it, the horse snaked its neck forward, huge teeth bared and snapping. Lachie jerked back just in time, leaving the animal's teeth clenching only air. 'Shit!'

She batted the horse away. 'Sorry. This is Sod, who likes to live up to his name.' Giving the horse another push on the nose, she held out her hand again.

He eyed the horse and then took it, surprised at the firmness of her grip. As he let go, Billy gave a yap. He nodded at the dog. 'This is Billy.'

She eyed the terrier and then him, a slight smile quirking her mouth. Immediately he felt defensive. So Billy wasn't a collie or kelpie, but he was a good dog and better than that savage horse.

To his surprise she crouched down and reached out for Billy, who wagged his tail in greeting before flopping onto his back to have his belly scratched. Laughing, she obliged, tickling his side until his leg beat crazily and his little body writhed from side to side in ecstasy.

'Cute,' she said, standing, and for a brief moment her smile made her very pretty, the sort of girl he'd look twice at if he saw her in the street or a bar. Then the wariness returned, and her lips compressed once more. She turned to her brother. 'Are you staying?'

Angus shook his head. 'I need to get back. We've five runners at Randwick tomorrow.'

She bit her lip. 'Maybe come up to the dairy for a cuppa? When you've finished with the manager.'

The manager.

That thumped him back to earth. He should have remembered girls like her didn't associate with the hired help. Angus led her away, speaking quietly. Lachie turned aside, shoved his hands into his pockets and surveyed the drive, wondering if he shouldn't collect his stuff and get the hell out of there.

Except where would he go? Not Delamere, and he couldn't face going back to more labouring. He was a qualified agronomist, but he knew from experience good jobs were hard to come by. Plus he had Nick to think of. Lachie didn't want to see him struggle like he had at uni, trying to balance work and study and barely succeeding at either. Nope, he was staying, whether Brooke Kingston liked it or not.

A clatter of hoofs caught his attention. Brooke sat on Sod's back, staring at her brother with her mouth turned down.

Angus put his hand to her knee and rubbed. 'I'm on your side. Remember that.'

She nodded and after casting a resentful glance at Lachie, urged Sod forward.

Angus walked to Lachie's side as she rode into the dressage arena, the horse tossing its head as though in a temper. 'Sorry. She's a bit upset.'

'Must be hard for her.'

'Yeah.' He kept his focus on his sister. 'Poor bugger hasn't been the same since the accident. She keeps insisting she's fine but I worry about her. We all do.'

Lachie nodded. He knew what it was like to worry about family. Not a day passed when he didn't fret about Nick or his mother. Sometimes, when he managed to push his anger and disappointment aside, he even worried about his father.

'Listen,' said Angus, facing him, his expression serious. 'Would you keep an eye on her for me? I know she keeps trying to drive the float, but it always ends up in some sort of panic attack.'

Lachie held up his hands as if to ward off the request. Angus seemed like a good bloke and he wasn't averse to helping out, but Lachie's degree was in agriculture, not psychology. He'd be more likely to make things worse than better. 'Look, I'm sorry, but I don't know the first thing about that sort of stuff.'

'You don't need to. All she needs is a bit of support. Someone to tell her nothing's going to go wrong.' He stared back at Brooke. 'I'd help her myself but I'm rarely here. And it's not something you can do over the phone.'

Lachie followed his gaze. Brooke eased Sod into a canter, the two flowing around the arena as if they were melted together. She brought him back to a halt before easing straight into a canter again, the horse moving as though directed by some invisible button. To his untrained eye they looked magnificent, like the horses at the Olympics. Muscles stood out on Sod's powerful hindquarters, his clipped, dark-brown coat glossy with good health. He held his neck arched, his body compressed, as if Brooke held him wound up like a tight spring.

'What about professional help?'

'She won't accept it. Besides, that'd probably mean moving to Sydney and Brooke's relying on the old saying that "possession's nine-tenths of the law", which is why she's staying put.' He smiled. 'My sister always did have a stubborn streak.'

Lachie suppressed a sigh. Stubborn. Great. All that told him was Brooke Kingston wasn't going anywhere in a hurry.

He cast around, suddenly realising Billy had disappeared. Unthinking, he whistled loudly for the dog. Billy raised his head from the foliage on the other side of the arena and, responding to the command as he'd been trained, broke into a sprint. Releasing a high-pitched yip, he bounded out of the grass, jumped the low white rail and in a streak of white, hurtled straight across the arena and into Sod's path. Startled, the horse skittered to the side, the whites of his eyes showing as he tossed his head and fought the tight grip on his reins. As Brooke cast a filthy look Lachie's way Sod wrenched at the bit, snatching a length of rein, then dropped his head and in a spectacular display of temper, released a furious series of bucks.

And to Lachie's utter horror, Brooke didn't last the distance.

FOUR

BROOKE COULDN'T TELL if it was the bitter wind, pain or humiliation causing the tears in her eyes, but of one thing she was certain—the new manager's idiocy had caused her unceremonious dumping, and heart-flipping good looks or not, she wasn't about to forgive him for it.

She scrambled to her knees as Angus pounded across the sand. The last thing she needed was more of his sympathy. Today had proven hellish enough.

He knelt down next to her, concern darkening his blue-grey eyes. 'You right?'

She nodded. A lump the size of a fist blocked her throat and threatened more tears. She gripped his arm and hauled herself up, hunting for Sod. Lachlan had him, the reins held tight under the horse's chin. Sod shook his head furiously, but Lachlan shook the reins with equal aggression and ordered him to cut his nonsense. To her surprise, Sod regarded the man for a moment before pressing his head against Lachlan's shoulder and rubbing hard.

Rotten, traitorous horse. She couldn't even trust him to take a piece out of her enemy. Although, given the size of the new manager, perhaps Sod was right to exercise restraint. The man was built like a colossus.

She dusted her backside, Angus still holding her arm and fixing her with a sympathetic look, the one that made her want to crawl away and hide. Andrew had regarded her the same way only that morning, when she'd collapsed out of his truck, falling to her knees as she gulped in air, fighting the awful terror that sucked all the oxygen from her lungs, heightened her pulse to an impossible rate and made her head feel as though it had broken from her body and floated into the clouds.

'You can let go now. I'm fine,' she said to Angus as Lachlan approached. The manager's gaze swept slowly over her face and body, assessing her with gold-flecked hazel eyes surrounded by luscious dark lashes and a sober expression. Although there was nothing sexual about his appraisal, the intensity of it was such that she had a weird urge to cross her arms in front of her chest.

'I'm sorry,' he said, holding out Sod's reins. 'It won't happen again, I promise.'

And she knew from his voice and the formal way he held himself that it wouldn't. Lachlan Cambridge possessed the straight-gazed focus of a man whose word mattered. She took the reins, looking away, disconcerted by the way he studied her. Billy sat by his master's feet, staring at her with equal intensity. Everyone appeared to be waiting for her to say something.

Why couldn't she laugh? Why did this stupid ache keep gripping her throat? She should be dusting herself off and leaping back into the saddle instead of standing there gormlessly, like a pathetic child. She'd never been pathetic in her life. Yet that's the way people looked at her these days, like someone to be pitied.

Or worse, taken advantage of.

She swallowed and dug at her courage, returning her attention to him. 'Make sure it doesn't. Sod's a valuable horse. He could have injured himself.'

'And so could you,' said Angus, initial sympathy giving way to anger. 'Where the fuck's your helmet?'

'I was only riding in the ménage.'

'So what? You still could have hurt yourself. You of all people know how dangerous riding can be. Remember Scott? You want to end up like him?'

'Scott was an accident.' A terrible, tragic riding accident that left Angus's best friend damaged forever.

'And so was Sod dumping you just then. Wear your fucking helmet.' Shaking his head, he let out a long frustrated breath. 'You've given me enough to worry about without adding this.'

'Don't, Gus,' she said. 'I'm fine.'

'You're not and you know it.'

She threw a glance at Lachlan, standing steady and silent with Sod, one hand stroking the horse's nose as he watched the exchange. Her hand crept to her wrist. She rubbed the special pressure point, willing her anxiety away. No doubt he'd be on the phone to Mark the moment Angus left, relaying all that had happened. How she wasn't looking after herself. How she still wasn't coping. How she needed help. Knowing Mark, he probably made spying on her a condition of Lachlan's employment.

She straightened her shoulders. 'I *am* fine. All I need is to be left alone.'

Taking Sod from Lachlan, she led him a short distance away and checked his gear, while Angus stomped off to fetch her helmet.

He handed it to her with an annoyed shake of his head. 'Wear the bloody thing, will you?'

Grudgingly, she plonked it on and fastened the straps. She knew she should wear a helmet, and her parents would have a fit if they found out she didn't, but she adored the rush of air through her hair as she rode, the sensation of freedom and oneness with her horse. There was something almost primitive about it, and it was a feeling she never wanted to lose. Time with her animals was precious. The accident had taught her that well.

Angus gave her a leg-up and retreated to the edge of the arena with Lachlan. Out of the corner of her eye, she caught the two men looking at one another, eyebrows raised, sharing one of those 'Women!' expressions. Well, to hell with them. She didn't care what they thought. All she wanted was to be left in peace with her horses, secure in the home she loved.

Ignoring them, she exercised Sod at the far end of the arena, first at a walk, then a trot, before finally easing him into a canter, gradually decreasing the size of the circles they made until he almost swivelled on his hocks. Despite his hissy fit, he knuckled down to work. Sweat sheened his dark coat and white flecks of foam dripped from his mouth. Collected training like this took effort and Sod habitually misbehaved, but today he pranced around like a dressage horse, obedient and supple, transitions seamless, his response to her aids immediate. She would have grumped at him for showing off if it weren't so pleasurable.

She caught sight of Angus and Lachlan as she brought Sod back to a walk and let him stretch on a loose rein for a few minutes. The men had moved to what she assumed was Lachlan's vehicle. They leaned against the tray with heads close together, observing her and leaving her with no doubt she was the subject of their discussion.

The gravelly ache returned to her throat and she stared between Sod's ears. Today needed to end, and quickly. It'd been a disaster from the moment she'd woken in the fridge-like dairy with the fanciful idea that maybe if she tried to drive Andrew's float, with one of his horses in it, her problem would disappear.

He'd been as eager as she to test her theory. Though hints of strain remained, since the accident they'd both tried hard to act normal around each other. Needing her friend desperately, Brooke followed Andrew's stoic lead, ignoring the strange looks he some-times threw her way. Looks filled with hurt and another emotion she struggled to interpret; for the sake of their friendship she chose not to dwell on them. Without his and Chloe's unrelenting support she didn't know how she'd cope. They distracted her with visions of a normal future, discussing the coming spring show season as if everything was fine. That they'd all be competing as they usually did—Chloe on her show hack Elvis, and Brooke and Andrew with their showjumpers.

Yet her grand idea had failed spectacularly. And now she fretted she'd made it worse.

It was bad enough when it was her own horses, but the thought she could cause harm to someone else's, someone she cared about deeply, had drowned her in panic. Sweat had soaked her shirt before she even turned on the engine and Andrew's jokes and humorous wagers hadn't soothed. They only made her realise how much was at stake.

Her hand shaking and slippery with sweat, she'd crunched his truck into gear and, trembling feverishly, released the clutch. A heartbeat later, she'd yanked on the hand brake and was scrabbling for the door handle, black, blinding panic stealing her breath, her mind only on escape.

Andrew had held her to his chest until she calmed, stroking her head and back with tenderness as she sobbed, protecting her from the blustery wind with his warmth, and clutching her as though she was the most precious thing on earth. Then he spoiled it by cupping her face in his palms and looking at her with those lovely pleading eyes and telling her he could solve everything. She could leave Kingston Downs and move in with him at Willowgrove. He'd look after her and her horses, make things right again. No more stress, no more family worries. Just the two of them, working together, doing what they loved. Jumping for the stars.

Despair at what would become of her, of the life she adored, had her considering his offer, but only for a moment. It'd never work. She didn't love him, not the way he wanted, and to live with him, even as friends, would only make things worse.

So they'd parted, both feeling miserable, and all she wanted was to lose herself in work and her horses. Instead, she arrived home to find her brother and that good-looking goliath in residence. And as if that weren't enough, she'd fallen off right in front of him.

Yep, it was definitely time for the day to end.

She gathered the reins and directed Sod into the showjumping arena. The clever thing to do would be to go for a gallop through the lanes, far away from Lachlan Cambridge and her brother's scrutiny, but today was Sod's jumping day and she wasn't going to change her routine for them. Besides, she wasn't about to run. This was her ground, and she'd damn well stand it.

Half an hour later, she brought Sod to a walk and slapped at his neck, delighted at how well he'd gone. She'd worked drills over small fences, concentrating on putting him at the optimum take-off point each time—basic exercises that helped them both train their eyes. Sod hadn't put a hoof wrong, and his uncharacteristically positive attitude helped lift the weight that had sat on her shoulders all morning.

The men had disappeared, although both vehicles remained in the yard. As she rode back to the barn, she hunted around for them but couldn't spy where they'd wandered to. Once inside, she slid off Sod and set about untacking him, yabbering nonsense as she worked, telling him how pleased she was with his performance, what a good boy he was, how she'd reward him with a few carrots in his feed. He ruffled his muzzle through her hair as she unstrapped his front near-side boot but he didn't bite, and for the first time that day she smiled. Perhaps today marked the start of their true partnership.

''Bout time you did that.'

Brooke jerked her head up, almost catching Sod on the chin. She stroked his cheek in apology before regarding her brother. He lounged against the tack-room grille, smiling at her.

'Did what?'

'Smile.'

She sighed and ducked under Sod's neck to reach his off foreleg.

'I do it a lot, Angus. You're just not around to see it.'

'That's not what I've heard.'

'Oh, yeah? Who's been telling tales?'

'Pretty much everyone. They're worried about you, Brooke. We all are.'

She tossed the boot aside and moved on to Sod's hind brushing boots. Not taking the hint, Angus remained at the grille, leaving her no choice but to face him when she'd finished stripping the boots. She leaned against Sod's neck, rubbing his face and fondling his ears, grateful for his solid warm bulk. 'I'm all right, Angus. Honestly.'

He nodded but his expression revealed he didn't believe her. Annoyance shot a flush up her neck but she didn't want to spoil her mood with a fight. Instead, she set about rubbing down Sod and brushing the sweat out of his coat.

'Mum wants you to come to Sydney this weekend,' said Angus when he'd finished putting Sod's tack away.

She sighed. She hated leaving Poddy alone, even if only overnight. Though the horse had Venus for company, Brooke still fretted he'd get into trouble and she'd lose him, like she lost darling Oddy. Andrew and Chloe didn't mind checking up on him for her, but it wasn't the same. Poddy needed her close. *She* needed to be close. Yet she also had to keep her family off her back, and part of her plan to do that was to help out more with the racing stables. Unfortunately, her mother interpreted 'helping out' as spending more time sucking up to owners instead of the stable work she'd envisaged.

'Do I have to?'

'Come on, you look good all frocked up.'

Brooke ceased rubbing and leaned her forehead against Sod's flank. She loved her mother, but Ariel's concern for her and insistence that Brooke needed to move home was stretching their once solid relationship. Brooke still hadn't forgiven Ariel's betrayal. She wasn't sure she ever would.

'She gets me down, Gus.'

Angus moved to her side to stroke her hair. 'I know. But she means well.'

'Then why is she trying to take me from what I love?'

At the choke in Brooke's voice, Angus gathered her up and

hugged her tight against his raw-boned body. 'Hey, stop worrying. It'll work out, you'll see.' He let her go and, holding her at arm's length, smiled. 'You're tough, remember? And if you don't start cheering up I'm going to dob you in to Nan. Then there'll be trouble.' He chucked her chin as she returned his smile. 'There. That's more like the Brooke we know and love.'

The mood lighter, they finished cleaning Sod together, chatting about horses until they led the rugged-up animal to his paddock for an afternoon's graze and relaxation. She followed Angus back to his car, looking around for Lachlan.

'What have you done with the new manager?'

'His name's Lachie, Brooke, and he's a good bloke.' He held her gaze. 'None of this is his fault, you need to remember that.'

'I know.' Though that didn't stop it hurting.

He opened the car door. 'Promise me you'll play nice.'

She rolled her eyes. 'I'm always nice.'

'Want a bet?'

'You sound like Andrew.'

Angus grinned. 'Wish I had the money to back it up like he does.' His shifted his gaze to the left, past the machinery shed, and lifted his chin. 'I think Sod's found a new friend.'

Lachlan stood at the gate to Sod's paddock, Billy tucked under one arm, using his free hand to stroke Sod's nose as the horse inspected the dog. Brooke held her breath. Sod was liable to take a chunk out of either of them. But the animal's benign mood continued and after several sniffs Lachlan dropped Billy to the ground, where he sat obediently as Sod lowered his head and subjected him to another inspection. Deciding the dog was harmless, Sod wandered off to graze.

With Billy bouncing through the long grass at the side of the lane like a black-and-white jack-in-the-box, Lachlan walked past them to the cottage, his palm held up in a farewell gesture. Brooke followed his progress. God, the man was built. Not to mention fit-looking with those long, strong legs, broad shoulders and flat stomach. She'd expected the manager to be older, perhaps someone in his forties with a wife and kids. Yet Lachlan appeared not much older than her. As for dependents, it appeared ankle-high Billy was it.

'Good-looking bloke,' Angus said slyly. 'Just your type, too.'

She swatted his arm. 'Oh, shut up.'

He laughed and gave her another hug. 'Call me if you need anything.' He kissed her cheek. 'Come down this Saturday. Galapagos Flyer's racing in the Winter Stakes and it's always a good day at Rosehill. And Dad would love to see you.'

She watched the LandCruiser until it reached the end of the drive and turned onto the road. Angus had been the lone dissenter on the family's decision to oust her from Kingston Downs and employ a manager, but as he explained to her afterwards, their parents genuinely believed this was best for her, and with Mark adding his vote, there was little he could do. All he could offer was a lean shoulder to cry on and a promise to remain her advocate.

She sighed and glanced at the house. Lachlan stood near his dark red Hilux watching her. After a few seconds' more cool appraisal, he shoved his big hands into his pockets and wandered over.

'I'm heading in to town to the supermarket. Can I get you anything?'

'No. I'm right, thanks.' Now he was close, he seemed even bigger. His shoulders extended broad and square, and he must have stood close to two metres tall. Billy snuffled around his feet, looking like a rat in comparison.

'Okay, but if you remember something, here's my mobile number.'

He held out a scrap of paper. She took it, staring at the number, uncomfortable. She wanted to hate him but it was hard when he came across as so straightforward. Angus was right, this wasn't Lachlan's fault.

He shifted a little, as though wanting to say something, then changed his mind and with a nod walked off, Billy scampering behind.

Shoving the number into her pocket and hunching her shoulders against the winter wind, she wandered past the dairy towards the one hill on the property. It was a rise near the road that overlooked Kingston Downs' beautiful landscape where, over the years, numerous pets had been laid to rest surrounded by gums and spiky grevilleas, their graves marked by rocks. Only her grandparents' dogs had crosses, but the nailed-on arms had long fallen away. Brooke still remembered the collies' names—Athena and Zeus. Powerful names that evoked images of majesty and romance, and a style of name she'd followed since childhood with her horses.

She wandered to the farthest corner of the hill, to the saddest and most recent grave. It'd been a week since her last visit to Oddy's resting place and in her absence weeds had taken hold between the native sarsaparilla tubestock she'd planted in the fresh dirt. In a few months the sarsaparilla would flower vibrant purple and the grave would be massed in happy colour. A fitting memory to a beautiful animal whose life had ended so tragically. She sat next to the grave, hugging her knees, and surveyed the landscape, too despondent to bother plucking the weeds.

She closed her eyes against the ache of Oddy's death and immediately flicked them open as the image of him dying invaded her mind's eye. She wished she could reach inside her head and scrub it clean of that night, and remember only the good times, the happy whickers he made whenever he saw her approach, and the sweet welcoming nudges that made her heart swell and want to hug him to bits. Instead, she was left with the weight of his agonising death. His harrowing, guttural cries as Sod and Poddy thrashed on top of him. His helpless flail as the sheared-off piece of aluminium dug deeper into him, slicing through arteries and veins, destroying his big loving heart.

Tears built in her eyes. She blinked them away, hating their hot sting, wishing for something to assuage her terrible guilt, but she doubted anything with that power existed. Her culpability was something she'd have to live with and learn to accept.

The same as she'd have to accept the new manager taking over her home.

She dug her fingers in the soft ground at her side. 'What am I going to do, Odd-job?'

But only the rising wind breathed in her ear. She hugged her knees again and stared sadly towards the river. It wove like a vein through the landscape, nourishing the land, bringing life and prosperity as it chugged and gurgled its way to the sea. A constant in a world so bent on change.

With only Sod in work and Lachlan taking over she would have little to fill her days. All the tasks that were once her responsibility now belonged to him. The crops and pastures, the maintenance of fences, irrigation equipment and machinery, the checking of troughs and the distribution of hay—all the things that had structured her life and provided her with quiet satisfaction were gone. Now all she had left were a half a dozen spelling racehorses, Sod and a couple of youngsters still on their winter break, parents blind to the hurt their benevolence caused, and a brother who viewed the world through the lines of a profit-and-loss statement.

And looming over it all, blackening the horizon like a cloud filled sky, hung a terrifying phobia with the potential to cost her everything she held dear.

FIVE

IN THE DAYS after his arrival, Lachie sensed Brooke's scrutiny wherever he ventured on Kingston Downs. If he was in the horse paddocks, checking troughs or fencing, she'd somehow conspire to ride by on either a horse or a quad bike. If he was amongst the lucerne, inspecting plant growth, soil moisture, or monitoring for weeds, disease and insects, he'd spy her leading Poddy and Venus to the edge of a nearby stand for a treat. Only on Saturday, when she disappeared to Sydney, did he feel at ease, but even then she'd left him explicit instructions on Poddy's care and extracted a promise to call her if anything, no matter how minor, happened to the horse.

He understood it—in her shoes he'd probably be the same—but her vigilance remained exasperating. He had no idea what he could do other than give her time to get used to the situation. Confrontation was out of the question, especially given her cold reaction to Billy's misdemeanour on the first day they met, but they'd have to talk at some stage. There were aspects of the farm he needed to discuss. Yet he let it slide, promising himself each day he'd approach tomorrow.

With winter only half gone, Lachie took advantage of this relatively quiet period in the farm's schedule to introduce himself around the district. Come spring he'd be flat out, once the irrigation and haymaking season commenced, and although he was confident in his ability to manage the property, nothing beat local knowledge and experience.

The time he spent with the Department of Agriculture's district agronomist proved invaluable, as did his chat with the Pitcorthie Rural Supplies' agronomist and irrigation specialist. But he learnt the most from Kingston Downs' two neighbours, and not all of it about the property. While both welcomed him warmly, neither could hide their disappointment at his arrival and their deep sympathy for Brooke.

'She's a good lass, that Brooke,' said Greg Hitchcock, who ran the dairy farm on Kingston Downs' northern side with his wife and three cherub-cheeked young children. 'She's worked hard to make that place what it is. Bloody terrible her family treating her like this. Lass deserves better after what happened.'

The southern neighbour, an elderly widow named Nancy Burrows, who ran moppy-headed alpacas and a few sheep on her thirty-hectare lot, made her dismay clear over a pot of tea and delicious homemade ginger biscuits in the warm but rundown kitchen of her weatherboard cottage.

'Oh, no!' she exclaimed when Lachie explained his role. 'And after all the poor love's suffered. She must be heartbroken. You know about the accident, of course.'

'Only a bit.'

Nancy shook her head and tutted. 'Terrible thing. She swerved to miss one of Colin Grayson's steers and hit a culvert. Flipped the gooseneck right over with her horses trapped inside. She managed to get two of them out but the other had been sliced right open and bled to death in front of her. They had to prise her off him, poor love. Didn't say a thing, just stood there white-faced and covered in blood, holding out her hands and staring at them as if she didn't know what they were for. Only came to life apparently when the vet arrived and wanted to destroy Poseidon. She always was potty about that animal.' She frowned. 'So if you're there, where's she living now?'

Lachlan shifted in his seat, not enjoying the conversation. 'In the dairy.'

Nancy's face had dropped in horror. 'That place? She can't live there! She'll catch her death. Her parents ought to be ashamed of themselves. I'll go and talk to the poor love. She can move in with me.'

The idea that his employment had forced Brooke out of home and into substandard conditions didn't sit at all well with Lachie. Angus had assured him the dairy was habitable—not luxury living by any means, but a decent conversion with all facilities and used on several occasions without complaint by Kingston Lodge's stable workers. Still, his conscience nagged. He bided his time until one afternoon, a few days after his cuppa with Nancy, when Brooke disappeared towards Pitcorthie in her LandCruiser, he seized the opportunity to take a closer look at the dairy. A few minutes' wait to verify she wasn't coming back and Lachie headed up the track to the old building.

He circled the outside, feeling like a creepy peeping Tom but determined to set his mind at ease. The building had only two windows, one of which, from the frosted louvres, he took to belong to the bathroom. Through the gauze curtains of the other he could see a large open-plan living and kitchen area, dominated by a six-seat pine table loaded with magazines and horse gear. The floor was covered in large white tiles and the walls were painted pale blue with simple shelves attached. Photographs of horses in various poses covered the pine planks. A narrow pine stand topped by a mid-sized flat-screen television with what looked like a DVD player alongside occupied the left-hand corner of the room. Next to it, a door led off to another room, through which he could just make out the edge of a bed. Opposite, in the right-hand corner, towards the thick timber front door, stood a freestanding slow-combustion wood heater with a stack of cut timber piled in a basket alongside.

The old lady had been wrong. The place was fine. Not great but, as Angus had said, liveable.

Yet for some reason, Lachie still felt uneasy.

———

The Monday after his arrival, Lachie pulled in to the yard after a trip into the nearby town of Muswellbrook to find the float out of the barn and attached to Brooke's four-wheel drive. She sat on the lowered ramp, Sod standing as far away from the float as his lead rope allowed. As he passed, she turned her head to the side, so all Lachie caught was a curtain of hair, but something about the slump of her shoulders and the way she clutched at her wrist told him she wasn't right.

Leaving the groceries in the car, he walked over, Billy snuffling behind, and stopped by Sod to stroke his nose. Clearly in a foul mood, the horse lunged at him, but a grab of his headcollar and a shake soon put paid to any biting nonsense. Brooke's head stayed turned, but now Lachie was closer and in a better position he could see her eyes were wide and glistening.

The float's centre partition stood angled across to make the opening wider and more inviting. Inside, on the rubber matting, sat a plastic bucket of horse mix. A webbing lunging rope was tied to one side of the gate and ran in a long line to a tangled pool near Sod, as though thrown down in a tantrum. Given what Lachie suspected had occurred he would be insane to try and help, but Angus's entreaty for him to keep an eye on his sister, and the sympathy he had for her predicament made him want to reach out.

Leaving Sod to his sulk, he sat down next to her, feet resting on the ramp, knees up with his hands loosely drooped over them, as if he and Brooke sat down every day like this for a chat. At least the weather had turned from the cold grey days of the previous week to bright, crisp winter. Sunshine gave him some hope she wouldn't bite his head off.

He watched Billy hunt around the horse yards for treats, eyes closing in delight as he discovered a piece of hoof clipping and flopped down to chew contentedly.

'Are you okay?' he asked after several long seconds had passed.

She answered without turning. 'Fine.'

He thought on that response. Clearly she wasn't fine, but what to do? He stared at Sod, who looked back at him, blinking, and took a single step forward. Brooke turned to the horse and he caught the red rims of her eyes and her grim mouth. They waited, hopeful that the horse would come closer, but Sod simply stared back.

Lachie reached behind for the feed bucket and placed it in front of his feet before returning to his relaxed pose. Nostrils flaring and ears pricked, Sod stretched out his neck, knees bending, and leaned forward as far as he could manage without tipping on his nose.

Lachie smiled at the comic stance. Any moment now the horse would have to take a step. Sod couldn't reach the bucket without doing so. Lachie dug his hand into the sweet-smelling mix of chaff and grains and let it run through his fingers. Sod's nostrils flared even wider, and a frown appeared above his eyes as though he was disappointed by Lachie's mean tease.

'You'll have to come closer if you want some,' he said to the horse.

But Sod wasn't about to be fooled. He jerked on the lead, wrenching it out of Brooke's loosened hands and trotted a short distance away, rump turned, head down as he tore hunks of grass from the patch growing near the barn's rainwater tank.

Brooke turned her head away again, gripping her wrist like it was broken. A single tear slid down her cheek. Hating the sight of it, Lachie placed his hand on the rubber matting next to her. Not touching, just wanting her to know he was there.

'It'll be all right. He'll get better.'

She dropped her wrist and turned on him, eyes huge. 'What would you know? I've been doing this for weeks and not once has he set foot in the float.' She sagged, the flare of fire lost. 'He never will.'

'He's just scared. Like you.' At her sharp look he shrugged. 'I heard about the accident. It must be hard.'

She stared at him, saying nothing, her jaw clenched, her mouth thin. She held her distress contained but it was there nonetheless. Despite his brain warning him not to be sucked in, his heart went out to her.

'I'm not scared,' she finally managed. 'I'm just . . .' She spread her hands as though seeking the words in her palms. 'Grieving.' Liquid pooled in her eyes. 'I lost Oddy, and Poddy's . . .' She grabbed her wrist and rubbed frantically at a spot on the inside, shoulders shaking.

With a dog's sensitivity, Billy did what Lachie felt he couldn't. Precious scrap of hoof still hanging from his mouth, he trotted over to take position by her side and raked a paw down her thigh, whining in sympathy. Smiling shakily, she released her wrist and stroked his head.

Lachie waited until he thought she'd regained her equilibrium. 'I'd like to help.'

'You can't. No one can.'

He digested that, picking bits of grain from his fingers. Sod had recovered from his sulk and stood regarding them, bottom lip quivering as though he were imagining his nose buried in the bucket. Maybe she was right and no one could help. Horses had long memories and if Nancy's description of the accident was accurate, it was unlikely Sod would ever float again. As for Brooke, maybe he'd be better off leaving her well alone.

Except he couldn't. Not after seeing her like this. His inner white knight wouldn't let him, and something about her drew him.

'Anyway, what are you still sitting there for? Shouldn't you be running off to phone Mark?'

He gave her a puzzled look. 'What for?'

'To tell tales about me, of course.'

'I think you might have me confused with someone else. My job is to run Kingston Downs. Nothing more.'

'Right.' She stared straight ahead.

'Look, Brooke, I don't know what ideas you have about me but I'm just here to do a job, not get involved in any family arguments. Those I can get plenty of at home.' He placed the bucket behind him, ready to stand. 'You seemed upset. I just wanted to help.'

He dusted his palms on the front of his jeans and rose. Casting a last glance her way, he walked forward and grabbed Sod, batting the horse away when he tried to nip and ruffling his ears when Sod bunted his shoulder in affection. He led the horse by the halter back to the float and handed the lead to Brooke.

'I'll leave you to it, then.'

Lachie tapped his leg, signalling for Billy to come. The dog tilted his head and looked from Brooke to him and back again before trotting to Lachie's side, hoof scrap hanging from his mouth like a curly cigar.

Two steps from the float she spoke.

'I'm sorry. I'm not normally like this.' She regarded him with huge brown eyes overflowing with apology, and he thought again how pretty she was, but in a sad way that tugged at his insides. It made him wish he could make her smile. 'I'm just finding this hard.'

He nodded. 'I can imagine.'

'Can you?'

He thought of Delamere and how he'd feel if, after finally taking it over, someone came and told him it was no longer his to run. 'Yeah, I think I might.'

————

Lachie pushed open the door to the Pitcorthie pub and surveyed the room, hunting for Sam O'Donnell and trying to get his head around the number of people crowded about the bar. The Pitcorthie Rural Supplies agronomist had called that afternoon to invite him out for a beer and, he suspected, to sound him out about playing for the local rugby team. It being a Thursday night, he'd expected the pub to be dead, but instead it buzzed with people and chatter.

Heads turned as he shut the door and took a moment to orient himself. The pub appeared the same as the dozens of others he'd been to. Timber floor and half-panelled timber walls, on which hung local sports club banners, framed jerseys and team photographs, and a bar that extended in a wide U-shape from the rear wall.

A series of small tables were arranged to the left of the entrance, their timber tops marked with drink rings and coasters. Several groups of women occupied the seats, the young ones ogling him openly, the older ones regarding him with sly interest. Behind them, through a door adjacent to the bar, he could make out the fancy carpet and reflected light of a poker-machine room.

Past the bar to the right, on a plain carpeted area, stood a pool table lit by a long, low-slung light. Screens showing racing odds sat high above a corkboard with racing fields tacked to it and a counter containing rows of betting slips. Tucked into a corner and flashing what was left of its lights stood a jukebox contributing the Rolling Stones' 'Start Me Up' to the general rowdiness.

Spying a freckle-faced, lanky man wearing the rural uniform of a garish striped shirt, RM Williams boots, and jeans with a leather hobble belt through the loops, Lachie moved to the right-hand side of the bar, nodding greetings on the way to those who made eye contact. Judging by the fluoro safety stripes on their uniforms, most were miners. The upper Hunter was overcrowded with coalmines that sucked many workers off the land. Lachie had considered it himself, but couldn't bring himself to do it despite the high wages on offer. The other patrons seemed to be a mix of farmers, council workers and people from town.

Sam shook his hand, a broad smile lighting his sleepy blue eyes.

'Glad you could make it. What can I get you?'

'Just a light, thanks.'

Sam signalled for the barman and turned back to Lachie. 'Rockin', isn't it?'

Lachie nodded, casting around the room once more before focusing on Sam. 'Unusual to see a country pub this busy on a weeknight.'

'Cashed-up miners with nothing else to spend their money on. Good for the town and especially good for Nate here.' He winked at the spectacularly broken-nosed barman who'd worked his way round to them. 'Making a fortune, aren't you, mate?'

'I wish.' He eyed Lachie eagerly. 'Is this him?'

'Yep.'

Nate grinned even more widely than Sam. 'Friggin' awesome.' He held out his hand. 'Nate Osbourne, manager of this muckhole, captain of the Pitcorthie Panthers. Lock, I take it?'

'Generally,' said Lachie, amused. Given Nate's eager expression he had a feeling the Panthers were short a lock forward, and probably a few other positions. 'Although I haven't played for a couple of years so I'm a bit rusty.'

'So, ah, you interested?'

'In a game?' Lachie shrugged. 'Sure, but only if there's a slot. I don't want to take anyone's place.'

Sam rolled his eyes. 'Nothing to worry about there. Most weeks we're lucky to field a side. And believe me, I could do with some help in the second row. At the moment, I'm it.' He took a sip of beer. 'How's Saturday suit?'

On the other side of the bar, Nate held an empty schooner glass under the light-beer nozzle, hand resting on the tap, fairly jigging as he awaited Lachie's answer. Though the publican was only of average height, his polo shirt was stretched taut over a barrel chest and thick biceps, a clear reminder that despite his cheery demeanour he wasn't a man to be messed with.

'Sounds fine.'

Nate pulled the tap, eyes glinting with relish. 'Sandy Hollow won't know what hit them.'

'We hate those bastards,' said Sam.

'It's their fault we've won the wooden spoon two years running.'

Lachie blinked. 'You finished bottom last year?'

Nate gave him a wry look and jerked his head towards the crowd. 'This lot would rather drink than play sport. No bloody loyalty.'

'We play short a lot,' explained Sam.

'Right.' Lachie took Nate's proffered beer and stared at it for a moment, wondering if he shouldn't think about looking for another club—but Sam and Nate seemed friendly enough and he'd already said he'd play. Besides, teams like this were usually the best fun and that was all he was after. Just a game on the weekend and the companionship of other men. He needed to make friends. Couldn't stay moping around Kingston Downs, trying to avoid Brooke.

'You'll need some kit,' said Nate, then screwed up his crooked nose as he assessed Lachie. 'Probably have to order it in special but anything green will do for the weekend. Things are pretty casual in our grade and Sandy Hollow's kit's bright yellow so you should be right. Socks you can buy from Musgrove's, same as shorts. Talk to Patrick there. He's our fly half.'

Sam rested his back against the bar as Nate moved away to serve. 'So how're things working out at the Kingstons'?'

Lachie took a sip of beer before answering. He had a feeling he needed to tread carefully with the subject. 'I've only been there a week and a half but pretty good so far. Property's in good nick.'

'So's Brooke Kingston,' said Sam with a wink.

Lachie's hand tightened around the glass.

'Andy Chiang's in there, though, and you and I are too poor to compete with the likes of him.' Sam thought for a moment. 'And, in my case, too married.'

Lachie remained silent. He'd never been one for gossip and he wasn't about to start, especially about the Kingstons, but Sam continued.

'Bad accident she had. Screwed her up a bit, poor bugger.' He focused his sleepy eyes on Lachie, waiting for a comment.

Lachie shrugged. 'I don't know much about it.'

'Swerved to avoid a steer,' said Sam, turning to lean over the bar to order another beer. 'Ran off the road. Made a real mess. Vet said it was a miracle any of the horses survived, although that champion showjumper of hers is rooted. Shame. She won a lot on the horse. Town was proud of her.'

To Lachie's relief, the conversation moved on, Nate drifting across to join in during quiet moments. He stayed for another round, resisting Nate and Sam's pleas to sign up for the pub's hapless cricket team as well. Given the currents tugging the Kingston family, he wasn't confident he'd be around come summer. Not that he'd expected the job to be long-term; after all, it was only a stopgap until Nick finished uni and things changed at Delamere, but he had hoped it'd last longer than a few months.

He declined another shout. Two was enough and even though he only drank light beer, he wasn't about to take chances with his licence, and he couldn't afford to be out drinking either. Money was tight and he had to think of Nick.

After farewelling Sam and Nate, and arranging a meeting time at the pub for Saturday, he headed for the door. As he reached to open it, he noticed the back of a girl's head—a slim-shouldered girl with a messy golden-brown bob. She sat opposite a stunning brunette who gazed at him with sparkly blue, heavily made-up eyes full of invitation, and a bust about to flow over the top of her low-cut bright-blue top. Making up the trio was an olive-skinned, ebony-haired Asian man, who regarded Lachie with an expression as cold as the brunette's was hot.

'Leaving so soon?' asked the busty stunner with a coy finger-twirl of her polished mane when he hesitated at the door.

At the brunette's enquiry, Brooke turned her head, half smiling in curiosity—a smile that fell as she recognised him. 'Oh, hi,' she said without warmth.

The brunette leaned forward, spilling even more cleavage. She looked at Brooke, eyes as wide as a night-startled possum. 'This isn't him, is it?'

Brooke nodded.

'Oh. My. God.' She slumped back in her seat and stared at Lachie with her mouth half-open before returning her focus to Brooke. 'You never said—'

'Chloe,' said Brooke in a warning tone, cutting off whatever she was about to say. She threw Lachie a resigned look. 'Lachlan Cambridge, this is Chloe Daniels and Andrew Chiang.'

'Everyone calls me Lachie,' he said, offering his hand to Chloe, which, to his amusement, she held in her silky-skinned clasp for far longer than courtesy required. Andrew shook with a tight grip, dark eyes not matching his thin-lipped smile.

He stood back, unsure, and glanced at Brooke, hoping for a cue as to his next move. Chloe kept staring, boggle-eyed, while Andrew's focus was on Brooke. Brooke's hands had disappeared under the table, but from Lachie's vantage point he could see her doing the same strange movement to her wrist as she'd done when he found her at the float with Sod.

When no invitation to join them came, he cleared his throat and returned his hand to the door handle. 'I'm on my way home if you need a lift.'

Slowly, Brooke turned her face to him. For a fleeting moment raw hurt filled her eyes, then her stare dulled and her expression went blank.

'I'm fine,' she said, not meeting his gaze, before deliberately turning her back on him.

'Right.' He didn't need another hint. He nodded to Chloe and Andrew. 'Nice to meet you both.'

He pushed out into the night and stood for a moment on the footpath. Muffled laughter and chatter wafted with his plumed breath on the gelid air. He looked over his shoulder at the pub door, frowning as he went back over their brief encounter, trying to figure out what he'd said or done to create that look in her eyes. Though he examined every word and action, no explanation came. He doubted he'd ever find one.

With a last glance at the pub, he shoved his hands in his pockets, hunched his shoulders against the cold, and crossed the road to his car, wondering what sort of fool stood in the freezing night wasting brainpower on what Brooke Kingston might be thinking.

Better to stick with women like Chloe. She might be a bit over the top, but at least understanding came easy.

SIX

'BLOODY HELL, BROOKE,' said Chloe, looking at her aghast. 'Do you think you could have been any ruder?'

But Brooke wasn't thinking about her manners. Her mind rattled with the word Lachlan had thrown out so casually. *Home.* She stared at her beer glass. It should be a nice word, a comforting word. Instead, it had sliced through her. Kingston Downs was *her* home, not Lachlan's, yet he made it sound like he'd already claimed ownership.

'Earth to Brooke.' Chloe tapped the table in front of her with a sparkly pink acrylic fingernail. 'Yoo-hoo.'

With Chloe's call, she thumped back to reality. She groaned and held her hands to her shame-flamed face, peeping through her fingers at her friend. 'Oh, God, I was rude, wasn't I?'

'Very,' said Chloe, 'and that's not like the Brooke we know and love.'

'I know, I'm sorry. But I can't help it. I just want him off Kingston Downs.'

Chloe grinned, exposing her very white but gapped front teeth—a flaw she was desperate to correct but couldn't afford to. 'God knows why. That man's a walking sex machine. Good-looking, built like the proverbial, and that arse!' She released a long, theatrical sigh. 'I could spend hours perving at it.'

Brooke felt Andrew's gaze. She hadn't told either of her friends what Lachlan was like, other than reporting that he seemed reasonably competent and owned a Jack Russell. But Andrew knew her well enough to know that Lachlan was smack in her man-zone. Her previous boyfriends had all been similar types—tall, well muscled, and attractive in an unpolished, ruggedly rural way, although with his size and thick-lashed hazel eyes, Lachlan Cambridge inhabited a different league.

'Doesn't matter what he looks like,' she said. 'I just wish he'd leave.'

'I know, I know. It's all horribly unfair and he shouldn't be at Kingston Downs.' Chloe leaned across to squeeze her fingers. 'But we're talking total hornbag here. And I mean *total*. Maybe you could keep him just a little while? For me?'

Brooke cast a glance at Andrew, who smiled and shook his head. As though tuned in to their conversation, the pub's ancient jukebox began belting out the Hoodoo Gurus' 'Miss Freelove '69'. Brooke bit her lip to stop herself laughing and thought, as she had countless times in the past, how blessed she was to have friends like Chloe and Andrew. They had their hiccups, sure, but she wouldn't trade them for anything. Chloe was funny, vibrant, and possessed a heart as big as Australia—a heart some believed she shared around too freely. Brooke occasionally squirmed at Chloe's promiscuous nature, but she understood it came from a combination of Chloe's innate generosity and her endless hunt for Mr Right. Brooke's great wish was for her friend to find a man who shared the same good humour and love of life that Chloe had, and settle down. Once, she'd even teasingly suggested Andrew, but Chloe had given her such a strange look she'd never mentioned it again.

As for Andrew, they were getting over their troubles. Slowly.

'Okay,' said Chloe, releasing Brooke's hand and eyeing them, 'who's up for a bet?'

'No one bets against a certainty, Chloe,' said Andrew.

She looked at Brooke, who raised her palms. Like Andrew, Brooke knew exactly what Chloe wanted to bet on—how quickly she could hook up with Lachlan. 'Not a chance.'

Chloe leaned back, pouting. 'Oh, come on. He might be one of those religious types, or have a girlfriend already. Who knows? He might even be gay.'

'Not the way he was looking at your cleavage,' Andrew countered.

'Yeah, he did seem a bit impressed.' She eyed Andrew, the corner of her mouth twitching. 'Six weeks or I shave my head.'

'Six weeks? Not with your track record.'

'All right, then. A month.' She tilted her head, blue eyes playful. 'Come on, what are the odds of a bloke like him *not* having a girlfriend?'

Andrew pursed his lips, considering. 'And if I lose?'

Chloe reached out to ruffle his perfect hair. 'You lose yours, Samson.'

Brooke hid a smile. One thing Andrew did care about was his appearance. Having his head shaved would hammer a deep dent in his vanity. 'Go on,' she urged when he continued to hesitate. 'Take a chance.'

He sighed and ran a hand through his sleek cut. 'I'm going to regret this.'

'You might, but you and I both know the thrill of the gamble's worth it.' Chloe held out her hand. 'Shake.'

'What are you going to produce as proof?'

'His jocks.'

Brooke screwed her nose up.

Chloe rolled her eyes. 'Well, what else am I going to use? The only other thing is the . . . you know, the . . .' She made a moue of distaste. 'You know!'

'Urgh,' said Brooke, cottoning on. 'No way! That's just too gross.'

'So, we're happy with jocks then?'

Casting Brooke a 'what the hell am I doing?' look, Andrew reached out and shook. 'A month, Chloe. And I hope like hell he turns out to be gay.'

———

Early the following morning, once Brooke had fed Sod and led Poddy and Venus to their paddock, she braced herself and walked to the cottage. Though the air was winter-morning arctic and a wind chill plunged the temperature even lower, sunrays saturated the sheltered verandah, creating an oasis of warmth. Two pairs of oversized boots— one long rubber, one short leather, both clean—stood neat sentry next to the doormat. Alongside, Lachlan had placed a raised aluminium- framed dog's bed, its mesh base topped with a thick sheepskin and an old bundled-up quilt.

As she reached the top verandah step the quilt twitched, then a little black nose followed by little black eyes tunnelled free from the fabric. Billy's mouth parted in a welcoming doggy smile, his tail raising the quilt as it thumped. Wriggling out of his cocoon, he jumped down to sniff her ankles before flopping onto his back in the hope of a belly rub. Grinning, she obliged, calling him a silly Billy when his leg thumped in crazy ecstasy. Brooke had her horses, but she missed having a dog around the place, and while she would have preferred a collie, Billy was a still a little cutie.

'He'll let you do that all day,' said Lachlan from behind the screen door, startling her. She hadn't realised the main door was open. The screen's springs creaked as he stepped out, a slice of Vegemite- smeared toast in his hand. 'Loves it.'

'My collie used to, too.' She ruffled Billy's head and straightened, casting a look over Lachlan. After the previous night's rudeness she'd expected hostility but she caught only wariness in his sunlit hazel eyes.

He nodded to the door. 'Did you want to come in for a cuppa?'

'No,' she answered quickly, then winced at how rude that must

have sounded. Again. Discourtesy was becoming a habit in his presence and that was so unlike her it made her squirm inside with contrition. She forced a smile. 'Thanks. I'm fine.'

'Okay.' He took a bite of toast and chewed, his gaze on hers, a
small frown knitting his brow. 'Is there—'

'About last—'

'Sorry.' He waved the toast at her. 'You first.'

Brooke bit her lip, fingers creeping to her wrist and pressing. 'Last
night. In the pub. I was very rude. I'm sorry.'

He said nothing for a moment, eyeing her in that quiet way he
had, as if he were weighing her words and his response very carefully.
Billy sat on his haunches, head swivelling between them. Finally,
Lachlan shrugged. 'I guess you didn't expect to see me there.'

'No.' She released her wrist, relieved to have her apology out of
the way. Lachlan took another bite of his toast, still watching her. She
turned her attention to the lawn, where a magpie was hunting in the
fresh-cut grass. Being winter, the buffalo produced little growth and
she'd let it go, but Lachlan had trimmed the edges and mown stripes
into the lawn, the neat sward marred only by a few holes where he'd
dug out weeds. She nodded toward it. 'You're more conscientious
than me.'

'I thought it needed a bit of a tidy.' He sucked in a breath. 'Sorry.
That sounded like a criticism.'

'Probably deserved. It *was* a bit messy.' She threw him a smile to
show she hadn't taken offence and slapped her palms against her
thighs. 'Right. I'd better leave you to it. If there's anything you need,
just yell.' As she turned to leave, Billy let out a sharp yap. Laughing,
she crouched down to give him a goodbye scratch. 'And you, my little
silly Billy, are welcome to a belly rub anytime.'

'There is something.'

She had to twist her neck right back to see his face. God, the man
was tall. Today, instead of his usual jeans, he wore twill navy work
pants with a matching shirt tucked in at the waist. Though not tight,
the material showed off the contours of his thighs and the leanness of

his hips. He wore his shirtsleeves loosely rolled, exposing muscled forearms with gold-tipped dark hairs. His chin was clean-shaven, his short hair slightly damp. As she breathed in she caught an enticing waft of citrus and scrubbed healthy male.

'When you have time, maybe you could show me around. Give me a bit of a history of what you've done here.'

She looked back at Billy, now flopped on his back with his legs wide apart, expecting another belly scratch. Yes, she did know Kingston Downs backwards. Yes, she had offered her assistance. But why should she help him? Surely it was in her best interests to see him fail as a manager.

'Brooke?'

She focused on Billy, for some reason unable to look at Lachlan. Last night, after the pub, she'd promised herself she'd treat him with courtesy. As Angus said, it wasn't Lachlan's fault that he was at Kingston Downs. He'd been employed to do a job and if he was anything like the man she suspected him to be, he wanted to do it well. But helping him felt like giving in.

He crouched down next to her. 'I know you resent me being here, and I don't blame you, but it won't be forever. It's obvious you've worked hard on this place and when the time comes for me to move on, I'd like to hand it back knowing I haven't undone everything you've achieved.'

She continued to stare at Billy, embarrassed by the flare of heat in her cheeks and acutely aware of Lachlan's proximity, his size, his smell, and, most of all, his understanding. 'You're making it very hard for me to hate you. You know that, don't you?'

He ducked his head and smiled. 'Maybe that's my cunning plan.'

She bit her lip, trying not to smile in return, feeling guilty that she'd even considered trying to undermine him. He didn't deserve that.

'I'm free now, if you like.'

'Good,' he said, standing. 'I'll just grab my jumper and boots.'

While he sorted himself, she wandered through the garden, Billy trailing behind, reflecting on his comment about this not being forever, wondering what plans he had. Whatever they were, they hadn't stopped him making himself at home. He'd already started pruning the peach tree in the small mixed-fruit orchard that ran along the side of the house, another chore Brooke had let slide. Cuttings lay in neat piles ready for burning, and although only half the job was done, already the tree was beginning to form the optimum vase shape.

'You look like you know what you're doing,' she said, hearing footsteps behind her.

He'd donned a dark-brown polar-fleece jumper with Central West Constructions embroidered on the chest in yellow and the neck zippered up against the cold. A faded baseball cap covered his brown hair, and she recognised its blue and gold stripes and the crest of Sydney University Football Club. The combination of brown, blue and gold brought out strange, almost tortoiseshell hues in his eyes.

'Mum taught me. She keeps a small orchard at Delamere.'

'Delamere?'

'My parents' property.'

She waited for him to elaborate but he didn't. Instead, he whistled for Billy. The terrier's head bobbed up from the long grass of the adjacent paddock, then lowered again as he scrambled back toward them. Ears and muzzle covered in dewdrops, he sat panting at Lachlan's side.

Smiling, he shook his head at the dog before regarding her. 'Shall we start?'

Enjoying the morning quiet, they sauntered toward the machinery shed and the bay where Lachlan now parked his Hilux. The mist that had hovered over the river when Brooke led Poddy and Venus out had lifted with the sun and breeze, and the landscape felt aglow with promise. In the distance, the craggy sandstone hills of the Wollemi National Park ascended majestically, their timeworn contours cupping the southern edges of the upper Valley.

'I figured we'd walk,' said Lachlan when she paused near his ute.

He looked up at the sky and the rising sun. 'It's a nice day and it's not as if we have thousands of acres to cover.'

'If you like. Besides, it's not like I have much else to do.' She grimaced, wishing she could tie her tongue in a knot. 'Sorry. Not your fault.'

'We seem to be doing that a lot today. Apologising, I mean.'

'The awkwardness of strangers. Although, out of the two of us, I'd have to say I own the most errant mouth.'

She led him down the lane to the paddocks, and unlatched the first gate on the right. Like many others on Kingston Downs, the paddock was small, less than two and a half hectares, and surrounded by dark timber and coated-wire fencing. Kaleidoscopic dewdrops hung sparkling from the wires, and snail trails glittered on the posts. At the far end, at Kingston Downs' boundary, a row of muted green gums pitched long shadows.

Casting a critical eye over the ground cover, she walked to the centre and halted. Though grass ran up to her ankles and patches of white clover still thrived, compared to its neighbours the pasture appeared tired. Around the many manure patches, the grass grew coarse and stemmy, and weeds shot up thick leaves and flower heads. Other areas were cropped to ground level, the plants weak and sour looking from overgrazing and shallow-rootedness.

'This is RL1,' she said.

'Right lane one,' Lachlan replied, nodding. He smiled a little when she regarded him with a disbelieving expression. 'It's how I would have named them.'

'Right.' But she wasn't sure whether to believe him or not. Angus could have told him her naming system. She'd check later to make sure, yet she doubted he'd lied. He didn't seem the type to play games —too contained and considered.

She dragged a foot through a clump of ryegrass. 'As you can see, it needs renovation. I'd planned to do it in the autumn but with the—' She looked quickly away from his sympathetic gaze, continuing as though nothing had happened while her fists clenched at her weakness. 'Horses are rough on pasture. They're fussy eaters and won't graze around dung or eat anything that's too old or rank. And they'll completely defoliate the species they find the most palatable, which makes it hard to not only maintain good cover and weed control, but can also affect the nutritional balance of the pasture and in turn the horses' wellbeing.'

She walked a short distance away and squatted, pointing at a patch of green with newly sprouted dandelion seedlings. 'See here? This is probably all that remains of the Golkonda Italian ryegrass I oversowed as a trial last year. Horses love the Italian types, especially the tetraploids, which have bigger cells and less fibre and are easier to digest.'

He crouched opposite her, his expression loaded with interest. 'It's an annual, though, isn't it?'

'More short-term. You can get a couple of years out of it if you manage it properly.'

'What about perennial ryegrass? Don't the horses like that?'

'They'll eat it no problem in the growing season, but if you put an Italian alongside a perennial they'll eat the Italian down to the ground and leave the perennial. So it makes pasture selection a balancing act. Nothing beats an Italian for winter productivity but without perennials you're oversowing every year.' She bit her lip and stared towards the river. 'Anyway, it's all a bit moot now. With so few horses there's more feed than they could ever eat. I'd be better off turning most of the place over to lucerne. It's where the money is and it'd at least get my rotten brother off my back.'

Suddenly, she realised what she was saying. She looked back at him. 'Sorry, I forgot. Not my problem any more.'

He gave her another of those assessing looks before straightening up. He shoved his hands in his pockets and scanned the paddock for a moment, before regarding her once more. 'Tell me about your renovation process.'

Brooke might be acting boorish but she wasn't thick. The change of subject signalled clearly what he thought of her pettiness. Heat

crawled over her cheeks. She reached out for Billy, on rodent high
alert near her knee, ears pricked, nose in the dirt, paws together and
body quivering.

She bit her lip in shame at her behaviour. 'You must think I'm
such a cow.'

'No. I just think you're hurting.'

'And taking it out on you.'

He smiled when she looked up. 'Don't worry. I'm big enough to
handle it.'

Unable to help herself, she smiled back. No matter how bad her
conduct, his reaction remained constant. No censure or complaint,
just understanding. She'd never met anyone like Lachlan Cambridge.
Giving Billy an affectionate head rub, she rose to answer his
question.

'On the horse pastures, I only direct drill. There are disadvan-
tages, I know, but it's cheaper than full cultivation and most of all it's
better for the soil. In the past I suppressed pasture growth through
either topping or spraying, but last year I asked Greg Hitchcock—he's
the dairy farmer to the north of us—if I could borrow some of his
heifers and use them to hard graze instead. You'll see the result
in LL4.'

'It didn't work?'

'Not as well as I hoped.'

He nodded. 'Plants respond differently to grazing. They recover
faster.'

'So I discovered. By the time the seedlings were at the two-leaf
stage, the older pasture was already too vigorous and swamped the
new growth.' She placed her hands on her hips and studied the
paddock, wondering how to solve the dilemma.

'You could spray in bands down the drill rows.'

'I know.' She sighed and flopped her hands to her sides. 'I'm just
trying to get away from spraying altogether. And no, I'm not a rabid
greenie, if that's what you're thinking. It's simply that I can see a time
in the future when we won't be able to do it at all, or it'll be so highly

regulated and costly it won't be worth the while. You only have to consider how bad it is with irrigation nowadays.'

'What about the lucerne? Tough to not use chemicals there.'

'It is, but I know a few farmers who've gone organic. It's hard, but small-bale organic hay sells at a premium in Sydney. Not just for animal feed, either. Some home gardeners buy it for mulch. There's a market there.'

'And high profitability from reduced inputs.'

'Exactly.'

He gave her a look she couldn't fathom but it left her feeling warm, and this time not with embarrassment.

They moved towards the gate, Billy leaping ahead, his nose grubby with dirt.

'So is this a strategy you want me to follow too?' Lachlan asked when they entered the lane.

She hesitated, unsure how to answer. Kingston Downs was his responsibility now. Her dreams were on hold.

'If it's any help, I'm fairly sympathetic to the idea.'

Brooke didn't know if this surprised her or not. Despite her initial antipathy to him, Lachlan was proving an altogether different man than she'd expected. The sort of man, if things were different, she'd like to get to know properly.

'With the horse paddocks, I'd like you to. The lucerne's another matter. That'd require a serious change in management, not to mention a long transition period before certification. Plus given how much cash the hay crop brings in, you'd never get approval from Mark.'

'Have you run the idea past him?'

She shook her head. 'I know what his reaction would be.'

'But perhaps if you explained it . . .'

Brooke made a disparaging noise. 'Mark doesn't care about the environment or 'best practices' or anything else philosophical. All he cares about is cash flow and profit.'

She opened the gate to the next paddock and led him into it, explaining its history as she walked. He listened attentively, asked smart questions, and most of all, treated her like an equal, which not only made her feel proud, it also made her recent treatment of him seem even surlier.

They worked their way around the property, discussing each paddock in turn, enjoying the rising morning, until they reached Poddy and Venus's paddock. From the moment she opened the gate, the horse and pony crowded round for attention. Venus bunted her woolly head against Lachlan's thigh, making him laugh with her demand for affection. His laugh was a warm sound, deep and honest, which Brooke liked.

She kissed and stroked Poddy's nose, watching Lachlan as he scruffed Venus's forelock like she was a big dog. Given the Shetland's tiny stature against his size, she almost looked like one.

Brooke also found herself admiring his easy way with the horses. No fear, no nerves—not even with Sod—just easy rapport.

'You like horses?' she asked when they'd completed their greetings and indulged the horses enough.

'Yeah. They're funny animals. Not smart like dogs, and ruled more by their instincts, but they're sweet-natured mostly.'

'So, can you ride?'

'Not like you.' He dug his fingers into Venus's mane and scratched. The pony's eyes closed in pleasure. 'We had horses as kids but they're gone now.'

'We?'

'Me and my brother, Nick.'

'Older or younger?'

'Younger.'

'And is he at . . .' She searched for the property name he'd used but it eluded her. 'At your parents' place?'

'No. He's at uni in Armidale studying to be a teacher.'

Lachlan let go of Venus and moved towards Poddy, and ran a big hand down his neck. His fingernails were clipped and clean, she noticed. Not manicured or pampered, simply neat. Neat and big, like everything about him.

'He was your champion, wasn't he?'

She kissed Poddy's nose. 'Still is.'

'He's a good-looking horse, that's for sure. Such a shame he can't showjump any more because of his eye.'

'Not because of his eye. He broke his—' She clung to Poddy as an invisible fist grabbed her throat, and quickly ducked her head to hide her expression. She squeezed her eyes shut, willing the images away. Sensing distress, Poddy shuffled.

'You don't have to talk about it.'

She shook her head. She wasn't going to give in to this. Not in front of Lachlan. She dropped her hands from Poddy and pressed her fingers into her wrist, counting out the beats.

Exhaling slowly, she faced him again, under control. 'It's okay. He shattered his third tarsal bone trying to kick free. With proper treatment it's not always a career-ending injury but unfortunately for Poddy it looks like it is. He's not lame, but the latest X-rays showed calcification in the bone. If I put him back into work he'll only break down again.' She bit her lip, eyes watering. 'I love him too much to see him in pain.'

Annoyed at being ignored, Venus bustled between them. Lachlan steered the Shetland gently aside and focused on the demanding pony, giving Brooke a chance to wipe at her tears. She didn't know if he'd done it on purpose but was grateful all the same.

'I think Venus has a crush on you,' she said when she'd recovered. The pony's eyes were half-closed, her lip quivering in delight at his ministrations.

'Like Billy with you, she's sussed out I'm a soft touch for a scratch.'

He regarded her for moment, eyes roaming her face, hunting, she suspected, for further signs of distress. There wouldn't be. Not today. She'd already embarrassed herself enough. Satisfied, he pulled up his sleeve and checked his watch. Brooke did the same, surprised to see it was almost ten. They'd been at it for nearly three hours. Lachlan appeared as amazed as she was. 'Time flies.'

'Yeah. I had no idea.' They stared at each other.

'Well, I suppose—'

'I guess—'

Lachlan grinned and indicated for her to speak first. 'Brains and beauty before brawn.'

His compliment, though made as a joke, left her momentarily confounded. Poddy plonked his head on her shoulder and blew warm breath into her ear and snapped her out of her fuddlement. It meant nothing. A figure of speech. Nothing more.

'I was just going to say we'd better go and do some work.'

'Exactly what I was about to suggest.'

The horses followed them to the gate, Venus neighing forlornly as they shut it behind them, and continued up the lane. They said little on the way. Brooke felt shy in Lachlan's presence, but she wasn't sure why. There was no doubt he was nice, and attractive too, and perhaps under other circumstances they could be real friends. But the fact remained that while he was here at Kingston Downs the life she adored, her home, all she loved, was at risk. And the longer he stayed, the stronger the pressure to move to Sydney would become.

Her family's well-meaning coercions, though tempered thanks to Angus, were already near unbearable.

How bad they'd be in a few months' time, she didn't want to contemplate.

SEVEN

FRIDAY LUNCHTIME FOUND Brooke balanced on the rail surrounding Willowgrove's undercover ménage alongside Chloe, watching Andrew work his impressive new Holsteiner colt, Marchment. The horse had only arrived that morning. Chloe should have been in the salon, but like Brooke, she couldn't resist sneaking away for an ogle.

Large fluorescent lights lit an interior larger than Kingston Downs' dressage and showjumping arenas combined. At the far end of the ménage, a two-tier spectator stand rose from the special sand and fibre surface. Protective padding layered the walls of the two long sides, on one of which Chloe and Brooke sat perched. Music filtered through expensive speakers strategically placed for acoustic clarity. Andrew usually fed crowd noise through them to acclimatise his youngsters, but today he'd chosen the sort of hyped-up dance music Brooke loathed but which he and Chloe adored.

The horse was, as Andrew had bragged, magnificent. A leggy colt with perfect conformation and gaits that flowed like silk. Generations of selective breeding showed in his build and haughty posture. Marchment was an animal well aware of his stunning looks, and showed off accordingly with head tosses and a strutting, look-at-me manner. A perfect complement to his equally swaggering master.

'That outfit's ridiculous, I'll have you know,' Brooke called as Andrew cantered past on the snorting animal. As though wanting to coordinate with his mount, he'd dressed in black, but with audacious highlights. His breeches sported contrasting scarlet patch pockets over the hips and scarlet rubbery knee grips running in diagonal stripes down the inside leg. A scarlet chest pocket emblazoned his black, body-hugging seventies-style shirt. Even Marchment's saddle-cloth and browband stood out, brightly blood red against his dark, glossy coat.

'You like it?'

'No. It makes you look like a bull ant.'

Chloe choked back a snort.

Andrew laughed and eased Marchment to a walk before stroking a palm down the front of his own chest, stretching the fabric tighter over his slim but athletic build. 'It's Italian. Very fashionable in Europe at the moment.'

Brooke rolled her eyes. She loved her friend but God, the man could be vain. 'Fashionable on the continent maybe, but only cause for sledging in Australia.'

Tossing her a 'you think you're so clever' sneer, Andrew turned Marchment away, calling over his shoulder as he headed to the other side of the arena, 'The problem with you, Brooke Kingston, is that you have no fashion sense at all. Your poor mother must be in despair.'

'He has a point,' said Chloe, nudging her.

'Nothing wrong with being a dag. Anyway, that outfit *is* ridiculous.'

Chloe tilted her head to the side, considering. 'I don't know. I think it's quite sexy.'

Brooke stared at her and blinked, astonished by the expression on Chloe's face. An expression which, if she didn't know her friend better, she could almost interpret as longing.

Chloe darted her eyes at Brooke and her face switched to one of her sparkly-eyed, cheeky grins. 'But don't you dare tell him I said that. Andrew has a big enough head as it is.' She slid off the rail. 'Hey, bull-ant man, can I've a ride?'

'You talking about me or my horse?'

'The horse, doofus. The other one you can only dream about.'

He cantered towards Chloe and halted Marchment perfectly square, as though he'd just completed a dressage test. 'You think you can handle him?'

'Don't you know?' she said, throwing him a wink, 'I'm an expert at rides.'

He dismounted and ran a hand down her long hair, expression teasing. 'You better be, otherwise it's bye-bye Goldilocks, hello Baldy.'

Chloe didn't bite. She merely raised a perfectly plucked eyebrow as her mouth quirked with smug confidence.

With Chloe organised and astride Marchment, Andrew joined Brooke on the fence. 'So what do you think?'

'Impressive. Have you jumped him?'

'Only over small stuff. Still a bit of work to do there. He has talent, though.' He regarded her. 'You should think about getting a new horse. Marchie's half-sister is up for sale.'

Brooke observed Chloe as she carefully rode Marchment around the arena, her brow furrowed as she concentrated on getting a feel for the horse. Her friend looked as beautiful on horseback as she did on the ground—slim, long-legged, soft-handed and fluid. No wonder she won so many hacking competitions. She could make any mount look stunning.

'I don't know.'

'You need to think about the future, Brooke.'

'I do. All the time. That's the trouble.'

'Hey, stop worrying. You'll get better.'

Brooke turned away, biting her lip against her disquiet, wishing she had Andrew's faith.

He reached across to squeeze her hand. 'I'd do anything to make things right for you, you know that.'

'I know, and you're sweet but it's not your fault. The blame's mine.'

'No, it's not.'

She shook her head and pulled her hand from under his to cross her arms over her chest, covering the ache inside. He could argue all he liked but the truth remained. The accident was her fault, its tragic consequences hers alone to deal with.

His gaze stayed on her, burning, reminding Brooke of all he longed for. All she couldn't give him.

'Don't,' she said softly when the intensity became too much.

His mouth thinned. Anger tinged his voice. 'I'm still allowed to care about you, you know. What happened between us doesn't change that. We're still friends.'

She wanted to believe him, to cling to the notion that they were as solid as always, but she couldn't forget his confession. Love didn't just disappear overnight.

She swallowed, wishing she knew how he really felt. Realising the only way to find out was to ask, she opened her mouth to speak but changed her mind at the sight of Chloe cantering towards them. Perhaps another time.

'That was pretty awesome,' said Chloe, halting Marchment as squarely perfect as Andrew had done. 'Like riding a rocking horse.' She dismounted, moving forward to fondle Marchment's ears as she kissed his cheek. 'We should put you in a hacking class. That'd make all those other pretties sit up.'

'Don't give him ideas.' Andrew jumped to the ground and took the reins from Chloe. 'He already thinks he's God's gift.'

'Bit like his owner then.'

Andrew poked his tongue out at her. Cross-eyed, Chloe returned the compliment until both broke into laughter, and for a brief moment, Brooke experienced a twinge of envy at being left out. Stupid, given she'd never once felt envious of her friends' easy relationship—but she'd changed so much since the accident. And not necessarily for the better.

Andrew jerked his head towards Brooke, all anger gone. 'Help me convince our stubborn friend here she needs to buy a new horse.'

'Andrew's right. You need something to keep you occupied. A young horse might be the challenge you need.'

Brooke dropped from the fence and stroked Marchment's silky neck. 'What's the point? It's not like I'll be able to take it anywhere.'

Chloe exchanged a rolled-eye look with Andrew. 'Oh, aren't you a Miss Misery Guts!'

'Yeah,' said Andrew. 'What happened to the Brooke we're used to?'

Brooke's fingers clenched around Marchment's fine mane. 'I've tried. I can't do it.'

'You can.'

'We believe in you.'

A spark lit in Andrew's eyes. 'You'll beat it. The Chiang-man says so.'

'And, as we all know,' said Chloe with mock seriousness, 'the Chiang-man here is never wrong.'

Brooke looked from Andrew to Chloe and back again, and laughed. They might share their ups and downs but God, she was lucky to have them in her life. 'I don't deserve you two.'

Chloe slung her arm around Brooke's shoulder. 'No, you don't. But we're here anyway.' She focused on Brooke's face. 'You *will* be able to do it. It mightn't happen overnight but in time you'll get your confidence back. You just have to keep working at it.'

Yet later that afternoon, as Brooke sat with her hands death-gripped on the steering wheel of her LandCruiser, all she felt was the rawness of failure.

Her stomach clenched as Venus's annoyed whinny sounded through the car's open window. Despite the cold, Brooke's hands were sticky with sweat. No sound came from the LandCruiser's engine and unless she took hold of herself and turned the ignition key, none ever would.

Gritting her teeth, she closed her eyes and rested her forehead against the steering wheel, trying to channel the resolve that had seemed so intense on leaving Willowgrove. Andrew and Chloe had faith; why couldn't she?

'You okay?'

She looked up to find Lachlan standing near the door, eyeing her with a worried expression, and quickly looked away again. 'I'm fine.'

'If you don't mind me saying so, you don't look it.'

'I said I'm fine.' She closed her eyes. 'Oh God, I'm sorry. I'm just . . .' She threw up her hands, hating her rudeness, this awkward, horrible situation.

'Grieving,' he said, tossing the word she'd used before back at her.

He took a step closer and curled his hand over the door. She stared at him. His eyes were doing that tortoiseshell thing, and his mouth held a gentle curve. Standing there, he seemed big and safe and strong and *kind*. Like Angus, except musclier and with much, much longer eyelashes.

'It's not grief,' she said suddenly. 'I'm scared, like you said. It's Oddy's screams. I can't make him stop. He just gets louder and louder and then I can't breathe . . .' She slapped the wheel in frustration. 'I need to beat this but he *just won't stop*.'

'Maybe I can help.'

'How?'

He shrugged. 'I don't know. I don't know anything about psychology but I can offer big shoulders to cry on. I could even be your punching bag if you'd think it'd help.' He bent and picked up Billy, who greeted her with an excited doggy grin. 'Or you can just borrow my dog. He doesn't mind being cried on.'

'How do you know?'

A shadow stole the brightness from his eyes. He glanced away. 'Long story.'

Brooke leaned back and stared through the windscreen, thinking.

Perhaps a stranger was what she needed. Someone dispassionate, who wouldn't suffer along with her. So what if she gave up her pride? She had little left as it was.

'Would you sit with me?'

He smiled. 'I think I could manage that.'

She smiled back, feeling the fluttering return of her optimism. 'I guess I'd better warn you that I'm really unattractive when I cry. And I mean *really* unattractive.'

'I'm sure I'll manage.' He dropped Billy to the ground. 'Do you want to try now?'

Venus let out another whinny. Brooke's mouth parted. Distracted by Lachlan she'd forgotten about the pony.

'Maybe you need to try some animal other than a horse.'

'Like what?'

In lieu of an answer he gave an enigmatic smile that made her heart do a weird flip-flop. 'Why don't you unload Venus and then wait here? I'll be back shortly.'

'Where are you going?'

But he didn't answer. Instead he strode across the yard to his Hilux and stepped inside. Seconds later he was heading up the lane.

Brooke climbed from the car, lowered the tailgate and led the irritated pony to her yard next to Poddy. The minutes passed. She stood by her beloved champion, caressing his long nose and muzzle, waiting. Kingston Downs lay hushed and slumbery in the late afternoon sun. The wind had died, leaving the landscape at peace, out of balance with her internal disquiet. In the front paddocks, a couple of thoroughbreds enjoyed a mutual scratch of each other's necks. Fresh country smells—cow and horse manure, pasture and moist, fertile soil —scented the air. But of Lachlan there was no sign.

Her shoulders slumped. Perhaps he'd chickened out. She couldn't blame him. Taking on her troubles was too much for anyone.

She looked up as the hum of a vehicle carried from the road. Attuned to Kingston Downs' environment, she noted the gear change. With a kiss on Poddy's nose she ducked out of the yard as

Lachlan's Hilux coasted down the drive, sunlight flashing off its red roof and chrome roll bar. Through the windscreen she could see Billy perched on Lachlan's lap, little paws up on the window's edge. As the ute passed she noticed the tonneau cover was pulled back and tucked in, and despite her relief at his return, the worry of what it might contain made her insides twist tighter.

He braked alongside the LandCruiser and with a 'Sorry it took so long', flipped down the tailgate and leant into the back to gather something grey and woolly into his arms. The sheep let out an indignant bleat as he hauled it towards the float and sat it on its backside, its upper body gripped between his knees.

'Meet our gallant test pilot,' he said, untying the rope securing the sheep's legs and scruffing its head. The ewe kicked and jerked, attempting escape, but Lachlan held her firm.

Brooke couldn't stop staring at the ewe, which rewarded her scrutiny with another grumpy bleat. The merino's weird, pale-brown eyes, with their oval pupils, gave it an almost demonic appearance. She told herself it was just a normal sheep, but the fist gripping her insides grew claws. Her mouth dried as she thought of towing the float with a living creature—even a demon-eyed one—in the back.

'She's one of Nancy's,' Lachlan continued when she remained silent. 'Don't worry, we won't go anywhere. We'll just sit. Dorothy'll be fine.'

'Dorothy?'

He muttered something she didn't catch. 'It's her name.' He stared at Billy, who regarded Dorothy with bright, excited eyes, before turning back to Brooke, his voice firm. 'She'll be fine. I won't let anything happen to her.' He paused. 'Or you. I promise.'

She nodded, wanting to believe him, wishing she could steal his certainty.

'Good. Now, could you lower the tailgate for me, please?'

She did as she was told, standing back with her arms crossed as he hoisted a kicking Dorothy into the float before quickly retreating to shut the gate on her. Locks in place, he moved to stand in front of Brooke. 'Ready?'

'Not really.'

He studied her more closely, roving those magnetic eyes over her face, assessing. 'If you're not okay with this I can take her back to Nancy's.'

She yanked hard on her courage. 'No. I need to do it.'

'Good. I didn't think you were the type to give up.' He tilted his head toward the LandCruiser. 'You jump in and get settled while I move the ute.'

He busied himself securing the Hilux's tailgate, leaving her to walk lead-footed to the LandCruiser. She halted beside the driver's side door and stared at it, praying for courage she wasn't sure she possessed. The gold lettering and logo of Kingston Lodge Racing grew fuzzy edges as the monster in her head roused. Automatically, her fingers crept to her wrist.

One, two, three.

She could do this. Lachlan was here. He'd promised Dorothy would be safe. It'd be okay.

Throwing a look his way and encountering an encouraging nod, she straightened her shoulders, reached for the door handle and climbed into the car.

With the Hilux safely parked in its bay, Lachlan lifted himself and Billy into the four-wheel drive and angled his bulk slightly towards her. Billy sat on his lap, glittery black eyes as watchful as his master's. After the cool outdoors, the confined space seemed oppressive. Brooke became hyperaware of Billy's doggy odour and the strong scent of lanolin on Lachlan's clothes. Sweat prickled her brow. She leant toward the window, sucking in air, fingers dug into her wrist, counting, counting, counting.

'It's okay. We'll just sit here. Talk maybe.' Lachlan's voice was gentle, his expression the same.

'What about?'

'I don't know. You?'

'You mean how crazy I am.'

He shook his head. 'You're not crazy.'

The float thumped as Dorothy butted a wall. Brooke closed her eyes. *One, two, three. One, two, three. One, two, three.*

'That thing you do with your wrist. I read about it on the internet. It's for anxiety, isn't it?'

She nodded, keeping her eyes closed.

'Does it work?'

'Yes. No.' Brooke shook her head. Biting her lip, she looked at him, pleading for understanding. 'It's probably all bullshit but I'm so desperate I'm willing to try anything. I have to get better. I have to take things back to the way they were before. If I don't I could lose Kingston Downs, and this place is my home.' She pressed her hand to her chest. 'A part of me. The thought of losing it . . .'

'You don't have to explain. I feel the same way about Delamere.' He smiled at her, and something passed between them. Empathy perhaps, understanding. 'Stupid to feel that way about a bit of dirt.'

'I know. No one seems to understand. Except for Angus. He's like that with Kingston Lodge.' She contemplated the steering wheel. The LandCruiser's keys dangled from the ignition, safely off. She didn't have to turn them. She could just sit, talk for a while. Get to know Lachlan. Dorothy would be fine as long as she didn't drive anywhere.

'Tell me about Delamere.'

He nestled back into the seat and stared out the windscreen, his face relaxed. Billy turned twice, delicate paws treading a nest, and curled up in his lap. Lachlan placed his hand on the Jack Russell's head and gently stroked as he talked. Brooke experienced an absurd longing to swap places with the dog.

'Not much to tell, really. I love the place but it's nothing special. Sheep and cattle fattening, lucerne in rotation with cereals. The usual thing for the area.'

'And what area's that?'

'The Jemalong Irrigation District, west of Forbes. Delamere's about fifty k's from town. Just over four hundred hectares. It used to be bigger but Dad had to sell off some land a few years back.' Tension appeared around his eyes and mouth. 'Things haven't been run as well as they could have been.'

'Is that why you studied agriculture at uni?'

'Yeah.' He smiled at her. 'That and because they wouldn't let me in to law.'

'Did you really want to be a lawyer?' She couldn't imagine it at all. Although she had no doubt he'd look as good in a suit as he did in work clothes.

'No. I just wanted to earn enough money to turn the place around.'

'Not a lot in agriculture.'

'That's an understatement. But there's much to be said for knowing happiness is where your heart lies, and mine's buried in the land.'

'So what are you doing at Kingston Downs? Why aren't you putting all your expertise into Delamere?'

'Dad and I had a bit of a falling out.' He pointed to the ignition. 'Why don't you turn it on?'

Immediately her stress returned. She shifted, blinking, and wiped her hands down the front of her jodhpurs. 'I'm not sure that's a good idea.'

'You'll be fine.'

'It's not me I'm worried about.'

'Dorothy has plenty of wool padding. Anyway, you'll only be turning on the engine, not moving. No harm in that.' He pointed to the handbrake. 'As long as that stays on we won't be going anywhere.'

She looked at him, feeding on his faith.

'You can do this, Brooke. I know you can.'

She stared at the dash. Slowly, she lowered her gaze to her keys. A scratched sterling silver and Swarovski crystal-encrusted letter B hung from the main ring, a birthday present from Chloe. She reached forward and let the cool metal touch her palm. Fingers tightening,

Brooke glanced at Lachlan, who nodded his encouragement. Her foot hovered over the clutch. She swallowed and closed her eyes. Already her breath was raggedy.

'It's okay. I'm here. I won't let anything happen to you or Dorothy.'

Anxiety ran like an electric current under her skin, but Lachlan's voice, his certainty, fortified her. She *could* do this. Inhaling shakily, she engaged the clutch. Her fingers gripped the plastic end of the key. Quiet dominated, as though the world held its breath, waiting for Brooke to move. Focusing on the diesel engine's coil light, she turned the key. The other keys jangled, the sound harsh in the hush. The coil light lit and three heartbeats later went out.

She looked at Lachlan, fear making her eyes feel huge. The last time she'd done this the panic and terror had been unbearable.

He leaned toward her, challenging her. 'Come on. Show me how brave you are.'

She shook her head. 'I'm not.'

'You are.'

He sounded so sure, so positive. She bit at her lip. He was right. She had to be brave and beat this. The tension in her leg holding the clutch made her thigh tremble but she wasn't about to let go. If she didn't do it now, she'd never do it. And the thought of that sent her mind spiralling. With a final glance at Lachlan and a suck of breath, she turned the ignition.

The diesel chugged. She flicked the gearshift into neutral and jerked her foot off the clutch, holding her hands up as though the LandCruiser's steering wheel had become a vicious animal.

Billy placed his two front paws on her thigh and looked up at her with his head tilted. She lowered her hand to stroke his head, seeking calm. He nuzzled and licked at her palm in understanding.

'You okay?' asked Lachlan.

'No.' She looked at him. Her heart seemed to be pounding in arrhythmic beats. Sweat soaked her armpits and back. Her mouth felt thick and her scalp tight, and though the clutch was no longer engaged the tremble in her thigh remained. 'But I think I'll be all right in a minute.'

'Good. Just remember you can stop at any time. All you have to do is open the door and get out.'

'I know.' She gave him a shaky smile. 'Thanks.'

'You're welcome.'

For a long moment they held each other's gaze, and beneath the buzz of her nerves, Brooke sensed another connection being made. Something stronger than empathy. An alliance. A silent deal that together they could beat this.

A bang from the float shot her stiff with shock. She whimpered, hands fluttering in panic as red images flashed across her mind.

Lachlan caught her fingers, his touch solid and reassuring. 'Shh. There's nothing to worry about. It's only Dorothy letting us know she's there.'

He lowered her hands to Billy and released them with a comforting squeeze. Billy wriggled under her touch, his tail swinging, delighted with the attention. Though the engine's diesel tick rattled her insides, Brooke found that with Lachlan's touch the swell of panic had subsided. Not completely, but it was no longer out of control. She'd be all right, just as he promised. They weren't going anywhere.

'Angus tells me Kingston Downs used to belong to your grandparents,' he said, restarting their conversation.

She nodded, knowing he was doing it to distract her and grateful for it. 'They moved to Port Douglas four years ago. Pop found the winters too cold in the Valley.' Seeing Lachlan's raised eyebrows, she explained. 'He had severe arthritis, probably from all the broken bones he received when he was a jockey.'

'I didn't realise he was a jockey.'

'And an owner-trainer, among other things.' She smiled as Billy sneaked fully onto her lap. She ruffled his ears. 'And what do you think you're doing?'

'Taking advantage of you, I suspect,' said Lachlan. 'Push him back to me if you don't want him there.'

'No, he's fine.' And he was. She found Billy's affection soothing.

'So your pop passed away?' Lachlan prodded.

'Just over two years ago now. When they moved, Pop leased the property to Kingston Lodge Racing, then when he died it went to Dad, who transferred it to a family company with all of us as equal shareholders.' She stared out the side window, eyes stinging as she remembered Mark's talk of buyer interest in the property. If her pop was still alive, no one would have even countenanced selling, but times had changed. Everyone had a stake in the company and Kingston Downs was worth a small fortune. A good offer would be hard to refuse, especially now when it wasn't pulling its weight businesswise.

'So is your nan still in Port Douglas?'

'Yes. And living the life of a merry widow.' She smiled, thinking of the spritely old lady who had no intention of acting her age, despite now being in her seventies. Last time they spoke her grandmother spent nearly their whole phone call discussing her new iPhone and mobile games addiction, after complaining that Brooke still hadn't responded to her Facebook friend request. 'Nan's great fun. You might meet her one day. She flies down every now and then to terrorise us all and to tell Dad where he's going wrong.'

'I hope I'm still here to meet her.'

Brooke dropped her eyes. If she had her way he wouldn't be. As soon as she sorted herself out she'd be back in charge, and Lachlan Cambridge would be out of a job. Her throat tightened at the thought. She ran her hand down Billy's white back, wondering why she should feel bothered by the idea. The only thing she owed Lachlan was thanks for his kindness.

A bleat sounded. Her head snapped up. She'd forgotten about Dorothy, about the engine being on, about being in charge of the float. The hand on Billy's back stilled.

'So, have you always showjumped?' asked Lachlan.

'Pardon?' She curled her fingers against her temple, frowning. 'Sorry, I just . . .' She dropped her hand. 'I suppose so. I used to do a lot of dressage, too. I still do with the young ones, but showjumping is my first love.'

'Must be exciting.'

'It is. Especially when you're jumping off against the clock. Poddy used to be—' She halted, her tongue sticking on the words. She glanced at Lachlan and quickly looked away again. She knew that expression. It was the same as Andrew's had been when she'd tried to drive his float at Willowgrove. She hated how weak it made her feel. Hated this horrible anxiety, this pathetic feeling of helplessness. This useless person she'd become.

She had to make it stop.

'Here,' she said, lifting up Billy and handing him over to Lachlan. As soon as the dog was in his hold, she pressed down hard on the clutch. Her palm hovered over the gearstick. Just one movement and it'd be engaged. A push down on the handbrake and a slow release on the clutch and they'd be moving. It'd be easy.

'Brooke, I don't think—'

'I'm fine.'

Her heart compressed in rapid beats. Sweat broke out once more across her forehead. The noise in her head grew. She ignored it. If she did this fast, she could beat it. She'd read about flooding on the internet, where phobia sufferers were plunged into their greatest fear and forced to endure it until the fear disappeared. She'd tried it on her own without success, but this was different. Lachlan was with her.

She pushed the gearstick into first. The memories began clamouring, the noise louder. Her head throbbed with them, but still she forged on. Billy whined. Lachlan hushed him. She could feel their eyes on her.

'Okay,' she said breathlessly. 'Okay.'

The handbrake went down. She slapped her hands to the steering wheel and gripped it tight. Shakily, she eased the pressure on her leg. She felt the gear engage. As the car lurched forward the building scream unleashed its full power. Agonising images filled her mind. Oddy's thrashing body. Her scarlet hands. The sticky hot blood. The flare of his nostrils. Oddy's unbearable pain as he suffered.

'No, no, no!'

'Brooke!'

The LandCruiser lurched and stalled. She fumbled with the door, moaning. Her fingers slipped on the handle. Something gripped her lungs. She had no breath. Her panic turned wild.

The door flew open. She fell out, crawling on her knees to escape. Stones dug into her hands and knees but she kept scampering. Somewhere, underneath the scream, her brain registered a dog's sharp yaps and the call of her name.

Suddenly she bumped into something solid. Arms reached under her armpits and lifted her. Her face pressed against soft fabric and big hands stroked her head and back. Lanolin and citrus and dog filled her nose.

'Shh, Brooke. Shh. It's okay, I have you. You're safe. Dorothy's safe. Everything's fine.'

She let out a sob as the worst of her panic subsided. Her hands formed fists in Lachlan's jumper. Despite his warm embrace, her sweat-covered body shivered with cold.

'I'm sorry,' he said. 'I should have stopped you.'

She clung to him, heart still galloping, head still filled with fading red. 'Oh, god. Make it end. Please. Just make it end.'

'I can't. Only you can.' He stroked her hair, the movement rhythmic and soothing. 'It'll take time, that's all.'

He held her as she let loose her despair. Finally, the tightness in her chest eased and her breath slowed to shuddery heaves. She raised her head from his chest and stared at the gold lettering on his jumper. His hold on her relaxed and she sat back on her heels, wiping at her wet cheeks. Lachlan remained on his knees, watching her closely.

'Better?'

She nodded, cheeks blooming with heat. She couldn't remember ever experiencing a more embarrassing day.

He smiled. 'I thought you said you looked really unattractive when you cried.'

'I do.'

'A bit tear-stained maybe, but I don't think you could ever look unattractive.'

She stared at him. 'Why are you being so nice?'

He shrugged. 'Perhaps I just want to keep my job. It's never smart to get on the wrong side of the boss's sister.'

But Brooke didn't believe him. This wasn't about currying favour. Lachlan had gone out of his way and, she suspected, against his better judgement to help her. Strange behaviour for a man whose best interests lay in *not* helping.

'Did Angus put you up to this?'

His gaze slid away. Without answering, he stood and held out his arm for her to grab. She took it, taking his silence for assent. Disappointment left her numb. She wanted him to be helping because he wanted to, not because he felt obliged.

They dusted their knees. She couldn't look at him and sensed he felt the same way. For a heartwarming moment they'd shared a connection. Assuming she hadn't imagined it.

'You should go and rest for a while,' he said. 'I can bring the horses in.'

'No. I'll do them. You sort out Dorothy.'

'Do you want me to take her back to Nancy's?'

Brooke looked into the distance, across the horse paddocks to Kingston Downs' highest point. Pain speared her heart as she thought of Oddy rotting in the soil.

After what she'd just been through it'd be so easy to concede defeat. To walk away from her fear and panic into the bosom of her well-meaning family in Sydney. Start a new life working at the stables with Angus and her dad, learning to be like her mother. Leave her beloved home behind.

Easy, perhaps, but cowardly. And what had Lachlan said? *There's much to be said for knowing happiness is where your heart lies.*

'No. She can stay in a stable for tonight until we can organise somewhere sheep-proof.' She met his gaze. 'I'm not going to let this beat me.'

He nodded. 'I'm glad.'

And though she couldn't be certain, in his tone she thought she caught a hint of not just satisfaction, but also pride.

————

Just after five, after she'd put the horses to bed for the night, Brooke drove in to Pitcorthie and parked out the front of Chloe's Cuts. The salon faced the main street—a squat, white-walled and black-framed building wedged between the community bank and Pitcorthie's newsagency-cum-post office. In the centre of the shop's large front window was a black and silver scissor logo. Bright light poured through the window and the glass-panelled front door, the logo casting strange shadows on the darkening footpath.

There was no privacy at Chloe's Cuts, which was exactly how Chloe liked it. Often, if they could see she wasn't busy, friends would drop in for a gossip on their way to or from the bank or the post office, while in quiet times Chloe could keep herself amused with the action on the street.

Brooke stopped for a moment to watch her friend expertly wielding her scissors around the head of a Nintendo-focused boy. A younger boy sat in the chair behind, legs swinging in boredom. She suppressed a smile. Poor Chloe loathed cutting children's hair but as a small-town salon owner and local, she wasn't in any position to refuse.

Sensing scrutiny, Chloe turned to the window and waved, rolling her eyes in mock exasperation when Brooke entered. Her client didn't look up from his game, but Brooke recognised Matty O'Don-

nell and his brother Jeremy by their droopy eyes and extensive freck-
ling. From his seat beside his brother, Jeremy regarded her with a
snot-nosed blank stare before focusing once more on the black and
white tiled floor.

'Hey, Matty. Hey, Jeremy,' said Brooke. 'How are you both?'

'Good,' replied Matty without breaking his rapid fingerwork.
'Jeremy's sick.'

'So I can see.' She threw a look at Chloe, who grimaced.

'But we're not cutting his hair today,' Chloe said, before adding a
quiet 'Thank Christ'. She continued on in the overbright, nervous
voice she reserved for children, a species she found unfathomable.
'But we need you looking slick for your concert tomorrow, don't we,
Matty?'

'Yeah.'

From the other seat, Jeremy sneezed loudly. For a brief moment,
a yellow-green hank of snot hung from his nose before he wiped it on
his sleeve. Chloe's blue eyes widened in horror. Trying not to laugh,
Brooke hunted around under the front counter for a tissue and
handed it to Jeremy, who gave his nose a desultory wipe and passed
the tissue back to her. Carting it by her fingertips, she dumped it in
the bin, before taking another chair as far away from Jeremy as she
could get.

'Where's Jas?' Brooke asked, referring to the boys' mother.

'At Kennedy's. She'll be back in a moment. So how're things with
the sexpot?'

'You mean Lachlan,' answered Brooke, frowning a warning.
Chloe was so clueless around kids she was liable to break into a
discussion about her bet. 'I'll tell you later.'

'Sounds interesting.' Chloe eyed her. 'You look tired.' She
stopped snipping and inspected Brooke more closely. 'Have you been
crying? Has he done something to upset you?'

She held up her hand, shaking her head. 'It's nothing.'

'Doesn't look like nothing.'

The timely arrival of Jasmine O'Donnell put a stop to any further probing. She bustled in, plastic bags full of groceries cutting into her fingers, and a harried expression on her round, normally cheerful face.

'Sorry I took so long, Chloe. I ran into Trev and he's a lovely old thing but he just wouldn't shut up and then I couldn't find any SPC spaghetti and Jeremy won't eat Heinz, and Sue had to hunt out the back for it and . . . oh, hi, Brooke. How's tricks?' She frowned as she took a good look at Brooke's face. 'Everything all right? You look a bit tired.'

'Fine, thanks, Jas. Sod's been giving me a hard time, that's all.'

'Ahh.' Jas and Chloe exchanged a look.

Brooke probed at her wrist, preparing herself for what might come next. People were only being kind when they offered sympathy and concern, but it made her want to scream. It didn't help that everyone believed she was wasting her time with Sod, that the accident had broken something in his temperament which could never be fixed. But she knew better. All it would take was time and a lot of patience.

'So how's that new manager of yours? All Sam can talk about is what an unbeatable second row the Panthers will have now he's signed on—bloody rugby, I tell you—but word around town is he's quite the hunk.'

Brooke shrugged, unwilling to give anything away. 'He's okay.'

'Okay is *not* how I'd describe Lachie Cambridge,' said Chloe, dusting the back of Matty's neck with a brush. 'Anyway, Jas, you'll be able to see for yourself tomorrow.' She grinned. 'But hands off. The man's mine.'

'A snap of your fingers and half the men of Pitcorthie would be yours, Chloe darling,' said Jas, hugging a sodden Jeremy to her side. 'Except for my husband, who values his manhood too much to stray. Although there are some days when I'd beg for someone to take him off my hands.' She winked at Brooke and dug into her handbag for her purse as Matty, still game-engrossed, slid off his chair and headed towards the door.

As soon as the O'Donnells had gone, Chloe turned to Brooke and plonked her hands on her hips. 'Okay, what happened?'

With a sigh, Brooke explained, although, as she relayed the afternoon's events, she found herself playing down Lachlan's compassion. Instead of the truth, she made it sound like his help was grudging instead of kindly offered, and gave no hint of her softening attitude towards him. She wasn't sure why, except she felt a compulsion to keep it secret, as if her feelings were too young, uncertain and fragile to risk exposure. Even to Chloe.

'You know what you need?' announced Chloe, after reminding Brooke for the umpteenth time that fretting about her problem would only make it worse. 'You need a big pamper session.' She strode to the front door and flipped over the *Closed* sign, flicked the lock and hauled down the blind, then with clicking heels strode to the back of the salon to push open the door to the beauty room. 'You. Inside. Now.'

'You don't have to do this, Chloe.'

'I do. Now stop arguing, get in there and strip.'

Brooke halted. 'You are *not* giving me another Brazilian.'

'No, doofus. I'm going to give you a massage. Then we're going to do something about that diabolical haircut. Everyone thinks that God-awful bob's my work. As if!'

Three-quarters of an hour later, her muscles aching pleasantly, Brooke watched Chloe in the mirror as she assaulted her hair, her friend snipping expertly away as she outlined her plan of attack for Lachlan's seduction. Now they were back out in the salon, away from the dim lights, calming Celtic-inspired music, scented candles, and Chloe's orders to relax, conversation had resumed.

'So, given he's such a rural sort, I figure I'd go for the down-to-earth country girl look tomorrow. It'll be too cold at the ground anyway to wear anything too revealing, and if he's one of those shy types I wouldn't want to frighten him off by being too forward.' She whizzed her castored seat around to Brooke's left side and eyed her work critically before whizzing back to the right. Brown hair fell in alarming hanks, but a distinct style was now emerging—a short, gamine look that accentuated Brooke's cheekbones and made her eyes look enormous. 'A bit of flattery here, a special smile there and he should be putty. God, I'm going to enjoy shaving Andrew's head.' She concentrated on snipping for a few minutes before resuming their chat. 'Are you heading to Sydney tomorrow or are you going to pike again?'

'I don't know. Probably.'

Brooke rubbed at her eyes, suddenly overcome with tiredness at the thought of driving to Sydney in the morning and coping with her family for another day. Maintaining the pretence she was fine, when the afternoon had proven so clearly that she wasn't.

The despondency she'd felt on arrival at the salon sank leaden on her again. 'Maybe I should've taken Andrew up on his offer. It'd make everyone's life easier—the family could use the capital from the sale of Kingston Downs to invest in another place closer to Sydney, and I'd be free to concentrate on showjumping. Things would probably be fine with Andrew. I mean, it's not as if we're not close. He's one of my best friends. I love him. Just not the way he wants.'

Chloe's scissors halted mid-snip. She looked at Brooke's reflection, appalled. 'I can't believe you're even questioning that you did the right thing.'

'But it would've solved a lot, wouldn't it?'

'For who?'

'Well, both of us, I guess.'

'But you don't love him.'

'Yes, I do.'

'No you don't. Not the right way. Not—' Chloe's jaw snapped shut, her pretty face hardening in a manner rarely seen. She raised her scissors, mouth tense as she gave two savage snips. 'This conversation's stupid.'

Brooke closed her eyes, wondering why she'd even brought it up. Chloe was right. It was a stupid conversation. She would never have done it to Andrew. She wouldn't have done it to herself, for that matter. But it was as though her friend's plans for Lachlan flicked a switch on her negative thoughts.

'You're right. I was just being an idiot.' She stared at her hands. 'I just feel so crap after today, like I'm never going to get better.' She looked up. 'And I feel useless, too. With Lachlan there I have nothing to do except work on Sod.'

'So bring Elly back into work. Do what we said and find yourself a new horse to train. Get off your bum and do what you do best. You're so good with the young ones—it'll do wonders for your confidence.' Chloe smiled, back to normal, and grabbed Brooke's shoulders from behind, shaking gently. 'Whatever you do, just stop being such a bloody misery guts. You're driving me insane!'

EIGHT

THE OLD GUMS lining Pitcorthie's sole rugby field rustled, creaked and swayed in protest as an arctic wind gusted across the ground. Noisy clangs rang through the air as it caused a loose sheet of corrugated iron to flap on the canteen's rusting roof. A crowd stood in front, chattering as they waited to be served, desirous of a hot cuppa to fend off the cold or lured by the comforting smell of barbecuing onions and sausages. Spying a loose bootlace, Lachie bent to retie it, wondering yet again what the hell had possessed him to join the Pitcorthie Panthers. There had to be better things to do than freezing to death on a winter Saturday.

Bootlace secured, he performed another stretch and surveyed the ground. In the centre of the field, the referee and linesmen probed with toes and tamped down sods with shaking heads as they completed their inspection of the torn-up playing surface, a legacy of the morning's junior competition. A low steel cyclone-wire fence, dotted with bright sponsors' signs, surrounded the field. Dozens of cars were parked nose-in against it, their passengers tucked inside against the cold. A few well-rugged souls braved the elements, standing in groups with their backs against the wind and scarves and jackets pulled tight.

Lachie spied Chloe perched against the bonnet of an older model Nissan Patrol, her hands around a steaming foam cup and slim legs stretched out. She wore dark denim skinny jeans tucked into long, light-brown boots, and a cropped, dark-blue double-breasted jacket with gold buttons and embroidered epaulettes. A dark-green and white scarf hugged her neck, the ends tucked inside the jacket front, adding further padding to her already ample chest.

Though the wind had caused tendrils to escape and dance around her face, most of her glossy brown hair was tied back in a thick, wavy ponytail. With her delicate features shown to their fullest, she looked even prettier than when he had met her in the pub. Yet when she cast her sparkly blue-eyed gaze his way, mouth widening into a broad gap-toothed smile as she lifted a hand to wave, Lachie found himself unmoved. Even during their first meeting he'd sensed something amiss. What it was, he couldn't quite pinpoint, but he couldn't shed the feeling her interest lacked sincerity; that it was put on to impress those around her more than him. But she was Brooke's friend and that meant extra courtesy was in order. He pointed to his shoulders, indicating her epaulettes, and gave a military salute, smiling when her mouth widened with laughter.

Resuming his stretches, he scanned further afield, hunting for Brooke on the off-chance she'd stayed local instead of heading to Sydney. He hadn't seen her since yesterday evening, when she'd taken off into town, and by the time he'd wandered out this morning the horses were in their day paddocks, the yards mucked out and her LandCruiser gone. Though he knew she was due at Kingston Lodge, disappointment left him feeling hollow. He'd wanted to talk to her before she left, to tell her to keep faith, but most of all he wanted to make sure things were still okay between them.

He still felt weird about yesterday. Half of him believed himself an idiot for getting involved, but the other half—the half unable to forget the torment he'd seen in her eyes—remained desperate to help.

She'd tugged something inside him, something he hadn't felt since Tamsyn had walked out of his life. Something he didn't want to feel, but whose pull he couldn't resist.

It was the tour around Kingston Downs that did it. Her passion affected him, just as her expertise surprised. She knew her stuff— from which pasture and lucerne species performed best, to the intricacies of irrigation management. What he'd thought would be a casual wander around the property had turned into a three-hour tutorial, with him the student. She hadn't been afraid to quiz him on his expertise either, asking pertinent questions, sifting through his knowledge to see if there was anything she could use to enhance her own. By the time they'd left Poddy and Venus he'd been in danger of developing a teenage crush. Which was why one glimpse of her sitting in the car so distressed had him acting like an idiot.

All he wanted was to do his job, see Nick through uni, and go home to Delamere when the time was right. Getting sucked into helping the boss's sister with her issues didn't feature, but he couldn't resist the look she'd given him. Clear brown eyes wide with hope, as if he was her last chance, the man who could change everything. The next thing he knew, his ego had taken over his brain and he was offering to come to her rescue.

And what a mess he'd made of it.

He lifted a leg and balanced it on top of the fence, leaning forward to stretch his hamstrings. His teammates milled around in their green jerseys with wide white Vs pointing down the front, clean white shorts bright, rubbing hands and complaining about the cold. Lachie estimated the team's average age at somewhere around thirty, and while their camaraderie and enthusiasm were undeniable, it was apparent from their lack of warm-up procedure that these were men who considered their bodies more shacks than temples. But they were a friendly bunch, and Lachie didn't really care if they were hopeless. He just wanted to have a run around and enjoy being part of a team. So long as he didn't earn an injury in the process.

Sam O'Donnell, the other lock, emerged from the change rooms, closely followed by Nate Osbourne, their studs clicking on the concrete as they crossed to the fence. Unlike Lachie, who wore headgear, Sam used black tape wrapped around his head to keep his ears in place, which lowered his brow and made his sleepy eyes appear even sleepier. In his Panthers' kit, with his acutely bent nose, intense eyes and menacing game face, Nate appeared a different man from the friendly publican Lachie had met on Thursday night. He stopped at the fence and waved his team over. Lachie donned his helmet, leaving the chinstrap loose, and lined up with his team. On the other side of the amenities block, their yellow jerseys bright, the Sandy Hollow Hornets did the same.

'Right, lads,' said Nate, slapping his hands together. 'Today's a big game and as you all know there's a lot at stake. And we're not just talking points here. We're talking pride.' He thumped his chest. 'Pride and honour. Not just our individual pride and honour or even the Panthers', but Pitcorthie's. Our town. That place we call home. So let's get out there and do it proud.' He caught them all by the eye. 'For Pitcorthie, lads.'

Pumped up, the team responded in unison. 'For Pitcorthie!'

Satisfied, Nate nodded then turned and jogged onto the ground. Invigorated and game hungry, his fourteen teammates followed, their puffed-up chests swelled further by the yells, cheers and whistles of the parochial crowd.

Lachie ran short sprints to warm up, still feeling unprepared despite his stretches. At lunchtime, in the warmth of the pub over juice and plates of sandwiches, Nate had introduced him to his teammates, describing with good humour each of their strengths and weaknesses, even ribbing his own missed tackles and wayward passing—bad failings for a centre—before moving on to a detailed description of the opposition and their likely tactics. Lachie had left the pub for the ground with the feeling he was in for an interesting game. Unlike most weeks, this Saturday they were fielding a full fifteen, and that charged the men with purpose.

The crowd groaned when Nate lost the toss and the Sandy

Hollow Hornets elected to kick into the wind. While this put the Hornets at a disadvantage in the first half, in the second they'd have the breeze at their backs and the lowering sun behind them as well. As he moved into position, Lachie gripped Nate's shoulder in sympathy.

'Don't you worry, Lachie,' said Nate, as upbeat as ever. 'Be the only victory they'll see today.'

The referee handed the ball to the Hornets' five-eighth, who gripped it ready for kick-off. Lachie secured the strap of his helmet and pulled his mouthguard from the top of his sock and threaded it into his mouth, heartbeat thumping as adrenaline began to surge. A quick check with the two captains and the referee raised his whistle. For a few seconds quiet descended, then a shrill blast broke the air, bringing with it another cheer from the crowd. Lachie crouched in line, one hand on the ground for balance, ready for the charge. The game was on.

————

By half-time, despite the Panthers' brave-hearted defence, the Hornets had scored and converted a try. The Panthers were only four points behind, though, thanks to a penalty goal, well kicked by Logan Price, their yarpy-mouthed scrum half. Lachie had run himself ragged, and came off the ground with his chest heaving, covered in mud and sweat, and his shoulder aching from a fiercely implanted and scraped boot.

Out of the wind in the change room, Nate gathered them around, rallying them with another pep talk. 'Fantastic effort, lads. We've really got them worried.' He patted Sam on the head; his sleepy eyes drooped even further with fatigue. 'Great effort, Sammy.' Patrick, whose agility, accurate kicks and rapid decision-making had gained them a lot of ground, got slapped on the shoulder. 'Brilliant work, Pat.' He singled out each of his teammates, heaping praise, until he reached Lachie. 'And you, mate, were friggin' awesome.'

Lachie shook his head, embarrassed.

'You bloody were.'

Sam gave him a look. 'What grade did you say you played for Uni?'

'First.'

His team regarded him with astonishment. Until now, Lachie had avoided the question, not wanting to create too much expectation, but even though he felt he hadn't played well, his superior talent was unmistakable. He'd won every lineout bar one, tackled ferociously, and sent passes hurtling like bullets. The only blemish was the missed lineout, when the sneaky Hornets, sick of having their throw-ins snatched, passed short instead. The Panthers player nearest the touchline was so startled he forgot to tackle, leaving the Hornets' forward free to charge over the line, much to the crowd's and the forward's amazement.

'Jesus,' said Nate, before shaking himself and clapping his hands together to regain their attention. 'But this is a team sport, lads, and we're going to keep playing like a team until we grind those bastards down. It'll be tough, and it'll take every ounce of guts we have, but mark my words, we're going to do Pitcorthie proud and win.'

Lachie took a swig from his drink bottle, listening attentively as Nate outlined tactics for the second half. Though out of the wind, the change room, with its damp concrete floor, single brick walls and exposed roof, remained frigid. As his sweat-soaked body cooled and threatened to tighten loose muscles, Lachie kept up a routine of stretches. The others did the same, taking their cue from him.

'Remember, lads,' said Nate, coming to the end of his speech, 'this is for Pitcorthie.'

'Pitcorthie!'

The chant kept coming as they ran out for the second half, earning yet another wild cheer from the Panthers-stacked crowd. As he jogged into position, Lachie scanned the perimeter. Though the wind remained gusty, the afternoon sun had broken through to cut the cold. The close score had enticed spectators from their cars, and they gathered tightly around the fence in green and white mobs inter-spersed with clumps of yellow-clad Hornets fans.

Patrick took the kick-off for the Panthers. Lachie sprinted after it, catching the Hornets' full-back as he attempted to duck past, turning him as they fell and forcing the man to release as he faced the wrong way. The Panthers pounced for the clean-out, securing the ball before flicking it along the line, the crowd screaming in delight at the turnover.

The try line beckoned, but the Hornets' defence continued to hold their ground. A collective groan issued from the sidelines as the Panthers' wing lost the ball forward for the second time in the game. Seeing his teammate's dropped head, Lachie quickly ran over to offer a few words of encouragement before joining Sam for the scrum. They couldn't afford to lose heart. Too much was at stake.

Thirty minutes passed without either side scoring. The ground was so dug up it looked like a herd of wild boar had rampaged through. Lachie's lungs ached as he sucked in cold air. His legs burned, his ribs throbbed where he'd been jabbed with an elbow, and his rucked shoulder pulsed, yet the pain registered only vaguely. The play of the ball was all that mattered.

Despite Nate's shouts of encouragement and Logan's endless yarping, the Panthers were flagging. As the Hornets had planned, the wind was working against the Panthers, and now the sun, low in the sky, shone into their eyes. The team was exhausted. Any break in play saw the men's heads drop as they bent over to lean their hands on their thighs. Lachie looked at Nate, whose grim face said it all, then at the clock, before casting around to the others. Defeat hung on their shoulders and weighed their tired, dragging legs. They'd need a miracle to get home. It was up to him to create one.

Awarded a penalty, the Hornets kicked into touch. The Panthers ran into position, ready for the lineout, Lachie towards the touchline. If the pass was short, he'd use his agility to cut it off. If it was thrown high, he'd snatch it from the air. Either way, the Hornets weren't laying a finger on it.

'We can win this, Panthers,' he told them, watching the opposition closely as the Hornets' hooker stood on the side waiting to throw in the ball. 'There's still time. One try. That's all we need.'

Nate joined in. 'Come on, lads. For Pitcorthie!'

The ball came in high. Supported by his prop, Lachie leapt, plucking it mid-arc and passing it to Logan, who passed immediately to Patrick. Patrick hesitated a moment, then catching Lachie's rapid run and call from behind, flicked the pass his way. Ball securely tucked, Lachie barrelled ahead, weaving his way past flat-footed players, working his way to the wing.

He made it to the halfway line before being brought down. Immediately he released, rolled away, and leapt to his feet again. The ball headed inside. Another pass and another tackle, but this time the men stayed up. Lachie joined the maul, driving into the Hornets' defence, muscling them back. The ball came out, passing along the line and gaining more ground until another maul formed. The twenty-two-metre line approached, galvanising the Panthers.

Lachie glanced at the clock. They had a minute, two at most, but momentum was in their favour. The tryline was theirs to attack, the Hornets as tired as the Panthers. They could win.

As soon as the ball came out he broke from the maul and sprinted across the ground. He'd seen a hole. All he needed was an accurate, lightning pass and he could run through to the line. He yelled to the five-eighth. Quick as ever, Patrick changed direction and fired the ball his way. Lachie intercepted and with the ball jammed against his chest, charged.

Legs pumping, he crossed the twenty-two-metre line, hunting around for support. None appeared. He gripped the ball harder as a flanker sprinted across to halt his run. He swerved, arching his back, leaving the attacker clawing air. The tryline loomed. Twelve metres. Ten metres. The full-back thundered toward him but Lachie knew he possessed enough pace to blast through.

'Lachie!'

Nate's call came from the wing. He glanced across. His captain was unmarked, and though Lachie knew it was a risk with Nate's self-confessed slippery hands, he didn't hesitate. He passed. As the spectators gasped, the ball speared straight onto Nate's chest. Arms locked around it and a grin splitting his face, he took two huge strides before swan diving for the tryline.

The crowd erupted as the referee pointed and blew the try. Panting and grinning, Lachie ran to Nate, slapping his back and rubbing his hair in celebration before leaving him to a pile-on by his ecstatic teammates.

'It's not over yet, lads,' said Nate, finally extracting himself. 'We still need the conversion to win.' He regarded Lachie. 'You want to take it? You deserve the glory.'

He shook his head. 'Not my forte.'

Nate picked up the ball and glanced at Logan. Lachie understood what he was thinking. Kicking for goal with the match in the balance was a huge responsibility, and perhaps one a captain should bear. Nate caught his eye. Lachie gave him a subtle nod of encouragement.

'I'll kick,' Nate announced to his team. 'That way if I fuck it up you can all blame me.'

'You won't,' said Lachie.

And he didn't, although it wasn't the prettiest of conversions. The ball wobbled off his boot, hit the cross bar and ricocheted skyward. Silence hung over the ground. Hearts stuttered in chests. Breaths suspended in lungs, then the ball tumbled to the other side and the Panthers were bellowing in triumph. Lachie found himself at the bottom of another pile-on, nose full of sweat and dirt, his head full of victory and his heart swollen with his love for the game and all it stood for.

When the on-field celebrations died down, he trudged toward the change room, taking a moment to scan the sidelines. Chloe stood at the fence, bouncing up and down in excitement. Andrew stood next to her, applauding but without great enthusiasm. Lachie surveyed the rest of the ecstatic crowd, his heart leaping as he spotted a blue Land-Cruiser in the far corner. A slight figure sat perched on the bullbar, and though a scarf was wrapped high around her neck and a green beanie covered her head, there was no mistaking Brooke. Their eyes locked and he caught a smile. Then she slid off her perch, held out her hands, and began a slow clap.

And though she faced the entire team, somehow that simple gesture felt just for him.

———

After the raw conditions outside, the thick, beery air and laughter-filled din of the pub felt warm and welcoming, and replete with community spirit. Discarded Panthers' scarves hung like green snakes from the backs of chairs. Someone had threaded Nate's dirt-encrusted jersey onto a pool cue and suspended it pointing outward from above the bar like a military banner. The jukebox pumped a tinny version of Queen's 'We Are the Champions'. Several Panthers, Nate at the centre, arms slung around shoulders and beers precariously held, sang along in discordant delight, a warning to all that Saturday night would last long and loud.

Lachie pushed the door closed and paused for a moment to scan the room for Brooke. He spotted her with Chloe and Andrew near the jukebox. Her hands were sunk deep into her jeans pockets and her chest sunk inward as though hunched against cold. Despite the warm fug and her flushed cheeks, the Panthers beanie remained on her head. Andrew stood with his arm resting on the ledge behind, not touching her, but relaying a clear message.

She caught Lachie's scrutiny and smiled slightly.

Noticing his arrival, Chloe waved him over, but she was too late. A whoop went up from the bar and in seconds Lachie was dragged towards it.

Attention on his performance escalated to embarrassing proportions. 'I just played the game,' he kept telling anyone who'd listen but the praise kept coming with the beers. He drank two, refusing further shouts despite assurances of lifts home and beds for the night. Lachie didn't need a hangover, and he wanted to make sense when he talked to Brooke.

Finally, he managed to escape by telling his teammates he needed a have a word with Brooke about the farm. The moment he wandered over, Chloe pulled on his arm and stood on tiptoe in an attempt to kiss him. Catcalls erupted from the bar. Avoiding direct attack, he turned his head and permitted her a brief peck on the cheek before straightening. Laughter and jibes broke behind him. He smiled wryly. No matter where you went, rugby teams were all the same. Thwarted but unfazed, Chloe maintained her hold, hugging him possessively to her side.

'You were amazing,' she said, fixing him with sparkly, invitation-filled eyes.

'Not really. I just played the game.'

She nudged him playfully. 'You're too modest.'

He shook his head and eyed Brooke. Her cheeks were flushed, the skin beneath her eyes shadowed, and her lips seemed dull and dry. Fatigue, or perhaps worry, sagged her posture.

'Are you okay?' he asked.

'Just tired. Nothing a decent night's sleep won't fix.'

'Congratulations,' said Andrew. 'You played well.'

'Thanks. It was a good game.' He cleared his throat and regarded Brooke again. 'How was Sydney?'

'I didn't go.'

'Too scared what her mother would say about her new haircut,' said Chloe.

'Actually,' said Brooke, flicking looks at Chloe and Andrew, 'I did what you've been nagging me to do and went to look at a horse.'

Immediately they began firing questions. What horse? Whereabouts? What's it done?

'You should have called me,' said Andrew. 'I could have come with you.'

'I wanted to look on my own.'

'So, are you going to tell us about it, or what?' demanded Chloe.

Brooke threw an exasperated smile at Lachie as if to say, 'See what I have to put up with?', then set about answering. 'I found him last night while trawling that new online sale site and liked the look of his photos so I rang the owner. He said he'd bred him for tourists to use as a trail-riding horse but he turned out too big—no surprise given his dam's a Clydesdale—so he gave him to his daughter to ride and she mucked around doing a bit of dressage and jumping—just low-grade Pony Club stuff—until she lost interest. Anyway, he looked like he had potential so I thought I might as well check him out.' She smiled at Chloe. 'And yes, it gave me a good excuse not to go to Sydney. Turns out he's a beauty. Perfect shoulder, strong hindquarters, a bit dopey-looking but sweet-tempered. And best of all, cheap. So I bought him.' She refocused on Lachie. 'I was hoping if you're free sometime during the week we could drive down to pick him up.'

'I can do it,' Andrew butted in.

Lachie remained silent. He wasn't about to get involved.

She shook her head and continued to look at him. 'Maybe Tuesday?'

'For God's sake, Brooke, I'll do it. I've told you before I don't mind.'

Sensing now might be a good time to retreat, Lachie shrugged. 'Work it out and let me know. I'll fit in with whatever you decide. I'd better get back to the boys,' he added, indicating the bar and the still joyous Panthers. Though what he really wanted was to go home and laze in front of the fire after double-checking with Brooke in private that she really was okay. Something about her body language niggled.

Chloe gave his arm a squeeze. 'Stay a bit. Anyway, you haven't seen what I've done with Brooke's hair yet.'

With a sigh, Brooke slid the beanie from her hair, scrunching up her nose as Chloe leapt in to run her fingers expertly through the short crop. Satisfied, Chloe stepped back, arm held open in presentation.

Instead of the messy bob he was used to, Brooke's hair clung to her head in boyishly short tendrils. The hair alongside her ears had been cut into a point, giving it a pixie-ish quality. With her hesitant smile she looked fragile and vulnerable but also very beautiful. The cut emphasised her soft eyes and gentle mouth, and did nothing to curb his burgeoning attraction.

He rubbed his hand over the back of his neck, sifting through comments for something appropriate to say while Brooke's gaze darted nervously over his face.

'Well?' asked Chloe, frowning. 'What do you think?'

'You did a good job. It suits her. She looks . . .' He turned to Brooke. His words were for her, not Chloe. 'You look very pretty.'

Surprise and pleasure widened her eyes and parted her lips, and his heart hiccupped in reaction, rising and falling in an adolescent crush flip-flop.

Disconcerted, he took a step backward. 'Right. I'd better see what sort of mess the boys are making of themselves.'

He smiled politely at all three of them before hurrying to the bar and the safety of his teammates.

But not before registering the narrow, frosted expression on Andrew's face.

NINE

LACHIE OPENED the screen door and let the cool morning brush his tired face. As though mocking him, Billy scrambled from his quilted cocoon and bounced from his bed, black eyes bright and clever, tail wagging frantically, electric with Jack Russell energy. Smiling and taking care not to spill his cup of tea, Lachie bent down to stroke Billy's silky ears before wandering to the edge of the verandah and leaning against a post. He surveyed the dull sky. Another rain front had brewed overnight and with the abatement of yesterday's wind, it lumbered over the Valley like a giant grey tarpaulin, blocking the sun and leaching the land of colour.

He yawned and scratched at his unshaven chin, thinking how well the weather suited his mood. Despite a long soak in a Radox-laced bath and an early night, he'd woken feeling sluggish. His rucked shoulder throbbed and his leg muscles were stiff and sore from exertion. As he'd dressed, he'd discovered purpling bruises he couldn't recall receiving, and an angry red stud scrape down his left bum cheek. All reminders that if he intended to keep playing, he'd better do some proper training and toughen up. With a bit of luck, he might even convince the Panthers to join in.

He smiled into his tea as he remembered the pub, the raucous fun and camaraderie. The pride he'd felt at being accepted into a community, a feeling he'd never quite regained after uni, when he'd set aside his ego for Tamsyn's sake, called a truce with his dad and returned to Delamere. Maybe he'd changed since uni, or maybe it was because he'd chosen not to play rugby and concentrate solely on the farm. Perhaps it was the scars that Tamsyn's unexpected dumping left behind. Whatever the reason, it felt good to belong again.

That he left the pub when he did was a smart move. The night was definitely deteriorating. Slurred words, discordant singing, and rumblings of swapping from beer to rum or bourbon were all, in his experience, sure signs of trouble. Not to mention a sore head. His body ached enough this morning without adding that to the mix.

His thoughts drifted to Brooke and the way she hadn't seemed quite herself in the pub. He left the post to walk to the verandah steps and gazed up the track, towards the dairy. Brooke's car sat near the front door, where she usually parked it. Smoke plumed from the chimney. She was home and fine and he should mind his own business, but as he leaned out to toss out the dregs of his tea his mind registered the yards. Three horses stared expectantly back at him.

He frowned and glanced at his watch. Eight a.m. By now Poddy and Venus should be in their day paddock. Brooke always fed them early before leading them out. Sod usually stayed put until after he'd been worked. Perhaps she thought the weather too miserable for them, yet it'd been worse on other days and the routine had remained unchanged.

'What do you reckon, Billyboy? Something not quite right here?'

Lachie eyed the horses for a few seconds longer before deciding to investigate. He couldn't shed the niggling doubt that something was wrong, and unless he did something, it'd never leave. He'd check the horses and wander up to knock on Brooke's door, just to be safe. And if she didn't appreciate his invasion of her space, he'd cover up his concern by asking if she'd come to any decision over picking up her new horse.

Rugged up and booted, Billy tearing nose-down ahead, Lachie headed to the yards. Poddy kept his good eye on him as Lachie ducked under the rail and went to the feed trough. A few flakes of chaff remained in the corners. He checked Venus's while she bunted his sore thighs, demanding attention. The pony's trough was vacuumed clean, as he'd expected. He paused to give Venus a good scratch before ducking through to Sod's yard, where he found more traces of chaff. Lumps of manure were scattered across the sand, dispersed by Sod's restless parading. Poddy's and Venus's yards contained neat, khaki piles in the corners.

'So you've been fed but not cleaned out,' he said to the handsome brown horse, scrubbing his ears and nose. 'So what's that mean then, huh?' Sod lowered his head and rubbed hard against Lachie's chest. He let the horse indulge, running his hand under his neck rug to check he wasn't too hot or cold. Sod was fine but Lachie's unease remained.

Stuff it. If he didn't check he'd worry all day.

Whistling for Billy, he left the horses and strode up the lane, hunched against the cold and wishing he'd remembered a hat.

He stopped at the blue-painted door, double-checking for a bell. Not finding one, he banged the end of his fist against the timber and waited, hands shoved into his coat pockets. A good twenty seconds passed without response. He took a few steps back and looked from the car to the roof and the tendrils of drifting smoke. Maybe she was asleep or in the shower. He refocused on the door and rubbed the back of his neck. He'd only known her two weeks, and while their farm walk and his ill-fated bid to help her had tempered her resentment, he could hardly call their relationship close.

Leg cocking complete, Billy nosed his way to the door and parked his rump down on the dirt-encrusted coir mat. He glanced expectantly over his shoulder at Lachie before staring once more at the timber. With a sigh, Lachie dropped his hand and gave the door another rap, this time harder. It remained firmly shut.

Casting Billy a 'this is all your fault' look and cursing his own stupidity, Lachie tried the handle. The door creaked open. Cautious and uncomfortable, he poked his head through the gap and though it was warmer than outside, no blast of interior heat struck his skin. He threw Billy another glance, his unease escalating.

'Brooke?' He pushed the door wider and crossed the threshold into a small entrance room. A worn oilskin coat lay tumbled on the floor below the coat rack, as though Brooke had tossed it at a hook and walked on, unconcerned if it caught or missed. A pair of scuffed Blundstone boots, elastic sides puckered with wear, lay on their sides in the centre of a dark-blue and gold Persian-style runner. He listened for a moment, expecting shower noise or a hairdryer, but the only sound was the crackle of wood. Frowning and easing the front door closed behind him, he stepped over the boots and with another call of her name, followed the runner into the main living area.

Brooke sat hunched on one of the pine dining chairs, swaddled in a blanket, dangerously close to the wood stove. Sweat streaked her brow and dampened her newly short hair. A deep flush covered her cheeks but the rest of her skin was so pale it appeared almost translucent. As she turned her face toward him her lips trembled with fever.

She regarded him with pained, watery eyes before staring once more at the blazing fire. 'Please go away.'

'You're sick.'

He looked around, still frowning. With the fire burning so hard the place should be boiling, but it was almost cold. He cast his eye over the ceiling – unpainted plasterboard with dabs of compound cement over the studs. No cornicing, and given the temperature, no insulation either. He shook his head in disgust. Though tiny, the space between the ceiling edge and the walls was enough to siphon every scrap of warm air from the place. Nancy had been right. The dairy was an icebox.

'Come on,' he said, moving toward Brooke with his hand out, ready to help her up. 'Let's get you to the cottage where it's warm.'

A tear trickled from her eye. 'Please, Lachlan. Just leave. I can look after myself.' A shiver surged, chattering her teeth. She blinked and her eyes widened. Suddenly she cast off the blanket and stood, swaying, in a pair of pink and white flannelette pyjamas, thick black socks pulled over the legs almost up to her knees. 'The horses.'

'Perfectly happy in their yards.' He gently rewrapped her in her sweat-dampened blanket and pressed his hand against her clammy forehead, grimacing at the burn of her skin. 'I think we need to get you to a doctor.'

'It's just a cold.'

'Looks more like the flu. Have you taken anything for it?'

She shook her head, then groaned and reeled as the movement left her unbalanced. 'Don't have anything. I never get sick.'

'There's always a first time for everything.' He placed a hand on her back. 'Can you walk or do you want me to carry you?'

'Neither. I'm fine where I am.'

'No, you're not.' And he wasn't about to argue about it, either. In one easy movement he scooped her up, tucking her to his chest as he headed to the door. For a moment, the colour in her cheeks seemed more from outrage than fever.

'What the hell do you think you're doing?'

'Looking after you.'

'Put me down!' She wriggled in protest but stopped abruptly, closing her eyes and cupping her palm to her head. Dehydration had probably added a severe headache to her woes.

'Are the keys in your car?'

Abandoning the fight, she mumbled a yes. Without another word, Lachie carted her to the LandCruiser and tucked her onto the passenger seat. He drove her to the cottage, coasting slowly past the horses so she could see they were fine, and assuring her he'd take care of them once he had her settled. Billy galloped ahead, tongue flapping, a streak of white against the mud and grass as he led Brooke home.

Lachie pulled up close to the verandah and, ignoring her protests and wobbly attempt to walk, hoisted Brooke into his arms, carried her into the house and laid her gently on the cottage's squashy fabric couch. It wasn't ideal, but the untouched spare room was cold, its double bed stripped. The thought of her in his bed made him uncomfortable, so until he decided what to do, the lounge remained the best option.

'Don't move,' he instructed, and set to work.

With the fire well stoked, Brooke's head supported by a downy pillow, fresh blankets covering her shivery body, and a full glass of water on the coffee table to add to the two he'd already made her drink, Lachie stood back to observe his charge, thinking hard over his next move. Playing nurse wasn't in his job description and though he wanted to be kind, the situation was awkward.

He could phone the local surgery. The number was included on the contact list Angus had given him on arrival, but if Brooke had the flu, which seemed clear, a doctor would do little more than prescribe rest, fluids and cold and flu tablets. Instructions Lachie could ensure she followed himself, once he managed to find a Sunday trading chemist.

Nancy would be happy to help. The old lady adored Brooke and had warned against letting her stay in the dairy. Chloe would also come to the rescue, and thanks to her accosting him in the pub as he was leaving last night, to more braying from the boys, he now had her number. Yet both options would entail Brooke moving off Kingston Downs, and he had the feeling she wouldn't appreciate that one bit.

'Brooke?'

'Mmm?'

'Will you be all right for a while?'

She turned her face toward him, sickness watering her eyes, no longer defiant but fearful and helpless. 'Why? Where are you going?'

'To find a chemist. You need something for that fever.' Sensing her need for reassurance, he crouched down beside the couch, resisting the urge to run a soothing hand across her heated forehead. 'I'll be as quick as I can. In the meantime, you just rest.'

Leaving the house phone and his number on a scrap of paper by her side, he headed for the door.

'Lachlan?'

He halted, ready to turn back in case she needed help. Instead, she smiled shakily, watery soft eyes regarding him with a kind of awed gratitude.

'Thank you.'

He nodded and left the house, buoyed by simple, heartfelt words that made him feel stupidly tall and noble.

————

Armed with cold and flu tablets, throat lozenges and a jar of chest rub, Lachie sat in his ute in Muswellbrook's main street and rang Angus.

'Lachie, how're things?' asked Angus cheerfully. 'Everything all right up there?'

'Fine, except that Brooke's sick.'

'Shit. What's wrong? Is she all right?' Worry filled Angus's voice and Lachie knew he'd called the right brother. Mark might be the money man, but after some of the comments both Angus and Brooke had made, Lachie suspected he wasn't the most compassionate of people, especially when it came to his sister.

'Flu. Chemist says it's going around, but she should be all right with rest. I've taken her to the cottage and bought some stuff to help with the fever and aches, so she should be okay. But the reason I'm calling is about the dairy. There's no cornicing and no insulation. Even with the fire going flat out it's still cold. It's no wonder she got sick.'

'She can't keep staying there then.' Angus let out a long breath. 'Fuck. She'll have to come to Sydney.'

'Maybe, but with your go-ahead, I could have a shot at fixing it. Then she wouldn't have to.' When Angus remained quiet he added, 'It's not a hard job.'

'Yeah, but can you do it? I mean properly.'

'I had a job laying batts after high school with a decent company.

And I worked for a plasterer during uni holidays for a bit of cash, so I can look after the cornicing too. The dairy's only small. I'd have the whole thing sorted in a day or so. I just need your permission to book the materials up.'

'You're a regular jack-of-all-trades,' said Angus, sounding impressed.

Lachie smiled wryly. Angus had no idea. In the years when he'd first left home and moved in with his gran, he'd done anything to earn money. Sometimes labouring during the day and working a bar at night. In one memorable six-month period, when he'd set his sights on university, he'd worked three jobs, living on next to nothing as he scrimped and saved, callused hands clenched tight around his dreams of a better future.

'I call it having a long and varied career. So can I go ahead?'

'Yeah, why not? I'll sort Mark with the account. Fuck. Why didn't Brooke tell me the place was so bad?'

'Probably didn't want to worry you.'

'More like she didn't want to hand Mum and Mark another reason for her to move home. They're already on the warpath after she didn't turn up at Warwick Farm yesterday. Mark's still making noises about selling Kingston Downs. Apparently that solicitor called him again this morning. On a Sunday! What sort of solicitor calls on a Sunday? Not even our owners do that to us, and they're as demanding as they come.'

Lachie kept his mouth shut. This wasn't a conversation in which he wanted to participate.

'Fuck, sorry, Lachie. You don't need to hear this. And don't worry, your job's safe. There's not a chance in hell we'll sell Kingston Downs. Not while Nan's still alive. The old girl'd see us hung, drawn and quartered first.' Angus's tone became businesslike. 'Look, if you could sort the dairy out, that'd be great. And thanks for looking after Brooke. I know you don't have to and I appreciate it. Poor bugger tries to act tough but she's vulnerable right now. Nice to know someone else is keeping an eye on her.'

On his return, Lachie found Brooke asleep, head tilted to one side and her right arm curled up to her chest so her knuckles rested just under her chin. With her flushed pink cheeks and schoolboy haircut, she looked like a child.

He picked up her empty water glass and took it to the kitchen to refill, then removed a blister sheet of cold and flu tablets from the packet. Returning to the lounge, he placed the medicine and the water on the coffee table and gently shook her awake.

'What?' she mumbled, rousing sleepily and regarding him with owlish eyes, which widened into confusion as she tried to sit up.

'It's Lachie. You're sick. I brought you to the cottage, remember?'

She flopped back and closed her eyes, rubbing a hand over her face.

He indicated the water and the blister pack. 'Take some. The chemist said they'd help ease your fever and aches. Then we'd better get you into bed so you can sleep properly.'

After she took the drugs, he ignored her protests and carried her into the spare room, staying close until she settled. 'Is there anything else you need? A book or something?'

'No, just sleep.' She pulled up the blanket and made a face. 'I stink, don't I?'

'It's just the fever. You'll be right.'

A miserable expression crossed her face. She raised her hand to her forehead and squeezed her eyes shut as though in pain. 'I'm so sorry,' she said, the words almost a sob. 'You shouldn't have to put up with this.'

'Hey, stop it,' he said, crouching beside her. 'It's okay. I don't mind. You're sick. Someone has to take care of you.'

'But—'

'No buts. Come on, sleep now.' He tucked the blanket back around her. 'I've a few things to take care of outside now, but I'll be back to check, and you have the phone and I'll have my mobile, so if you need anything you just call, okay?'

She nodded.

He smiled at her. 'Don't worry. You'll be all right.'

———

The day proved busy and nothing like the quiet Sunday Lachie had intended. The horses were easy enough but sorting out Dorothy, who let her frustration with being locked in the stable be known with an endless succession of grumpy bleats and wall bunts, proved more problematic.

Being designed purely for horses, Kingston Downs had nowhere that was sheep-proof. Though he searched all over the property, he could find nothing with which to make a temporary enclosure for Dorothy, leaving him no choice but to call on Nancy. The old lady happily loaned him some rusting star pickets and a few rolls of ringlock, but on hearing Brooke was ill, took a great deal of reassurance before she was satisfied Lachie had it all under control. Even then, she didn't seem fully convinced, and it came as no surprise to discover Nancy tiptoeing out of the house later that afternoon, when he returned yet again to check on Brooke.

'I'm sorry, Lachie dear, but I was worried.'

'That's okay. I thought you might come and check on her anyway. How is she?'

'Still feverish, poor love. You'll need to make sure she drinks plenty of water. I'll make some soup and bring it over tonight, just in case she's up to eating.'

Lachie swallowed a shard of resentment. Nancy only wanted to mother Brooke, yet for some reason her interference annoyed him. He might be a man, but that didn't mean he couldn't care for Brooke properly.

As if she'd read his mind, Nancy let out a little gasp, her furrowed cheeks pinkening as she pressed her fingers to her mouth. 'Oh, what must you think of me! There I go intruding again.'

'You're fine, Nancy,' said Lachie, softening. 'I appreciate the help and I'm sure Brooke does too. Anyway, if she's all right I'll get back to work.'

Nightfall cast deepening shadows over Kingston Downs by the time he finished all that needed to be done, but the horses were now feeding contentedly in their raked yards, Dorothy was head-down in the enclosure he'd built in RL1, the spelling horses and paddocks had been checked, and he had all the measurements required for the dairy's cornices and batts. And though he'd winced at the intrusion while collecting them, in his arms he carried clean clothes and toiletries for Brooke.

He found Nancy in the kitchen, flowery apron fixed tightly around her front, reading the local paper. The house felt tropically warm and smelled of whatever was bubbling in the two large pots she'd set on the stove. His stomach gave a grumble as he registered the delicious scent.

'Something smells good.'

Nancy rose and began to strip off her apron. 'Chicken and vegetable soup for Brooke when she's up to it—and I hope you don't mind, but I made you a nice beef casserole. I know what you boys are like.' She waggled a finger, expression stern. 'Never looking after yourselves properly. There's a loaf of fresh bread and I popped an apple and rhubarb crumble in the oven for later.'

Whatever residual umbrage Lachie felt toward Nancy vanished, melted by the old lady's sweet motherliness and generosity. He stooped to plant a kiss on her cheek. 'Can I marry you when I grow up?' he asked, grinning, before ducking away as she blushed and batted her hand at him in embarrassment. 'How's Brooke?'

'Asleep again. Poor love's caught a nasty wog. Her fever still hasn't broken. I'd say she'll be out of action for a few days. Well,' Nancy said, tucking her apron over her arm. 'I think I've stuck my nose in enough. Now, if you need anything, you just let me know.' She hesitated at the door, gazing back at Lachie with concern deepening the lines of her corrugated face. 'Take care of her, Lachie. I'm so terribly fond of Brooke.'

'Seems like everyone is.'

'That's because she's a nice girl.' Suddenly her eyes glittered and a sly smile tilted the corner of her mouth. 'She'd make a good match for a handsome boy like you.'

'Goodnight, Nancy,' said Lachie, shaking his head and holding the screen door open. What was it about the elderly that made them take such glee in matchmaking?

When Nancy had trotted off next door, Lachie went to check on Brooke. He stood in the spare room's doorway with the bundle of clothes, watching her.

'I can feel you staring at me,' she said, not opening her eyes.

'Sorry. I just wanted to see how you were.' He took a few steps inside and laid the clothes on the edge of the bed. 'I brought you some things. Sorry if they're not right. I kind of just grabbed whatever was on top in the drawers.'

She eased up in bed, wincing at the movement, and frowned at the pile, gaze lingering on the underwear lying beneath her hairbrush and toothbrush. Lachie's skin heated with embarrassment. He hoped she wouldn't comment. He felt bad enough as it was for rifling through her belongings.

To his relief she smiled weakly. 'I suppose that's a hint I should have a shower.'

'It'll probably make you feel better.'

Shivering and manoeuvring painfully, she slid out of bed, gripping his proffered arm for balance. As she straightened, the waistband of her stripy pyjamas flopped to one side, exposing a sliver of pale hip. Any other time he'd think it cute, but she looked so forlorn he could only feel sorry for her.

'Can you manage?' he asked when she let go of his arm and shuffled forward, arms wrapped around herself against a chill only she felt. Her lips trembled and she breathed in short jerky pants.

'I think so.'

'The bathroom's to the left. I'll fetch you a towel.'

She flashed him a filthy look. 'I think I know where it is, thanks.'

He said nothing as she continued past. No point in making it worse. He wasn't an insensitive man. He understood that every minute he occupied her home caused Brooke hurt, but he wasn't going to let her make him feel guilty for taking a job he needed.

At the door she stopped, hand on the jamb, head down. 'Oh God, I'm sorry. You've been so nice.' She made a choked noise, like a wrenched sob.

Lachie stepped forward and placed his arm around her shoulders. 'Hey, it's okay.'

'It's not!'

'It is. You're sick and feeling miserable. You're allowed to snap.' He squeezed her shoulders. 'Now come on, let's get you to the bathroom.'

While she showered, Lachie changed her sweat-soaked sheets and laid out her night-time flu tablets, mentally running through his chores for the next day as he worked. He'd need to do a load of washing, feed Sod, Poddy and Venus and muck their yards once he'd led them out for the day. Plus he had to check on Dorothy and the other horses, and complete his scheduled weekly walk through the lucerne stands to check the lucerne flea population. Brooke had said so far it had been kept under control but numbers could rise quickly, and left untouched the pest could have a significant impact on yields. The property's two young stands in particular required close monitoring. Only when those jobs were complete could he head in to Pitcorthie to pick up what he needed for the dairy. Finishing both the batts and the cornicing in a day may have been a bit optimistic, but the sooner he finished, the sooner Brooke could settle back where she belonged.

His mind skipped to the cute image of her in her pyjamas. He remembered the way his arm felt around her slim shoulders, how protective she'd made him feel. Irritated with himself, he let out a harsh sigh. He'd felt the same way about Tamsyn once, and she'd broken his heart so badly that nearly twelve months on it still hurt.

And if there was one thing he knew, there wasn't a chance in hell he'd let the sister of his new employers do the same.

———

Two days later, when Lachie wandered into the cottage at the end of a wearying day, he found Brooke on the couch, curled with her feet tucked up in the corner of the lounge, watching the news. While she was still obviously sick, he was relieved to see her fever had broken. Her skin had lost its greasy sheen and the colour in her cheeks was now a healthy pink instead of a burning red. The house was cosy with warmth and the smell of Nancy's made-for-spoiling-men home cooking. Seeing Brooke up and on the mend added to the odd feeling of contentment Lachie had been experiencing since her arrival. With Nancy bustling in and out, cheery smiles and wonderful cooking smells wafting in her wake, and the strange comfort of another— albeit ill—person's presence, the cottage had the air of a real home instead of a shelter where he ate, bathed and slept.

He returned her welcoming smile. 'You look much better.'

'I feel a lot better, thanks, except for this cough. How are the horses?'

'Fine, but I think Poddy misses you. He keeps staring at the house like he's waiting for something. Venus is her usual self and Sod has been good. He only tried to bite me once today.'

In fact, the horse had been more than good. Much to Lachie's gratification, that afternoon he'd managed to coax Sod a few steps up the float ramp. With a bit more time and patience, he felt confident Sod would make it all the way on. The horse seemed to respond to his voice, size and no-nonsense attitude, trusting him when Lachie encouraged him onward.

'Probably enjoying his holiday. Everything else okay?'

'Don't worry, the place hasn't fallen apart.'

'I didn't mean to imply—'

He held up his hand. 'I know you didn't.' He indicated the kitchen. 'So are those smells yours or Nancy's doing?'

'Sorry, not mine. I can cook pretty well but not like Nancy.' She paused and shifted a little. 'You've made quite an impression with her.'

'I'm good at charming little old ladies.'

'According to her, you've charmed all the locals.'

He shrugged. 'I don't know about that. Anyway, if you're right for a moment, I'm off to shower.'

When they were both clean and fed—Brooke with a small portion of Nancy's Lancashire hotpot and Lachie with hotpot and a large bowlful of one of the best bread and butter puddings he'd ever eaten—they settled back in the lounge. The television murmured softly in the background. Lachie balanced his laptop on his knees and studied the news and commodity and stock prices before moving on to the long-range weather forecast and the rainfall statistics for Pitcorthie and the Jemalong Irrigation District. Though his eyes were on the screen, half his mind remained tuned to Brooke.

'Are you okay?' he asked when she readjusted her blanket for the third time, suppressing a cough that sounded like it'd been drawn from somewhere around her feet.

'Just a bit chesty.' She moved her chin, indicating the laptop. 'What are you looking up?'

'The news. Weather. Boring stuff.'

'Not wasting time on Facebook?'

'Not my thing.' He glanced at her. 'Is it yours? I can post something to your wall about you being sick if you want.'

'No, thanks. Nan might see, then she'd tell Mum or Mark and I'd never hear the end of it. Plus I fibbed a bit and texted to Chloe and Andrew that I just had a cold instead of the flu. I've been enough trouble as it is without them adding to the fuss.'

Lachie remained quiet, thinking about his call to Angus on Sunday. He'd made no mention of it but she'd find out eventually. Better to come from him. 'Just so you know, on Sunday, when I went to the chemist, I called your brother.'

Panic flitted across her face. She sat up, fingers curling into her blanket, deep cough heaving her chest, making it hard for her to get the words out. 'You called Mark?'

'No.' He set the laptop aside and leaned toward her. 'Not Mark. Angus.'

'Oh.' Relief sent her back against the pillow. 'What did he say?'

'That he was worried.'

'I suppose now he knows the dairy's like a fridge he thinks I should come to Sydney.'

'No. Once I told him I could sort it out he seemed okay with you staying.'

'You're going to fix the dairy?'

'Not going to. Done. I finished the ceiling off and laid insulation, so now it should stay warm for you. I fixed the loo cistern while I was there too. And that loose cupboard.'

She appraised him for a while, before smiling wryly and shaking her head. 'You've been here, what? Two weeks? And already you've charmed the entire district, almost single-handedly won the most important rugby game of the season, played nurse to an appallingly ungracious patient, looked after the farm and my horses, and now you're telling me you've fixed the dairy, including the leaky loo. Is there anything you can't do?'

'Plenty. I can't sing, for starters.' And nor could he make his father see sense or make Tamsyn love him the way he'd loved her, but they were other stories.

'Makes two of us. Andrew says I sound like a strangled cat.' She coughed again and slapped at her chest. 'Right now I feel like one.'

They lapsed into quiet. In the background the fire crackled. A phone company's jingle emanated from the television before giving way to a car ad.

Lachie cleared his throat. 'You and Andrew . . .'

'Friends.'

'But he'd like to be more than friends?'

She frowned. 'Why do you ask?'

'No reason.'

She waited for him to elaborate but Lachie already felt he'd said too much. He reached for the laptop again. He hadn't sent Nick an email for a while and they needed to sort out what they were doing for their mother's birthday, plus he had a few other mates he wanted to catch up with. He opened a blank email and began his laborious two-fingered typing, making even more mistakes than usual, aware of Brooke's contemplative gaze lingering on his face.

'So what do you think of Chloe?'

He swallowed. How to answer? Chloe was sexy, stunning and vivacious, but he doubted Brooke wanted to hear that, particularly now when she wasn't feeling her best. Navigating women's egos was a minefield and he didn't want to hurt Brooke, even accidentally.

He tapped out a few more letters, feigning nonchalance. 'She seems nice.'

'She's very beautiful.'

'But so are you.' His fingers stopped. He stared hard at the screen, wishing he could dissolve into ones and zeros and whoosh off into the ether. What the hell possessed him to say that? Maybe he'd caught her fever. He closed the laptop lid. 'I, ahh, might go to bed. You probably should too.'

She didn't move. She simply stared at him with a strange unfocused look on her face he couldn't interpret. A sort of dumbfounded, uncomprehending expression, as if she thought he'd lost his marbles. Given what just came out of his mouth, it was highly likely he had.

'Brooke?'

She blinked and settled her eyes on him. 'Yes. Bed. Good idea.'

As she brushed her teeth, he filled her glass of water and checked to see she still had enough night-time drugs and warm blankets. Satisfied, he stood at the door, hand on the light switch, waiting for her to snuggle down, desperate for escape and the solitude of his own room where he could brood over his big mouth in private.

'All settled?'

She nodded, her small frame dwarfed by the timber bed, and for a brief but intense moment their gazes locked.

'Thank you,' she said softly. 'For everything.'

Later, as he lay on his own bed, hands behind his head, staring at the ceiling, he puzzled over how, once again, she'd made a simple statement resonate. How so much of what she did roused something inside him, and made him feel tender and almost possessive towards her. How this whole place seduced him with its sense of home, of all the things he'd once hoped to find at Delamere.

And it left him worrying that he was being tempted along a path down which even his dreams had never wandered.

TEN

BROOKE WOKE on Thursday morning at first relieved to find the last of the aches and fever gone, only to discover a few seconds later they'd been replaced with a cough so deep each convulsion felt like fish hooks jerking inside her lungs.

The humiliation seemed endless. She hung over the side of the bed, hacking and moaning, aware Lachlan would be in to check on her any second, but unable to stop. Cough or no cough, she had plans for today. Plans that required his cooperation, and she wouldn't earn it by sounding like an emphysemic hag.

Bare footsteps padded across the polished floorboards. 'Here,' said Lachlan, handing her a glass of water.

She clutched it in her shaky grip and drank between half coughs and ragged, heaved breaths. The fit over, she sank back onto the mattress with her palm on her aching chest. Lachlan stood at the edge of the bed in a pair of faded jeans, the zip done up but the top button still loose, and a dark blue twill shirt hanging open over his chest. A fine line of inky hair ran up from his waistband and curled around his neat belly button before trailing toward his chest. The pale bronze skin of his torso stretched smooth over taut, well-developed muscles of the type seen more often in elite-sports change rooms than farm cottages.

Brooke blinked, wondering if this was a cough-induced hallucination. Two-metre-tall rugby-playing rural types didn't stand by her bed looking sleep-ruffled and concerned and unbelievably sexy every day. Yet there Lachlan stood, evaporating every drop of water from her mouth and turning her insides fluttery and hot.

Catching her intense appraisal he stepped back, fingers reaching for his jeans button. She glanced away, embarrassed by her blatant ogling and flustered by her body's reaction to him.

'Sorry, Lachlan. I didn't mean to wake you.'

He shrugged. 'I planned an early start anyway. Weather forecast's perfect so I'm going to spray the Aurora stand while I have the chance.'

She closed her eyes and nodded. She'd noticed last week that particular lucerne stand needed a clean-up, but Lachlan's words only reminded her that a short time ago the control of winter grasses and broadleaf weeds was her task. She released a long breath. Now was not the time for tears. Hauling back the blanket, she swung her legs from the bed, determined to get the day, and her plans, underway.

'Would you like some breakfast?' Lachlan had backed up to the doorway, filling it with his impressive V-shaped build, jeans fastened and hugging his hips, his shirt buttoned and tucked in. 'There's Vita Brits, or I can do you some toast.'

'Toast and a cup of tea would be great, thanks.'

He left her hunting for clothes, but the clean pile folded neatly on the dresser comprised only nightwear, socks and a windcheater. She tugged on the socks and jumper over her pyjamas. They'd do until she made it back to the dairy. Her canary-yellow pyjama bottoms might make Sod's eyes boggle, but no one else on Kingston Downs, least of all her, could care less how daggy she appeared.

The appetising smell of toast drifted through the kitchen. A pot of tea, steam rising from its spout, sat brewing on a trivet in the middle of the table, with an open packet of Vita Brits, butter and a jar of Vegemite placed alongside. Lachlan had set two places at right angles to one another. Without thinking, Brooke took her usual seat at the head of the table, still a fraction light-headed after suffering another coughing fit in the bathroom. She reached for the mug of tea in front of her, frowning when she saw it was black instead of milky, then put it down quickly and scraped her chair back when she realised what she'd done.

'No, stay,' Lachlan said, his hand light on her shoulder. He shifted his mug and placed a clean one in front of her and filled it with steamy tea, before handing her the carton of milk. A few minutes later he passed her two slices of toast.

'Would you like me to bring you anything from the dairy?' he asked when he sat down with his bowl of cereal and last week's copy of *The Land*. 'Books or magazines . . . ?'

'No need. I'll be going back today.'

His spoon halted halfway to his mouth. 'Another day or so here won't hurt; that cough sounds bad.'

'It's just a cough, and I have things to do.' She leaned forward. 'Speaking of which, would you be free this afternoon?'

He chewed slowly, eyeing her. 'Why?'

'I was hoping you could drive me to pick up Robert.'

Confusion furrowed his brow. 'Who's Robert?'

'The horse I bought on Saturday.'

He dipped his spoon into his cereal and moved it about, but didn't eat. She could almost see his brain working. She liked that about him, the way he always thought about his answers. There was a reassurance in it, a recognition he would never do anything stupid or harmful. That he cared—about himself, about others. About her.

'I don't think that's a good idea. Not with that cough of yours.'

'I'm twenty-four. I think that makes me old enough to make decisions about my own health, don't you?'

He said nothing. It was another thing Brooke noticed he did whenever he sensed a row, and a characteristic she'd liked. Except at this moment, the trait irked. It was as if he thought her a child not worth arguing with.

A hush descended, broken only by the old cottage's grumpy awakening as it stretched its cold timbers and settled into the morning. Every creak, ping and crack made the tension worse. She sat back with her arms crossed, frustrated and, although she knew it was puerile, more than a bit disappointed. Now she'd have to call Andrew. Or a horse-transport company. Word would soon filter back to Kingston Lodge if she took that option, but she had to do something. The owner had been paid and it wasn't right or sensible to leave him or Robert languishing.

Lachlan flicked another page on *The Land*. Though he acted interested in the articles, she sensed his mindfulness, as if they were connected by a strip of elastic that kept shrinking, compelling surreptitious glances between them, eyes flicking away before meeting.

She rubbed her face, thinking of Andrew and how eager he'd be to help. How he'd laugh and joke all the way to Salt Ash, making silly bets and talking nonstop about horses. But no matter what he said, she wasn't convinced things were back to normal. She couldn't shake the memory of how he'd looked at her as they sat on the ménage wall at Willowgrove.

Despondent, Brooke rose to take her plate to the sink, the hunger she'd felt now a cold rock in her stomach. She stood, staring out the window at the orchard and beyond to Nancy's, admiring a vista she once took for granted. That she'd thought she'd have forever. Liquid welled in her eyes. A life here, with her horses, her friends, her home, seemed so little to want, though she knew in her heart how huge it all was, how lucky she was to lead the privileged existence she did. So many people had nothing. No home, no purpose, no love. She still had all these things and had no right to feel sorry for herself simply because she couldn't tow a float with a living creature inside. It was selfish and stupid and wrong.

Yet it hurt. So badly.

'Brooke?'

She stared at him, adrift. Carefully, as though he was approaching a flighty horse, he reached for her wrist. She peered down, frowning as he gently prised her fingers from where they'd dug hard into her flesh. She hadn't realised she'd been touching the pressure point. He held her hands apart, his touch gentle. His dark-lashed hazel eyes skimmed over her face.

'You should go back to bed.'

Tugging her wrists free from his hold, she turned away. 'I can't. I need to call Andrew and sort Robert.'

'Is the horse really that important?'

Her throat convulsed in a cough. She held it in as much as she could but it rattled and scratched. 'Yes.'

'Christ, Brooke, listen to yourself. How can you expect me to help you when you're coughing like that?'

She wanted to yell at him that it wasn't just Robert. It was her need to *do* something. To feel useful. To engage in the one thing that made her feel strong and talented, that kept the hydra in her head at bay. Training showjumpers was what she loved, what she was good at. With the farm out of her hands it was all she had left.

He gripped the back of a chair. Arms braced, he turned his head towards her, and though his tone was calm she couldn't miss the serious intent behind his words. 'I know you think I'm treating you like a child, but you have to remember my position here too. You're the sister of my employers, and while it's not my job to look after you, I doubt they'd be impressed if I let you catch pneumonia. I need this job, Brooke. Not forever, but for now. And I don't want to jeopardise it.'

'You think I'm being selfish.'

'No, but I do need you to understand how much being here means to me. I could get a job labouring or driving a truck in the mines, but working on the land is what I love. And every day I'm here I'm learning more. From you, from everyone else. Knowledge that I hope to take home to Delamere and use to turn the place around. Make it into something to be proud of.'

He stopped, expression unsure, as if he didn't know from where all those words had suddenly come. He pushed off the chair and straightened. 'I'm sorry.'

'For what?'

'I don't know. Laying all that on you.'

She smiled. 'Maybe I deserved it.'

'No. You didn't.' He sighed and rubbed at the back of his neck. 'All right. I'll take you to pick up Robert. But first you need to clear it with Nancy.' At her raised eyebrow he smiled crookedly. 'I think I'm more scared of what she'd do to me if anything happened to you than your brothers.'

———

Soporific winter sun streamed warm and sweet through the windscreen of the LandCruiser as it journeyed down the New England Highway, the road much busier now as they neared Rutherford, at the lower end of the Valley. Brooke stretched and eased her head back against the seat, slowly emerging from the sleep she'd fallen into less than fifteen minutes after turning onto the highway. Billy raised his head from her lap to eye her before settling his chin on his paws once more. She laid a hand on his back and stroked, listening to the quiet rumble of the wheels and the soft music Lachlan had feeding from his phone into the stereo.

He glanced at her and back at the road, smiling, his hands easy on the wheel, his touch sure. The sleeves of his crisp blue striped shirt were rolled up to expose strong forearms and an expensive looking chrome-banded watch. Bone-coloured jeans sat snug around his thighs, long legs ending in a pair of polished but worn brown leather boots. Clean-shaven, smelling of soap and that same citrusy scent, his short dark hair neatly combed, he looked like a male model for the legendary bush outfitter RM Williams.

'You're awake then?'

She smiled back. 'Sorry. Couldn't help myself.'

'How's your chest feeling?'

Besides clearing the trip with Nancy—who had proven even harder than Lachlan to talk around—Lachlan's other rule was that they call into a chemist for a chat and some cough medicine before commencing their journey. Fortunately for Brooke, after quizzing her closely and accepting her fudged answers, the pharmacist agreed she'd be fine as long as she kept warm and drank plenty of water. Though it left her drowsy, the medicine he'd suggested eased her chest and made her feel human again.

'Still a bit rattly, but better, thanks.'

She surveyed the landscape and grimaced at the sight. Each time she reached this section of the New England Highway she seemed to discover suburbia creeping another tentacle into the Valley. Swathes of new, identical-looking houses intermeshed by sleek bitumen roads extended into the distance. The constructions were so close together their eaves almost kissed.

'I remember when this used to be paddocks,' she said.

'Lot more money in subdivision than running a few cattle. People like their big houses and small bits of dirt.'

'Not me.'

'Me neither, but a home isn't just a building. It's what you make of it, the people you love in it.'

'That's very profound.'

His gaze slid to hers, a smile twitching his mouth. 'Don't you know? I'm a very profound kind of guy.'

She laughed. 'So I'm learning.' Her laughter gave way to a cough. She thumped her chest and, exhausted, leaned her head against the window and let out a groan. 'I'm so over this flu.'

'Don't worry, you'll come good.'

They passed through Rutherford and into Maitland, slowed by roundabouts, lights and thick traffic. As they hit the other side of town, where the speed limit returned to eighty, Lachlan turned up the stereo, fingers tapping on the wheel. Brooke tuned in, curious to know what music he liked, but she didn't recognise the song or the band.

The music swelled from a quiet melody into a sweeping, rocked-up chorus, the lead singer's gravelly voice making the lyrics sound even more heartfelt.

'I like this music. Who is it?'

'A Sydney indie band called Blackheart. Tamsyn put me onto them.'

The moment the words were out, Lachlan stiffened. The line of his jaw sharpened and his mouth thinned. Though the traffic was less dense and the road a broad dual carriageway, he kept his focus straight ahead, hands gripped at ten to two on the wheel. Whoever Tamsyn was, he hadn't intended to say her name.

Brooke stroked Billy's soft head, admiring the dog's pretty black and tan ears, trying not to ask the obvious question when her heart kicked with the desperate need to know who this Tamsyn was. And more importantly, what she meant to Lachlan.

Finally, she could hold it in no longer. 'So who's Tamsyn?'

'Just a friend.' He indicated the bottle settled in the holder in front of the centre console. 'You should drink some of that water. The pharmacist said it was important to keep your fluids up.'

Aware she'd just been fobbed off, Brooke did as she was told, her mind racing. Tamsyn. Whoever she was, she wasn't 'just a friend'.

Neither spoke until they reached Hexham, where Brooke indicated for him to take the exit to the bridge crossing the Hunter River, then to follow the signs to the airport. Twenty minutes later, at Salt Ash, she directed him past the Pony Club grounds, finally pointing to a red mailbox at the head of a palm-lined drive.

'That's Robert,' she said, indicating an enormous dark-brown horse grazing in the front paddock. At the sound of the LandCruiser, Robert's head jerked up. Warm optimism curled inside Brooke as she admired the line of his noble, white-striped nose, the massive shoulders and muscled rump, the calm, intelligent eyes. Even from this distance she could sense the horse's latent talent, the raw promise of greatness.

'Christ,' said Lachlan, peering through the windscreen. 'He won't be too strong for you, will he?'

'No way. He's as gentle as lamb.'

The changeover progressed smoothly. Anton Gulliver, Robert's owner, was a chubby, florid man with an unruly bush of hair the same colour as his two overweight golden retrievers, and a nature as amiable as his horse. He kissed Robert goodbye with genuine tears in his eyes and a request that Brooke keep him informed of his wellbeing, a favour she was more than happy to provide. She knew what it was to love an animal, and Anton clearly adored all his.

'Don't worry, he'll be spoilt rotten, I promise,' she assured Anton through the window, sympathetic tears filling her own eyes as she held Billy's comforting body close in her lap.

'Thank God for that,' said Lachlan as they turned back onto the main road, the unease that he'd shown since the mention of Tamsyn seemingly forgotten. 'I was worried he wasn't going to fit.'

'Oh, come on. He's not that big.'

'He's big enough.' He glanced at her. 'Will he really make a good showjumper?'

'I think so. He has the conformation for it and he rides beautifully. It's like sitting in an armchair, and I like his temperament. He's so calm and sweet, but last week the moment I showed him at a jump he really came to life. His head bobbed up and his ears pricked and he had that real 'let me at 'em' feel.' She paused, her heart clenching at the memory. 'Poddy had that.'

'Is that why you bought him? Because he reminded you of Poddy.'

'Actually, I bought him because he reminded me of you.'

Lachlan grinned. 'What? Big and dopey-looking.'

'Robert's not dopey-looking. He's a gorgeous horse.' She turned away, biting her lip, wondering if he understood the implication of what she'd said. Her gaze slid back his way. Though his eyes remained on the road, his mouth held a hint of a smile. She stroked Billy's head, feeling as silky within as his soft fur.

For most of the journey back up the Valley, Brooke dozed. Despite her nap on the way down, she couldn't prevent her eyes drooping as the rhythmic rumble of the road and the tranquilising soft music weaved their magic. She roused again halfway between Singleton and Muswellbrook, to the mines of the upper Hunter and the cooling towers and stacks of the Bayswater and Liddell power stations.

'Okay?' asked Lachlan, glancing at her.

'Fine.'

'Robert's been good. Hasn't moved.'

'Anton said he was a good floater.'

He glanced at her again, hands twisting on the wheel. She waited, alert to his body language, the shifts and grips, the pensive expression. The signs he wanted to ask something but was wary of doing so. The road narrowed back from four lanes to two. Trucks whooshed by, rocking the car and the float. Lachlan pulled down the visor as the sun streamed low through the windscreen and returned his hand to the wheel, twisting.

Brooke watched him closely, curious.

'Can I ask you something?' he said finally.

'Sure.'

He hesitated, then went for it. 'Are you worried? About the promise you made to Anton?'

'What do you mean?'

'You told him he could come and visit Robert whenever he liked at Kingston Downs.'

'So?'

'But you mightn't always be there.'

'I will.' She set her jaw. 'I'm not leaving, no matter what Mum or Mark or anyone says.' She expected further argument but to her surprise he shook his head, smiling as though he found her determination funny. 'What?'

'Angus was right. You *are* stubborn.'

'Runs in the family. Nan's worse.' She stroked Billy's shiny sunlit coat. 'I'm sorry, for what it'll mean for you. I know you need this job.'

'I'm sure I'll survive. Anyway, until we get you sorted I doubt I'll be going anywhere soon.'

We. The word had a nice sound, a rightness that made her feel fuzzy.

'You still want to help? Even after the other day?'

'Yeah.' He grinned at her, shiny-eyed, the gold-green flecks in his eyes sparkly as they reflected the sinking sun. 'I've always been a sucker for a damsel in distress.'

The sky had turned indigo by the time they turned in to Kingston Downs, the horizon a pale-gold glow of rapidly fading sun. Grazing horses raised their heads at the lights in the drive. Robert released a loud whinny that was repeated around the farm, calls of greeting and curiosity. With night coming in fast, Brooke hurried to unload Robert and bring in Poddy and Venus. She let Lachlan deal with Sod, confident the horse wouldn't be able to put anything over him.

Poddy nudged her as she led him up the lane and warmed her face with welcoming breaths, and she returned his affection with kisses and pats in between telling him about their new arrival, her voice flushed with enthusiasm and an emotion she was trying to ignore. It felt like a secret flowering of trust between her and Lachlan and, perhaps, something more complex. And exciting. Venus bustled alongside, greedy for dinner, ears twitching as she listened in.

Sod squealed and stomped when introduced to Robert, nostrils flaring, eyes widening, body quivering with animosity, but the gentle half Clydesdale didn't react. He stood calmly, taking in his surrounds with interest, while Sod carried on like a pouty prima donna until Lachlan ordered him to settle down and show some manners. After a few more snorts and foot stomps, Sod calmed and Lachlan rewarded his good behaviour with mane ruffles, ear tugs and assurances he was still his favourite. News Brooke digested with bemusement. Sod wasn't anyone's favourite. Most thought him a nutcase. Herself, on occasion, included.

When the horses were settled and tucking in to their night-time feeds, Brooke leaned cross-armed over Robert's yard and watched him in the moonlight. Deeming Venus the safest companion, she'd placed him next to the pony, and the contrast between the two made her smile. Both were shaggy-coated, with unruly manes and thick feathers running down their fetlocks, but side by side Robert stood so tall and strong he made Venus look like a child's toy.

'Cute,' said Lachlan, coming to join her from Sod's yard where he'd been placating the deeply sulky horse with more scratches and head rubs.

'Very.' A cough rasped her chest, reminding her she hadn't taken any medicine since lunchtime. With no sun left, the air temperature was dropping fast, the cold tickling her lungs. 'I suppose I should head to the dairy before this gets any worse. You'll call me if you hear them playing up, won't you?'

'Why don't you stay in the cottage another night? Then you'll be able to keep an ear out yourself and you can help me clear up some of Nancy's leftovers. There's enough food in the fridge to last a week.'

She gazed back at Robert, hesitant. It made sense to stop with Lachlan, but she'd already put him out enough. He was, as he'd explained that morning, an employee and, when it came to her, in a difficult position. She didn't want him thinking she was exploiting his kindness.

'With the fire being out for so long it'll take ages for the dairy to heat up.'

He was right, but still she hesitated.

He lowered his head to look at her, a teasing smile curving his mouth. 'The cottage has bread and butter pudding.'

'I've been enough of a burden already.'

'You're not a burden, Brooke.'

'I wish someone would tell that to Mark.' She sighed and pushed off from the rail. 'All right, but only because I wouldn't like to see you get fat because you felt you couldn't let Nancy's cooking go to waste.'

He patted his flat stomach as they headed to the cottage. 'No chance of that. Metabolism of a bull.'

———

Legs curled up under her, Brooke flicked through channels on the television hunting for something to watch while Lachlan finished tapping out emails on his laptop. The fire crackled and snapped, enveloping her in cosy heat and contentment. Dinner sat pleasantly heavy in her stomach. She'd barely eaten all week, but one sniff of Nancy's heated leftovers and her belly had rumbled into life. By the time she and Lachlan had finished, poor Billy had been left only well-stripped bones and Lachlan was forced to make up his bowl with tinned dog food.

Giving up on finding something decent, she settled on an American crime show, the cast of which seemed implausibly attractive. The lead detective had a chiselled jaw and a cocky swagger to match his athletic body, while the female profiler brought in to work with him tossed cascades of glossy hair and regarded the detective with limpid eyes. Sexual attraction crackled between them as they worked the case. Meaningful looks, sly touches, and hasty steps backwards as they reached the boundaries of their professional relationship underlined a lust the show's writers would never allow to be consummated. If they were smart.

But the mystery sucked Brooke in and before long she was sprawled belly down along the couch with her chin resting on her knuckles and her legs up and crossed at the ankles, mind rattling along with the characters.

'It was the janitor guy,' said Lachlan. 'The one who slipped out the door at the start.'

'I thought you were typing.'

'I was, but it's not hard to keep up with all those flashbacks they keep showing.'

She focused back on the screen, not wanting to miss anything. 'I reckon it's the bloke with the puffed-up poodle, the one who reckons he heard the crash.' She pointed as the camera panned to show the character staring at the building where the murder took place, a smug half smile quirking his mouth. 'See. Look at that smile.'

Lachie shook his head. 'Janitor guy.'

'Evil smiling poodle man.'

They watched intently as the show raced toward its climax.

'Shit,' said Lachlan as the detective arrested poodle man.

Brooke twisted to poke her tongue out at him.

He reached across to tweak her big toe. 'Hang on a minute, Miss Clever Trousers.'

She swung around in time to see the detective cuff the janitor as well. But as the picture switched to the two men locked up in interview rooms, detective and profiler arguing over their guilt, someone thumped on the cottage door. Eyebrows raised, Brooke looked at Lachlan, who shrugged before setting his laptop aside and getting up to answer.

The moment the door was open, Chloe's voice filtered in and for the first time Brooke could recall, her heart didn't skip with delight on hearing her friend. Instead a cold, shameful jealousy slithered its way into her gut and stayed.

Chloe bounced inside, dark curls tumbling, pink-cheeked and red-lipped from the cold, casually sexy in a pair of black leggings and knee-high boots, and a long cream jumper that skimmed her hips and showed off her hourglass figure.

She pointed a scarlet fingernail at Brooke. 'You, my lying friend, are in trouble. You told us you only had a cold but we ran into Nancy outside of Kennedy's just before and she told us you've been as crook as a dog.'

As the 'we' registered Brooke broke into a coughing fit. By the time it passed Andrew was sitting beside her on the couch, leaning in close, eyebrows furrowed with concern.

'Why didn't you call me?'

She reached for her water glass and took a sip, buying time to catch her breath and cope with the accusation staining his voice.

Aware of his proximity, she carefully placed the glass back on the coffee table, using the movement as a cover to shift her body a fraction away from Andrew's. 'It was just the flu. Nothing serious.'

'That cough isn't nothing, Brooke.'

'I'm fine,' she said, forcing a smile. 'Really.'

'Well, you know who the culprit was,' said Chloe.

'Could have been anyone. People were sneezing all over the place when I was in Muswellbrook the other week.'

'No way. It had to be Jeremy O'Donnell.' Chloe rolled her eyes when Brooke gave her a blank look. 'In the salon. Friday night. Remember? Snot going everywhere. Little bugger's given it to half of Pitcorthie by the sound of things. Not to me, though.' She beamed at Lachlan. 'I never get sick.'

'Always a first time for everything,' said Lachlan, throwing Brooke the tiniest of winks to remind her she'd said the same thing. 'Now, can I get you a drink? Tea, coffee, beer, red wine? No white wine or spirits, sorry.'

Chloe clutched his arm, smiling up at him, her body close. 'Red wine sounds lovely.'

The cold creature in Brooke's stomach squirmed.

Lachlan turned to Andrew. 'Beer?'

'Thanks.'

His sympathetic gaze landed on Brooke. 'Milky tea?'

She shook her head, alert to Andrew's watchfulness. The way he tensed at Lachlan's considerate tone.

Chloe followed Lachlan to the kitchen, leaving Brooke alone with Andrew. He looked rock-star gorgeous in a pair of skinny black jeans, a white T-shirt with a metallic silver motorbike motif on the front and a striped black and brown blazer with the sleeves pushed up. With his golden skin and sleek black hair, his perfectly formed mouth and dark naughty-boy eyes he was beautiful; yet Brooke felt nothing. No tingle across her skin, no lazy flip-flop of her stomach. Only the unselfconscious familiarity of someone she'd known and trusted forever.

Yet in whose presence she could no longer relax.

'You and Lachie seem to be getting on well,' he remarked.

'He's been kind.'

She stared at the crime show's rolling credits. Whoever the killer was, she and Lachlan would never know.

'I take it that monster in the end yard is your new horse.'

'Yes. We picked him up today.'

Andrew pursed his lips in annoyance. 'Are you going to Sydney on Saturday?'

Brooke sighed. She didn't want to think about Saturday but her mother had already left several messages, all of which she'd replied to via text for fear of breaking into a coughing fit and alerting Ariel to her illness. 'I don't know.'

'You should. If nothing else but to keep the peace.'

'I know. I just don't want to.'

Andrew pressed his shoulder against hers. 'I'll hold your hand. I'm going down anyway. Mum has a runner in the Farnlee Handicap.'

'I think it'll take more than that to get me through the ordeal.'

'Don't worry, I'll take care of your mother. Ariel adores me.' He batted his eyelashes, back to his normal teasing self. 'But how could she not?'

'I'll think about it. It'll all depend on this rotten cough.' And whether she could think up a decent excuse between now and Saturday.

Chloe's laughter tinkled from the kitchen. Brooke clenched her teeth and focused on her hands, ashamed of the ugly feeling that writhed each time she looked at Chloe with Lachlan.

She knew her friend, had witnessed Chloe's moves dozens of

times, laughed at them and teased her over her brazenness, yet observing her with Lachlan now brought no amusement. Each hair flick, sexy smile and slow look from under perfectly mascaraed lashes only turned Brooke's insides colder. Lachlan's expression remained impassive, but she knew he'd crumble like all the others. No one was immune to Chloe. Not even Jackson, though he'd done his best to hide his attraction. She'd seen it, though, when he'd had too much to drink, and while Brooke couldn't blame him—he was, after all, a typical bloke—each incident cut a little piece of her heart away.

Lachlan returned with the beers, Chloe close by his side. She ignored his offer of a seat and perched on the arm of his chair, arm casually slung along the back, legs stretched out and her hip brushing his arm. Talk circled, led by Chloe, but Brooke barely participated. Her lungs felt tight, her insides chilled. The start of a headache pulsed at her temples.

Andrew let out a long sigh and turned to Brooke, speaking quietly. 'Looks like I can kiss my hair goodbye. I knew it was stupid to take her on.' He leaned into her, head on her shoulder, looking up at Brooke with a puppy-like expression. 'Will you still love me when I'm bald?'

She smiled and tousled his glossy black cut, glad for his silliness.

'Don't worry, Chiang-man. It'll grow back.'

'I'll be ugly.'

'You won't. Bald men are meant to be hot.'

'White bald men, yes. Black bald men even more so. But Asian bald men?' He shook his head. 'We're talking seriously unhot.'

'Do you really think Chloe will do it?'

'Come on, Brooke. What do you reckon? When was the last time someone knocked Chloe back?'

'There was that guy at the Royal Easter Show last year.'

'I meant straight men. Gay guys don't count.'

Brooke grimaced. 'None that I'm aware of.' She frowned. 'So why did you make the bet if you knew you were going to lose?'

He shrugged. 'You know me. Couldn't help myself.'

But the words were said without meeting Brooke's eye, leaving her wondering. She pressed her fingertips to the corners of her forehead and rubbed, willing the ache away. Everything felt out of kilter. She couldn't work Andrew out. She couldn't work herself out. The two people she loved like family were acting weirdly. Chloe trying too hard; Andrew professing one thing then acting the opposite, making bets he didn't have a hope of winning. As for herself, every second Chloe remained in the cottage only made her jealousy worse.

The dull achy pulse around her temples became a pound.

'I'm going to bed,' she announced suddenly. She stood, legs stiff, and forced herself towards the hall door, each step weighed down with confusion and her swirling, ugly emotions.

As she turned into the hall, she glanced back. Chloe's head was turned, not toward Lachlan as she'd expected, but toward Andrew, the smile she'd worn since her arrival faltering. Andrew's gaze was fixed on Lachlan, eyes stony and mouth set, hand tight around his beer.

Which left Lachlan, the only one of the three looking at her.

And, at that moment, the only one of the three she felt sure of.

ELEVEN

FOR ONCE, Brooke was glad of the Saturday morning drive to Sydney. It gave her time to think and she had a lot to contemplate – the turbulence affecting her childhood friendships for one, her feelings for Lachlan another. Not to mention her family and its ill-judged protectiveness.

The M1 motorway ground beneath her, through cuttings and over bridges, laden with traffic, although thankfully not as thick as on a weekday. Showers were forecast for later and, to the south, grey clouds edged into the azure sky. They looked like her head felt. Overloaded, bleak.

She rubbed her hand across her hair and let it drop, irritated by her tangled emotions. A knot of anger, jealousy, shame, anguish and yearning, with the last as sweet as it was stupid.

Both Chloe and Andrew had phoned the night before—Chloe to discuss her progress with Lachlan, Andrew to ask if she wanted a ride to Sydney. An unsettled night's sleep on Thursday had done nothing to assuage Brooke's irritation with either of them and she'd been terse, using faked excuses to get off the line. Now shame sucked at her insides. She had no right to be jealous of Chloe, and her unease about

Andrew was unfair. What happened in the gooseneck didn't preclude them from being friends. She was reading too much into everything.

The motorway dipped, rolling down towards the Hawkesbury River and the huge bridge spanning it. The brown-green waters swept majestically on either side, the land tumbling to the edges as though trying to shake its coating of trees and shrubs into the water. She gripped the wheel as a semitrailer thundered past on the inside, building speed for the steep climb out, and she wished she had Lachlan's easy confidence at the wheel. But the accident had stolen that, as it was slowly thieving everything else.

Lachlan. She had to stop thinking about him in ways that were impossible. In a month, a year, at any time, he could be gone, building his dreams at Delamere. Forbes wasn't far from Pitcorthie—four hours at the most—but it might as well be in another state. His heart pumped Delamere-tainted blood the same as hers did with Kingston Downs. Why start something that could never be finished? Better he sleep with Chloe, trigger their years-old pact of no trespassing on one another's man-turf, and put himself out of reach of even her fantasies.

On Thursday he'd come to her room after Chloe and Andrew had gone, knocking softly, leaning against the jamb, watching her as she sat on the edge of the bed, hands draped between her knees, shoulders slumped. 'I have some paracetamol if you need,' he'd said.

'I'm okay.'

'You sure?'

She'd nodded, wishing he'd go away so she could think, but he stepped inside and crouched in front of her, taking her hands, thumbs rubbing the knuckles. And all she'd wanted to do was bury her face in his big chest and cry.

'Brooke, if you need someone to talk to . . .' He stopped and looked at her fingers for a moment, before raising his gorgeous, worried eyes to hers again. 'About anything. I'm here.'

Even now, she could still feel the longing his words had inspired.

The traffic slowed as the climb out of the river basin exacted its toll on less powerful engines. Brooke indicated and changed to the outer right-hand lane as the LandCruiser's superior torque drew her past the other vehicles. In under an hour she'd be at Randwick, facing her family, trying to act normal when all the time she'd be waiting for the pressure to start, the subtle and unsubtle reminders that Sydney was the best place to repair her cracked life.

She wished she could have explained to Lachlan, perhaps asked his advice, knowing he would think hard on any answer, but she'd fobbed him off with another 'I'm okay' and the excuse that she was tired. And then lay awake in the darkness, imagining what it'd be like to be Chloe, and hating herself.

She'd avoided Lachlan yesterday as well, unable to look at him except to say thanks for mucking out the yards—a job she would have done but which he insisted on completing, citing her need for rest. The other times their paths had crossed, he'd regarded her with puzzlement, scrutinising her in that way he had. She kept her expression blank, giving him nothing, afraid of what she might reveal if she didn't hold herself together.

Even with the fire and the new insulation keeping in the heat, the dairy had seemed cold and soulless when she'd settled in for the night after almost a week away. Not once, in the years she'd been living alone at Kingston Downs, had she ever felt lonely. But the dairy smelled sterile, the atmosphere was cheerless and nothing, not her magazines and books, the equestrian paraphernalia strewn around or the photographs of her beloved horses, could recreate the warmth and intimacy she'd experienced in the cottage with Lachlan. After a shower and an uninspiring dinner of eggs on toast, she'd slumped at the kitchen table tracing lines in the pine top, overcome with hollowness.

Later, restless and tense after the calls from Chloe and Andrew, she'd trudged to the yards and perched on the rail of Poddy's yard, the horse's lovely head resting in her lap, and savoured the quiet contentment of his adoration. She'd whispered to him, revealing the secret stirrings of her heart, and gained succour from his steady loyalty, miraculously intact even after all the horror she'd put him through.

A whicker from Sod had broken the spell. Poddy shifted, ears pointing to the cottage. Brooke cast a look over her shoulder and in the shadow of the verandah thought she saw a figure move, but by the time she'd slid off the rail and turned around it was gone. Lachlan—if he'd been there at all—had disappeared.

———

Close to Royal Randwick, Brooke flicked the indicator and turned down Doncaster Avenue. She cruised past the discreet entrances of other trainers' yards before arriving at the most discreet of all, Kingston Lodge. Only a small brass plaque next to the front door of the modest bungalow that fronted the road revealed this was home to a successful stable.

A red-brick lane led down past the house and opened into a small carpark containing Angus's LandCruiser and Mark's zippy Audi. Christopher Kingston's Mercedes usually completed the trio of blue but to Brooke's disappointment the space was empty. She glanced at the house—Angus's residence and also the hub of the stables' administration—but the blind in her father's office was drawn. Unusual, but perhaps he'd merely finished office work for the day and had now ducked out on an errand.

She slid in behind Angus's and Mark's cars, parking them in and leaving her father's space free. She wouldn't be there for long. The clock was already nearing ten and Ariel expected her at Bondi Junction at eleven.

Brooke passed through a brick archway into Kingston Lodge's small but pristine complex. The yard was rectangular, with three sides of red-brick stables facing a grassy inner garden. Several shady gums spread limbs and leaves over one end, sheltering a picnic bench and a battered trolley barbecue, a site that, over the years, had witnessed the opening of many bottles of champagne, wine and beer.

Tears had been shed there, too. Over horses, hearts, and the myriad tragedies of life.

The fourth side opened onto a multi-use area containing an undercover rotary horse walker, a concrete wash bay, and a flat, raked-dirt area to trot the horses up for their daily inspections. The stable half doors were all painted Kingston Lodge Racing blue with small, brass-framed blackboards fixed to the lower doors, each with the horse's name neatly written in white chalk. Bales of straw sat in tidy stacks against the outer walls, some with pitchforks propped behind in readiness for mucking out. Not a single scrap of dung or straw tainted the swept walkways. Several horses regarded her with interest, ears pricked, eyes bright, their coats glossy with robust health and the dedication of their strappers.

Brooke headed towards the rear of the yard, where Angus stood talking to a strapper who held the lead of an extremely fit-looking chestnut. She tickled soft muzzles and ruffled forelocks along the way, smiling as the yard's champion, Galapagos Flyer, whickered in recognition. And so he should, given all the mollycoddling she'd provided the horse during his spells at Kingston Downs. She paused to give the adored old campaigner a kiss and a scratch before continuing her walk towards Angus. In a pair of jeans and a body-hugging Kingston Lodge Racing wool jumper, and with his air of calm authority, her eldest brother looked like a younger version of their father. Angus's smile shone with pleasure at the sight of his sister. A smile that never ceased to lighten Brooke's mood.

Patting the chestnut on the rump as the strapper led it away, Angus strode to meet her, kissing her cheek before standing back to eye her new hairstyle. His gaze sparkled with mirth as he shook his head. 'Mum's so not going to be happy with you. She hasn't stopped bragging about how beautiful you looked after your makeover. I take it this is Chloe's doing?'

'Who else?'

'At least it's better than that eastern suburbs bob. Made you look about forty. This, on the other hand, makes you look like a pervert's schoolgirl fantasy.'

'Gee, thanks.'

'It's a compliment, Brooke.' His gaze flitted over the rest of her, expression sobering. 'You've lost weight.'

'I've been sick, remember?'

'I know that, but Mum and Mark won't. You know what they'll think.'

'They can think all they like. I'm perfectly fine.' She glanced to the right and the walkway leading to the house. 'Is Dad around? I wouldn't mind a word with him.'

Angus shook his head. 'He's in Melbourne. McCurdie's racing in the Bletchingly Stakes at Caulfield.'

The Bletchingly. Shit. How could she forget the Melbourne Spring Racing Carnival? It was only the biggest on the racing calendar and of major importance to the yard. Christopher Kingston would be tied up with it for weeks, commuting between the two state capitals, his attention on his horses—their preparations and their performances.

Her heart sank. When she'd turned off the motorway something had happened. The sleepy depressive drone of the high-speed road had disappeared, replaced with the fits and starts of aggressive city traffic, horn honks and ill-tempered drivers burning to reach their destinations. Five minutes, one cut-off and one near miss from a P-plater who looked suspiciously like she was texting, and Brooke had caught their infection. She'd sat up straight with her hands fisting the wheel, her mouth and eyes narrowing, the determination she always harboured rousing like a lioness. This horrible year would not beat her. She would assemble her allies and stand strong.

But the ally she'd hoped to recruit today was interstate.

Angus slung a comforting arm around her shoulder. 'Anything your superhero big brother can help with?'

'Not really. I was just hoping to get Dad onside, that's all.'

'He'll be back tonight. You can talk to him at home.'

She shook her head as Angus steered her across the lawn. No way would she be staying. 'I'm heading home as soon as the Farnlee's over. I need to get back to Poddy.'

'You're going to have to rejoin the family one day. You can't keep using Poddy as an excuse. The horse is fine. Lachie's there and he's a pretty capable bloke.' He caught her eye, eyebrows wiggling. 'Anything going on in that department?'

An image from Thursday night dashed across her mind's eye. Lachlan in the recliner, Chloe close, fingers dancing across the back of the seat, anticipation shivering the air. 'No.'

'But you want there to be?'

'*Angus.*'

His eyes widened. 'You do!'

'No, I bloody don't. Anyway, Chloe's staked a claim.'

'Bugger. Never mind, there's always Andrew. Marry him and he could buy you a dozen Kingston Downs. Now,' he said, halting in front of a box containing a rather unattractive, roman-nosed, flea-bitten grey. 'Meet our new arrival, Cunning Cavalier. Came from Marty Cranbourne's yard. Ugly, isn't he? But the connections have this weird belief he's going to be the next Gunsynd.'

She rubbed the horse's forehead. 'And will he?'

Angus shrugged. 'Who knows? Bloodline's nothing to get excited about and he's not exactly setting the course on fire at trackwork, but weirder things have happened when a horse changes stables. Although this one's already been through a few.'

'Flyer looks good, as always. How are the others going?'

'All right. Things have been a bit tough lately but we'll survive. We always do.' He glanced at his watch and sighed. 'Shit. I gotta go.'

'Can I help with anything?'

'No. With McCurdie at Caulfield we only have two runners today and Sally has them both under control.'

She scanned the yard, desperate for something, anything, to keep her at the Lodge. 'You sure? There must be something I can do.'

'Stop looking for excuses to stay,' he said, kissing her cheek and squeezing her arm before pushing her toward the arch. 'Go on, before Mark realises you're here and comes out to nag. And trust me, with the crappy mood he's been in lately you don't want that. Between him and Mum, Mum's definitely the lesser of two evils.' He gave her another gentle shove. 'I'll see you later at the track. And Brooke?'

She swung around. 'What?'

'Be nice. She's only acting like she is because she loves you.'

With heavy feet Brooke trudged back to the LandCruiser, laden with contrition, yet wondering why, if her mother loved her so much, Ariel was so determined to make her leave the place where she was happiest. There was no question she adored her mother—Ariel was kind, clever and loving—but her well-meaning attentions eroded Brooke's confidence, increasing her anxiety that she'd never recover from what had happened.

She slid behind the wheel and started the engine, and, inhaling deep breaths, tried to reignite her spirit, but the harder she tried the more it refused to kindle. Not even the nail-biting drive to Bondi Junction made it flare. By the time she turned into her parents' street it had extinguished completely, leaving her flat and dreading the afternoon ahead.

'Oh, Brookie, your gorgeous hair!' Ariel cried when she opened the door. 'And you looked so beautiful before.'

Brooke raised an eyebrow. 'And I don't now?'

'Of course you do, but . . .' Ariel shook her head as she raked her eyes over her daughter, assessing her offspring with maternal efficiency. 'What are you doing to yourself?' She grabbed Brooke's wrist. 'Look how thin you are.'

'Mum, please don't start. I'm fine. Honestly. Now, can I come in or are you going to keep me standing on the doorstep all day?'

'Oh, have a listen to me. There I am nagging and I haven't even said hello.' She gathered Brooke in a tight hug. 'It's lovely to see you. I know you think I'm a silly sausage but I adore our mother–daughter days and I missed you last week. Saturday just didn't seem the same.'

Arm around her shoulders, Ariel guided her into the kitchen. Her mother's tense back and overly jolly voice kept her on high alert. Ariel wasn't finished, merely regathering before another attack.

'So how's your painting going?' Brooke asked as she perched on a seat at the breakfast bar while her mother set about making coffee—a task that mainly involved positioning two handleless glass latte cups under the automatic espresso machine's spout.

'Really well,' said Ariel, her face immediately brightening. 'I managed to finish another one this last week.' She gave the cups an unnecessary fiddle. 'It'd be nice to have more time to dedicate to it but so much of my day seems to be taken up with other commitments.'

'Are you still doing the media stuff?'

'Yes, unfortunately. It was fun when I first started but now I find it all so very boring. Habillé have asked me to be their racewear ambassador this spring carnival.' Her face took on a pinched expression. 'I'm rather inclined to say no.'

'You can't seriously be thinking of turning down one of the biggest fashion brands in the country, surely? Imagine all the parties you'd get to go to.'

'It's not all champagne and canapés, Brooke. It's a job.'

'A very glamorous job that you'll breeze through like you always do. And think of the extra publicity for the yard.'

'Yes. We mustn't forget the yard,' Ariel said tightly before removing the cups from under the espresso machine and passing Brooke her latte.

Alarmed by the brittleness in Ariel's voice, Brooke studied her mother, aware she'd spent so long observing the world through the prism of her own worries, she'd become detached from the troubles of others. It was time she paid attention.

Though as beautiful as ever, Ariel wore an air of tiredness. Tension lines etched the borders of her mouth and eyes, while a downward tilt dragged at her lips. And in her eyes lurked a cloud of what Brooke had interpreted as motherly concern, but which, to her shock, now seemed more akin to sadness.

Worry rattled through Brooke. Her mother was always so composed and confident. This wasn't like her at all.

'Mum?'

'What?'

'Are you okay?'

Ariel frowned slightly. 'Of course. Why do you ask?' She patted fingers over her face, eyes and mouth widening with feigned fear. 'Am I looking *old*?'

Brooke grinned. 'No. You look twenty years younger, as usual. But you do seem a bit, I don't know, strained maybe.'

She waved a hand. 'Oh, don't you worry about me, I'll be all right.' She smiled reassuringly, back to her usual possessed self. 'Now, tell me what you've been doing with yourself.'

Brooke took a sip before replying, feeling terrible for the half-lie she was about to tell, but equally unwilling to reveal the truth of her days at Kingston Downs. 'You know, riding, keeping an eye on things.'

'In other words, very little.' Ariel put down her cup and reached for Brooke's hand, preventing her daughter from tucking it under the bench. Brooke clenched her teeth against the urge to snatch it away so she could rub at her wrist. The lecture was coming, and from the sincere and empathetic look on her mother's face, nothing would stop it. 'Please, Brooke. Come home. It's so obvious you're not doing well. Look at you—you've lost weight, given yourself a radical haircut. You can barely sit still you're so desperate to rub your wrist. Yes, I noticed. We all have, and it worries us sick. You need help—a therapist who can help you work through your problems and give us back the old Brooke, the one everyone adored because she was always so happy and full of laughter. Come to Sydney, even if it's just for a few months, so we can get you right.'

Brooke breathed in hard through her nose, jaw iron tight, teeth hurting from the pressure. She would *not* cry. Not here.

'I told you, I'm fine. I'm happy. And Lachlan's helping me with my floating problem.'

Her mother's mouth pursed at the mention of Lachlan's name, the pressure on Brooke's fingers coming a little harder. 'I see. And Lachlan is qualified, is he?'

'No. But he's kind and patient and together I know we'll beat this.'

Ariel released her hand and Brooke had to concentrate hard on keeping it above the bench. 'It sounds like you and he have developed quite a bond.'

'Not really. He's just offered to help, that's all.'

'I would have thought he'd be kept busy enough looking after Kingston Downs. It's no small responsibility he's been given.'

'He *is* busy with Kingston Downs,' said Brooke quickly, alarmed by the frost in her mother's tone, and fearing she'd landed Lachlan in trouble. 'I've been keeping a close eye on him and he's knows exactly what he's doing. Mark was lucky to get him. Good managers are hard to come by.'

'I'm sure,' said Ariel, though she didn't sound the slightest bit impressed. She glanced at the kitchen clock. 'Well, I suppose we'd better make ourselves glamorous. We're having lunch with the Cameron Syndicate and they're too important to be kept waiting. Even more so since they haven't had a winner since February.'

'Must have dud horses.'

'Yes. Dud horses your father sold them.'

There it was again, that edge of strain.

Forewarning buzzed through her veins as Brooke remembered Angus's words about the yard. She knew lean years existed in racing, when winners seemed elusive, and Kingston Lodge had had its fair share, but this was the first time she could remember anyone talking about it.

'Is everything all right? I mean, with the yard?'

'Of course,' replied Ariel, but this time there was no mistaking her splintery tone. Brooke's fingers shot to her wrist as anxiety took hold. Her mother headed for her bedroom, hand held out for Brooke as though she were six years old, choosing to ignore or failing to

notice her daughter's distress. 'Now, come along. I've just remembered a little black Audrey Hepburn dress I have that might fit you. A
bit of makeup, a nice jacket and heels and you'll knock that lovely
Jason Cameron for six.'

———

Brooke stood in the owners' stand watching the track as the starters
circled for the Farnlee Handicap. As it wasn't a carnival event, the
crowd on Rosehill's famous lawn was thin and drab, lacking the party
atmosphere, excitement and colour of the major meetings. Though
she didn't look at all out of place, the Hepburn-inspired dress, a
cropped black and white houndstooth jacket, and heels that squashed
her toes and made her ankles ache made her feel ridiculous. At least
she'd managed to escape the fascinator Ariel had wanted to pin to
her head.

Dutifully, she smiled at Jason Cameron, son of the Cameron
Syndicate's chairman and an overinflated twerp, as he moved into the
seat beside her. He'd done the same at lunch, sidling up to sit next to
her and spending the rest of the meal big-noting himself. He was
good-looking, in a citified sort of way, with a trendy spiked haircut,
dark-chocolate eyes, and clean, smooth skin that spoke of judicious
use of male skincare products. But his personality left her cold. For
the sake of the yard and to not embarrass Ariel, Brooke had politely
tolerated the self-absorbed prat when what she'd really wanted to do
was pour her glass of red wine into his lap.

Sensing movement, she turned to see who'd taken the right-hand
seat, stomach clenching when she met her brother's gaze.

'Mark.'

'Brooke.' He leaned across her to shake hands with Jason. 'Jason,
how are you? Good lunch?'

'Very good, and made all the better by the excellent company I
shared.' He threw Brooke a wink that made her look quickly to the
barriers. Shit. The idiot was coming on to her.

She indicated her seat to Mark. 'Here, take my place so you can talk business with Jason.'

'No, we're fine. We had a good chat yesterday.'

'Oh. Right.' Brooke bit her lip, wondering if she could use the excuse of a toilet break to escape, but only a few horses remained to enter the barriers and she wanted to watch the race.

She glanced across the stand, past her mother who was charming Jason's prettily plump mother, to where Andrew sat with his mother, Lee. They'd chatted earlier, Andrew barely able to contain his mirth at her outfit, and trying his best to raise a laugh from her when she responded only half-heartedly to his teasing.

He smiled and discreetly pointed to Jason, before making a wanker gesture with his fist. Brooke rolled her eyes and gave him a 'you have no idea' look, then quickly stopped as Jason turned to see who she was grinning at, his face clouding as he recognised Andrew.

Brooke turned back to the runners. Two barrier attendants in safety vests and helmets held their arms locked behind the Camerons' horse, Dalliance, pushing the excited, bit-snatching animal into the stalls. Lee's galloper, Tiny Torpedo, was already in place. With the last of the field locked in its gate and the light above the barrier flashing, the crowd hushed, eager for the burst of horses.

Light's on. And they're racing in the Farnlee Handicap. Tiny Torpedo jumped well, followed by Mangaman and Shirley's Pride. Then Dalliance and Bossybritches . . .

A cheer rose, only to be silenced by nervous tension as the horses settled into their strides. Jason gripped his race book. Further along, Ariel and Jason's mother clutched arms. Brooke glanced at Andrew and Lee, leaning forward intently, mouths moving as they urged Tiny Torpedo on.

All eyes, it seemed, were on the race. Except Mark's.

He leaned in close to Brooke's shoulder, his voice low. 'How's life up at the holiday farm? Enjoying yourself?'

Brooke kept her focus on the blur of colour at the back of the track. She wasn't going to play this game. It wasn't worth the angst. She had plenty of that already.

'Better make the most of it while you can.'

She shot him a look. What was he on about?

. . . Shirley's Pride is looking good coming up to the twelve hundred, Tiny Torpedo a half length behind followed by Bossybritches and Mangaman. Then it's Dalliance to Our Boy Peter . . .

Mark's eyes slid to Jason and then behind to check no one was listening. 'I just got off the phone to Dad. McCurdie had to be scratched from the Bletchingly.'

Brooke's eyes widened. 'Poor Dad. He must be disappointed.' The Bletchingly Stakes had kicked off the Melbourne Spring Racing Carnival since the early nineties. It was an important race, and not only because of its Group 3 status and $125 000 in prize money. As a good opener to the season, it attracted a quality field and was considered an important performance indicator for the later, more prestigious and lucrative races. With McCurdie's excellent bloodline and solid performance as a two- and three-year-old, he was considered a future race winner. 'I hope it's nothing serious.'

'Tendon.'

'Shit,' said Brooke, feeling ill.

Coming up to the eight hundred and it's still Shirley's Pride, with Bossybritches on the inside alongside Tiny Torpedo, Mangaman, Our Boy Peter and Dalliance . . .

'Yeah, shit. And you better start praying Dalliance comes home.' Mark leaned in even closer, his breath hot on her ear. Alarm shot down her back. This wasn't intimate, it was menacing. Her mouth dried. 'You wouldn't realise being stuck up there in your little sanctuary but times are tough, Brooke. We had a lean autumn carnival, and those two horses Dad spent over a million on at the Inglis sales? Still unsyndicated.'

She looked at him, her anxiety skyrocketing. In the stands, the crowd began to rise but Brooke's legs felt so jellified she didn't have a hope of standing. 'But you've attracted new owners, new horses. Like that Cunning Cavalier.'

'Been through half a dozen stables already,' said Mark, grabbing her elbow and bringing her to her feet, fingers squeezing tight when she wobbled. 'We're the connections' last resort.'

'Come on, Dally,' yelled Jason, on his feet and banging his race book.

Coming up to the turn now and it's Bossybritches in the lead followed by Tiny Torpedo, a half length to Shirley's Pride and Dalliance who's moving onto the rail . . .

'If we don't syndicate those horses or start producing some decent results, things are going to have to change.'

An avalanche of ice fell through Brooke. She snatched at her wrist, pressing hard and counting. Desperate for control. 'What do you mean?'

'I mean, it's about time you took your head out of the clouds and realised this is a business we're running, not some fucking pony club.' His voice roughened with the effort of keeping his anger and their conversation close. 'It's all right for you—the only person you have to worry about is yourself, but the rest of us have lives and responsibilities. If the yard goes under it's not just you who loses out. It's all of us, and I, for one, am not prepared to let that happen. Not now that—' His jaw clenched, then he took a steadying breath. 'Remember that buyer I told you about? His solicitor called again yesterday. That's how keen he is.'

Two hundred metres to go and it's still Bossybritches but Tiny Torpedo has hit her straps and she's coming home, Shirley's Pride's still hanging in with Dalliance, followed by Mangaman who's fading fast . . .

'I know you don't want to face it, Brooke, but you need to. Kingston Downs is on the line.'

Jason leaned forward, hands clenched, his face red. 'Come on, Dalliance!'

Tiny Torpedo has her neck in front . . .

'No.' Brooke shook her head. He couldn't be serious, but Mark's face revealed his determination. 'You can't. Nan and Angus and I won't let you.'

'Unless things pick up, we won't have the choice.'

And it's Tiny Torpedo a length to Bossybritches and Shirley's Pride, a neck to Dalliance . . .

As Tiny Torpedo streaked past the finishing post the Chiangs and their guests erupted, rushing the air with loud whoops, cheers and whistles.

The Camerons muttered words of disappointment, shooting accusing glances at Brooke, Mark and Ariel. To Brooke, every look was like a knife cut. Her anxiety rocketed, each breath shallower and faster than the last, threatening to plunge her into a full-blown panic attack.

She pressed harder and harder on her wrist, fingernails cutting into her flesh. *One, two, three. One, two, three.* She closed her eyes, using every ounce of strength to force calm, thinking of Lachlan, his strong arms holding her, his tender hands stroking her head, whispering that he had her. That it would be all right.

Mark leaned in closer. 'Start praying, Brooke.'

But Brooke already was.

TWELVE

'BROOKE?' Lachie took another step towards Poddy's yard, the aches and small agonies of his rugby-battered body forgotten. Though he'd ordered Billy to stay on his bed, the little dog had followed from the cottage, drawn, as he was, to the hunched figure in the yard. Harbouring none of Lachie's wariness, Billy sat by Brooke's feet, looking up, right paw rising and falling as if he wanted to touch her but couldn't summon the bravery to do so.

She kept her head buried in Poddy's mane, the horse standing quiet and solid, as though he sensed his mistress's need for strength. Except for the Blundstone boots on her feet, she appeared to be still dressed in her racewear. The white houndstooth checks of her jacket glowed almost phosphorescent in the moonlight, the bottom of her knee-length black dress like a shadow.

The door of the LandCruiser hung open, the interior light emitting a soft orange bloom across the yards. The other horses watched, ears held forward, breaths steamy in the cold night air. Hesitant to intrude, Lachie studied her posture. Her arms were around Poddy's neck, one hand fisted in his mane. She held her head tilted and bowed as she pressed the side of her face into his coat. Her shoulders curved inwards, hunched, as though against the cold, yet some innate sensitivity told him it wasn't the cold she fought. He took another step closer, focusing hard. And then he heard it. A choked sob so quiet and cut off it could have been a trick of the night.

His indecision evaporated. He ducked under the rail and turned her towards him, arms wrapping around her trembling shoulders. 'Hey, it's okay. Whatever it is, it'll be okay.'

She shook her head into his chest but didn't reply. Not knowing what else to say, he held and comforted her as best he could, keeping her warm with his body.

Finally, she pulled away, wiping at her averted eyes. 'God, you must think I'm pathetic.'

'No.' Pathetic was the last word he'd use to describe Brooke. Clever, gorgeous, brave and vulnerable, but never pathetic.

She shook her head, not believing him. 'I'm so sick of crying on your shoulder.'

'They're big shoulders. They can take it.' His hand curled with the urge to tuck his fingers under her chin and turn her face to him. 'You want to talk?'

'No point. Anyway, I feel a bit better now I've had a good cry.' She reached out to stroke Poddy's nose. In the moonlight, the horse's sunken eye socket appeared dark and ghoulish, but Brooke didn't seem to notice. All Lachie sensed was her profound love for the animal. 'Thanks for looking after the horses.'

'You're welcome.' He lowered his head to meet her eyes. Mascara smudged sooty circles under her lashes and tears made her eyes limpid, yet through the sadness he glimpsed an inner strength no sorrow could diminish. He smiled, trying to cheer her up. 'Would you like to hear some good news?'

'Please. After today I could do with it.'

'The Panthers won again. Beat the Ellerston Eagles for the first time ever. It's a wonder we can't hear them celebrating in the pub from here.'

Her head jerked up. 'You're joking.'

'Nope.'

A moonlit grin of unvarnished delight spread across her face. 'But that's fantastic! And all thanks to you, no doubt.'

'No, not my doing. The boys played their hearts out. I think last week fired them up. Nate didn't drop the ball once and Patrick's passes were like lightning.'

Her fingers stilled on Poddy's nose. 'Did Chloe turn up to watch?'

'Yeah.' Chloe had been there in full colour, screaming from the sidelines, running up to him at the end of the game and attempting to kiss his muddy mouth. He'd turned away, embarrassed by her brazenness. The Panthers laughed and teased him for being shy, but shyness had nothing to do with it. He simply didn't trust Chloe. Unlike Brooke's spontaneous reaction, with her lit-up, happy smile and wide honest expression, Chloe's attentions felt calculated and overblown, as though he were a prize instead of a person. A trophy to be paraded around and shown off. 'I didn't see Andrew, though.'

'He was at Rosehill. His mother's horse, Tiny Torpedo, won the Farnlee Handicap. Dad's horse came fourth.'

'Oh.' Lachie looked away, annoyed at the flare of resentment he felt on hearing Andrew had been with Brooke. A thought hit him. He looked sharply back at her. 'It's not him, is it? Why you're upset?'

'No. It's . . .' She stilled, a glaze of worry setting her face, before a false smile cracked it away. 'It's nothing. Don't worry about it. I was just being stupid.'

He didn't believe her, but if she didn't want to talk about it then he wasn't going to push. Given she'd been in Sydney, it was probably a family thing—and that was something he'd best stay well out of.

'I have other good news,' he said. 'Something you'll like even more than the Panthers winning.'

'Oh, yes?'

'I managed to get Sod here,' he nodded towards the horse, 'to walk to the top of the float ramp.'

She looked from him to Sod and back again. 'You're kidding me.'

'Nope.'

If he'd thought her delight at the Panthers' win was amazing, it had nothing on the way she looked now. Her entire face was transformed, glowing with happiness and admiration, making him feel absurdly proud.

She clapped her hands together. 'But that's brilliant! How did you do it?'

'With a lot of patience. I just kept talking to him, trying to reassure him it was okay.' He grinned. 'And I had carrots.'

She laughed, the sound rich and warm in the night. 'You bribed him!'

'Only a bit. Anyway, it works with Billy.'

'And there I was thinking Billy only behaved because he loved you.'

'He does. I feed him, he loves me. Simple.'

She ran her hand down Poddy's neck. 'I wish humans were as easy.'

Lachie tilted his head at the sky, thinking of Tamsyn, how he missed the signs completely. The mistakes he never wanted to make again. 'So do I.'

An awkward silence fell, interrupted by Billy's snuffling and Sod's restless movements. He wanted to carry on the conversation, to keep her smiling, but a hint of frost hung in the air. Cold seeped under his jumper and crept icy fingers along his flesh. For Brooke, in her flimsy racewear, it had to be worse. She'd only just recovered from the flu. He didn't want her getting sick again.

He pointed towards the cottage. 'Do you want to come in for a cup of tea or something? There's a bottle of red wine open.'

She shook her head. 'No. I need to go home and get changed out of this stupid outfit.' She looked down at herself and waggled a booted foot. 'Blunnies. Now that's more me.'

He couldn't agree more. Casual suited her, not that stiff, tailored artifice. And she looked good in jodhpurs. Really good. 'Okay, but I'll be up for a bit if you change your mind.'

'Thanks. And thanks for . . .' She waved a hand at herself. 'You know.'

'Any time.' He cupped her upper arm and regarded her earnestly. 'You sure you're all right?'

'Yeah,' she said, holding his gaze in a way that made his stomach somersault. 'Thanks to you.'

Words that kept Lachie smiling all the way back to the cottage.

———

Though Lachie tried to focus it elsewhere, his mind kept drifting back to Brooke. That was the trouble with driving—too much time to think. The trip to Delamere for his mother's birthday gave him plenty. What he should be concentrating on was his father and how to keep his temper with the obstinate fool, but all he could think of was how good Brooke made him feel. Heroic, almost. Like he could do anything.

Christ, he admired her. Her bravery and determination. He even appreciated her stubbornness. Each time she tried to drive the float he could see the terror as it took her over, yet in the five days since she'd been back from Sydney she'd tried again and again. Brooke said she felt safe with him watching her, but as proud as that made him feel, her distress left him floored, to the point where he was beginning to dread the sessions as much as he suspected she did.

They'd made small progress. She could sit in the car with the engine running without issue now. He'd even managed to get her to hold her foot on the clutch and put the car in gear and hold it there, and while her breath would become ragged and sweat would break out over her face, her hands would shake and her legs would tremble, she could do it. Anything more, though, ended in a full-blown panic attack that turned his insides out and left Brooke a gasping mess.

She needed proper help, professional help. Convincing her of that fact, however, was going to be a challenge.

He glanced at Billy, paws up on the passenger-side window

frame, tail wagging at the passing landscape. On this side of the Great Divide, the land stretched in wide plains to the horizon. Winter crops, healthy after solid rains, turned the country into a patchwork quilt of green. Any day now the paddocks would transform into a blaze of yellow as vast plantings of canola came into flower. Through the windscreen the sky draped the world in an endless cloth of blue, cloud-free and magnificent. He leant his arm against the window and let the sun warm his skin as his phone siphoned music through the car.

He drove through Parkes and continued on the Newell Highway towards Forbes, thinking how different it was here to the Valley. This was the land of his childhood. The sweeping Central West where flood followed drought, and the highs and lows of farming provided joy and agony in equal measure. He had family here, and memories. So many memories.

Typically, when he reached this close to home excitement would flood his veins, but today resignation and a twinge of annoyance at having to leave Kingston Downs flattened his mood. Perhaps the bad times—the arguments, the hardships, his shattered heart—had finally overwhelmed his memories of the good he'd once experienced here. But as his mind drifted back to Brooke once more, he wondered if it wasn't something else, something he needed to shut down fast.

From Forbes he cut off the highway and headed west. The country looked good, slowly repairing after years of devastating drought, of the drying, dying river and no water allocations, of heart-breaking days when wind blew up whirly-whirlies of dust where lush crops and pastures once thrived. They had been harsh years, savage times now burnt into the local psyche. Lachie knew of one farmer who'd committed suicide, unable to stand another day of hopeless-ness. Harry Cambridge, with no more livestock to sell, sold parcels of precious Delamere land to survive—an act that had nearly sent Lachie walking again. But he had Tamsyn to think of then, a future, dreams, and he'd stayed.

He turned into Delamere's tree-lined driveway, his heart finally lifting as he spotted Nick's battered ute parked in the shade cast by the farm's four-bedroom, pale-green weatherboard house.

Unlike the rest of Delamere, the house and garden—his mother's territory—were immaculate. A wide verandah, upon whose swept timbered floor a six-year-old Lachie once raced laps on his bike, protected the house from the elements on all sides. Winter flowers— like those in the perfectly pruned orchard nearby, evidence of Minette Cambridge's green thumb—cascaded in vibrant colour from terracotta pots placed on either side of the verandah posts. Four cane chairs with well-stuffed, bright-yellow cushions sat against the western wall, the perfect perch for Lachie and Nick to enjoy a beer and talk while the sun went down.

A giant form shadowed the front screen door as Lachie pulled up behind Nick's ute. Convinced the figure was his dad, he braced himself for his old man's disapproving gaze and hard-set mouth. Instead, the door swung open to reveal his grinning brother. Lachie's stomach and shoulders relaxed at the sight. He returned the grin and then laughed as his mother bullied past Nick, her smile full of welcoming warmth, her eyes glistening with happy, love-filled tears.

Lachie alighted quickly, taking the stairs two at a time, and grabbed Minette in a bear hug, lifting her off the ground to swing her around as he always did, while Billy yapped and ran circles in delight. The Cambridge boys inherited their size from the paternal side and while their mother wasn't tiny, she was diminutive enough to appear doll-like alongside her boys, who took great pleasure in picking her up for hugs.

Her joyous giggles were one of the best things about coming home.

'Happy birthday, Mum,' said Lachie, noisily kissing her cheek before placing her down to admire a country-girl prettiness that never seemed to fade, no matter the creeping of years. A few more lines creased her eyes, mouth and neck, and grey peeked through the roots of her dark-brown hair where the colour had grown out, but her hazel eyes, so like his and Nick's, retained their loving sparkle, her mouth its adoring smile. 'You don't look a day over thirty.'

'You're such a liar,' she said, swatting playfully at him. 'But it's so good to see you.'

'Great to see you, too, Mum.' And it was. He adored his mother. He turned to Nick. At twenty-two his brother's face still held a trace of boyish innocence but his body was that of a full-grown man. He stood a centimetre shorter than Lachie—a fact the brothers double-checked at least once a year—his frame showing all the strength and bulk of a typical Cambridge. Lachie thrust out his hand. 'Hey, shortarse.'

Nick took it and they enjoyed a brief man-hug, grins as wide as Minette's.

'Still ugly, I see,' teased Lachie.

'Still a boofhead.'

'But a good-looking boofhead.'

Nick rolled his eyes. 'You just keep telling yourself that if it makes you feel good.'

The joke was an old one. From boyhood, Nick had possessed the sort of looks that made people stop and stare. By the time he reached adolescence, wherever he went, girls swivelled so fast for a second glimpse they tripped over their feet. With his long dark eyelashes, and eyes even more green-golden than Lachie's, skin that tanned with the merest kiss of the sun, a perfect straight nose and a kissable mouth, Nick was the poster boy for handsome. Feeling it was his fraternal duty to prevent Nick gaining a big head, Lachie had always teasingly put him down.

'Leave your brother alone,' said Minette, slapping at his arm. 'You're both gorgeous. Now, come inside and tell me all about your new job, Lachie. I've baked your favourite jelly slice for you, but there's lemon cake too if you want.'

'Slice sounds perfect, Mum.' He bent to plant another kiss on her cheek. 'It's really good to see you.'

Moisture returned to Minette's eyes. 'And it's wonderful to see you.' She looked from Lachie to Nick. 'Both of you.'

At the sound of the screen opening they all turned towards the door. Harry Cambridge stepped out of the house. Expression as cemented as his wife's was animated, he moved towards Lachie, leaving verandah boards groaning behind him.

The expression Lachie had anticipated. His father had never been one for displays of affection, and the rancour between father and son made greetings difficult. What he hadn't expected was his father's diminished frame. The Olympic-swimmer-sized shoulders were as broad and muscled as ever, the hips as narrow, the legs as long and powerful as Lachie remembered, but they'd lost their edges, like an eroded Greek statue, sandpapered down by the elements and time. His father wasn't thin—not sick or frail—more essence-deprived, as though his thick skin had sprung a slow leak.

Shocked, Lachie flicked a look at Nick, who returned it with a minute 'don't ask me' shrug. Out of the corner of his eye, he caught the purse of his mother's lips, the worry crinkling her brow. Whether it was for Harry or a reaction to the sudden tension, he couldn't tell.

Stomach clenched, Lachie focused on his father. He held out his hand, keeping his tone neutral. 'Dad.'

Harry gripped his palm and fingers too hard, as though needing to prove his strength. 'Son.'

'How's things?'

Harry sniffed. 'All right.'

'You've lost a bit of weight.'

'Hard work'll do that to a man.' Harry jerked his chin towards Lachie's ute. 'How's that flash bus going?'

'Good. No problems.' He rubbed his neck and hunted for something else to say, but his brain remained jammed on his father's appearance and what it could mean. Perhaps nothing. The man was in his fifties, afterall.

Harry looked him up and down, eyes narrowing as he took in the new shirt with its polo pony logo, which Lachie had bought off

Patrick at mate's rates when he collected his Panthers jersey from Musgrove's Menswear. His lip curled. 'Looks like you're fitting in.'

'It's been good,' Lachie replied, refusing to bite. He was here to celebrate his mother's birthday and catch up with Nick, not fight with his father. Delamere had seen enough bile. He could resist, be strong. Like Brooke.

Except his father had a way of getting deep under his skin, working and working with his bitter, jealous barbs about his neighbours, their thriving crops, fat sheep and well-finished cattle. So Harry had lost his father at fifteen. So an inexperienced, unskilled, and barely literate boy had been forced to become a farmer and run a business as his grief-stricken and shocked mother succumbed to depression. But that didn't mean he couldn't learn. All he had to do was ask for help, but that would cost Harry too much of his manhood. Stubborn fool.

Minette tucked her arm in Lachie's. 'Come on. A cuppa awaits and I want to hear all about your new job.'

He smiled at her, grateful for the break in the tension. 'And I have a special present I want to give you.'

'Your being here is present enough.'

'Oh, and what about me?' objected Nick.

'No one cares about you, shortarse,' said Lachie, earning a jab from his mum's elbow.

'I meant both of you.' She glanced at her husband with a cheer that seemed forced. 'Come on, Harry. Let's get some cake into you. Can't have you fading away on me.'

Lachie's eyes met his father's, and for a brief, intense moment, Lachie thought he saw regret, perhaps even guilt, flicker across Harry's face. Then it passed, replaced with the disapproval Lachie had tried and failed for so long to inure himself to.

Copying his father, he set his jaw, steeling himself for the afternoon ahead. They could pretend happy families all they liked. If Harry's welcome told him anything, it was that true reconciliation remained a long way off.

———

Nick emerged from the house and handed Lachie his beer. They leaned against verandah posts, staring out across the land towards the tree line of the river. Lachie surveyed the run-down irrigation plots and cereal paddocks with a weariness that bordered on defeat.

Nothing had changed. Perhaps it never would.

After afternoon tea, he and Nick had driven around the farm, barely talking as they took in Delamere's unhealthy winter crops, the thin lucerne stands, ground so overworked it had turned to powder. Harry had stood in the tractor shed, feet apart, wiping his oily hands on a rag, watching as they drove off. Nick had asked him to come along. Tossing Lachie a look he couldn't interpret, his father refused. Just as well. Harry had made a smart comment moments before about Lachie finding his niche in the Valley with all the Pitt Street farmers. Lachie had retorted that he'd rather be at Delamere, which resulted in a shot back 'And whose fault is that?', which had nearly seen Lachie lose it.

But as the day passed, as Lachie tuned out dark thoughts on the years of hard slog that lay ahead and concentrated on inspecting pastures, fences and stock, adjusting again his mental notes of all the improvements needed to bring the property up to scratch, he found his once insuppressible enthusiasm for the place waning. He could barely summon it now. All he could think was what a waste Delamere was.

He took a slug of beer and frowned, confused by his feelings. He wanted to be here. This was home, his dream, and yet he couldn't shake the idea that something had altered. Something deep inside himself. Maybe Delamere reminded him too much of what he'd lost, what he feared he'd never regain. Maybe he was simply tired from the drive and tension of the day.

Maybe it was the way Brooke seemed to constantly interfere with his thoughts, and his fear of what she might attempt in his absence.

He pressed his hand over his shirt pocket, feeling the hard surface of his phone, wondering if he shouldn't call her, check everything was all right, that she hadn't tried to tow the float by herself.

Nick gripped his shoulder, interrupting his brooding. 'We'll sort it out one day,' he said, voice low to prevent it carrying it into the house.

'What's this *we* business?' Lachie replied, copying his brother's tone. 'Another year and you'll be off teaching brats and earning more bucks than you ever would at this place.'

Something unreadable flashed across his brother's handsome face. 'This is my home too, Lachie. Teaching's only an insurance policy. That was the deal, remember.'

'I know. I just want something better for you.' Better than the heartache and frustration Lachie faced at Delamere. He lowered his voice even further. 'Has Mum said anything to you about Dad?'

'I asked but all she'd say was that she was trying to get him to the doctor.'

'She thinks he's sick?'

'Must do.' Nick picked at his stubby label. 'Maybe he's depressed. Wouldn't be the first bloke around here.'

'No.' And given the state of things, depression wouldn't be a surprising diagnosis. 'Do you think we should say something to him? See if he'll talk?'

Nicked gave a half-bark of wry laughter. 'I'd like to see you try.'

The two exchanged a look, one of shared knowledge.

Lachie drifted back to staring into the sunset while Nick regarded Billy with exasperated amusement. The terrier had found an ancient tennis ball and had taken to walking around with it in his mouth, dropping it at the feet of any human he came across, head swivelling between the ball and the human, eyes pleading for it to be thrown. Initially, Nick and Lachie indulged him, but as the ball became wet with slobber, their interest waned. Billy's, however, hadn't.

Nick shook his head at the dog. 'It's your own fault, slobberchops.'

Billy put a paw on his ball and whined.

'Oh, all right.' He nudged Billy out the way with his boot and kicked, firing the ball down the drive. Lachie laughed as Billy dove off the verandah and streaked after it, almost tumbling end over end as he skidded to a halt and snatched the ball in his mouth. 'That dog's nuts,' said Nick.

'No he's not. He's great.' Billy galloped back and dropped the ball at Lachie's feet, tongue lolling as he panted. Lachie reached down to give him an affectionate pat. 'Best dog I ever had. Isn't that right, Billyboy?'

In response, Billy picked up the ball and dropped it again, flopping down with a reproving look to gnaw on the rubber when his master chose to ignore his unsubtle hint.

They lapsed into silence. Around them, beyond the house lights, the night settled, quiet except for the occasional call of a nocturnal bird and the swish of the breeze through trees and grass. Lachie tucked a hand into his pocket. A chill sharpened the air, but he had no intention of moving inside—not yet, anyway. Maybe when his father had gone to bed.

Nick broke the hush. 'I've met a girl.'

Immediately, Lachie's mind went to Brooke. He shook her away and regarded his brother, peering closer as he detected the unmistakable moonishness of love in Nick's face. 'Shit.'

Nick gave him a 'piss off' sneer.

'You're meant to be studying.'

'I am. Gaby helps me.' A secret smile tilted his mouth, leaving Lachie in no doubt about what their study involved. 'She's in her last year of teaching so she knows what's up. Anyway, you should be grateful I met her. I might have quit otherwise. All that study gives me the shits, and I miss this place a lot. And you're not one to talk. You met Tamsyn at uni. Didn't stop you from passing. Speaking of which, I suppose you've heard.' Nick took a mouthful of beer. 'Looks like she got her wish.'

Lachie stared at him, alarm raising goosebumps on his skin. 'What do you mean?'

Nick's eyes widened as he realised his error. 'Fuck. You don't know.'

'I don't know what?'

Nick sucked in a deep breath. 'There's no easy way to say this so I'll give it to you straight. She's married.'

'What?' Lachie forced his voice to normalcy but it still emerged rushed. 'When? Who to?'

'Month or so ago. Some rich cotton farmer from Mungindi, apparently. I only know because she changed her Facebook status and then I checked her wall and it was all there.'

Lachie turned to face the rising moon and stars, feeling numb. 'So it's really over.'

'Of course it's over. It was over before it even started.'

He set laser eyes on Nick. 'What's that supposed to mean?'

'It means she never loved you, and the only person who couldn't see that was you.'

Lachie's fist closed hard around his beer.

'I'm sorry, bro,' said Nick, placing his hand on Lachie's shoulder. 'But she wanted the farmer fairytale, like on the telly. One look at you and she thought she'd found it, but then you brought her here.'

Lachie tried to think, to go back to the day he'd driven her down Delamere's drive. He knew the property was run-down, that compared to others in the district it appeared broken, unfixable, but he'd thought she'd see its potential, recognise that a prosperous future could rise from the powdery soil and rampant weeds. The district was home to some of the best livestock-finishing properties in the country. In time, Delamere would join their numbers. He'd make sure of it.

She'd said little, been polite but cool to his parents. He'd put it down to nerves. After all, he'd been as bad when he'd met her parents, not wanting to stuff anything up in case it jeopardised his chances with Tamsyn. He'd never considered she might have been disillusioned—that she'd found Delamere, and him, wanting.

And he'd warned her before they visited, told her how things were. She said she didn't mind. That she loved a challenge. That nothing mattered as long as they were together. Had she lied?

'How do you know all this?'

'Overheard her on the phone one night, talking to a friend about what a shithole Delamere was. She thought it was going to be like you, but instead she found this.'

Lachie rubbed his forehead, hating what he was hearing, knowing it explained so much. 'Why didn't you say anything?'

'How could I? You were so in love with her you couldn't see straight.'

Nick was right. Lachie's brain had disengaged the moment he met Tamsyn. Not only was she very pretty, with cascading blonde hair and eyes the colour of the sky, but when she smiled his heart would flutter and float like a released balloon. Besides finishing uni, making her happy became his only purpose in life. He'd even reconciled with the old man so they could have a future together. At Delamere.

He thought back to Kingston Downs and the ring sitting in the top drawer of his bedside table. The diamond he'd wasted too much money on but couldn't bring himself to get rid of. But he would now.

That dream, at last, was over.

———

He drove home the following morning with his head full and Billy's paw on his leg, the sensitive terrier releasing the occasional sympathetic whine. Since Nick's revelation about Tamsyn Lachie had felt lost, overflowing with unanswered questions, doubting his ability to see people for what they were. Wondering what other screw-ups he'd made.

Only when he spied the pristine paddocks and fences of

Kingston Downs, so different to Delamere, did his mood lift. His family home, despite his mother's best efforts, rang with bad memories of frustrations and fights. Of disappointment and heartache. Whereas Kingston Downs' neat blue and white cottage, with its short timber verandah and cosy, if incongruously furnished, interior evoked feelings of warmth and happiness, the way a proper home should.

He cruised down the drive, Billy yapping excitedly as he spotted Brooke near the yards. She stood on a plastic crate, a pair of clippers in her hand, beside a stoic Robert, who appeared not in the least perturbed at the piles of thick hair building around his feet. Lachie waved and slowed, caught by the sight of her T-shirt riding up from the waistband of her tight brown jodhpurs. His foot pressed the brake as his gaze dropped to her bum.

Her jodhpurs were the style with an inlaid suede seat, designed to help the rider grip the saddle, but Lachie couldn't help but notice how the contrasting arc hugged the globes of her rear, accentuating their muscular leanness. Putting the car into neutral and muting the stereo, he wound down the passenger-side window and leaned across to talk to her, easing Billy out of the way as the dog tried to take centre stage.

She turned off the clippers and smiled at him. 'How was it?'

'Good. Mum liked her present.'

'That's great. Nancy makes lovely stuff.' She waved the clippers at Robert. 'What do you think? Different horse, isn't he?'

In the sunshine, the clipped surface of Robert's coat took on a lighter, almost purple-grey hue, but it shone with good health and exposed his massive muscular frame. Where thick feathers had covered his hocks and hoofs, now strong-boned, clean legs ended in broad feet, a rear one of which he rested on its toe in relaxation.

'He looks good.'

And so did Brooke. Though slim and fit, her body still curved in all the right places. Places he'd like to touch. He blinked, stunned with himself, and eased back to the driver's seat to stare straight ahead. Where the hell did that come from?

He glanced back at Brooke, who regarded him with bemusement, and forced a smile. 'I'd better leave you to it.'

She nodded, but when he drove off towards the machinery shed, he watched the rear-view mirror. The clippers remained stationary, her gaze never leaving the ute. And as he walked to the cottage with Billy on his heels and his overnight bag in his hand, he could still feel her scrutiny, and savoured the surge of pleasure it gave him until common sense slapped him back to reality.

He put off doing what he knew he must—taking his time to sort his dirty clothes and put on a load of washing, checking and filing the letters that had arrived in the last two mail drops, casting an eye over this week's copy of *The Land*. Finally, he returned to his bedroom and slid open the top drawer of his bedside cabinet. The blue velvet box sat in the corner. White flecks of lint speckled the fabric from when he'd tossed it in with his clothes on its various travels.

He stared at it, waiting for the pain to start, but the emotion affecting him most strongly was relief. He reached into the drawer and drew the box out, holding it loosely, elbows on his thighs and leaning forward, hands dangling between his legs. Mouth grim, he opened the lid. The single one-carat diamond blazed as bright and clear as the day he bought it. The carefully cut facets reflected and dazzled with kaleidoscopic intensity. Unable to afford the purchase straight off, he'd placed the ring on layby, paying it off week by week, working himself stupid, taking every bar shift he could fit around his uni schedule. Tamsyn didn't know what he'd done. He'd kept the purchase a secret, wanting to surprise her with the white gold and diamond ring that caught her attention each time they walked past the jeweller's window. Her disappointment when she noticed it gone from display told him that he'd chosen well.

Except he hadn't. By the time he made the final payment she'd already decided it was over. Delamere and Lachie weren't for her. And unlike everyone else, it seemed, he never saw it coming.

He pulled out the ring and shook his head at the inscription.

Tamsyn. Love always, Lachie.

What a joke.

With a sigh he replaced the ring and snapped the box closed, before rising and tossing it onto the dresser with his other Tamsyn reminder—the Longines watch she'd bought him for his twenty-seventh birthday with nothing inscribed on the back, not even a 'Love, Tamsyn'.

The two items said it all. He loved her. So much he'd even had his feelings etched into an engagement ring, whereas Tamsyn only loved the fairytale she thought he could give her. They never stood a chance.

He'd keep the watch. Like the music she'd introduced him to, he liked it, and he might be angry and sad and hurt, but he wasn't petty. The ring, though, was history.

The same place he should have consigned Tamsyn long ago.

THIRTEEN

THE MONDAY FOLLOWING his trip to Delamere, Lachie leaned against his ute with his legs stretched out in front, enjoying the sunshine. He should be working, fixing the leaky water trough he'd discovered, or servicing machinery, checking the pumps and irrigation lines, the paddocks, horses, doing a dozen things, but watching Brooke in the ménage on Robert was like watching ballet. And it held him mesmerised.

The two of them moved with perfect harmony, as though hearing the same tune in their heads. She applied her aids so subtly Lachie could barely discern them—a shift of her weight here, an increase in leg pressure there, a flex of her soft hands—but Robert read them, and he responded with controlled grace, elegant despite his size.

Walk to canter, then halt. A rein back, then straight into canter again. A slim, supple girl on a giant horse, in absolute control.

God, she was amazing.

She brought Robert back to a loose-reined walk. His head hung low and relaxed. White foamy slobber fell from his mouth as he chewed his bit, nostrils wide from effort. She ruffled his mane, chattering to him, her cheeks flushed pink with pleasure and exertion.

Lachie caught snatches of words on the light breeze—superstar, champion, special—and found himself foolishly wishing she meant them for him.

After a lap of the ménage at a walk, she brought Robert back into hand. The horse gathered himself, body compressing, his huge power constrained by her quiet aids. Brooke urged him into a trot and steered him towards the far side of the arena where she had a series of coloured showjumping poles laid on the ground in a line, ending in a metre-high upright fence made from two cavaletti jumps stacked on top of one another. As soon as Robert spied the poles, his body language changed. The ears that had been swivelling suddenly darted straight ahead. His head rose, his nostrils widened and his controlled trot lifted, his legs bouncing off the sand as though on a trampoline. Eagerness shivered across his tensed muscles.

Brooke had been right. Point Robert at a jump and he became a different horse.

The door to the barn clanged, breaking his enchantment. Chloe emerged, dressed in skin-tight beige breeches, long black riding boots and a cobalt-blue polo shirt one size too small. Behind her, as sleek and shiny as her boots, strutted a haughty black horse, a white star bright in the centre of its forehead.

Hips swaying, she led the horse towards Lachie, smiling sexily, dark-lashed blue eyes glittery, her nipples evident through the over-stretched weave of her shirt. He looked away, swallowing. He'd known she was there, recognising the battered Nissan Patrol attached to a worn horse float, and had made a mental note to avoid her, but when he'd driven back from the paddock to fetch some multigrips he'd been distracted by Brooke on Robert. Now he was caught.

'Shouldn't you be at the salon?' he asked when she approached and leaned her backside against the ute, close to his.

'Monday's my day off. Couldn't think of any better way than to spend it here with the horses, Brooke . . .' Her gaze flashed with invitation. 'And you.'

Keeping his expression dispassionate, he concentrated on holding his hand out for the horse to sniff before stroking its nose. She'd catch on soon. He hoped. 'Good-looking animal.'

'This is Elvis. Best-looking horse in the Hunter.'

'The name suits him.' Although given the animal's dark magnificence, the arrogant way he held his head, and his look-at-me strut, perhaps Black Beauty would have been more appropriate. 'So what's Elvis's talent, other than looking pretty?'

'Not much. He's a show horse, so prancing around looking pretty is what he does. Very well, I might add.' She tickled Elvis under the chin. 'Elvis here was champion hack at the Maitland Show back in February.'

'So what's he doing at Kingston Downs? Don't tell me that after reaching those heights he's looking for a career change as a showjumper?'

She nudged him. 'No, doofus. Brooke's going to give me a hand with his canter transitions. His off side's fine but for some reason he's really stiff on his near side. It could simply be me dropping my weight without realising—wouldn't be the first time I've fallen into that habit —but I'm worried it could be something else with him. Maybe a back problem. Brooke will be able to work it out. She always can.'

At the mention of Brooke, Lachie turned his attention back to the ménage. 'She's good, isn't she?'

'Very. She was such a mess after the accident we were worried she was going to give it up. Losing Oddy and then learning Pod's career was over really knocked her around, but she's come good. Except for the float thing.'

In the ménage, Brooke laughed and slapped Robert's neck as he gave a happy pigroot after the final jump, before easing him around for another run. The sound of her laughter and the delight on her face made Lachie's insides tumble.

'So, tell me, Lachlan Cambridge,' said Chloe, eyeing him sideways, 'is the reason you're playing hard to get because you already have a girlfriend, or are you just plain shy?'

He threw her an amused look. How like Chloe to come right out with it. How he should answer, though, was another question. Telling her straight out that he wasn't remotely interested might be hurtful, and he liked her too much for that.

'Why?' he asked, hedging. 'Are you offering?'

'Maybe. But right now from you I'd be happy with a quick shag.'

He laughed and shook his head. 'Sorry. I'm not into quick shags.'

'I can do long ones.'

'Of that I have no doubt. And I'm sure it'd be very pleasurable, but I'm fine.'

'You sure?'

'Positive. Thanks, though. It was . . .' he paused, trying to think of the appropriate phrase, 'kind of you to offer.'

Releasing a long sigh Chloe crossed her arms and sagged back against the ute. 'Bugger. The direct approach has always worked in the past. You'd be surprised how often I get lucky.'

'Actually, I wouldn't.'

'Anyway, you haven't answered my question.'

'Which one?'

'The "are you just shy or have you got a girlfriend?" one.'

'Oh, that one.' He glanced at Brooke and quickly away. 'No. I don't have a girlfriend.'

Chloe must have caught something in his voice. She smiled knowingly. 'Ahh, broken heart.'

He thought of the afternoon just two days before when he'd taken out Tamsyn's ring, braced for a stab of pain that didn't come. How he'd tossed the box on the dresser like a piece of rubbish, consigning it and her to history. How when he touched Brooke, saw her smile, heard her laugh, the world turned warm, as though his heartache had never existed.

'Yeah. But I think it might be getting better.'

'Better enough to have sex with me?'

'Sorry, but no.'

'In that case, I don't suppose you could lend me a pair of your jocks?'

He stared at her quizzically, mind working overtime. The sex request he could grasp, but his underwear? That was way out of left field. 'Now why would I want to do that?'

She eyed him for a moment, then shrugged, a smile playing on her lips. 'No harm in telling you now, I suppose. That night in the pub, when Brooke introduced us, I made a bet with Andrew that I could sleep with you within a month.'

Lachie's eyebrows shot up.

'Yeah,' said Chloe, having the good grace to blush, 'I know. A bit presumptuous of me, but we all thought you'd be easy.'

He resisted the urge to look at Brooke, hurt that she'd thought of him that way. Wondering if she still believed it. 'Except for Andrew.'

'No, Andrew thought you'd be easy too, but he never could resist a bet, and when Brooke egged him on that was the end of it.' She ran her hand down her long silky ponytail and waved the end at him. 'So unless I lie and produce a pair of your jocks as proof I managed to get into them, my head gets shaved.'

He winced. Chloe's cascading hair must have taken years to grow. 'That's tough.'

'Very. And not a good look for a hairdresser. Are you sure you can't lend me a pair?'

Lachie considered for a moment. The thought of vain Andrew having to shave his head held appeal, but then everyone would think he'd slept with Chloe.

'As much as I'd like to help, I can't. But I wouldn't worry. You're so beautiful it won't make a scrap of difference.'

She gave a nod of appreciation and then sighed. 'Thanks. I just hope you're right.'

As he pushed off from the ute to head back to work, Brooke left the arena and rode towards them. She was smiling but Lachie noted a pensiveness beneath it.

She flicked a look at Lachie before dismounting and addressing Chloe. 'Why don't you warm up Elvis while I sort Robert?'

'Sure.' Chloe threw Lachie a wink. 'If you change your mind . . .'

'I won't.' He turned to Brooke as Chloe led Elvis to the arena. 'Robert looked good.'

'He's going well.' She paused, hooping the reins over Robert's head and fiddling with the buckle. 'You and Chloe looked like you were having quite a chat.'

'You could say that.' He decided to take a risk. 'We were discussing her bet. The one she was always going to lose.' He held her gaze.

'Oh. Right. So you know about it, then?'

'I do.'

She bent down to scratch Billy, who had returned from his explorations and was sniffing for attention. The moment she touched his head he flopped onto his back and spread his legs in expectation of a belly rub. 'You aren't tempted?'

He stared at the sky, overcome with disappointment at Brooke's role in the bet. She'd considered him some sort of easy lay, just another bloke who didn't give a shit. He refocused on her. 'You really think I'd sleep with someone for a bet?'

Her eyes widened as she registered his tone. Abandoning Billy, she straightened. 'That's not—'

'I'm a man, Brooke. Not a teenager.'

She remained silent, biting her lip, hands tight around Robert's reins. The yard fell into silence, broken only by the carrying thud of Elvis's hoofs and a snort from Robert.

'I should get back to work,' he said, uncomfortable and worried he'd been too harsh. After all, when Chloe and Andrew made the bet, he'd been at Kingston Downs a week and a half. Brooke hadn't known him at all then.

He rubbed the back of his neck with his free hand, trying to figure out what to say, but Brooke dived in first.

'I never thought you'd sleep with Chloe just so she could win a bet. I thought you might have been tempted because you like her.'

'I do like her, just not that way, and I also prefer to think that when two people sleep together it means something.' He looked away, heat creeping up his neck. 'You probably think I'm old-fashioned.'

'Not at all.' She moved closer and touched his arm. 'It's nice.'

She smiled, eyes soft and lovely, flipping his heart over. Shit. He needed to pull himself together.

Helping Brooke was one thing. Falling in love with her wasn't on the agenda. Though as his heart continued to thump and his skin tingled from the hesitant caress of her hand he had the uneasy feeling it was already too late.

———

'Stop being a sook,' said Lachie, scruffing Sod's mane. The morning following their awkward conversation about Chloe, as Lachie helped her lead out the horses on the way to check irrigation lines, Brooke had asked if he could help her with Sod later that afternoon. Given Lachie's out-of-control feelings he'd wanted to keep away, but a promise was a promise, and he knew how much getting the horse to load meant to her. 'You're a big brave horse. If Venus can do it, then surely you can.'

Sod stood on the float ramp, sniffing the rubber matting, one step from putting a foot inside the scary interior. To make the float seem wider and more inviting, Lachie had removed the centre partition, and with a bucketload of encouragement he'd managed to coax Sod up the ramp, but that was as far as the horse would venture. Frustrated, Brooke had fetched Venus and walked her inside in the hope Sod would see there was nothing to be afraid of. But Sod's head held the same monsters as Brooke's, and they were proving hard to defeat.

'I don't think he counts Venus as a horse,' she said, scratching the pony's forelock.

'Take her out,' replied Lachie. 'She's only making it seem narrower.' And probably reminding Sod of travelling with the others when the gooseneck flipped, but mentioning the accident wasn't a good idea. Loading a fractious Sod made Brooke sad enough. As she led

Venus out, Lachie snuck a chunk of carrot to Sod. 'Come on, boy. Make her happy.'

He tugged on Sod's halter, heart leaping when the horse took a small step forward. 'That's it. Look how easy it is.' Lachie released the pressure and stroked Sod's neck while he examined him for signs of distress, but Sod's ears remained pointed forward, his breathing even, and his coat sweat-free. Encouraged, Lachie gave the halter another tug. Sod raised his right hoof, hesitant, hovering between fear and trust.

Lachie darted a glance at Brooke, standing at the end of the ramp with her hand to her mouth and her eyes wide with hope.

'Please, Sod,' he whispered. 'Show her how brave you are.' The horse's foot went down, dragging Lachie's optimism with it. They'd tried. And one step inside the float was still progress. Hiding his disappointment Lachie slapped Sod's neck and rubbed his silky coat. Sod had done his best. Maybe tomorrow he'd make it further.

Sod bunted him affectionately in the ribs, then to Lachie's astonishment, he looked straight ahead, and with an 'oh, well, if I must' snort, took not one, but two steps into the float.

'You little cracker,' he whispered, resisting the urge to cheer. Instead, he buffed Sod's head with medal-polishing enthusiasm, praising the horse to the hilt and sneaking him another chunk of carrot from his pocket.

Sod now stood half in, half out of the float, further inside than he'd ever ventured before. The temptation to reward him for his effort by leading him out was great, but one glance at Brooke and the joy pinking her cheeks made Lachie want to try for more.

He bent close to Sod's head. 'You think you can take another step for me?'

Sod's ears swivelled, listening. Lachie didn't know if it was something in his manner or voice, or perhaps it was simply his size, but Sod respected him. Had done, he realised, from their first introduction.

He curled his fingers on the cheek strap. 'Come on, boy. A couple more steps. Easy work for a big brave horse like you.'

The encouragement worked. With no further ado than a shake of his head, Sod walked the entire way into the float, gave the haynet a cursory sniff, and poked his nose towards Lachie's pockets in a demand for carrots.

Lachie emptied them out, stuffing orange chunks between Sod's greedy lips as he scratched the horse's forelock, casting ecstatic grins between Sod and Brooke, who stood at the base of the ramp with both hands over her mouth, eyes huge and glistening with happy tears.

When the carrots were gone and Sod began to show signs of restlessness, Lachie led him out, easing aside to let Brooke fuss and plaster kisses over the animal's nose, her joyful babbles warming him the way no sun ever could. Only when a bored Sod nipped her on the arm did Lachie retake control and, after ordering the horse to mind his manners, lead him to his yard.

Rug secure, haynet tied and water checked, Lachie gave Sod a last proud scratch before ducking under the rail to join Brooke leaning against the fence.

'I can't thank you enough,' she said.

'It's early days. The real trick will be getting him to travel. But it's a start.'

She rested her chin on her hands, staring at her horse. Sod snatched at his feed, unaffected by the late afternoon's activity, while Venus tried in vain to snake her fat neck under the rail separating their yards in the faint hope of hoovering up scraps. Billy sat in the corner of Sod's yard, blissfully chewing a hoof clipping he'd scrounged. 'I can't help thinking that if Sod can do it then so can I.'

Encouraged by Sod's success, Lachie's thinking had drifted down the same line. 'You want to give it a go?'

'Yeah, why not? The float's out.'

'And Venus is conveniently at hand.'

Brooke eyed the pony, now on its knees, neck flat and head

twisted sideways, eyes narrowed in determination, lips flapping comically as they attempted to secure a single stalk of fallen lucerne, and shook her head. 'Not Venus.'

'What about Billy? It'll save me fetching Dorothy. And he won't grump.'

She bit her lip. 'I don't know.'

'If you're worried about hurting him, don't be. That dog is indestructible.'

'You sure?'

'I wouldn't offer him if I wasn't.' He whistled for Billy, who immediately trotted over, coveted hoof scrap poking from his jaws. Lachie scooped him up and with Brooke following, strode to the float.

A few minutes later they sat in the LandCruiser, engine running, Brooke's hands gripping the wheel. Already her brow was speckled with sweat, her breathing laboured. Doubt pricked at Lachie's conscience. She was so happy when Sod loaded, so confident. Now, despite his patient encouragement and the rock-steady faith that worked so well with Sod, her fear continued to escalate. No matter how he longed to help her, this was out of his realm.

'We don't have to do this, Brooke.'

'I want to.' Her mouth held a stubborn line. 'If Sod can do it, so can I.'

'Sod's a dumb animal. You're a clever human. It's not going to be as easy.'

She looked at him with an expression on the verge of crumpling. 'You don't believe I can do it.'

Hating the despair in her eyes, Lachie shifted in his seat, torn between wanting to reach out for her and keeping his distance. 'You can do anything you put your mind to, but I don't want to see you upset because you can't cure yourself in an instant. This will take time.'

'But that's the thing. I don't have time.'

He stilled. 'What do you mean?'

She shook her head. 'I can't say. It wouldn't be right.'

He didn't probe further, respecting her need for privacy, but that didn't stop him from working her words over. He suspected it was something to do with the night he found her crying into Poddy's neck. That was a week and a half ago. Last Saturday the Sydney Spring Racing Carnival, which despite its name ran each year from August to September, began in earnest with the San Domenico Stakes day at Royal Randwick. Brooke had dutifully driven down to Sydney, but he could see from her tight expression as she kissed her horses goodbye and headed for her car that the journey was made under sufferance. He imagined this week would be no different.

'Brooke, if there's anything I can do . . .'

'Thanks. But it'll be okay.' She twisted her hands around the wheel. 'I just need to get sorted.'

And once she was, he'd be out of a job. Goodbye, Kingston Downs. Goodbye, Brooke. Hello, wherever. He stared at the dash, wondering how he ended up in this mess. A month he'd been here. A heartbeat in the scheme of things. Yet the idea of leaving made his breath feel short.

What did it matter? Brooke's wellbeing had to be what counted.

He pointed to her leg. 'You feel up to engaging the clutch?'

She swallowed and inhaled shakily before closing her mouth and nodding. Grim-faced, she pressed on the clutch until it reached the floor.

'That's great. You're doing fine. Nothing to worry about.' Not wanting to push, he let her stay like that for a moment. 'Are you ready to put your hand on the shift?'

'I don't know.'

He recognised the build of panic in her voice and quickly tried to ease it. 'That's okay. You don't have to. You can just sit. The car's in neutral. We're not going anywhere. There's no rush.'

She blinked, spilling a single tear from her left eye. Each point of her knuckles jutted hard and white against her stretched skin. He knew she wouldn't make it, that this attempt would be no different from the others. Any moment and her distress would get the better of her and he'd despise himself for letting it get that far. Maybe she'd hate him a little bit for letting her.

'It's okay. You can stop now.'

Jaw clenched, she gave a rapid shake of her head.

'Please, Brooke. It's not working.'

Another tear plummeted down her cheek. As it reached her chin he made a decision. No matter what she wanted, he wasn't going to sit back and let her fall apart. Before she could stop him or argue, he reached across and turned off the ignition. Then he pushed himself out of the car, strode to the driver's side, hauled open the door and dragged her into his arms.

He expected a fight. Instead, she let him hold her to his chest.

'Don't do this anymore.'

'I have to.'

'Then get proper help.'

'I don't need proper help. I have you.'

I have you.

He swallowed. Three words and she'd turned what he'd hoped was a stupid crush into something greater, something far, far worse.

He forced himself to let go and hold her at arm's length. Out of kissing distance. 'I know you don't want to hear this, but your family's right. You need proper help. Even policemen and soldiers, people who have been through unspeakable horrors, understand they can't treat themselves, that they need a professional to help them cope with the terrible things they've experienced. It's not a sign of weakness.' He cupped her face, running his thumbs under her eyes to clear her tears, resisting the urge to drop them to her mouth, to stroke away the soft trembling of her lips. 'You're special, Brooke, but not unique.'

'I don't want to leave here.'

'So we'll find you someone local.'

He knew he should drop his hands, step away, break the tension between them, but he was caught, held by a need he wished didn't exist. A need that had simmered, unacknowledged, half-dormant, from the moment he'd arrived at Kingston Downs. The need that had boiled over the moment he let the last shreds of his love for Tamsyn float free.

Her gaze darted to his mouth and back up. He swallowed, lost in her clear brandy-coloured eyes. Eyes no longer pooling with yearning for his comfort, but for something else, something more. Something he shouldn't give.

But so desperately wanted to.

Blood pounded past his ears, loud, intense, as though in warning. Everything tightened, from the tiniest muscle in his body to the very air surrounding them, as if the world held its breath, expectant. He couldn't remember ever wanting to kiss someone so badly.

Her body swayed, weight shifting to the balls of her feet. She placed a hot hand on his chest, eyes hooding as her mouth parted.

His pumping blood became a roar.

With a single, brief caress across her lips, Lachie let his hands slip away and took a heavy step backwards. Regret hung between them, congealing in the stunned silence. He shoved his hands in his pockets. Even if it felt like shit he'd done the right thing.

For both of them.

'Poor Billy must be wondering what's going on,' he said for want of something else to say.

She blinked and gave a little shake of her head, as though she'd been far away and needed to bring herself back to earth. She touched her lips, the place where only a few seconds before his hand had been. Then she focused on him and snatched her fingers away as though afraid she'd touched poison. The gesture made him sag a little bit inside. He should have known he'd overstepped the mark, that he'd misread the signs. After all, he had a pretty solid history of believing in emotions that didn't exist.

'Yes. Billy. Of course.' Folding her arms protectively across her chest, she looked down at her watch before throwing him an awkward smile. 'And I'd better bring in the horses.'

'What's the time?' He didn't need to ask. The dropping sun and cooling air told him it was nearing five, but he took his cue from her, acting normal when he felt anything but.

'Ten to five.'

'Poddy will be wondering where you are.'

'I'd best get to it then,' she said, dropping her arms. Casting him one last look, she turned towards the barn. Three steps later she halted, head twisting over her shoulder. 'Thanks, Lachlan.'

He nodded, watching as she continued inside for the leads, wishing that, just once, she'd call him Lachie. But even after all they'd been through he was still Lachlan. Friend, perhaps, but still the farm manager. Professional relationship only.

And if he didn't want to get hurt any more than he already would, he'd better make sure it stayed that way.

FOURTEEN

BROOKE PRESSED her head against the tack room wall, waiting for the rumble of the tractor to fade. One wave, one sexy morning-bright smile from Lachlan and she'd turned into a crazy, love-sick mess. Although that was a lie. She'd been a crazy, love-sick, *embarrassing* mess since Lachlan led Sod into the float three days ago, and it was only getting worse.

She should be angry, not mooning around like a poddy calf. That was her job Lachlan was heading down the lane to complete. So what it if was only small? She was still the one who'd slaved her guts out preparing the new lucerne stand. She should have been the one driving the tractor and seeder, seedbox filled with the pre-pelleted lucerne seed Lachlan had picked up yesterday from Pitcorthie Rural. Seed that *she'd* pre-ordered. Yet underneath her sweaty, heart-poundy infatuation lurked not anger, but a strange feeling of contentment, as if Lachlan's presence at Kingston Downs made the world right. That he belonged, like her, to the Valley.

'Idiot,' she muttered, pulling away from the wall and gathering up her all-purpose saddle and a cavesson bridle fitted with a simple eggbutt snaffle bit. Brooke didn't have time for fantasies. Especially hopeless ones like that. She had horses to work.

She carried the tack outside, hooking the saddle over the rail of the nearest yard, in which a very pretty, white-blazed chestnut filly stood regarding her with blinky brown eyes.

'Ready for a workout, Elly?' she said, sliding under the rail and approaching the horse with soft coos.

Today was Electra's second day in work and although kind-natured, the filly retained her quivery ex-racehorse nerves. Brooke had picked her up cheap from a local trainer and promptly turned her out for six months to mature and settle. Realising she needed more distraction from Lachlan than Robert and Sod provided, Brooke had decided to bring Elly into work.

With the horse saddled, bridled and booted, Brooke led her toward the ménage, mind drifting to Lachlan, her skin prickling with heat as she recalled how close she'd come to exposing herself. The moment when she'd almost kissed him.

One more breath and she would have reached up on tiptoe, slid her arms around his neck, pressed her body against his and tilted her mouth for a kiss like a drunk, desperate spinster. What a fine reward that would have been for him after all he'd done. Lachlan had shown her nothing but kindness, and all she seemed capable of was embarrassing him and humiliating herself.

Except . . .

Brooke halted and touched her lips, remembering the way he'd cupped her face and run his thumbs gently under her eyes, across her mouth. The swirls of green-gold in his beautiful hazel eyes as they'd gazed at her. For a heartbeat she thought . . .

She dropped her hand. Lachlan had made himself clear from the start. His tenure at Kingston Downs might be temporary, but he needed this job and wasn't about to do anything to jeopardise it. Brooke remaining here placed him in an awkward position. Of course he would help her as best he could. It was only politic. Besides, Angus had asked him to.

And he'd knocked back Chloe, a woman no man ever said no to, and which could only mean one of two things. Either he genuinely didn't like Chloe that way, or his heart lay elsewhere. Perhaps with a friend called Tamsyn.

Confused by the sudden halt, Elly nudged Brooke and blinked her lovely eyes, the skin above them furrowing in a way that reminded Brooke of Oddy. Surprised, Brooke kissed the filly smack on her soft muzzle. This was the first time the memory of Oddy brought feelings of love instead of slicing pain. She was getting better.

And though her head said it was thanks to the panacea of time, her heart relayed a different message. Her recovery—if she could call it that—was all thanks to Lachlan.

No wonder she was in love. That man could do anything.

———

Workout complete, Brooke steered Elly from the ménage, rubbing her mane while praising her for her good behaviour. Though they'd done little more than walk, interspersed with an occasional trot or canter to stave off boredom, the eager-to-please filly had performed impeccably, concentrating hard on Brooke's aids. She deserved a relaxed hack around Kingston Downs.

They ambled down the lane towards the lucerne stands, reeled like hooked fish. The deep chug of the tractor, which had filled the air for the last hour, was gone, replaced with the quiet sounds of the countryside. As she neared the river and the last lane paddock, Brooke spied Lachlan crouched in the dirt, checking the newly planted seedbed. Her heart gave a little hiccup, her skin buzzing with excitement.

Billy greeted her at the gate with a sharp yap that sent Electra skittering and earned him a sharp rebuke from Lachlan, who stood and dusted his hands before walking towards Brooke. For a big man he moved with an athletic grace Brooke found mesmerising, covering the gap with an easy stride that made the distance appear shorter than it was.

'Sorry,' he said, letting Electra sniff his fingers before stroking her nose. 'Billy forgets his manners sometimes.'

'That's okay. She'll have to learn to put up with worse at shows. Half the battle is trying to keep them calm when there's so much going on.' Patting Elly's neck, Brooke pulled her feet from the stirrups and slid off, looping her arm through the reins and moving to lean against the top fence rail. 'No problems?'

'None. Seed depth is good. Just need to get the roller onto it.' He joined her at the fence, surveying the finely tilled seedbed. Thanks to months of dedicated preparation, the rich soil extended weed-free, crumbly and moist. Soil testing had shown the earth to be at the optimum pH, with high nutrient levels, and Brooke had made sure that the seeds had been lime-coated, treated with fungicide and insecticide, and inoculated with rhizobia—a special strain of soil bacteria that would form nodes on the plant's roots and fix vital nitrogen from the air. The constant cutting and removal of plant material during haymaking extracted a lot of nitrogen from the property.

'I'm looking forward to seeing how this variety performs,' she said, referring to the new-release SARDI-bred strain she'd selected for the paddock. If production reached the level she anticipated, she'd replace the larger, aging Aurora stand with it in a year's time. 'It's done well in trials.'

'I know a contract seed grower who grew it last year. He seemed pretty impressed.' He presented Brooke with one of his heart-skippy smiles. 'Can't fault the preparation, that's for sure. You did a great job.'

'Thanks. Pop always said that if you get the prep right then the rest will follow, and he was right. What varieties do you grow at Delamere?'

The heart-skippy smile collapsed. 'Old ones.'

'Like Aurora, you mean?'

'No. Like Siriver and Hunterfield.'

Brooke stared at him. Siriver and Hunterfield weren't simply old; in plant-breeding terms they were ancient. The modern, proprietary varieties produced higher yields with better leaf-to-stem ratios and increased disease resistance, and they persisted longer, spreading the cost of stand establishment over a greater period, reducing overall inputs and increasing profit. The seed was more expensive due to its Plant Breeder's Rights protection—a form of plant copyright—but in most cases the enhanced performance easily outweighed the cost.

'Yeah,' he said, reading her disbelief. 'I know. And it's not as if Dad's even growing them for seed. At least there'd be a bit of money in that.'

'Doesn't he know about the new varieties?'

'He knows,' Lachlan replied grimly. 'He just chooses to ignore their existence.'

'But why?'

'I wish I knew.' He squinted back towards the paddock. 'I used to ask him when I was a kid. All he'd say was that if they were good enough for his old man, they were good enough for him. But sometimes I think he's just too afraid to change because it would mean he'd have to ask for help.' He looked down and picked at a splinter of timber. 'He's barely literate, Brooke.'

'I'm sorry.'

'Don't be. It's his own fault. He could learn if he wanted to but he won't. If it weren't for Mum and Nick and me . . .' He shook his head. 'The farm's stuck in a time warp. Sometimes I hate him for it. Other times I just pity him.'

Brooke rested her hand on his back, wishing she could do more to comfort him.

He looked at her, mouth quirked. 'I don't know why I told you that. Must be feeling sorry for myself.'

'Hey,' she said, nudging him. 'None of that. Feeling sorry for yourself is my exclusive turf.'

His laugh sent her heart tripping.

'Which reminds me.' He reached into his shirt pocket. 'I meant to give you this earlier.' He handed her a neatly folded piece of paper and waited until Brooke had unfolded it before going on. 'She's a Newcastle-based psychologist who specialises in anxiety and stress disorders. According to her website she does a lot of work with road accident victims. I thought maybe she could help. Only problem is that she's booked up until mid-October.'

Brooke traced the name with her finger. Dr Elizabeth Dalgleish. The name sounded safe, yet it made her feel hot, scared. Wary. 'I don't know . . .'

'Call her.' He caught her eye and smiled. 'How are you going to get rid of me if you don't get better?'

That was the problem. Brooke didn't want to see Lachlan go. Yet if life was ever to return to how she wanted it, that's exactly what had to happen.

She bit her lip, panicked by the thought of him leaving. Tempted, so tempted, to rip Dr Dalgleish's name and number to shreds and cast it like confetti to the wind.

Uncertainty at her reaction tugged Lachlan's smile into a frown.

'It's what you want, isn't it?'

'Yes. No. I mean—' She closed her eyes, shaking her head, trying think clearly, but he stood so close she could smell him—that evocative citrus fragrance that came from his clothes or deodorant or something and seeped into her brain, fuddling it. 'I want to get better, I *have* to get better, but I know how important being here is for you.'

How important it had become for her.

'Don't worry about me. I'll be fine. I've lost jobs before. There are others around.' He smiled and leaned in close. 'The most important thing is you.'

She stared at him. He wore that expression again, the one that made her wonder, made her heart do that excited dance and set her tongue sticking in her mouth. For a few seconds he held her stare before breaking away to shove his hands in his pockets and look back at the paddock, leaving Brooke overwhelmed and electrified by that intangible *something* she thought had passed between them.

'Well, I suppose . . .'

'Yeah . . .'

But neither moved, the awkward, hungry memory of their almost-kiss two days ago rippling between them. Instead, they focused on Billy, back at his master's feet after inspecting a mouse hole. He flopped on his haunches and regarded them with one ear cocked, panting as he glanced from Brooke to Lachlan and back again. Seeking attention, Elly hung her head over Brooke's shoulder and blew warm breath on her face, but neither Brooke nor Lachlan seemed capable of movement. Bored, Billy gave up his contemplation and sank to his belly, chin resting on his paws, eyes closing.

Finally, Lachlan slapped the rail, shaking them from their daze. 'Right. I'd better get rolling.' He indicated Elly. 'Can I give you a leg up?'

'Thanks.' She slipped the piece of paper into the zippered pocket of her jodhpurs. Pulling the reins back over Elly's head, she positioned herself by the saddle, hands on the pommel and one leg cocked.

'Ready?'

She nodded and after a bounce let Lachlan raise her into the saddle. Carefully, he guided her foot into the stirrup then stood back, the sun catching highlights in his hair, handsome in his dark-blue twill work clothes and leather boots. Tall and strong against the backdrop of rich dark soil and verdant green, the Hunter River in the distance chugging its inexorable way to the sea, he caused Brooke's heart to race once more with the idea that this was where he truly belonged. Not at Delamere, but here, on Kingston Downs, with her.

As she rode away, the piece of paper, the first step to reclaiming her life, burned in her pocket.

———

Later that afternoon, as the day turned shivery with the lowering sun, Brooke stood in Venus and Poddy's paddock peering into her beloved horse's nostrils. A thin stream of watery mucus leaked from Poddy's nose. She stroked his cheek in sympathy then placed her hand under his rug to check for sweat. His coat felt slightly damp, but she'd have a better idea how severe his temperature was once she had him back in the barn.

'Come on, my poor baby,' she said, clipping the lead to his halter. 'Let's get you somewhere nice and warm.'

She led him up the lane, trying to keep her worry at bay, Venus following like a scruffy puppy. When Brooke had walked Poddy out that morning she'd thought he wasn't as happy as usual, but horses have moods like people and he'd shown no symptoms of illness, so she hadn't given it much thought. But the last nine hours had given the infection enough time to take hold and manifest itself in a runny nose and an elevated temperature.

The most important task was to quarantine him. Though she suspected a cold, it could be something worse, and she couldn't afford to expose the other horses. Venus, as Poddy's constant companion, would also require isolation, something that wouldn't impress a pony enamoured with a life of all-day grazing.

At the barn she placed them in a stable each, before setting to check Poddy over properly. She held up his tail and inserted a thermometer into his rectum, apologising for the indignity as she waited for a reading. Poddy took it with his usual stoicism. She patted his rump as she extracted the thermometer and inspected it. A shade over thirty-nine degrees. Definitely a mild temperature.

'Poor baby,' she murmured, stroking his warm neck and kissing his cheek. 'I know exactly how you feel, and it's not much fun at all.'

After washing her hands and disinfecting the thermometer, she checked Venus's temperature as well, but the pony remained as robust as ever. Satisfied, Brooke returned to Poddy's stable to fuss over him, replacing his canvas rug with a thick doona-style one, damping down his evening feed to help prevent cough, hovering as he ate, watching every mouthful to ensure his appetite was still strong. Telling herself over and over that a vet was unnecessary. Poddy had a cold. That's all. He'd be fine with warmth, rest and a bit of molly-coddling.

Unable to put off bringing in the other horses, she reluctantly scrubbed her hands again before heading back out into the chill of the falling evening. As she walked down the lane, the sky a magnificent swathe of peach and indigo, Lachlan appeared, striding back from the river, Billy bouncing alongside with a stick longer than his wriggly body clamped between his jaws.

'Need a hand?' he called as he neared.

'Thanks.' She passed him a lead rope. 'If you could take care of Sod, that'd be great. Poddy has a cold and I needed to sort him out, so I'm running a bit late with them.'

'Is he all right?'

'I think so, but I'll need to keep a close eye. I'd love it if you could keep a lookout too. If you see any of the other horses with runny noses or looking a bit off, let me know. They've all been vaccinated against equine influenza but—' She shrugged, not wanting to think about the danger.

'It's hard not to feel nervous.'

'Yes. I know it's just a cold—they happen, especially this time of year—but I worry about him.' She looked at her feet as guilt gripped her. 'I don't want him to ever be hurt again. He's suffered enough.'

Lachlan draped an arm around her shoulders and squeezed her to him. 'I'm sure he'll be fine.' His arm dropped as Sod let out a welcoming whicker and trotted towards the gate.

'He must really like you,' said Brooke. 'He's never once done that with me.'

Ducking through the gate, Lachlan scrubbed the big dark horse's face and affectionately tugged his ears. 'I don't know about liking me. I think he just wants more carrots.'

But Brooke knew better. From day one, Sod and Lachlan had formed a bond of trust and respect, the strength of which was proven when Sod allowed Lachlan to lead him into the float. Any other person and she might have experienced a stab of jealousy, but like everything with Lachlan, it only intensified her attraction.

'So what will you do with Poddy?' he asked as they walked Electra, Robert and Sod to the yards.

'I'll monitor both him and Venus overnight. Then, assuming there's no increase in his temperature and he stays eating and looks happy, it's just a matter of keeping him in for four or five days and making sure he stays warm.'

'I'll make up your bed in the cottage so you don't have to trudge back and forth from the dairy.'

'Thanks, but there's no need. I'll sleep in the barn.'

He eyeballed her with a mixture of worry and irritation. 'Brooke, in case you haven't noticed, it's freezing at night. You only had the flu a couple of weeks ago. You'll make yourself sick again. I can keep check on Poddy.'

'No. Poddy's my responsibility.'

Catching her tone, he stared ahead, jaw tight, mouth grim, but he didn't argue any further. Just as well. No matter how Brooke felt about Lachlan, when it came to caring for Poddy, nothing would break her resolve.

With the horses in their yards and settled for the night, Brooke ducked to the dairy to make a sandwich, grab some magazines and a warm coat before returning to the stable. She rechecked both horses' temperatures, relieved to find no change, and nestled into the corner of Poddy's stable with a wool rug over her legs to eat her dinner and watch over him.

At ten, Lachlan arrived with a thermos filled with milky tea and a plastic container of Nancy's jam drops, which Brooke accepted with gratitude. She expected him to leave. Instead, he settled beside her, back resting against the stable wall, legs drawn up and his hands dangling over his knees.

'All okay?'

She nodded and took a sip of tea. 'No change, which is good.'

'Are you warm enough?'

She indicated the horse rug over her legs. 'Snug as a bug in a rug, if a bit smelly.' She took another sip of tea and nibbled on a biscuit, grateful for the sugar hit. Poddy stood opposite, one hind leg cocked and rested on his toe, eyes dozy. The air smelled of wood shavings, horse and Lachlan. All the good things.

'I ran into Chloe when I ducked into town earlier.'

'Oh, yes?' As she normally did on a Thursday, Brooke had met with Chloe and Andrew last night in the pub but Chloe's mood was subdued, a state Brooke and Andrew put down to the imminent loss of her crowning glory.

'I asked her when shearing day was and she told me that she's not going through with the bet.'

Brooke frowned. Chloe? Renege on a bet? That'd be a first. 'Why not?'

'No idea. Not good for business, maybe.'

'This is Pitcorthie. No one would care. She'd probably get more people coming in just to look at her bald head.' Brooke made a face, thinking on Chloe's uncharacteristic behaviour. 'Andrew will have something to say about that.'

Lachlan shrugged. 'Maybe that's the point.'

She glanced at him quizzically. Yes. Maybe that *was* the point. But why? She chewed on that for a moment. Perhaps they'd had an argument, which would explain Chloe's quiet mood at the pub. But neither Chloe nor Andrew had mentioned one, and in the past, when any one of them had had an issue with the other, they'd always taken care to sort it out before it festered. Then again, maybe they hadn't wanted to bother her with their problems. It wouldn't be unlike them to be protective, especially after all that had happened.

Brooke returned her attention to Poddy. At least he was easy to understand. Unlike her friends.

'You love him, don't you?' Lachlan asked.

'More than anything.' She took a sip of tea and leaned back, gazing at her darling horse. Poddy's ears twitched as though he knew they were talking about him. 'Dad gave him to me for my eighteenth birthday. I couldn't believe my luck. For a green horse Poddy showed incredible talent. The first time I put him at a jump, his head and ears shot up like a periscope.' She smiled at the memory. 'Next thing I know he's coiled like a giant spring and tugging on the reins and I hadn't done a thing. It was a tiny cavaletti, barely half a metre high, but he couldn't wait to get at it. Like Robert, but even bolder. I couldn't believe it. It was if I'd been handed the keys to a supercar. I was thrilled and excited and scared all at the same time.'

He tilted his head with interest. 'Why scared?'

'I was afraid I'd ruin this perfect animal.' She dropped her head and stared at her milky tea. 'But I didn't. Not until the accident, anyway.'

'You have to stop blaming yourself,' he said gently.

'I know. It's hard, though. I love him so much. Too much, probably.'

Lachlan let some shavings run through his fingers. 'Do you think there's such a thing as loving too much?'

'I don't know. Maybe. With animals.'

'But not with humans?'

She frowned at him over her mug. 'Why?'

He shook his head. 'Doesn't matter.'

'Are you having one of your profound moments?'

He laughed, a lovely deep sound she couldn't get enough of. 'Must be.'

They lapsed into quiet. Brooke sipped her tea and finished her biscuit, watching Poddy but aware of Lachlan's presence, wishing he were closer. Wishing she could tangle her fingers in his and rest her head against his chest and listen to his heart beat.

There was so much about him she wanted to know. From his boyhood dreams, to his favourite colour, to whether he liked hot curries. But most of all, she wanted to nurture her fantasy that he was destined to stay at Kingston Downs. That Delamere and his other life didn't exist. Because one day, when he was gone, that would be all she had left. Dreams, fantasies and heartache.

She took another sip of tea, wondering where to start, wary he'd fob her off if she probed a sore spot. But it was his sore spots that mattered; those were what she wanted to understand.

'Why did you leave Delamere?'

'The first or the second time?'

'First, I guess.'

He paused and she could sense him gathering himself. 'Dad and I used to fight all the time. Every day I'd look around me and see all these thriving properties. And then I'd look at ours and wonder why it couldn't be like all the others, why Dad couldn't see what I could. I'd point out articles in *The Land* and the local paper about new innovations, or the top sale prices others were getting, and Dad would just ignore me. I'd visit my mates on their farms, spend the whole time feeling jealous, then come home and take it out on Dad.

'As I got older the fights grew worse. Then one day Dad did his nut and accused me of being ashamed of him.' He looked at his hands, remorse tugging at his mouth. 'I told him I was. I didn't mean it, I was just frustrated.' He looked at her. 'I still regret that moment.'

'You were young,' said Brooke, feeling for him.

'That's no excuse.' He breathed in deeply. 'I left after that. Moved in with my gran. Quit school, took any job I could find. Spent the next four years working my arse off and getting nowhere, moaning how different things would be if I had the run of Delamere.'

'So how did you end up at uni?'

'That was Gran's doing. She pointed out that for a person who spent so much time bitching about their uneducated father, I was doing a damn fine job of turning myself into him. Made me sit up and think. So I enrolled in TAFE, finished my HSC and applied for uni.'

'What did your dad think?'

'No idea. Dad and I weren't on speaking terms. Mum was proud, though.'

Brooke ran her finger around the edge of her mug. 'I can't imagine you arguing with anyone. You're always so careful about what you say.'

'Not when I was younger, I wasn't.'

'So what changed you?'

'Life.' He paused. 'People.'

Brooke flicked him a look, her attention caught by the way he'd spoken, as if he didn't mean *people*, but one person in particular.

'Life teaches you things.' He shrugged and smiled wryly. 'I just wish I'd learned faster. Then I wouldn't have made so many mistakes.'

'Ahh, but making mistakes is what makes us better people.'

'Now who's being profound?'

She smiled at him, thrilled with the small confidences he'd shared.

'Are you going to Sydney tomorrow?' he asked.

'No way. Not with Poddy sick. What about you? Are you playing rugby?'

'Yeah. We're playing at Cassilis. Speaking of which, I should get some sleep.' He rose, scraping shavings off his legs. 'Will you be all right?'

'I'll be fine. I have Poddy to keep me company.'

He glanced at the horse. 'Not much of a conversationalist.'

'He is. You just don't speak horse.'

'Maybe I should learn. Anyway, if you need anything, just bang on the cottage door.'

He gave Poddy a quick rub before sliding the stable door open and stepping through. Halfway through closing it, she called his name. He halted, head cocked.

She fiddled with a strap on the wool rug. 'Do you like it here? The Valley, I mean.'

'Yeah. I do. A lot. Sometimes . . .' He shook his head. 'It doesn't matter.'

'What? Tell me. Please.'

He caught her gaze and held it. 'It's stupid, I know, but sometimes I wish I could stay.'

FIFTEEN

LACHIE CLOSED the gate to the new lucerne stand and leaned his arms on it, smiling with contentment. He couldn't have timed it better. Light rain had fallen two days after sowing, followed by days mild enough to keep the soil temperature warm, but not hot enough to dry the seedbed. He rubbed his fingers together, dirty from when he'd dug them into the earth to check germination. Any day now the dark soil would develop a green tinge, as the seedlings poked their tiny first leaves above ground. Then the race would be on to beat the myriad insects hungry to feed on the juicy sweet plants, to keep the water up, and manage this and the other stands in the face of what looked to be a hectic haymaking season.

Hard work. Progress. Fatigue. Satisfaction. He couldn't wait.

He glanced at his watch, glad to see he still had an hour before he had to leave for rugby. The sun on his back was too pleasant to relinquish just yet and he wanted to think. Although that's all he'd been doing for the past week. Working and thinking and going crazy.

All because of a girl he'd once labelled a spoilt, stuck-up brat.

Not once had Lachie ever considered making a life anywhere other than Delamere. From the moment he'd skidded his old ute down the drive at age eighteen, he swore he'd be back. He'd made the same promise the second time, when the shock of Tamsyn's departure, flamed by his father's comments, had erupted into fury and carried him away once again. But he hadn't counted on Kingston Downs and Pitcorthie. And he hadn't imagined anyone like Brooke.

A week had passed since the night in the stable. A week of him thinking about what he'd admitted. A week of dreams choked with the raw yearning that had broken over Brooke's face when he'd revealed his secret wish to stay. A wish that grew stronger with each passing day.

Probably just as well they'd both been busy—Brooke tending Poddy and working her horses, him with the farm and a trip to Randwick to deliver Pompey Girl for Angus. Though he could have gone down and back in a day, Lachie had stayed overnight in Sydney, catching up with mates, hoping a bit of time away from Kingston Downs would give him perspective. But every moment away only reinforced his feelings, how much he missed the Valley. How desperately he missed Brooke.

'What do you reckon, Billyboy?' he said, crouching down to scratch the terrier's ears. 'Should we stick around?' Billy tilted his head back and forth, as though considering the idea, before releasing a sharp yap. 'Yeah, you'd love to stay, wouldn't you? You love your hoof bits and mice and all that nice shit to roll in. Good life for dogs at Kingston Downs.'

Easy. Except yesterday Brooke had bounced up to him, cheeks flushed, clear brown eyes wide, to announce she'd booked an appointment with the counsellor. The news made him proud and sad at the same time. She'd taken the first step to recovery, and with it, set the clock on his tenure ticking.

'Always other jobs,' he said to Billy, chucking him under the chin and rising. He'd put feelers out locally, see if anyone had anything coming up. Perhaps one of the studs might be interested. There'd be something.

Anyway, it was about time he faced the fact that the old man was never going to change. They'd never be able to work together. Except for that one ill-fated attempt after uni, Lachie had lived without Delamere for ten years. In that time he'd matured, learned and educated himself, all in preparation for his return home, and what had happened? The bleak recognition that in ten years nothing had altered. And never would.

The Valley gave him contentment. He could stay, and if his instincts were right and she felt the same about him as he felt about her, he could build a life with Brooke.

He grinned at his dog. 'Better kiss her first, though, hey, Billyboy.'

Tonight. When she arrived back from Sydney and stopped at the yards to check the horses. In the moonlight. Perfect.

And this time, there'd be no stepping away.

Still grinning, he strode back up the lane. A quick check on Poddy and he'd be off. The horse was over his cold but Brooke insisted he be monitored, and when Brooke insisted, Lachie couldn't say no.

Thirty metres from the paddock his pace faltered. Poddy stood by the gate with his head lowered, Venus close by, nudging his shoulder. Typically, the horses only moved to the gate when they had visitors, or something caught their attention, or it was time to come in. When Lachie passed earlier Poddy and Venus were in the centre of the paddock, happily grazing, where they should have been. Now they were both by the gate, as though waiting for him. And there was something weird about the way Poddy held his head, as if it had become too heavy for his body.

Something was wrong. Very wrong.

Stomach churning, Lachie broke into a jog.

'Hey, Poddy, what's the matter?' He unhooked the gate, frowning as he tried to fathom the sight confronting him. 'Oh, fuck!'

From the tip of his nose to his ears, Poddy's face had swollen to grotesque proportions. His good eye was a bare slit and his breath whistled as he tried to suck air through the bloated passages that were his nostrils. His normally glossy bay coat was black with sweat, and from the rise of the horse's rug Lachie could see the pained heave of his chest and the effort it took to draw air into his lungs.

He stared at Poddy, unsure of what to do. Then an avalanche of horror washed over him as the horse swayed and crumpled, groaning as his pain-racked body collapsed. The sound of this agony kicked Lachie into action. Mind racing, he crouched at Poddy's nose and stuck his fingers inside. Swollen flesh closed around them. He felt breath but it was faint. Nothing else mattered. He had to keep those passages open. He had to keep Poddy breathing.

Leaving the gate ajar, Lachie sprinted for the shed.

'Fuck, fuck, *fuck!*' he yelled, tipping over another box of junk when it failed to yield what he needed.

He stood and closed his eyes, trying to calm his panic and think. There had to be something he could shove up Poddy's nostrils to hold his airways open. Washing machine hose? Too big. Garden hose? Yes. Unstrapping his pocketknife from his belt holster, he sprinted for the cottage's yard, skidding to a halt in the orchard when he spied a length of black polypipe dripper line. Flexible garden hose would be better but this was closer, and every second counted.

'Hang in there, Pod,' Lachie whispered as he ran back to the paddock and knelt by the horse's head, cutting the length of polypipe in half. Heart hammering, he inserted one piece of pipe and then the other into Poddy's nostrils, wincing and apologising as he forced it past the swelling. A dribble of blood leaked from one nostril, cut by the hard, jagged plastic edges.

Once the tubes were in place, he leant his cheek in front of Poddy's nose, feeling for air. Poddy's whistling breath felt faint but it existed. Using one hand to drag his phone from his shirt pocket, he felt around Poddy's throat with the other. The horse's pulse flickered, rapid and uneven.

Fingers clumsy with fear, Lachie found the vet's mobile number.

'Tony? It's Lachie Cambridge at Kingston Downs. Look, I've got an emergency. Brooke's horse Poddy has gone down. His face is swollen and his nostrils are closing. Pulse fast. Looks like some sort of allergic reaction. I shoved polypipe up his nostrils to keep the airways open and it's working so far, but his breathing's still shallow.'

The vet fired back a series of questions, which Lachie answered as best he could.

'Could be snake bite,' said Tony. 'I'll be there in ten.'

'Follow the lane. You'll see me.'

He hung up and sat back on his haunches, overwhelmed with helplessness and fear. Venus nudged his shoulder and he stroked the pony for comfort. He needed to call Brooke, but without a diagnosis he didn't know what to say. And if Poddy was dying, or needed to be put down, better to not let her know he had suffered. Let her think it was quick. Save her anguish. She'd had enough to last a lifetime.

Ten minutes passed like an hour. An hour in which Lachie barely breathed for fear Poddy would die. He phoned the pub to advise Nate he'd miss rugby, asking him to keep the news about Poddy to himself in case word filtered back to Brooke. The remaining minutes Lachie filled comforting Poddy. He kept stroking the horse's cheek and talking to him, alarmed at the heat radiating from Poddy's skin but striving to keep his voice calm, even and soothing, wishing he could do something to assuage the horse's distress. Every breath tore, the shallow rhythm broken by an occasional agonised groan. Poddy's good eye remained half-closed, the skin around it crinkled with pain.

Tony Hall emerged from his specially modified ute in that unhurried urgent way that only vets and doctors possessed. Though much shorter and balder than Nate, Tony shared the publican's barrel-chested, thick-armed build, an asset when it came to treating large, often difficult animals. Lachie had introduced himself during his first week at Kingston Downs, and hadn't known what to make of the brusque vet. Sam and others, though, were adamant in their assessment—Tony was one of the best vets in the district, respected for his efficiency and no-nonsense attitude. What he lacked in bedside manner, he made up for in skill, and in a world of million-dollar livestock, that was all that mattered. If Poddy could be saved, Tony was the man.

In seconds, the vet was by the horse, checking his pulse and breathing, peering closely at the rampant swelling of Poddy's nose. With pursed lips and narrowed eyes he flicked through the tight hair of Poddy's face and nodded to himself before heading to the ute and rummaging in the back. Wary of breaking Tony's concentration, Lachie stayed by Venus, saying nothing, taking comfort from the pony's sturdy body.

'Snake bite,' Tony announced as he returned with a series of needles and drugs. 'Don't suppose you saw the culprit?'

'No.'

'I'll administer a polyvalent antivenene along with some painkillers and an anti-inflammatory. That'll get him out of pain and back on his feet at least. You did the right thing with the pipe. He probably would have died otherwise.'

'He'll be all right, then?'

Tony's focus remained on measuring out drugs but his expression was grim. 'Maybe.'

'What do you mean, maybe? Surely the antivenene will sort it all out?'

'Not necessarily,' replied Tony as he inserted a needle into Poddy's neck. 'If the animal survives the initial bite there's some hope, but snake venom is often contaminated with clostridium and salmonella. The risk of infection is high.'

'Okay,' said Lachie, trying to keep calm. 'They're serious bacteria, but with antibiotics he'll be all right.' He snatched at Tony's arm. 'Won't he?'

Tony released a noncommittal grunt. Leaving Lachie staring at Poddy, he collected his syringes and bottles and took them to the car.

Lachie's chest felt too small for the fear it contained. Poddy couldn't die. Not now, just as Brooke was coming to terms with the accident, when the future at last seemed bright. Tony had to be covering his arse. Bacteria wouldn't stand a chance against a horse as healthy and cosseted as Poddy.

Tony returned to the paddock. 'Let's try to get him up.'

It took the two of them a solid five minutes of pushing and coercion to bring Poddy to his shaky legs. Despite the drugs, the horse swayed and groaned. Tremors ran down his neck and through his body, his rug rising and falling with each heave of his big chest. Upright, his swollen and bloody nose appeared even more grotesque, and Lachie ached for the sweaty and pain-washed animal.

'I'll stay with him while you get the float,' said Tony. 'We need to get him to a stable.' He frowned and cast around. 'Where is Brooke, anyway?'

'Warwick Farm.'

'You better call her. She needs to be here.'

Lachie didn't want to think about Tony's tone as he jogged for his ute, but he couldn't shake the fatalistic note in the vet's voice. He reversed up to the main door of the barn and stepped out to slide the doors open, mind working overtime on how to break the news to Brooke. By the time he'd hitched the float and sat back in the car he knew he couldn't put it off any longer. Sucking in a breath he called her number.

'Brooke, it's Lachie.'

He tried to sound calm and normal but perhaps, as with Tony, it was his tone that had her immediately alert. Her voice came back, tremulous.

'What is it? What's happened?'

'It's Poddy. He's . . .' He drew in another long breath. 'It looks like a snake bit him. Tony's here now. He's treated him with antivenene and painkillers and we've managed to get him back on his feet.' He hesitated before ploughing on. 'I'm sorry, but he's in a bad way. You need to come.'

'Oh, God.' Her breath came fast and shuddery, then it disappeared, replaced with the sound of buffeting cloth and muffled voices. The noise faded and Brooke came back on the line. 'I'm heading to the car now. I'll be there as soon as I can.' She paused and he caught the sharp clip of shoes on concrete, moving at pace. When she came back her voice was charged with panic and effort. 'What sort of snake?'

'I don't know. Whatever it was had gone by the time I found him.'

'What's Tony's prognosis?'

'He's not saying.' He chose his next words carefully. She had a long drive ahead. The last thing he wanted was for her to panic. 'He's doing all he can but Poddy will be calmer with you here.'

'I'll be there as fast as I can.'

'I know you're worried, but don't rush. You need to get here safely.' He listened to her for a few seconds, to the shuddery exhalations and choked-down fear. 'Poddy's in good hands, Brooke. He's not going anywhere. He'll still be here whether you arrive in four hours or two.'

For the first time a bit of steel entered her voice. 'You make sure of it, Lachlan.'

SIXTEEN

BROOKE ARRIVED mid-afternoon in a hail of scattered gravel and panicky fumbles for the door latch. She scrambled out of the Land-Cruiser, hitched up her pencil skirt and sprinted for the barn's side entrance, stumbling as her high heel caught on the edge of its concrete slab. She grabbed the jamb for balance, eyes adjusting to the dull and dusty light within. The stable door stood open, Lachlan inside, his bulk shielding her beloved Poddy's face.

Lachlan turned and walked towards her, keeping Poddy from view. His face said more than words ever could. She closed her eyes for a second, fortifying herself, and before he could stop her, darted towards Poddy.

Her world lurched. She reached out for something to hold.

Lachlan grabbed her arm. 'It's okay, Brooke. I'm here.'

But Brooke knew nothing would ever be okay. Not for Poddy. Not for her.

She leaned against Lachlan for a moment, taking comfort from his strong embrace, telling herself she had to hold it together for Poddy's sake. She pulled away from him and straightened her shoulders, and with a sniff and a brush at her eyes, moved slowly towards the stable.

'Hey, Poddy-baby. It's me.'

On hearing her voice Poddy raised his miserable head and let out a pain-cut whicker. His head dropped again, nose almost into the wood shavings. She knelt by his head, talking quietly, lightly touching his cheek, the tip of his sagging ear, so afraid of the horror before her.

'Hang in there, my big brave champion.' Tears fell unchecked. Her throat ached with fear and grief. All the way home she'd prayed it wasn't this bad, but one look at the swelling and she knew Poddy would need a miracle to survive. Still, he had survived the accident, and Brooke would do her damnedest to help him survive this. 'You can beat this. You can beat anything. You're my darling champion with the biggest bravest heart there is.' She clutched his leg and leaned her head against his knee, sobbing. 'You can't die. You can't.'

She swallowed down her grief but it was too huge to contain. Tears leaked out, flooding her cheeks, dripping from her chin. She clamped her jaw, breathing hard through her nose, forcing herself to stop. This wasn't helping Poddy. She had to stop thinking of herself and concentrate on her darling.

Releasing Poddy's leg, she mopped her face on her cream silk blend top. Makeup and mascara smeared the sleeve but she didn't care. She hated it anyway. Like she hated her stupid cream and brown high heels and the fashionably high-waisted brown pencil skirt foisted on her by Ariel.

Ariel. If it weren't for her mother, Brooke would have been home, Poddy might not have been bitten and this nightmare wouldn't be happening.

'Where's Tony?' she asked, rising to face Lachlan.

'He had to go to another emergency but he'll be back.'

'What are his instructions?'

'Keep checking his temperature and monitor closely for any change in his demeanour. The painkillers should ease the worst of it and the anti-inflammatories are slowly bringing the swelling down.

Tony gave him a tetanus booster but there's still a chance of infection. He thinks he might have been treated early enough to prevent kidney damage, but we won't know for a while.'

Heart thumping, she glanced at Poddy's deformed face. The swelling had forced the skin covering his blind eye outward, like a giant, unlanced boil. His ears hung limp. The skin of his long nose stretched tightly over the inflammation. And in the lower centre, a lump rose, huge, painful and horrifying.

Anguish sent her hand to her mouth. The potential loss of Kingston Downs might terrify her, but it meant nothing in the face of Poddy's death. The farm was just dirt. They could always buy another. Poddy was a living, breathing, loving creature. An irreplaceable one of a kind.

'He's going to die, isn't he?'

Strong arms wrapped around her. 'Shh. Don't think like that. Poddy's a survivor, he's proved that once before.'

'I can't lose him, Lachie.'

His hold tightened, his mouth pressed into her hair. 'I know.' After a while he eased away, raising his hand to stroke her cheek with the back of his knuckles. 'I know you won't leave him, so I'm going to organise some things for you, okay?'

She nodded, grateful he understood.

'It might take a while but I'll have my mobile, so call if you want me.'

'Okay.' She held his gaze. 'And thank you.'

His expression softened and he smiled a fraction. Then he placed his lips to her forehead and held them there in a move so tender tears threatened again. 'Hang in there. Poddy needs you. I'll be back as soon as I can.'

When Lachie had gone, she returned her attention to Poddy and set about making herself useful. After taking his temperature she grabbed a bucket and a sponge and attacked his sweaty coat, talking to him all the time, reassuring him he'd be fine although the iceberg in her stomach said otherwise. She scraped the excess water away and, using towels, rubbed his coat dry then brushed it straight, wishing Tony would hurry up and return so she could talk to him.

Horses were as susceptible to snake bite as humans, and like humans, survival depended on the species of snake and the rapidity of treatment. Thanks to Lachie, Poddy had received swift attention, but if the bite was from an eastern brown snake he had little chance. With a red-bellied black she had hope, but even then the risk of secondary infection remained high. She pressed her face into Poddy's neck and closed her eyes as fear curdled her insides and the drying sweat under her thin clothes turned her skin to ice.

Footsteps sounded on the concrete. She recognised Lachie's heavy, straight tread. Stroking Poddy's neck, she blinked, wondering when she'd begun to think of him as Lachie instead of Lachlan.

'I brought you some clothes,' he said. 'I'll leave them on the lid of the feed bin. There's a bottle of water and a thermos of tea for you as well. I'll bring sandwiches when I come back. Is there anything else you need?'

'A miracle would be handy.' She smiled wanly. 'Sorry. You're being wonderful as usual, and I'm being an ungrateful cow again.'

'No, you're not, and even if you were, it wouldn't matter. You've more important things to worry about than me.' He glanced at his watch. 'I need to bring the other horses in and check on the farm, and you need to get into some warm clothes. I'll be back as soon as I can.'

As soon as he'd gone she stripped down and hurried into the clothes he'd brought, pulling on her boots as Tony arrived.

'Well?' she asked, after the vet had finished his inspection and taken blood samples.

'At this point, all we can do is monitor him.' He fixed Brooke with a steady blue gaze. 'But you must understand that his chances are slim. *Very* slim.'

'But they exist.'

'Yes.'

'Then save him. Like you did before.'

Tony sighed and patted Poddy's rump. 'I'll do what I can.' But his tone told her he thought Poddy had no hope. He laid a hand on her shoulder and squeezed. 'In the meantime, keep him warm and settled. And watch that temperature.' He crossed paths with Lachie on the way out, and jerked his head towards Brooke. 'And you watch her.'

Lachie joined her leaning against the stable wall, a plastic lunch box in his hands. 'I brought some sandwiches.'

'Thanks, but I'm not hungry.'

'Have you had any of the tea?'

She shook her head, unable to take her eyes off Poddy. Tony had administered more painkillers but Poddy's head remained lowered, his body language forlorn. The sight filled her with pity and anguish. She couldn't bear to think of him suffering. Not again.

Lachie took her hand, his skin rough but warm, and squeezed. 'I'll pour you a cuppa. It'll make you feel a bit better.'

Nothing would make her feel better. Not while Poddy was in danger. She slid down the wall and hugged her knees to her chest. How could this be happening to him? He was a sweet, innocent horse who deserved to live out his days happily grazing with his friend Venus. Not trembling in a drab stable, ravaged by poison.

She dug the heels of her palms into her eyes, wishing the world away.

'Hey,' said Lachie, sitting beside her and opening his arm. 'Come here.'

She sank into his embrace, her body tucked and cradled against his side, her head on his chest. She stared at Poddy with sore eyes while Lachie's heart beat strong against her ear.

'I'm so scared, Lachie.'

'Don't be. I'm here. I'll take care of you.'

'Why Poddy? That's what I don't understand. Why not Sod or Elly or Venus or Robert or someone else's horse?'

'No reason. It's just life.'

'Then life's shit.'

'Not always. Sometimes life's magical.' He traced his knuckles down the side of her face. 'Come on. Your tea's getting cold.'

She sat up, feeling strange, like she'd missed something, something important, but unable to fathom what. Lachie handed her a mug. She took a sip. The tea was tepid but sweet, milky and comforting. He offered sandwiches and biscuits but she refused. Tea she could tolerate, but food would never make it past the constriction in her throat.

As the hours passed, the light filtering through the barn's skylights dimmed and finally darkened. Brooke rose frequently to take Poddy's temperature and whisper comforting words to him, releasing long breaths when the reading remained elevated but steady. Her mobile rang several times. She answered Tony's calls immediately, relaying information to him, listening carefully to the vet's instructions. Angus's call she answered in monosyllables until he gave up on her. A few seconds later, Lachie's phone jingled. He excused himself and stepped out into the night. She didn't need to see the screen or hear his conversation to know it was Angus. If Brooke were her brother, she would have done the same.

The three calls from Ariel she let pass through to voicemail.

At ten, Lachie left for the cottage, returning twenty minutes later with damp hair and smelling of soap and Lachie-ness, his arms loaded with pillows and blankets, and another thermos of tea.

'You don't have to stay,' Brooke said when she realised he carried enough bedding for two.

'I want to.' He passed her a blanket and a pillow, and sat down next to her. 'Anyway, I'm just following orders. You look after Poddy, I look after you.'

'It's not your job, Lachie.'

He smiled and draped his arm around her shoulders, tugging her against his warmth, gifting her comfort where none seemed possible. 'Yeah, it is.'

The night extended, long and exhausting. Brooke kept trying to think of things to talk about but her mind was too filled with worry to think beyond Poddy. Lachie seemed content to keep the silence.

Each time she returned after tending Poddy he'd hold out the blanket and let her crawl into the warmth and security of his embrace.

As dawn crept slowly through the barn, Tony arrived. He took one look at her and shook his head at her dishevelled appearance. To everyone's relief, the majority of Poddy's swelling had dissipated overnight and he was at last able to breathe properly through his nostrils. Despite Tony's diligent disinfection of the bite zone, the marks had begun to weep, but Poddy appeared more alert and responsive to Brooke's attentions, raising her hope of his recovery.

'He's beating it,' she announced.

But the vet remained sceptical.

———

Despite Brooke's early optimism, Poddy's condition improved no further. For five days, except for brief toilet and shower breaks, she didn't leave the stable. Alerted by Lachie, Nancy bustled in with delicious casseroles, cakes and puddings, mumsily urging Brooke to eat up, but Brooke had no interest in food. She ate meagrely, not tasting any of it, surviving instead on the endless thermoses of milky tea Lachie supplied.

Numbness settled in. Her guard against the darkness.

People came and went. Chloe, Andrew, Nancy, Angus. Neighbours and Pitcorthie locals dropped by to offer sympathy and support, but Brooke didn't have the energy to deal with anyone but Tony. Though her relationship with Andrew had improved of late, with hints of their former ease returning, Brooke still expected an argument when she refused his offer to stay, but he barely protested. Mouth thin, he simply glanced from her to Lachie and nodded, as if he finally understood. She had someone else now. Andrew and Chloe might be her dearest friends, but in her blackest, most fear-filled moments it was Lachie, with his calm solidity, who kept her fragile insides from shattering.

She ceased answering her phone, leaving Lachie to take the brunt. He fielded every call, except those from her mother.

'Talk to her, Brooke,' he said, holding out his phone for the umpteenth time. Ariel, like the others, had given up calling Brooke's mobile, bombarding Lachie with calls instead. 'Even if it's just for a few minutes. She's worried sick.'

Brooke shook her head. 'I can't deal with her right now.' She couldn't deal with anyone.

'A few words. That's all. She's your mother. She loves you.'

She rolled out a breath, knowing Lachie was right. 'All right.'

She took the phone and pressed it to her ear. 'Mum.'

'Brooke, thank God. How are you?'

'Fine.'

'And Poddy?'

'Poddy's . . . Poddy's hanging in there.'

'He's a strong horse. He'll fight.' She paused. 'Brooke, darling, I want to come up and stay with you. Help you through this.'

'Like you've been trying to help me these past months? No, Mum. You stay in Sydney where you belong. I'll stay here where I belong. Where I should have been all the time.'

'Brooke, that's not fair.'

Disbelief and fury turned Brooke's voice glacial. 'Don't talk to me about what's not fair. My beautiful Poddy's fighting for his life. That's what's not fair.'

Suddenly the phone jerked from her hand.

'Ariel, it's Lachie.' He moved swiftly to the door but she caught his words. 'I'm sorry. She's upset . . . I don't think that's a good idea right now . . . Maybe later, when Poddy's better . . . I will. I promise.'

Brooke's pointless anger faltered. She leaned her head against the stable wall and let the numbness wash back over her.

'I'm sorry,' she said when Lachie hung up. 'I just can't deal with her right now. I know she's not to blame. I know I'm not either.' She turned dull eyes onto him. 'But I can't help thinking that if I'd been here . . .' She pressed knuckles hard against her teeth as tears, always so close, stung hot.

'Hey, stop it.' He crouched down next to her, pulled her hand away and gently rubbed it between his big palms. 'Poddy doesn't need you upset. He needs you strong.'

For Poddy's sake she tried.

Though Lachie came to check on her during the night, he retreated to the cottage to sleep. The farm couldn't be neglected, and they both understood the danger of mixing fatigue with machinery. The nights seemed colder without him, lonelier, and in the dark quiet the monster she'd been slowly taming roused and breathed its filth into her mind, blaming her for Poddy's suffering. For not having the fortitude to stand up against Mark and her mother. For not fighting for what she loved.

Poddy's condition remained fragile. The cold he'd suffered the previous week had left his immune system weaker than normal. Despite heavy doses of antibiotics, infection took hold, and the bite area developed into a large open wound. Layer by layer, the skin peeled away until a sore the diameter of a tennis ball opened up. Tony had warned of the complication, but the reality of that ugly suppurating hole knocked Brooke sideways. She comforted Poddy as best she could but sometimes, when the horror became too great, she huddled in the stable corner, knees drawn up, trembling, as the hope she once possessed leaked slowly into the night.

At dawn on the sixth day the last of it disappeared.

Brooke woke from a doze and rubbed her eyes. Suddenly she stilled. She peered into the hazy light as a creeping sense of wrongness sent goosebumps down her back. Hands braced against the stable wall she moved upright, eyes not leaving Poddy, dread weighing her limbs.

Across the smell of wood and manure came the scent of corruption, sweat and pain. Swallowing hard, she took a careful step forward. Poddy's good eye stared dully back at her. Ears that had swivelled with life and attention hung limp. His tail was raised in distress and his once glossy coat was sweat-stained and devoid of shine. Wheezy breaths scraped the quiet like sandpaper.

Working fast, praying against all instinct that she was wrong, Brooke checked Poddy's temperature. She stared at the thermometer, swaying in shock as she registered the result.

'No. Please, no.'

She wrapped her arms around him and buried her face in his fevered neck, choking on the knowledge that the worst of Tony's warnings had come true. Poddy's once powerful body could no longer withstand the infection. In all likelihood it had reached the bone.

'Brooke?'

She kissed Poddy's cheek and stepped away. Time mattered now. She couldn't afford grief.

Lachie's gaze flicked from her to Poddy. He placed the thermos and a plate of toast on the ground before standing in front of her and cupping her cheek. Her lip trembled at his touch, the sympathy in his expression threatening to unravel her. She grasped his fingers and held them against her skin, then breathed in hard, willing herself to say the words.

'Can you fetch the rifle for me?'

'Don't you want to wait for Tony?'

'No. He's suffering. I can't . . .' She shuddered in a breath. 'He's endured enough.'

'I'm sorry. I know how much you love him.'

Her mouth wobbled as grief rose like a solid prickly mass in her throat. Using what little strength she had remaining, she clamped down on it. She'd indulge it later. Once Poddy was out of pain.

'Thank you. Now, please, can you bring the rifle?'

He nodded and walked briskly to the cottage where the property's .22 was safely stored in a steel cabinet in the spare room. The keys were once Brooke's responsibility but Angus had passed them to

Lachie. At the time she'd seen it as a betrayal. Now she was grateful for the time it granted her.

'You stay brave, Poddy-baby,' she said, standing on his good side, stroking his cheek. 'You stay big and strong and you never forget how much I love you. You're going to see your old friend Oddy now. He'll have missed you.' A sob broke. 'Like I'm going to miss you.'

She ran out of words. The stream of love she'd wanted to offer him was sluiced away by tears she couldn't stop. She stroked Poddy's cheek, his neck, his shoulder, his ears, an ache throbbing in her chest as she tried to memorise every muscle, every contour of his big courageous body.

Hearing Lachie's return she placed her lips against Poddy's white star, kissing him for the last time. 'Be brave, Poddy. I love you.'

She stepped away, breathing hard, digging into her core, mining it for steel.

No more room for sentiment. She had a task to complete.

Lachie stood outside the stable with the gun, barrel angled to the ground. She approached, preparing herself to take it, for the feel of warm timber and cool metal, the machinery of death.

'Thanks,' she said. 'Greg Hitchcock has a front-end loader we should be able to borrow. Maybe you could get it for me? We'll bury him up with the others.'

'Sure.'

She waited for him to move, to pass her the rifle, but he stood there looking at her as though it was her who should be moving. 'It's time,' she prompted, holding out her hands.

His face dropped. He took a swift step backwards. 'No way, Brooke.'

'He's my horse,' she said, angry at him for delaying. This needed to be done fast. 'It's my responsibility.'

'Like hell it is. And I'm not going to stand here and argue over it either. It's cruel to all of us. So say your farewell then go lock yourself in the cottage and don't move until I say you can.'

She recognised the jut of his jaw, the squared feet and shoulders, the tense body, and knew there was no point fighting. The wash of relief made her dizzy. Lachie would make sure it was done right, without shaking hands and blurred vision. A swift and painless end.

'Thank you,' she whispered, before turning to her beloved horse once more. 'You be good for Lachie. You be brave and stand still and soon it'll be over.' She kissed his star, his cheek, the soft hair above his good eye, hands caressing, stroking, memorising. 'I will never forget you, my champion. Never.'

She turned away, tears dripping, mouth contorting.

'Go now,' said Lachie. 'And take Billy with you.'

She nodded and walked to the door, determined not to look back, but the elastic band of love holding her to Poddy was too great. One hand clinging to the frame, she took him in, locking him deep and safe in her heart.

Her darling Poddy. Her friend.

Tears splashed. She blinked, needing her vision clear, but they fell relentlessly. She gave in. Photographs, video and memories would be her comfort now. And her never-ending love.

'Promise me you'll make it quick,' she whispered.

'I promise.'

SEVENTEEN

LACHIE WATCHED Brooke as she snatched up Billy and ran from the barn. At the cottage door she halted and glanced back, expression stricken, clutching Billy high against her chest the way a frightened child clutches a favourite soft toy. He willed her onward, understanding the plea in her eyes, the fear for Poddy. Only when he pressed a hand over his heart and then opened his palm to her, reinforcing the promise he'd made to make Poddy's death quick, did she finally mouth 'thank you' and step inside.

Aware of Poddy's increasingly laboured breaths, he worked fast. Though he'd lost condition, Poddy still weighed close to half a tonne. Lachie needed him to fall within easy access of the front-end loader, which meant leading him into the space at the rear of the shed near the big sliding doors, an area that had the added advantage of being easily washed down. He didn't want Brooke remembering Poddy in death, marked by a bloody stain. She'd already witnessed enough.

To make room, he slid open the doors and drove the truck out, leaving it parked close as an extra shield in case Brooke tried to watch from the cottage. The space cleared, he loaded the gun and with the safety on, laid it flat next to the float. He stared at it for a moment, his stomach tensed against what was to come. Though it was a necessary part of life on the land, he hated shooting animals. He hated the snap of the bullet, the sudden slump of extinguished life, the hollow feeling it left in his gut. But neither could he stand suffering. And Poddy was suffering badly.

Not wanting to hurt the horse with a noseband across his wound, Lachie led Poddy out of the stable using a lead rope wrapped around his neck. Racked with fever and pain, the horse made shuffling, slow progress, but he followed obediently, standing where Lachie positioned him with his head lowered, a gentleman to the end.

Heart thumping hard, Lachie picked up the rifle, flicked off the safety and took aim. Suddenly, the enormity of what he was about to do overwhelmed him. In Brooke's eyes he might never escape this act. This one shot could forever taint him as the man who killed her beloved Poddy.

He lowered the rifle and waited for his breathing to steady. He couldn't afford to think about the consequences for him and Brooke right now. What he needed to do was take steady aim and not fuck this up. For Poddy's sake, and Brooke's, he had to do this right.

Jaw set, he raised the rifle.

Poddy blinked his dull eye, resigned to his fate.

The shot cracked the morning calm, rushing birds to flight and sending horses squealing. As the last echo rattled into the distance, peace descended, as though the Valley's creatures had all bowed their heads to mourn in silence the passing of one of their favourite sons.

Lachie walked from the shed to look at the sky, aglow with the rising day. Across the paddocks came the low of dairy cattle moving to morning milking. A magpie warbled to a mottled juvenile from her fence-top perch before hopping down to join her offspring. Sod whickered from his yard, seeking attention and breakfast. The world roused again, embracing life, moving on.

Something he prayed Brooke could do too.

———

Lachie stood guard over the body until Nancy arrived. He should have called her before, had Nancy sitting with Brooke when she heard the shot, but he'd been too worried about getting her out of the way and saving the horse further suffering to think of it. While he waited, he phoned Tony and then Angus to pass on the news and assure them Brooke was being well cared for. He phoned Chloe as well, and her sobbing lament for Poddy and his special place in Brooke's heart did nothing to alleviate Lachie's unease.

Nancy's hand fluttered to her mouth when she saw Poddy's collapsed form, but to Lachie's relief, bar a moistening of her eyes, she held her emotions in check.

'Brooke's inside with Billy. It'll take me a while to bury Pod, and I don't want her leaving the house until it's done. She doesn't need to see this.'

Nancy placed a warm hand on his arm. 'I'll take care of her.'

'Thanks.' He kissed her cheek. 'I appreciate it. See if you can't get her to sleep. She hasn't had any proper rest since last Friday night.'

'Neither have you, by the looks of it.'

'I'll be all right. Just make sure she is.'

Nancy appraised him for a moment, her wrinkled mouth pursing. 'You're in love with her.'

He didn't see the point of denial. 'Yes.'

'I'm glad. Does she know?'

He shook his head and glanced at Poddy, now at peace and out of pain.

She patted his arm again. 'I hope you get a chance to tell her soon. When it'll give her joy.'

'Will it?'

Nancy smiled. 'Oh, I think so. But we have to get her through this first.' She sobered and crouched by Poddy's head, placing her age-spotted hand on his cheek. 'Goodbye, Poddy. You were a good horse. We'll all miss you.' She sniffed and rose, and with a final nod at Lachie, hastened to the cottage.

The morning passed slowly. Lachie rang Greg, who kindly

offered to drive the loader over after milking and give him a hand with the burial, explaining it'd take two of them anyway. To fill in time, Lachie dealt with the other horses. Sod misbehaved all the way to his paddock, skittering and shaking his head, spooking at everything and nothing. Robert and Elly were also nervous, but it was Venus who almost brought Lachie undone. She wouldn't stop crying out for Poddy. Swinging her shaggy head left and right, hunting for her friend, bunting Lachie's arm and looking at him with frowny eyes as though asking what he'd done with Poddy. Even when he let her in with Robert and Elly she stayed at the gate, whinnying hysterically and staring plaintively back up the lane toward the barn. Lachie walked away breathing hard through his nose, each high-pitched call shooting another spike down his back.

He cleaned the yards, making lists in his head of what else he needed to do, imagining ways he could comfort Brooke, knowing none would help. Greg's arrival gave him respite from his introspection, but only for while. Thoughts of Brooke remained close, his unease alongside.

With Poddy buried, he dealt with the barn, taking care to not leave any trace of Poddy's demise. As per Tony's instructions, he removed all the wood shavings from the stable, and scrubbed the walls and floor with disinfectant and left it to dry. Though he suspected Poddy's rug was salvageable, he carried it to the incinerator at the back of the orchard and burned it anyway. Lachie doused the halter and brushes in disinfectant and left them the sun, adding a reminder to his list to put them away at the end of the day.

Filthy, sweaty, but satisfied he'd done all he could, he walked slowly to the cottage, stopping on the verandah to rub Billy's head and thank him for being good to Brooke. The little dog seemed more subdued than usual, as though he too sensed the sorrow the day had brought.

'She's asleep,' whispered Nancy in the kitchen. 'But you go wash up and I'll sort you out some lunch.'

He paused by the spare room. The door hung ajar but not wide enough for him to see inside. He placed his hand on it, hesitant. He should leave her to sleep. Brooke was exhausted and grieving. She didn't need him right now.

After this morning, she might never need him.

The thought left him sinking.

He pushed on the door and stepped into the room. She lay curled on top of the bed with her back to him, a crocheted rug over her legs, still dressed in yesterday's clothes. As he stepped closer her hand moved and reached out for him. He took it and sat down next to her, stroking her hair.

'Lie with me,' she whispered.

Though his clothes were stained and his hands dirt-encrusted, he did as he was told, stretching out behind her, his body spooning her contours, arm circling her belly. He listened to her breathing slow as she settled, and felt his own fall into rhythm as he relaxed. Perhaps later, when she'd had time to think, she'd remember what he'd done, but right now, with her warm and small in his arms, with his heart beating against her back, Lachie savoured the small grace she'd offered, and loved her even more.

Footsteps halted in the hall, then the door creaked quietly shut and he was alone with Brooke. Gradually, like her, he fell asleep.

———

Lachie woke to a shake of his shoulder. Nancy leaned over him, her finger to her mouth, then gestured towards the door before disappearing from view. Careful not to disturb Brooke, he propped himself up and drank her in. She lay curled in his arm, soft, smooth-browed and deeply asleep, free for a short while from the pain. Resisting the urge to place a kiss on her slightly parted mouth, he instead set about extracting himself with as little disruption as possible, covering her with the rug before padding out into the hall and closing the door behind him.

He squinted at his watch, cursed at the time, and hurried to the kitchen. He'd been asleep for over three hours. Too long when so much work still lay ahead.

'Bad weather's coming,' said Nancy, handing him a ham and cheese sandwich. 'You need to get the horses in. I'll stay until you're done but I need to get home too.' She wrung her hands. 'My ladies get upset in storms.'

'How bad is it?'

'Bad enough for a weather warning.'

'I'll be quick.'

Gripping the sandwich in his teeth, he headed outside, checking the sky as he pulled on his boots. He recognised the build up of dark clouds to the west. As the weather intensified, the Valley would funnel the storm eastwards, dropping patches of heavy rain. They could be in for a wild night.

He led Venus in with Robert and placed them side by side in the yards, hoping the big calm horse would offer comfort to the upset pony, but the moment he released her, she turned her face to the barn and whinnied plaintively. Taking pity, he took a moment to scruff her mane and fondle her ears, but Venus remained disconsolate. Only when he brought her evening feed did she give up her vigil and bury her nose in the trough.

With Brooke's horses and the sheds secure, and his rounds of the racehorses complete, Lachie returned to the cottage, sending a relieved Nancy home to her flock and settling in to listen to the storm and wait for Brooke to wake. He made phone calls, reassuring Chloe and Angus that Brooke was fine but grieving and exhausted, asking them to pass on the message. They could talk to her tomorrow. Tonight, Brooke needed sleep and space.

Darkness had long fallen by the time Brooke padded out of the bedroom. As she entered, he rose from his seat at the kitchen table. Her eyes were bleary, red and swollen, her hair messy, her movements sluggish. She pulled out a chair and sat, staring at nothing.

'I'd hoped it was a dream. I'd hoped—'

He reached across and tangled his fingers in hers. 'I'm sorry.'

'Me too.'

'Can I get you anything? Cup of tea? Glass of red wine? Something to eat?'

'I don't know.' She frowned and rubbed her brow. 'Maybe some wine.'

He squeezed her hand and rose to open a bottle. She needed to eat but he wouldn't force it. In a moment, when she was more awake, he'd heat one of Nancy's casseroles and hope the smell would rouse her hunger.

A blast of rain hit the window as he passed her a glass, followed by another squall that rattled the eaves. He watched the rain splatter and slide down the kitchen window. Neither of them was going anywhere in this, and a couple of glasses of red wouldn't hurt either of them. Bottle and glasses hooked in one hand, he rounded the end of the table, kicking the door snake snug against the draught as he passed.

He paused to touch Brooke's upper arm. 'Come into the lounge. It's warmer there.'

He stoked the fire, watching her out of the corner of his eye. She sat on the edge of the couch staring into her wine glass as if she couldn't decide whether to drink or cry. He wished he knew what to say.

'Do you know how this all started?' she asked, looking up. 'With a stupid bet, that's how.'

Recognising she wanted to talk, he hooked the poker in its rack, replaced the shield, and waited. The fire crackled and snapped, throwing heat onto his back.

'We were at the Ardellan Show,' she said hollowly. 'Everything was normal. Then Andrew made a bet that if he beat me in the C-grade jump-off I'd have to kiss him.'

Andrew. He should have known.

'Just another bet, no different from a hundred others we'd made. Except it was. And I knew it. I'd sensed it for months but didn't want to acknowledge the truth. I thought we could go on pretending it was all a joke.' She shook her head. 'How stupid I was.'

Rain hit the house in sheets, loud, insistent.

'I thought I'd win. But I lost.' She bit her lip and raised shiny eyes to the ceiling. 'God, how I lost.'

'Then what happened?' he asked when her lapse into silence showed no sign of ending.

She took a long slug of wine, and rolled the glass bowl between her palms. 'He came to the trailer. We had dinner, wine, talked about the horses. Andrew tidied.' She looked at Lachie. 'And then he wanted me to pay up.'

The way she said it made Lachie want to punch something. Carefully, before his clenched fist snapped the stem, he placed his wine glass on the carpet, forcing his expression to neutral.

'It wasn't right.' She took another slug of wine and reached for the bottle, the neck rattling against the rim as she poured. 'I had to push him away. He said he loved me. That he couldn't wait any more.' A tear dribbled down her cheek. 'I should have known. The signs were there but I kidded myself they were illusions, just him mucking around, and he always had these glamorous girlfriends who were nothing like me. And he *never* said. Not once.

'I didn't sleep well that night. I was tired and upset and the next day I couldn't concentrate. Poddy and Oddy were lovely, but Sod dumped me in the warm-up ring and by the time I came to leave I was so sore and exhausted I couldn't think straight. I was okay until we neared home and then—' She stopped, losing focus as she disappeared into her memories.

Lachie moved fast. He didn't want Brooke going there. Kneeling in front of her he prised the wine glass from her grip and set it aside before taking her hands in his. 'Hey. Look at me. It was an accident. No one to blame. Just an accident.'

She came back, liquid eyes trailing his face. 'A stupid bet, Lachie. One stupid, childish bet and all I love gets stolen from me.'

'Not all. You still have Sod.'

She released an unsteady half laugh and, pulling her hands from his, wiped at her wet cheeks. 'Yeah, I still have Sod.'

'And Robert and Elly and Venus.' And him, Lachie longed to add, but now wasn't the time. 'And Kingston Downs.'

Her expression dropped. 'Perhaps not for much longer. Mark says we might have to sell.'

'They won't do that to you, Brooke.'

'They mightn't have a choice.'

'I'm sure it won't come to that.'

'I hope you're right.' She smiled and touched his face. 'Thanks.'

'What for?'

'For being here. Looking after me. For . . . for Poddy.'

He stared at his hands, balanced on her knees, thumbs rubbing the surface of her jeans. 'I was worried you'd blame me.'

She frowned. 'Blame you? No. Never. You did what I couldn't do. What I should have done from the start instead of putting him through all that. I could never blame you for destroying him. I thank you for it.'

He raised his head and met her eyes, and Lachie felt the pull, that incredible yearning to touch her. To gather her to him, press his mouth to hers and breathe her in. But tonight of all nights, he had to resist. She was too vulnerable.

He pulled his hands away from her knees and rose. 'How about I heat us up something for dinner?'

'I'm not hungry.'

'Ahh, but you haven't smelled what Nancy made yet.'

She ate little, stirring hunks of meat and vegetables around her plate, pausing often to take a sip of wine. When Lachie carefully suggested maybe she'd had enough to drink she fobbed him off, telling him it'd help her sleep. He hoped it would, but he also worried what the alcohol would do to her dreams. She'd endured enough nightmares.

They watched television after dinner, another crime show featuring a robbery gone wrong, but Brooke's blank stare told him her

concentration lay inward, in a place he longed to touch. Three-quarters of the way through the show she rose, stating she was going to
bed. Lachie gave her half an hour to settle before checking, and found
her curled under the thick blankets, wet-cheeked but thankfully
asleep. Fatigue wearying his bones, he trudged to his room and lay on
the bed with his hands behind his head, staring at the ceiling,
listening to the creaking, rain-swollen timbers of the cottage as wind
tugged at its frame.

Wishing himself beside her again.

Lachie woke shivering and blinking into the darkness. He raked a
hand over his face, trying to orient himself. Easing his legs over the
edge of the bed he realised he'd fallen asleep still wearing his filthy
work clothes. In all the worry about Brooke, he hadn't thought to
shower.

He glanced at his bedside digital clock. At least it was only eleven
and not the middle of the night. With half a bottle of wine under her
belt, Brooke should sleep through the noise of the old pipes. Stripping
off his shirt and socks, he headed for the bathroom, sneaking a look in
on Brooke as he passed.

The bed was empty.

'Brooke?' He checked the bathroom and the toilet, continuing to
call out to her.

Anxiety rising, he dashed to the kitchen. Nothing. Then he spied
the angled draught snake, pushed out of alignment by the swing of
the door.

'Shit!'

He ran to his room, yanked on a jumper and sprinted barefoot
back to the kitchen. He wrenched open the door, sending it crashing
into the wall. Alerted by the noise, Billy barked and skittered to the
edge of the verandah, white body quivering in anticipation.

'Where the fuck'd she go, Billy?' he asked the dog as he pulled on
his freezing boots. He suspected he already knew the answer.

Boots on, he ran out into the yard, splashing through puddles,
Billy yapping at his feet. Rain pattered his shoulders and plastered

his hair. He scanned the yards. The horses eyed him, ears swivelling, alert. Sod whickered then tossed his head in alarm as Lachie sped past and yanked the barn door open. The interior was black, smelling of disinfectant and woodchips, noisy with rain on metal and empty. Leaving the door open, he sprinted down the track to the dairy and charged inside. No Brooke.

Which left only one other place.

Water channels furrowed the track up the rise, the surface torn from the heavy wheels of the front-end loader, and eroding further in the storm. As he ran along the track edge, the wet and slippery grass tangling with his legs, the rain intensified. Fear shot adrenaline down his legs. He pushed harder, slipping and stumbling, blind to his safety. Thinking only of Brooke. Billy galloped ahead, a white streak in the unlit night.

Halfway to the top he saw her. She laid face down on the muddy surface of Poddy's grave, arms splayed like a crucifix, hugging him through the soil. Lachie pushed on, the stiff backs of his boots blistering his heels, his fear and relief giving way to anger.

He slid to her side and grabbed her shoulders, rolling her out of the mud, the urge to shake her enormous. 'Are you fucking *nuts?*'

'I want him back!'

'You can't have him. He's dead, Brooke. Dead!' His anger, so hot when running, dissolved as he took her shivery, stricken form. Wrapping his arms around her mud-smeared body, he hugged her to him. 'And you're alive. Alive and precious. I know you want him back. I know you miss him, but lying here won't change the fact he's gone.' He cupped her anguished face as rain sheeted over them. 'Don't spoil his memory like this. He deserves better. You both do.'

Fat tears welled and spilled down her face, merging with the rain. 'It's my fault he suffered,' she sobbed. 'I should have been stronger. Listened to Tony. But I was selfish. I couldn't bear to lose him. And I made his last days miserable.'

'No. His last days were spent with you. They could never be

miserable. You did what you did because you loved him. No one can blame you for that.'

A flash erupted in the distance. He glanced upwards, listening for the rumble, counting the seconds. Close. Too close.

'We need to go.' He forced her to her feet. He couldn't carry her, not in these conditions. Grieving or not, she'd have to run.

They stumbled and slid their way to the base, Lachie keeping a tight hold on Brooke's hand, worrying she might run back to Poddy. Back on the main track he broke into a jog, pulling her along. Another lightning flash crashed through the sky, the resulting thunder even closer. The noise seemed to snap her out of her torpor. She increased her pace, sprinting with him towards the cottage.

At the verandah he released her hand. Safe under shelter they bent forwards, hands on knees, sucking in breaths.

'I'm sorry,' she said, panting. 'But I needed to see him. I had to apologise. It felt so important.'

'You could have done it in the morning.'

'I know. I'm sorry.'

He straightened, still breathing hard. She was soaked, her thin clothes clinging to her body, hair pasted to her scalp. Lips trembling with cold, her face smeared with dark mud.

'Come on,' he said, wrapping an arm around her shoulders. 'Let's get you inside before you catch pneumonia.'

She glanced down at Billy, wet, quivery, head swinging between them. 'And Billy. Poor thing's freezing.' Without waiting for an answer she scooped him up, the dog's tongue flicking at her face as he tried to kiss his thanks.

Inside, Lachie plucked Billy from her arms and ordered her to the shower. After stoking the fire, he raided the linen cupboard for an old towel before settling in front of the blaze to rub the dog dry. Worried Brooke might tell him off if he dumped Billy back out into the night, Lachie fetched the terrier's raised bed and blanket from outside and set it up in the corner of the lounge.

He plonked the ecstatic dog on top and regarded him with his hands on his hips. 'Move and there'll be trouble, understand?'

Billy understood. Without so much as a turn, he snuggled down, chin on his paws, regarding his master with an expression suspiciously like a smug grin.

The pipes ceased their creaking. Realising Brooke had no clean clothes, Lachie raided his drawers for a clean T-shirt and a pair of drawstring tracksuit bottoms and laid them outside the bathroom door, calling to let her know they were there.

He waited in front of the fire, trying to shed the muscle-deep cold, wishing he had some brandy or whisky to warm his insides.

Brooke emerged wearing only the T-shirt, her skin pink from the hot water, smelling like his shampoo and soap. She laid the tracksuit pants on the couch. As she bent, the T-shirt lifted, exposing her upper leg and a tiny sliver of firm bum. Underwear. He hadn't considered that. And now she wore none.

'They kept falling down,' she explained.

Lachie swallowed, mesmerised by the creamy skin of her thighs. His gaze travelled up to take in the swell of her breasts, trying not to stare at the hint of erect nipple. Desire tugged and swelled, fanned by her fragile sexiness.

He pointed stupidly to the bathroom. 'I'll, er, shower now.'

'Okay.' She walked toward the fire. 'I'll stay here.'

He escaped, feeling teenaged and idiotic. The shower helped. In clean clothes, smelling respectable, he felt normal again, in control. Throwing his reflection a last 'behave yourself' look, he headed back to the lounge.

He found her sitting cross-legged on the carpet in front of the fire, the wide neck of his T-shirt hanging off one smooth shoulder, the loose fabric caressing her curves, hinting at the soft contours beneath. Her body shielded only by thin cotton. Close to naked.

She smiled over her shoulder, sending his heart tumbling. 'Come sit with me.'

He sat awkwardly alongside her, knees drawn up and crossed at the ankles, arms strapping them in place. 'How are you feeling?'

'Crappy.' She tilted her head to rest it against his shoulder. 'Grateful to you.'

His right arm left his legs and wrapped around her. 'You don't have to be.'

She tilted her face upwards, mirrored flames dancing across her shiny eyes. 'I do.' She looked away and fiddled with the hem of the T-shirt. 'I'm so sorry for everything. I never used to be like this. But since . . .' She bit her lip.

'Hey, enough.'

'I just wanted you to understand.'

'I do. You've had a shit year. They happen, and they change us. The main thing is to keep looking forward.'

She nudged him. 'Mister Deep again.'

'Yeah,' he said, nudging her back. 'That's me.'

Rain drummed on the cottage and wind stretched the timbers, but the old house held fast, its interior protected, cosy and intimate. Bored with watching humans, Billy closed his eyes in canine bliss. Lachie relaxed, staring at the fire as it wove around the logs, content to have Brooke by his side, fantasising that maybe, one day, this might be for always.

'Lachie?'

'Mmm.'

'I want to go to bed.'

He hid his disappointment with a smile. 'Okay.' He rose and helped her up, keeping hold of her hand past the point when he should have let go. He wanted to say something before she went, some sort of hint as to how he felt, but the way she looked at him, so trusting and exposed, stole his words. Instead, he placed a long tender kiss on her forehead. 'Sleep well.'

'No. You don't understand.' She bit her lip, holding his gaze, sending wings fluttering in his chest. 'I want to go to bed with you.'

The room stilled. He stared at her, wondering if he'd heard right, scanning her face for signs of a joke. Instead, all he saw was sweet, nervous honesty.

And a woman made vulnerable by grief.

Christ, he wanted her. He wanted to kiss all her sadness away, take her to a place where only pleasure existed, where she felt safe and cocooned in his love. But not tonight. Not when she was so emotionally defenceless. Not when she might regret it tomorrow.

'I don't think—'

'Shh,' she whispered, pressing her forefinger to his lips. Then she dropped her hands around his neck and drew him to her. Her breasts pushed against his shirt, her sweet breath caressing his mouth as she urged him on. 'Don't think, Lachie. Just do.'

He hesitated, caught between what he thought was right and the demands of his heart and body.

She brushed her mouth across his. 'Please. Tonight. Just do.'

Electrified beyond reason, he did.

EIGHTEEN

ONE TENDER TOUCH, one exquisite kiss, and the grief Brooke had been clinging to so tightly subsided. It still throbbed in the background, but the edges were dulled. They no longer cut blades through her heart. Instead, as Lachie took the kiss deeper, her spirit swelled, ballooned by something marvellous, something rapturous and hope-filled.

Multiple times in her love-drunk hazes she'd imagined kissing him, but not once had she imagined it would be this magical. He'd started tentative, careful, just a light brush of her mouth, as though testing her sincerity, and she'd melted against him, wanting more. Sensing her need, he'd responded, cupping her face as he pressed his mouth harder against hers. Now, he kissed with a hunger that turned her inside out and drowned her in feelings of love, lust and desperate, insistent want.

And God, was it right. Perfectly, wonderfully right.

His hands slid down her neck, across her shoulders and down her bare arms, knuckles brushing her sides, each touch electric. He kissed his way across her cheek, warm, excited breath heavy in her ear as he nibbled at her lobe then left it to kiss a trail down her neck. He nuzzled the neck of her T-shirt aside to place fluttery kisses on her collarbone. Eyes closed, she arched her back, panting with pleasure as she let the glory of it swallow her.

He nuzzled his way back up to her mouth before drawing back to look at her intently. 'Are you really sure about this?'

She wrapped her arms around his neck and pressed against him. 'You're kidding, right?'

'No. I'm serious. I need to know.'

'I'm positive, Lachie. Absolutely,' she brushed her mouth against his, 'positively,' sucked at his lower lip, 'positive.'

She meant it. Heart and soul meant it. She loved him, and if the tragedies of the year had taught her one thing, it was to give and show her love, not hide it, because tomorrow could see it snatched away. Every hour, every minute, every second needed to be treasured. And even if this was only one night—a display of kind-heartedness and sympathy on his part—at least she'd have it to cherish and remember.

'If you change your—'

She pressed her finger against his mouth, shaking her head. 'No more worry. No more talk. Just do.'

Relief eased the uncertainty from his eyes. He grabbed her finger, kissed the tip, and taking her hand fully in his, led her to his bedroom, pausing briefly in the doorway to look at her for reassurance before leading her inside. He sat on the bed and drew her between his legs, his palms light on her hips, warm through the thin fabric of the T-shirt. She smiled and bent to kiss him, returning the pleasure he'd gifted earlier.

Trailing kisses over his mouth and face, down his neck, she twirled clumsy fingers at the buttons of his shirt, popping them one by one until she could spread the cloth apart and press her hands over his chest. Light hairs tickled her fingers. Solid, tight muscles moved against her palms. He traced fingers up and down her thighs, sending goosebumps tumbling deliciously up her back and across her shoulders, teasing his way past her groin and her fluttering belly to tickle more patterns over her waist.

Brooke broke her kisses and straightened. Holding his attention, she reached for the hem of her T-shirt. His eyes flared as she raised it up and pulled it over her head. Then he slowly dropped his focus to scan her body, hovering on her breasts, slipping lower, lips parting as his expression glazed with desire. Anticipation tingled and fizzed between them like a sherbet in water.

He leaned forwards and placed a single delicate kiss on the pale skin between her breasts. 'You're perfect.'

Brooke glowed as though a million fireflies fluttered under her skin. Overcome, she brushed a hand across his hair and grabbed the back of his head, kissing him hard, climbing closer until the exposed skin of her stomach joined his. Heat flared and became liquid, made molten by his words and touch.

He responded with passion to match her own, curling her closer, as though he couldn't touch her enough, rolling sideways to ease her gently on the bed, palms stroking, fingers skimming, mouth exploring. Lower, lower.

Their breaths, gasps and moans overtook the night. She wrenched at his shirt, wanting it off, wanting him fully naked, skin to skin. Releasing a beaded nipple, he helped with the task, movements as urgent as hers, tossing the shirt to the floor before lowering his head and sucking once more.

Desperation rising, she fumbled with his jeans, the button cumbersome and difficult. Finally, it popped and she slid her hand inside to feel his length, shuddering and closing her eyes as he returned the favour.

He played and teased and kissed and sucked until she couldn't stand the exquisite pleasure any longer. She wanted them together, made whole. 'Lachie, please.'

'Hold on,' he said, kissing her and propping himself up to pull open the bedside drawer. He drew out a pack of condoms, and flicked the lid before extracting a foil packet.

She smiled. Trust Lachie to be prepared. Prepared and thoughtful.

God, she adored him.

She helped slide the sheath on, loving the feel of him, his smooth size. Ready, he questioned her again with his eyes. She answered with a hot hungry kiss and a tug on his hips, drawing him towards her, to where she pulsed. Bracing his weight, he pulled away from her mouth and eased his hips closer, free hand gripping her thigh, eyes locked on hers as he nudged at her and slid a fraction inside. She arched her back, curling in ecstasy, her rapture mirrored in his face.

Gently, stretching the moment, he pressed a little deeper and held. Quivers skittered across her skin, leaving it puckered and electrified. Her mouth parted, shallow breaths coming rapidly. Waiting, waiting. Still intent on her, he nudged some more. Her eyelids lowered, hands clawing on his back, needy, so needy.

'Lachie, I can't—'

His mouth clamped on hers, shutting her off, and with a deep moan of desire he slid fully inside.

Nothing compared to the pleasure he wrought. Physical, emotional, total. This wasn't just sex—this was a level of intimacy she'd never experienced before. Love in its most intense form. Whether he felt the same love, she didn't know, and it didn't matter. Sharing the moment was enough; his tenderness and care were enough. And he did care. Every sensuous movement, every delicate touch, every blazing response told her that. So she floated, going with him, savouring and embracing what he gave her, what she'd never forget.

'You called me Lachie,' he said when they were done. He rested on his elbow looking down at her, hand caressing her sweaty belly.

'It's your name.'

'I know, but until this week, you always called me Lachlan.'

'This week changed a lot of things.'

'Yes, it did. But calling me Lachie is one of the good things.'

'At least one good thing happened.'

He raised an eyebrow. 'One?'

It took Brooke a couple of heartbeats to work out what he meant.

Then she laughed, a sound, given her heartbreak, both strange and good. As though she was healing already.

Perhaps, thanks to Lachie, she was.

'Oh, all right,' she said, curling her arms around his neck and dragging him down to kiss his delicious mouth. 'Maybe more than one good thing. Maybe two.'

'What's this "maybe" business?'

She smiled. 'Okay, definitely two good things.'

He snuck fingers to the inside of her thigh as he trailed kisses over her collarbone and down toward her nipple, his skimming, shallow breaths raising goosebumps across her skin. 'I think you need more good things. Two's not enough. What do you say to three?'

'I like three.' She gasped, thrills shooting through her insides as he stroked upwards and simultaneously nipped lightly at her nipple. 'Yes. I think three would be very good.'

———

Brooke opened one eye and then the other and smiled, smug with bliss. Lachie's bed. Sex. Love. She raised her arms and rolled over, ready to drape him in warmth and a good-morning kiss. Her arms fell as she registered the empty space.

She listened for a while, hoping for the rattle of dishes in the kitchen, the shower or the flush of the loo, but the cottage remained quiet, except for the familiar chorus of its morning creaks. Disappointed, she buried her face in his pillow, inhaling his scent, remembering the night before. Lachie, Lachie, Lachie. His name sang in her head and swelled her heart. The sex had been, to put it mildly, amazing, but it was the rest that hazed her mind. The softness in his eyes when he looked at her, the slow, indulgent way he caressed her body, the way he'd breathed her name. Signs, perhaps, that he shared her feelings. That last night was more than compassion, more than a way to make her forget Poddy.

Poddy.

Pain struck. Instant. Piercing. She buried her face deeper, hugging the pillow, expecting tears. Though her throat roughened, to Brooke's surprise her eyes remained dry. Whatever grief she held, Lachie had once again assuaged it. Not totally, but enough to halt the suffocating rush of panic like that which had attacked her last night and caused her to embrace Poddy's grave in a futile hunt for comfort.

She turned onto her back, wishing Lachie would come back. She wanted to apologise again for her behaviour and to thank him for his understanding. For taking care of her when he didn't have to. And she wanted to probe how he felt before she did something stupid, like blurt out how in love she was.

The jazzy jingle of his phone's ringtone echoed from the kitchen. Brooke held her breath, hoping he'd rush in to answer it, but after several rings the noise stopped. She glanced at the bedside clock, amazed to see it was after seven. The horses would be hungry, their yards in need of cleaning. Her stomach rumbled. And she needed breakfast.

Brooke slid out of bed, hunting for something to wear. Last night's T-shirt lay folded on top of the dresser. She padded over and pulled it on, wishing for something Lachie had worn instead so she could have a little bit of him against her skin. As she scouted for his shirt, her attention was caught by a blue velvet box, lying on its side against the mirror.

She glanced at the door, listening for him over the loud thump of her heart. The cottage remained quiet.

Brooke reached out, hesitant. This was Lachie's room. These were his things, not hers. She should mind her own business. Self-censured, she dropped her hand to her side, but the blue velvet box called. And it called loudly. This wasn't just any box. The size and shape said ring box. A ring box in Lachie's room on Lachie's dresser.

Anxiety nagged at her insides. Was it his ring or a ring for someone else? Perhaps it was an heirloom, a harmless thing.

A harmless thing. Of course it was. And one little look wouldn't hurt.

Relieved, she picked up the box and flicked the lid.

Brooke swayed and reached for the dresser. She shut her eyes but the vision of the diamond remained.

A solitaire diamond. An engagement ring.

Time ticked. Breathing hard, she reopened her eyes and stared at the thing in her hand, willing it away, but it kept glittering, teasing her with shards of light. Though aware of her growing hurt, she couldn't resist the need to know more. With clumsy fingers she extracted the ring and turned it to expose the inside.

Tamsyn. Love always, Lachie.

Tamsyn.

She stared at her sex-tousled reflection in the mirror. Her smug expression was gone, cut across with uncertain lines of doubt; was last night only kindness, a response to her grief?

Whatever the ring's explanation, ecstatic or heartbreaking, she'd find out.

Movements robotic, she tucked the ring into its velvet nest, closed the lid and carried it with her to the kitchen to wait.

NINETEEN

ANXIOUS TO GET BACK to Brooke, Lachie drove faster than usual down Kingston Downs' drive, causing the two resting race-horses in the front paddock to jerk their heads in surprise. A posy of jonquils nicked from Nancy's garden sat on the Hilux's passenger seat. Billy lay on the floor, his head on his paws, eyes raised in a martyred expression, extremely put out to have had his perch usurped.

He grinned at the dog. 'Better get used to it, Billyboy. That'll be Brooke's seat from now on.'

And, with luck, so would the space in his bed be hers.

The bed he couldn't get back to fast enough.

He'd left her sleeping and gorgeous, knuckle curled under her chin like a baby, lips soft and still a little pouty from the night before. After planting a light kiss on her shoulder and resisting the urge to caress the smooth rounded edge of her exposed breast, he'd snuck out of the house to feed the horses and do the yards, before dashing across to Nancy's for some flowers.

He'd wanted roses—luscious, heavily scented red ones—but the delicate white and yellow jonquils would have to do as a gift to the woman he loved. As would a long morning kiss. And more.

Lots more.

He slowed, not wanting to wake Brooke with a noisy arrival, and parked near the verandah steps. Snatching up the posy, he winked at Billy. 'Wish me luck.'

The little dog raced ahead as Lachie leapt up the stairs. All Lachie could think about was getting to Brooke, kneeling by the bed, kissing her awake and then, finally, telling her he loved her.

And then he'd make love to her again.

The thought had him tugging his boots off in a rush. Leaving them where they fell, he pushed open the door.

Brooke sat at the end of the kitchen table, her fingertips lightly resting on the lid of a blue velvet box as she regarded him with rounded eyes.

He halted, posy held dumbly, and looked from her to the ring box and back again.

Shit.

'I'm sorry,' she said. 'I shouldn't have looked but I saw the box and . . .' She shrugged and bit her lip. Then she held his gaze, her expression so pleading it made his heart clench.

'What does it mean, Lachie?'

'Nothing. It—she—means nothing.' He moved closer and laid the flowers on the table before crouching down to take her hands in his. 'There was once a time when I wanted to marry her, but it turned out she didn't feel the same. I kept the ring, hoping she'd change her mind. She never did. And then I met you.' He took a breath, preparing his words, needing her to understand it was over. 'When Nick told me Tamsyn had married someone else I got it out, figured it was about time I sold it. I never imagined you'd see it.'

She smiled a little. 'I shouldn't have looked.'

He returned her smile, confidence building. 'It would have been hard to resist, especially after last night.' He squeezed her fingers. The time had come. 'I don't love her any more, Brooke. I love you.'

Relief flooded her face. Taking a shaky breath, she pulled her hands from his and curled them around his neck, pulling him close until their foreheads touched and they were eyeball to eyeball. His stomach somersaulted in anticipation as he sensed her mouth curl.

'And I, Lachie Cambridge, am completely crazy in love with you.'

'Really?'

'Really.'

'Good, because I need to take you to bed again.'

Brooke quirked an eyebrow. 'Who says we need a bed?'

'You want me to make love to you here?'

'I don't care *where* you do it, Lachie,' she said with a laugh. 'Just so long as you stop talking and get on with it.'

Not about to disobey orders, he shut up and kissed her. It was desperate, stupid with happiness, and aflame with need, made more intense by her ardent, equally desperate response.

In seconds, his hands were inside her T-shirt, skimming her warm satiny skin. He hauled her up to the table, accidentally squashing the flowers. Her legs parted, drawing him between them as he kissed his way across her face and down her throat. Hands grappled to release his clothing. Dislodged by the frenzy, the ring box flew to the floor. Grinning at her, he tugged on the hem of her T-shirt and dragged it over her head, her lust-drugged gaze and exploring fingers nearly setting him off.

He wanted her now, here. Everywhere. Forever.

His mobile jangled. Intent on Brooke's left breast, Lachie ignored it.

She touched his hair, voice breathless. 'You want me to grab that?'

'No.'

He nibbled, enjoying her gasp, thinking he'd like to taste lower, moving his hands in readiness. The phone stopped for a few seconds before starting up again. He pulled away and glared at it.

'You should probably answer. That's the third time it's rung.'

He probably should, but he was busy and as horny as hell. And one look at Brooke's flushed cheeks and neckline told him she was too.

She tilted her head to the side. 'It could be important.'

He let out a breath. She was right. 'Don't move.' One hand holding up his lowering jeans, he moved to the end of the table and inspected the screen. He pressed answer, eyes raking over Brooke's trembling, pale body, contemplating where to kiss her next.

'This better be good, shortarse.'

'It's Dad.'

Lachie froze. 'What about Dad?'

Brooke slid off the table and scooped up her T-shirt, moving to his side to place a hand on the centre of his back.

'He's collapsed. They're flying him to Dubbo.'

'Shit. What happened?'

'I don't know. I couldn't get much sense out of Mum. All she said was she found him out by the hayshed. The paramedics called for the chopper.'

He tucked the phone under his chin and began buttoning his jeans. 'Heart attack?'

'No one knows for sure, but Mum didn't think so. He's been sick, short of breath, lost a shitload of weight. More since we saw him. It could be anything.'

Lachie closed his eyes, picturing his father from his last visit home. The stiffness of his once powerful body, the deep crags in his face; Harry Cambridge was an age-ravaged shell of the man he had once been. Lachie had known something was wrong, they all had, but all he'd cared about was sticking it to the old man.

But that didn't mean Lachie didn't love him.

He focused back on Nick. 'Okay, I'm leaving now.'

'Me too. I'll see you there.'

He hung up and immediately called his mother, but her number went straight through to voicemail. Most likely her phone still sat on the kitchen table at Delamere. She'd never seen the point of a mobile. He checked his own voicemail and found her breathless message. Anxiety shuddered through her voice and he cursed himself for having left his phone behind when he'd risen to sort out the horses.

He turned to Brooke. 'It's Dad.'

'What's happened?'

'I don't know. He's collapsed. They're choppering him to Dubbo.' He touched her face. 'I'm sorry. I have to go.'

'Of course. What can I do to help?'

'Look after Billy.' He rubbed the back of his neck, trying to think past the cloud in his head. 'And you'll need to move the irrigation pipes in the Aquarius stand.'

'Don't worry about the farm. I can take care of that. And Billy.'

He kissed her quickly and headed to his room to grab a few clothes. When he returned to the kitchen he found her rapidly assembling a cheese sandwich. A bottle of water already stood on the table.

'For the drive,' she said, handing over both. 'You haven't had breakfast.'

'Thanks.' He glanced at the door, needing to leave. His mum needed her boys. Maybe the old man needed them too. But Brooke made him hesitant. He didn't want to leave her so soon after Poddy's death, after the joys of last night, after their momentous admissions. 'I meant what I said. I love you.'

She smiled and reached up on tiptoe to kiss him on the mouth. 'And I love you. Now go, your family needs you. Call me when you know something.'

———

The news wasn't good. For the fourth day in a row, Lachie sat beside his father's bed, holding his mother's hand, while Nick continued his endless pacing as they waited for the results of yet more tests. Lachie had given up snapping at Nick to stop. Pacing soothed his brother, helped him cope with the news. All Lachie had was his mum's trembling hand.

'He wouldn't go to the doctor,' she kept saying. 'I tried and tried but he refused to go.'

'It's not your fault, Mum.'

How many times over the last four days had Lachie said that already? Too many, but that didn't stop Minette castigating herself.

That it was no one's fault didn't shield any of them from guilt's savage sting.

Cancer. Terminal. No one to blame but fate or God or whatever mean-spirited entity controlled their lives. Blinking hard, Lachie raised his eyes to the ceiling, choking back thoughts that wouldn't stop steamrolling him flat. This was his father waiting for death's call. A man who wasn't old. A man with a family who loved him, despite his faults. Lachie should have done something. If the doctors had caught it earlier, they could have dug into their bags of tricks and saved Harry—chemo or whatever they did—but unchecked the insidious cells kept working on his body, burrowing into places they had no place, destroying the man from the inside.

Lachie lowered his gaze to the bed. The shock his dad's appearance first elicited had dulled to a sad ache. The specialist was amazed his father hadn't collapsed earlier, and put it down to Harry's size and strength. No sign of that size and strength existed now in the gaunt creature with watery eyes and hands curled like bird's claws; his appearance made even worse by the loss of will to live. No fight, only resignation. Out of everything, Lachie hated that the most.

He stood suddenly. 'I need some air.' He touched his mum's hair. 'You'll be okay for a while?'

She nodded and returned her puffy-eyed attention to her husband.

'You want company?' asked Nick.

Lachie shook his head. He wanted to be alone. He wanted to think away from this stifling room with its thick haze of sorrow and antiseptic.

He headed out the front of the hospital and crossed the road to the park that fronted the Golden Highway. In vibrant contrast to the park's dusty-leaved gums and drying grass, the sky glowed electric blue. Trucks and cars rumbled past, but even their fumes couldn't mask the clean herbal smell of the open air. Halting, he stared eastwards into the shimmering horizon as the afternoon sun soaked his back.

East, where Kingston Downs lay. Where Brooke was.

Moving into the shade, he pulled out his mobile phone and eyed the screen. So tempting to call her, to let her distract him from his pain, but the moment the specialist passed his verdict, Lachie understood things had changed forever. Best leave whatever they might have shared to his imagination, reserved for the countless lonely nights ahead at Delamere.

Voices floated towards him, a couple of smokers escaping the hospital grounds. He slotted the phone back in his pocket and cast another look up the road. He'd get over it. Like he'd get over the death of his father. Like he got over Tamsyn. He had to.

His dream of running Delamere had finally come true.

And the price was losing two people he loved.

Two weeks after his father's collapse, Lachie returned to the Valley. Spotting the familiar blue and gold Kingston Lodge Racing sign, he indicated and slowed. Hard to imagine only two months had passed since he came to work at Kingston Downs. Two months that had changed his life.

Now his life would change again.

Only this time, he couldn't shrug the feeling it would be for the worse.

At the first glimpse of Brooke riding Sod around the ménage his heart hiccupped like a drunk. Until that moment he hadn't realised how badly he missed her. Too much of his energy had been spent on coping with his father, his mother and, to a lesser extent, Nick, for him to focus on his feelings for Brooke. Now, longing sucked at his resistance, calling him to stay, asking for the impossible.

At the sound of his ute she halted Sod, a grin splitting her face as she waved. Then she leaned forwards and with an excited whoop urged Sod into a canter, performing a lightning turn to chase the ute across the yard.

He pulled up next to the cottage and quickly alighted, desperate for her, but Billy made it first. The little dog hurtled around the corner of the house yapping hysterically, before launching himself at his master, claws scrabbling Lachie's knees as he bounced up and down. Grinning, Lachie hoisted Billy up and ruffed his head, enjoying the ecstatic reunion.

Not to be outdone, Sod skidded to a standstill and let out a welcoming whicker. Dumping Billy, Lachie approached to scratch the horse's forehead while Brooke dismounted.

'I think he missed me,' he said, trying to keep things light.

'We all did.' She moved close to touch his arm. 'How's your dad?'

He shrugged. 'Better now they've let him go home. He hated the hospital.'

'And your mum and Nick? How are they coping?'

He stroked Sod's silky muzzle. 'Getting through.'

'And you?'

He blinked as the pang hit. The truth was he wasn't coping. Each time he looked at his father he felt guilty. Earning the run of Delamere this way seemed so wrong, but he acted strong. For his mum's sake, for Nick's, but mostly for his dad, who wanted the property where he'd lived all his life to be in a man's hands. A man whose heart lay as buried in its soil as Harry's own had done.

'I'm okay.'

'You sure?'

He nodded, using the silence to control himself. 'What about you?'

'I'm okay.' She smiled. 'Like you're okay. In other words, I'm crappy, but coping.' The smile dropped. 'I miss Poddy. Sometimes I can't breathe I miss him so much, but each day it gets a bit easier. Each day I try to do what you said, and remember that it's the future that counts.'

Unable to help himself he reached out to brush her cheek with the back of his hand, his heart squeezing as she closed her eyes and pushed against it. The urge to hold her, to kiss her was like a roar in his head, but it would be better for both of them if he kept his distance.

He let his hand drop and returned his focus to Sod, whose eyes almost rolled into the back of his head at the extra hard head rub he received. 'Why don't you put the big sook here away so we can talk?'

'Okay.' But she didn't move. Instead, she pressed against him, arms circling. 'I missed you.'

'I missed you, too,' he whispered, lowering his face into her hair, breathing the sweetness of her, while pointless longing pulled harder and harder at his bones. 'Come on,' he said, letting her go.

He waited for her on the verandah steps, watching her fuss around Sod, admiring her riding-muscled body, the way the sun shot bronze highlights through her brown hair. Storing memories. In an hour, maybe two, he'd be gone. He couldn't afford more time. The latest verdict from his dad's GP was that it could be any day; the palliative care nurse thought it might be longer. Whenever his dad passed away, Lachie wanted to be there.

Brooke sat next to him, smelling of horse and leather and her own special scent. He soaked it in, as he soaked in the changing colours of the yard as fast-travelling clouds decorated it in shadows and light. As he soaked in the fragrance of grass and soil, the cottage's old timbers. The tormenting sense of home.

He stroked the soft edges of her hair. 'It's getting longer.'

'I'm growing it out. Back to the way I used to have it. Ponytail girl. More me.'

He found it hard to take his hand away, but like this conversation, it had to be done. Two days ago, he'd phoned Angus to formally resign. It should have been Mark he called, but when it came to

Brooke he trusted Angus more, and, as Lachie hoped he would, Angus had agreed to keep the news under wraps for a few days. Brooke needed to hear of his resignation directly from him, not her brother or anyone else. So Lachie had arranged to meet Brooke today. To talk, explain, pack his things and leave Kingston Downs and her forever.

He'd kidded himself it'd be simple. Now, in her presence, it felt impossible, but this was one farewell that couldn't wait.

He closed his eyes, bracing himself. The time had come.

Her hand clasped his, worry adding a tremble to her voice. 'Lachie?'

'I've resigned, Brooke. I can't come back.'

Her fingers tightened. 'Not even after?'

'No. I'm moving back to Delamere. Permanently.' Her shaky breaths scraped his heart but he kept going. 'So Kingston Downs is all yours again. We've both got what we wanted.'

She snatched her hand from his and balled it against her stomach, her body curling in on itself as though for protection. 'I knew this would happen. From the moment you told me your dad was dying I knew you mightn't come back, but I couldn't help hoping you'd change your mind. I kept thinking about the time you said you'd like to stay.' She shook her head. 'But deep down I knew you wouldn't. Your heart wasn't here.'

On that she was wrong. His heart lay with hers.

She stood suddenly, brave and strong and clever and sexy even in heartbreak. All the things he loved about her. 'You'll be in a hurry to get back to your dad. I'll help you pack.'

He stood and placed his hands on her shoulders, gaze on hers. 'None of this means I don't love you.'

She smiled, eyes glittering with moisture. 'I know. And it doesn't change the way I feel about you either. I still love you like crazy.'

They smiled at one another, high on their declarations, but then reality hit. He was going to Delamere. Brooke was staying here, the place she'd never leave, the place he didn't want her to leave. They loved, but their dreams, their lives, ran at tangents.

The realisation made him want to roar his frustration at the world.

His grip on her shoulders tightened. He didn't want to let her go. Not now. Not ever. 'We could try the long-distance thing.'

Hope flared and faded just as fast. 'It'd only make things harder in the end. Because there would be an end, wouldn't there?'

'No.' Closing his eyes, Lachie let out a breath. He hated it, but she was right. 'Yes.' His grip eased. He opened his eyes and steadied his gaze on hers. 'We'll keep in touch, though.'

'You bet we will.'

She reached up to kiss him, the connection fierce, sad and edged with recklessness, as though she didn't care that each second only made the fissures in their hearts deeper, the damage irreparable.

She drew away to give him another courageous smile. 'Maybe in another lifetime.'

'Yeah, another lifetime.'

But as they stood in the shadow of the cottage clinging together, Lachie knew he didn't want another lifetime. He wanted this one.

———

Packing ended too soon. The cottage had come fully furnished and Lachie owned little. All he needed was to throw his clothes into bags, grab Billy's things, collect toiletries, books and other junk he'd collected in his time there, and dump it in the back of the ute.

He carried the last bag out with leaden feet. Brooke hovered by the back of the ute, her falsely bright expression belied by the desperate way she hugged Billy to her chest. He threw the bag in the tray and began securing the tonneau, all too conscious of the rapid drip of time.

The last loop secured, he opened the driver's side door and turned to Brooke.

Smiling, she kissed the top of Billy's head and passed him over. 'I'll miss him.'

'He'll miss you. We both will.'

He placed Billy on the passenger seat. Every breath seemed obstructed, struggling to get past the rock of loss lodged in his chest. 'I guess it's time.'

She nodded, biting her lip, holding everything in like he was. She placed her hand on his shirt and closed her fist, tugging the cloth. 'You take care.'

'I will.' He stroked his thumb over her trembling mouth. 'I have to go.'

Aching, he placed a brief tender kiss on her lips and forced himself into the car. Delaying wouldn't change anything, and they'd said all they could.

He reversed slowly, watching Brooke as she wandered across the yard to Sod. He kept watching as he changed gear, as he rolled forwards, as he passed, and in the rear-vision mirror as the ute crawled down the drive.

She stood straight-shouldered, head up. She'd be all right, in time. They both would.

And then he saw her grip her wrist.

He braked hard, dumping Billy to the floor. Leaving the engine running, he threw a quick apology to Billy before leaping out and running back to Brooke.

'Don't,' he said, tugging her fingers from her wrist and closing his big hands around her small ones. 'You don't need this any more. You're better than some cheap internet trick.'

'I don't want you to go.'

'I know, but I have to. And you'll get through this, just as you've made it through everything else. There's a great future out there waiting for you.' He kissed her forehead. 'Do something for me?'

'What?'

'Every time you think you need to rub your wrist, think of this.' With the last word, he kissed his way down her face, over her eyelids, across her cheeks, until he reached her soft, pliant mouth. He put everything into it, heart, soul, his dreams, his love, his loss, giving her everything he owned, everything she'd need to be strong, to be all he knew she could be.

He backed away. 'No more wrist pressing. Promise?'

She smiled, damp-eyed, flush-cheeked and beautiful. 'Promise.'

'Good,' he said, satisfied, and glad he'd stopped, despite the urgency to leave. The memory of that kiss, the way she looked now, would sustain him for the years it'd take to get over her. He returned her smile. 'See you next lifetime.'

This time when he put the ute into gear, he kept driving.

TWENTY

BROOKE SAT in the grassy space between Poddy's and Oddy's graves, hugging her knees. In the distance, as they had for millennia, the Valley's bordering dusty sandstone hills maintained their ancient vigil over a land ripe with spring pastures and crops. Closer in, on her neighbours' properties, tractors rolled around paddocks, Friesians grazed, bright white newborn lambs cavorted spindly-legged near their mothers, and the river kept its flow, moving on, as she should.

As she never could.

Over the last two days, since Lachie's departure, she'd come often to this place to think, sometimes talking aloud to her boys, telling them all she felt, all her regrets, all the dreams she still wanted to come true. But most of all she fretted over whether Lachie was okay. While he had still looked as dark-lashed handsome as ever during his visit, even in the sunshine his gold-flecked eyes had appeared shadowed, his mouth slightly turned down, his strong body slowed by fatigue. Not by much, but enough that she'd noticed.

Except during his kiss. There'd been no fatigue in that.

She touched her fingers to her mouth, remembering, and dropped them as a blue car turned into Kingston Downs' entrance. She tracked its path, amused when it stopped at the end of the drive, near the turn-off to the dairy, as though the driver were unsure whether to try for there or the cottage. The visitor chose neither, parking instead alongside the barn near the yards.

Her mother stepped out and, shading her eyes against the sun, cast around. Brooke sighed. She'd known this was coming. Ariel had been trying to talk to her since Poddy's death. On the few occasions Brooke succumbed to answering her calls, she could barely manage monosyllabic replies. Even talking to Angus came hard. Although each day found her a little better, Poddy's loss, now topped with that of Lachie, had left her too raw for sharing confidences. Andrew and Chloe had tried their best to be supportive, telling her that it was okay to let it all out, but Brooke didn't want to talk about her pain, or how shredded with grief she sometimes felt. Her emotions, especially those relating to Lachie, were too precious to be anything but private.

And she couldn't risk showing any signs of weakness, especially in front of her family, in case it plunged her into another cycle of well-meaning intervention.

After checking the barn, the cottage and the dairy, Ariel finally spotted Brooke. She climbed the slope, elegant as always in a pair of dark denim skinny jeans, long brown leather boots and a crisp white shirt with a fashionable leopard-print silk scarf knotted at her throat. Her hair, perfectly styled, curled around a face that, for once, reflected her age. Despite careful makeup, today every one of Ariel Kingston's fifty years showed.

Remorse, so close these days, stabbed pointed fingers into Brooke.

'Hi, Mum.' She patted a clear space beside her, next to Oddy's native sarsaparilla-coated grave, now cascading with violet flowers. 'Take a seat. Just mind the bees.'

Ariel sat, copying Brooke's leg-hugging pose. Leaning her head back and closing her eyes, she inhaled a deep draught of the clean country air. 'Ahh, that's better.' Smiling, she surveyed the view. 'It's pretty up here.'

'Very. Especially on a day like today.'

Niceties over, Ariel tilted her head to the side and contemplated her daughter. 'So how are you, Brookie?'

Brooke thought on the answer for a moment. 'Not bad, considering.'

'I'm sorry about Poddy. He was a good horse. I know how much you loved him.'

Instinctively, Brooke lowered a hand to his grave. Tiny weeds had formed a soft green blanket over its surface. She hadn't yet decided what to plant in his honour. Maybe a white-flowering ground rose. Something pure; special, like him.

'I made a mistake, Brooke. I'm sorry.'

Surprised, she studied Ariel, absorbing the new lines around her mother's mouth, the guilt-tugged eyes.

'I was so worried about you,' her mother continued. 'We all were. You changed so much after the accident. All that life and spark suddenly gone. And that thing with your wrist.' Ariel's brown eyes filled. 'You turned me inside out with worry. I just wanted you home where I could look after you. But you never liked Sydney, not even as a little girl. You always ran here when you were hurt or worried. Never to me.' She bit her lip. 'I always hated that.'

Brooke dropped her head, awash with shame.

Ariel released a tremulous sigh. 'I should have listened to Angus. He understood, but he's always understood you better than I have.'

'I'm sorry, Mum.'

'For not being like me?' Ariel squeezed her arm, her smile watery but sincere. 'Don't be. We love you just the way you are. Except for that haircut.' She brushed her hand over Brooke's ratty, half grown out hair. 'You should grow it back long again.'

'I'm trying to, but it seems to be taking forever. Chloe offered to do hair extensions but I told her false tails were for show ponies. And that's one thing I'm definitely not.'

They shared a smile and Brooke sensed the first splicing together of the ravaged ends of their relationship. In time, the knots would knit smooth, and maybe even new ends would form and meet and join, bonding them stronger. Making up for the past.

'Brooke,' said Ariel after a while, her fingers twisting. 'There's something else you should understand, something I'm not very proud of.'

Curious and nervous, she waited for her mother to continue.

'I've come to realise my motivations for getting you home weren't entirely selfless. I was desperately worried, certainly, but I also thought that with you at home, you could take over some of the responsibilities I have.' She sighed deeply, a heartfelt, weary sound Brooke had never heard her mother make before. 'I'm so tired of promoting the yard, being a fashion ambassador, having to charm people I don't even like.

'I love you all dearly, but I'm more than Christopher's wife. More than Angus, Mark and Brooke's mother. I'm Ariel Kingston, and I have passions and dreams like everyone else. Passions and dreams I've forsaken for too long.'

'So what do you want to do?' asked Brooke, then realised she already knew the answer. 'You want to paint.'

'Yes.' Ariel clutched at Brooke's hand, emphasising her words with finger squeezes. 'I love it. I really do. An artist is what I want to be, not a walking advertisement for some company.'

'So follow your dream.'

Letting go, she turned to gaze into the distance. 'It's not that easy.'

'No, you're right. Of course it's not. I'm sorry. With all that's happened I keep forgetting how much trouble the yard's in.' At her mother's quizzical expression Brooke shrugged. 'Mark told me. He said we might have to sell Kingston Downs.'

Ariel's lips pursed. 'Did he now?'

'It's okay, Mum. If it has to be sold it has to be sold. He's right. Even with the hay crops it's a drag on the yard.' She swallowed, her throat rough with the thought of losing her beloved home.

Ariel gripped her arm, hard. 'Brooke, listen to me. We would never sell Kingston Downs. Never. We wouldn't do that to you.'

'But Mark—'

'Mark is being Mark. We've hit a rough patch. It happens. We'll get through it just like we got through the last rough patch. You don't need to worry. Kingston Downs is safe. It'll always be safe.'

The relief of hearing Ariel's words filled Brooke's eyes with tears. Over these past weeks she'd tried to ignore the threat of losing Kingston Downs. She didn't have the energy for it. Poddy and Lachie had sapped her emotions, but deep within her heart the fear of more loss lingered, preventing her from healing properly. Now, with her mother's promise, she could look forward, regenerate, conquer her issues. Find herself again.

Life would be almost perfect.

Almost.

'Did he tell you he's going to be a father?' Ariel's mouth lifted in a wistful smile.

'Who? Mark? You're joking!'

Her mother nodded. 'That's another reason he's been so stressed lately. Apparently his girlfriend's family isn't thrilled with the idea.'

'I didn't even know he had a girlfriend.' Now Brooke thought of it, she had sensed a change in him in the last few months, but she had too many of her own problems to dwell on it.

'Neither did we until last week. Chris and I had dinner with Mark and Nayla last night. Lovely girl, beautiful eyes. Her family are Lebanese and run a restaurant in Coogee near Mark's apartment building. Nayla works there, which is where he met her. Love at first sight, apparently.'

'Are they going to get married?'

'I imagine so. Nayla's parents are putting a lot of pressure on them, and they adore one another. You can see it in their eyes, the way they touch. It's so romantic.'

Romance. Adoration. Touching. The words tumbled through Brooke's heart, igniting a flare of envy. If the world were right, these were things she and Lachie should be sharing.

'You and Lachie became close,' said Ariel, hitting home in the way only mothers can.

'Yes.'

'And?'

'And nothing. He's gone home.' She stood and began brushing dirt off her jeans. 'Come on, I'll introduce you to my new horse, Robert. He's a sweetheart.'

Ariel made no further mention of Lachie but Brooke was well aware of her interest. No matter how Brooke tried to avoid it, his name kept popping out as she showed Ariel around Kingston Downs. Even during lunch, when they ate around the dairy's pine table instead of at the cottage, Lachie's presence echoed. With each mention, Ariel's mouth would twitch, as though suppressing a knowing smile.

'Thanks for coming, Mum,' she said as they stood by Ariel's car late in the afternoon. 'It should have been me doing the apologising. I was horrible to you after Poddy was bitten, but I couldn't stop thinking that if I was here—'

'You were upset.'

'Yes, but I shouldn't have laid any blame on you.' Brooke leaned her bum against the rear door and stared past the dairy towards the hill. 'It wasn't anyone's fault. It was just one of those shitty bad-luck things, like Lachie's dad getting cancer.'

'You miss him.'

'Poddy? Desperately.'

'I meant Lachie, Brooke.'

Brooke looked away, clamping her mouth against the ache.

Ariel slung her arm around Brooke's shoulders and squeezed. 'If it's meant to be, you'll find a way to be together.'

'How, when he's at Delamere and I'm here? Time to just move on.' She smiled to cover her despair. 'Speaking of which, I've an appointment with a counsellor next month. She specialises in the sort of thing I've been through.'

'I'm glad.' Ariel stroked her hair. 'It was never going to sort itself out on its own, even for someone of your determination.'

'So what about you? What are you going to do?'

'I don't know. What I always do, I suppose. Carry on, keep smiling. It's what we Kingstons are good at. Anyway, if Mark and Nayla decide to marry I'll be too busy organising a wedding to worry, and then there'll be the baby.' Her face softened. 'I'm really looking forward to that.'

'They might produce the little girl you've always wanted.'

'I already have the little girl I always wanted.'

'Who smells of horse.'

'Ahh, but it's a nice smell. Why do you think I married your father?'

They laughed and Brooke turned to hug her tightly. 'I'm so sorry I've been awful.'

'You haven't, and anyway, I'm the one who's sorry for being selfish.' She patted Brooke's back. 'Please don't be a stranger to us. I know you don't like to leave here but we love seeing you. And I promise no more lunches with owners, make-overs or dress-ups.'

'No more Audrey Hepburn outfits?'

'No more Audrey Hepburn outfits.'

'It's a deal then.'

As Brooke stood in the yard waving her mother farewell, she experienced a kind of peace, as though life really was moving on. It had been the toughest year of her life, but she was making it through. Slowly, admittedly, but getting there.

All she needed was to fill the hollow Lachie left.

———

Brooke sat in Chloe's salon draped in a black protective cape, staring at her tired face. Chloe whipped around on her castored stool, snipping at Brooke's ragged mess of a hairdo, humming to the stereo as she worked.

Five weeks had passed since Lachie left, and the spring hay season was leaving Brooke as exhausted as it always did. When she wasn't worrying about the weather and moving irrigation, she was on the tractor, trying to time mowing, raking and baling in an effort to produce the perfect bale. And when she wasn't on the tractor she was walking windrows, scrunching the cut lucerne in her hands, listening for the special crackle and breaking of the stems that would tell her the hay was ready, just as her pop had taught her. Too wet and she risked mouldy bales and overheating stacks. Too desiccated and she'd lose precious leaves. As a precaution, she'd even resorted to drying lucerne in the dairy's microwave oven to calculate moisture content. With so few racehorses spelling on the property, the farm's worth was now measured purely by its lucerne production. She had to get it right.

Five weeks. Funny how she continued to measure the days that way, as though there might be some end to Lachie's absence. She couldn't even bring herself to move back into the cottage, just in case. The dairy held memories—his kindness when she was sick, his jack-of-all-trades skill—but the cottage's rooms fairly vibrated with emotion, none more so than the main bedroom. She dropped her eyes to the black cape, reminiscing. Aching.

'Thinking of Lachie again?' asked Chloe, halting her snips.

Brooke looked up and smiled wanly. 'Sorry. Seems to be a habit these days.'

'Have you heard from him?'

'Last night. Only briefly, though.'

Too briefly, as if he found talking to her difficult. A rapid update on how he was, how his father and family were faring. A quiet query about how Brooke was coping on the farm, her progress with the counsellor, an expression of pride when she admitted her slow but steady improvement. And every word, every breath, misted with their unuttered yearning for each other.

Chloe slid a strip of damp hair through her fingers and levelled the ends with two efficient clips. 'How's his dad?'

'Fading.'

'Must be so sad for him.'

'Yes,' said Brooke, remembering the anguish in Lachie's voice as he'd described his father's deterioration. The way he wished he had more time to make up for the lost years. How he regretted his hotheadedness. She tried to tell him not to fret, to make the most of the time he had left, but his regrets ran deep, and no words could smooth the fissures.

'I wish he'd stayed,' said Chloe, looking over Brooke's shoulder and pursing her lips slightly as she tugged on the sides of Brooke's hair, comparing the trimmed lengths by feel.

The bright salon lights highlighted the gold threads developing in the brown, the result of too much time spent in the October sun. After much discussion, Brooke and Chloe had finally agreed on a shaggy bob until she had more hair to style. Brooke longed for enough hair to scrape it back into a ponytail but the pixie cut was taking forever to grow out, and hell would freeze over before she'd resort to extensions.

'You liked him,' said Brooke with a squirm of jealousy.

'I did, but not in the way you think.' Chloe sighed and wheeled her chair to the front, laid her hands in her lap, fingers tense around her scissors, and held her sapphire gaze straight. 'I never really wanted to sleep with him, Brooke. For starters he's not my type, but even early on, it was pretty obvious that he was only interested in you.'

'So why make the bet?'

'For the same reason I've made every other stupid bet with Andrew. To get his attention.'

'Why?' Brooke's eyes widened as understanding dawned. 'Oh, shit.'

'Yeah. Oh, shit indeed.'

'Okay,' said Brooke, trying to digest the news. 'Okay. You're in love with Andrew?'

'Yes. Unfortunately he's in love with you. At least with Lachie here I had a chance. Now . . .' Chloe raised her scissors and dropped them again in despair. 'Andrew will think he can win you back.'

'But I don't want him. I never wanted him. He knows that.'

Besides, Chloe was wrong. Andrew, while friendly, hadn't made a single move since Lachie left. If anything, he'd been distant. It was as though the moment in the stable, when she'd refused his offer to help keep vigil over Poddy, had finally proved to Andrew where her heart lay. And with understanding came change and healing. Now, unlike Brooke with Lachie, he'd moved on.

She frowned, mind switching back to Chloe's revelation. 'So if you're in love with Andrew, what about all those other guys?'

Chloe made a wry face. 'I thought if I pretended I was over him, I could make myself believe it. Like a self-fulfilling prophecy. And maybe I needed to prove to myself how desirable I am.' She touched her chest for emphasis. 'That *I'm* someone special too. Trouble is, it's become second nature. And don't worry, I'm very aware of what people say about me.' She shook her head, disgusted, although whether in Andrew, Brooke or herself, Brooke couldn't tell. 'It's stupid, I know, but I felt better about myself if I knew that guys were interested in me—even if it was never Andrew. I think deep down I understood we'd only ever be friends, but I couldn't help hoping. I didn't want to stop believing that it might happen. But then he went and fell in love with you.' Suddenly her face crumpled, bright blue eyes pooling.

'Oh, Chloe, why didn't you tell me?'

'I was desperate to, but I was afraid it'd make things weird between us. That it'd spoil our closeness. And to be honest I was a bit jealous. I knew it wasn't your fault but it still hurt.'

Hearing the pain in Chloe's voice, Brooke studied her friend, acutely aware of how much had changed between them over the course of this year. All those secret desires slowly eroding their once happy triumvirate. Desires Brooke had never even knew existed, but should have sensed.

'I'm so sorry, Chloe. I wish you'd said. I wish Andrew had said. But most of all I wish we could have fixed this years ago.'

'Me, too.' Chloe smiled a little. 'Might have saved me a lot of bad sex.'

'So we're okay? You and me?'

'Don't be a doofus, of course we are.'

Relief bursting across her face, Brooke flicked the cape to free herself, launched from her chair and wrapped her arms tight around Chloe. They embraced for a long moment before releasing each other, smiling despite their tears.

Brooke sat back while Chloe inspected her face in the mirror and ran the corner of a towel under her eyes to tidy the mascara smudges. Makeup fixed, Chloe picked up her scissors and squatted back on her stool, before scooting behind Brooke to resume cutting.

'So what are you going to do about Lachie?'

'Nothing. As I said to Mum, there's no point. He's there and I'm here. May as well be the other side of the world.'

'I really wish he'd stayed. Andrew knew right from the start Lachie was exactly your type. I knew it'd be easy to get him to agree to the bet—he wanted Lachie out of play.' She made a face. 'He's so transparent sometimes. Stuffed if I know how you never suspected.'

'I did. Sort of. I just didn't want to admit it. I was too scared it'd ruin our friendship.'

'Nearly did anyway.'

'Yes.' Suddenly Brooke smiled and clapped her hands to ease the tension. 'Right. So what are we going to do about you and Andrew?'

Chloe shrugged. 'Nothing. What's there to do? He's not interested. Whatever happens, one thing's for sure. I'm not making any more stupid bets. I'm worth more than that.' She caught Brooke's eye. 'Lachie did me a big favour knocking me back. It made me really think about my life, what I was doing to myself. I turn twenty-five in a few weeks. What sort of twenty-five-year-old shaves her head to get some bloke's attention?' Her mouth set in a determined line. 'We're not kids any more, Brooke. We're adults, and it's about time we all grew up. It's fine for Andrew. He's so rich he could buy someone's heart if he wanted to.'

'He couldn't buy mine.'

'No. But he's tried enough times. He's still trying to with all that Kingston Downs business.'

Brooke shot upright so fast Chloe's scissors flew out of her hand and clattered to the floor. She whipped around and, gripping the chair's arms, jutted her face at Chloe. 'What Kingston Downs business?'

'He's been trying to buy the property for months, Brooke.' Chloe's expression turned sullen, the bitterness she'd kept so well hidden slithering to the surface. 'I imagine it's meant to be his big present to you. The one offer you could never refuse.'

'It was *Andrew*?'

Chloe nodded.

'Oh God.' Backing away, Brooke put a shaky hand to her mouth as wave of nausea threatened to engulf her. 'But . . .' Brooke shook her head, trying to understand. 'Why would he do that to me?'

'Because he loves you. Why else?'

'But he doesn't! I've been worrying myself sick over this. If it weren't for Mum promising the family would never sell I'd still be panicking over it. Oh God, I need some water.' Tearing at the velcro tape securing her cape, Brooke tossed it aside and ran to the wash station. She turned the cold-water tap on flat out, using the shower-head extension to rinse the acid taste from her mouth. Even with her nausea under control, her trembles refused to subside. Andrew buying Kingston Downs? It defied belief.

She slumped into the basin's reclining chair and rubbed her hands over her wet face. Andrew. How could he? He was supposed to be her friend. As was Chloe.

Slowly, she dropped her hands and focused her cold gaze on Chloe. 'You knew and you never said anything.'

Her friend's gaze dropped. 'Only because Andrew let it slip. I'm sorry I didn't tell you, but he made me swear not to.'

'So why tell me now?'

Chloe walked to the chair and knelt by its side, her palm covering the back of Brooke's hand. 'Because I'm so over this; the secrecy, the lies, the heartache. Andrew needs to hear it from you, that even Kingston Downs won't change your mind. Otherwise he'll still hold out hope, and I just can't handle it any more.' Chloe wiped her cheek as a tear spilled down it slowly. 'And no, I'm not a complete idiot. I know Andrew might never be interested in me, but I need a chance to find out.' Voice choking, she held up her forefinger. 'One chance, Brooke. It's not too much to ask, is it?'

'No,' replied Brooke, sympathy softening her anger towards Chloe.

'So you'll talk to him?'

Oh yeah, Brooke would talk to Andrew all right. She needed to get to the bottom of this. He was over her, no matter what Chloe believed, so why try to buy Kingston Downs? It didn't make sense.

'Yes.'

'Thanks. It means a lot.' Chloe grinned through her tears. 'Who am I kidding? It means everything.' She kissed Brooke on the cheek. 'Come on, let's finish this trim. We need to keep you looking awesome in case Lachie comes back.'

'He won't,' said Brooke, lowering herself into the squishy cutting chair.

Chloe leaned down and wrapped her arms around Brooke's neck, looking at her in the mirror, expression alive with hope. 'But we can dream, you and I.'

Brooke smiled and clutched reassuringly at Chloe's arm. 'Sure we can.'

———

Jaw set, Brooke left the salon and drove the twenty-five kilometres to Willowgrove with her hands tight around the wheel and her mouth as thin as a knife slash. The anger towards Andrew she'd suppressed in Chloe's presence festered like an ugly boil. What sort of game was Andrew playing? He knew how stressed over Mark's threats she'd been, yet he'd been one of the causes. And what the hell did he want with Kingston Downs anyway?

She flicked the indicator and drove towards the main house, a sprawling white building surrounded by an English garden that wound around the house in a series of landscaped 'rooms'. As teenagers, she, Chloe and Andrew had spent countless summer hours exploring the garden's hidden nooks, delighting in the cool shadowed groves and the swathes of colourful flowers and plants, lazing on wood and stone benches, wading in the garden's decorative pools. Sharing the secret, intense language of adolescence.

She slid to a stop outside the end bay of the four-car garage, spraying up white gravel. Slamming the door, she took a moment to calm herself and think where Andrew could be. Even with the lowering sun, the temperature remained warm, the sky a summery peach and gold. She stalked around the edge of the house towards the pool and entertainment area, where, when he wasn't in the stables, Andrew tended to live in the summer months. Where the three of them had partied and laughed and loved as only long-time friends can do. Without troubles. Happy. Or so she'd thought.

'Brooke!' Andrew waved before kicking off the pool wall and sleeking through the water in clean fluid strokes. He emerged at the edge near her feet, dark-gold skin sparkling with water drops, teeth perfect and white as he grinned. The muscles across his shoulders flexed as he planted his hands on the pool edge and raised his body out of the water, eyes wide with happiness at seeing her.

Another woman might have been mesmerised by the sight of his lithe body, his laughing, handsome face, but Brooke remained, as always, unmoved.

'You look knackered,' he said, dripping beside her, oblivious to her crossed arms and furious expression.

'Why?' she asked.

He blinked, confused, before his eyes registered her stance.

Expression sobering, he headed towards the pool room, with its long bar and lounge area complete with a large, flat-screen television tuned to MTV, and game consoles of every make. 'Why what? Do you want a beer? I have Peronis, your favourite.'

'You know damn well what. Kingston Downs, Andrew. My home. Have you any idea the stress you've caused me?' She placed her hand over her heart. 'How scared I've been?'

He looked away from her, as though it pained him to meet her gaze, and quickly ducked his head to stare inside the fridge, fingers tense around the door edge. 'I didn't mean for that to happen.' For a long while he said nothing, then he pulled out two beers, shut the door and leaned against it. 'Chloe told you everything, I suppose.'

'You mean there's more than you trying to steal my home from me?'

'I wasn't trying to steal anything, Brooke.'

'So what were you trying to do then?' She crossed her arms and shifted her weight onto one hip. 'Explain it to me.'

He walked behind the bar, found a bottle opener and flicked the caps off both beers before heading towards her, one held out. When she refused, he shrugged and took a slug from his bottle, watching her. No laughter danced in his dark eyes now. This was serious.

'You think I was trying to buy your love.'

'Oh, come on, Andrew. You might do some dumb things some-times, but you're forgetting I've known you long enough to know you're not that stupid. So why?'

'Because of what happened, that's why.' Anguish twisted his face. 'Whose fault do you think the crash was, Brooke? I knew you were exhausted. I knew I should have followed you. But I was angry and hurt and too busy licking my wounds to do the right thing. And look what happened. I've told you before I'd do anything to make up for what you went through. Kingston Downs mightn't have brought Oddy back or cured Poddy, but it would've been something.'

'It was an accident. No one's fault.'

'I shouldn't have forced you to kiss me.'

'And I shouldn't have made the bet in the first place! For God's sake, Andrew, it was an *accident*. I never blamed you. The only person I ever blamed was myself, and thanks to my counsellor I don't even do that any more.' She grimaced. 'Well, not much.'

Confusion knitted his brow. 'You mean you never blamed me?'

'No!'

He placed the two beers on the floor and, without hesitating, wrapped his arms around her. Brooke stiffened, but Andrew made no move except to press his face into her shoulder. 'I'm sorry you were frightened about losing Kingston Downs.'

'You should have told me what you were doing. I was so stressed. And if you'd bought the place, I could have ended up hating you.'

He pulled away. 'That was a chance I had to take if I was going to make things right.'

'They were never wrong. Except for,' she flapped a hand, 'you know.'

'That's all over now. As you said, I might be dumb sometimes but I'm not completely stupid.'

'Except when it comes to Chloe.'

He threw her a 'huh?' look. 'What's Chloe got to do with anything?'

She let out a breath. Time for more truths. 'She's crazy about you.'

Laughter bubbled from his mouth. At ease now, he bent to retrieve the beers, shoving one into Brooke's hand. 'You can't be serious.'

'Deadly.'

His grin dropped. 'But—'

'Trying to cure herself,' interrupted Brooke, knowing exactly what he was thinking. 'And show you just how desirable she is.'

He shook his head, overcome with the same sense of disbelief Brooke had experienced. 'I suppose you knew?'

'I had no idea. She only admitted it this afternoon.' Brooke drank from her bottle. 'But I realise now there were signs. I just didn't read them. Like with you. And there I was thinking we knew everything about one another, when the reality was we knew so little. So much for friendship.'

'You're missing the point. It was for the sake of our friendship I never admitted how I felt. Do you think we'd have stayed friends all this time if I had?'

Brooke stared at the television, mind only half registering the video that was playing. Andrew's words held truth. This mess had occurred precisely because of their friendship. Because they all cared so much for what they shared.

'You're right,' she said. 'We would have fallen out long ago. But now we all know the truth, and that means things aren't ever going to be the same again. And we're going to have to deal with it. You and Chloe especially.'

He stared into the neck of his beer. 'I don't know if I can.'

'Take a gamble, Chiang-man.' She smiled and patted his shoulder. 'You never know, you might come out the winner this time.'

TWENTY-ONE

LACHIE ROSE, dressed and, as had become his habit these last seven weeks, headed immediately for his father's room. He paused outside the door, bracing himself. The cancer, so widespread and unstoppable, had reduced Harry Cambridge to a series of angles. Triangular cheekbones, sharp-edged shoulders, elbows and fingers bent like set squares, and eyes which, when they weren't closed with fatigue, narrowed in on Lachie like lasers.

'Hey, Dad,' he said as he knocked and entered. Though he kept his expression impassive, the sight of his father never ceased to send a cold rush through his gut. 'Where's Mum?'

His father lifted a hand and pointed a bony finger in the direction of the bathroom.

Lachie listened for a moment, satisfied when he heard the faint tinkling of the shower. Good. He wanted a moment alone with his dad, time to say the words he'd been aching to say for weeks but which he'd kept inside him, intimidated by those laser looks. Unsure what reception he'd receive. Fearful of contempt and rejection.

Steeling himself, he pulled up a chair close to his father's head and sat on its edge, leaning forward so Harry wouldn't miss a word. The palliative care nurse said it wouldn't be long now and he believed her far more than the GP who'd written his dad off a month ago. The Home Hospice mentor had made similar noises, preparing them for the inevitable. The one small mercy was that Harry would die at home, with his family around and Delamere's air in his lungs.

And, if Lachie's prayers came true, peace with his son in his heart.

Harry hitched those pain-filled eyes to Lachie's face and for a moment, Lachie thought he wouldn't be able to do it, but his resolve held and the words, long overdue, emerged.

'I'm sorry, Dad. For everything. For running out when I was a kid, to doing the same again last year. For never giving you the respect you deserved. For not being the son you wanted.

'I should have . . .' Lachie swallowed and breathed deeply. 'I never meant what I said. I was never ashamed of you. I just wasn't mature or smart enough to understand.'

Harry's hand rose from the blanket, clawlike fingers searching. Lachie leaned closer, uncertain, afraid. 'What is it? What do you need?'

'Hand,' Harry whispered dryly.

Lachie leaned back slightly. Hand? His dad turned his palm over and held it open. Lachie stared at it as something deep and painful cleaved his chest. A flood threatened, but he held it in check with a vice-like clench of his jaw. Not now. Not at this moment. Later, when he could walk away and give vent to his pain and grief and let his emotions dissolve in private.

Hesitantly, he placed his palm against his dad's and gripped it.

Harry's watery eyes fixed on him. 'Proud you're my son.'

Lachie's throat swelled. He bent his head. After all he'd done he didn't deserve his father's grace.

'Lachie.'

He looked up and, for the first time, he saw in his father's ravaged expression the approbation he'd sought since boyhood.

'Love you.'

'I love you too, Dad.'

His father's eyes closed, his grip slackening as weakness claimed him. Lachie kept hold of his hand, imprinting the feeling to memory.

Arms draped around his shoulders. His mother kissed his cheek. 'Thank you.'

'You heard?'

'Not all of it, but enough.' She hugged him harder. 'He always regretted driving you away.'

'I thought it was what he wanted.'

'No. He loved you. He wanted to work with you. He just didn't know how to communicate.'

'Neither did I.' He glanced at her, mouth crooked with regret. 'Except by arguing.' He looked back at his dad, now asleep in his morphine haze. 'I'm sorry, Mum. It must have been hard on you.'

'Doesn't matter. What matters is you're here now.' She straightened and patted his shoulder before kissing the top of his head. 'Go and have your breakfast. I'll keep watch.'

But Lachie was too full of emotion to eat. Instead, he wandered outside, Billy tracking alongside, and headed away from the house to the back of the machinery shed. The place he used to escape to as a boy when he was upset or angry. Where he'd yank grass from the dirt and throw stones and think defiant thoughts, unaware that with each moment he spent indulging his moods, his father had taken another unknown step towards death.

Morning sun lit and warmed the corrugated iron and turned the dew-covered, weed-infested area pretty with sparkling colour. He leaned against the shed wall, staring sightlessly across the farm, his mind rolling over his father's words, the intensity of his expression.

So many years. So much wasted time. And for what? Ego.

He slid downwards until he crouched with his arms draped over his knees, wondering how many more mistakes he was going to make with his life. Sensing his distress, Billy shuffled to his side and scraped a dirty wet paw down his work trousers, before cocking his head and whining.

Lachie stroked his head. 'Made a bit of a fuck-up of things, didn't I, Billyboy?'

He smiled indulgently at the dog, grateful for Billy's unrelenting adoration and innate ability to sense when his master needed comfort. He scooped the dog into his lap and tickled his chin. Excited by the attention, Billy tried to lick his face but Lachie nudged him away until Billy settled down and relaxed under the brush of his palm, and together they watched the sun climb and the dew evaporate and brightness gather over Delamere.

Peace with his father. A long time coming, but made.

———

Lachie dug his hand into his suit pocket and fingered his phone, a gesture he'd been making all morning. The compulsion to hear Brooke's voice, her soft words of condolence, made more poignant by her unmistakable concern for him, remained as huge as when he'd first noticed her missed call. Manners dictated he maintain his presence at the wake, and he didn't want to leave his mother. Any moment, and he feared her facade of quiet stoicism would crack.

He nudged his way to her side and bent to talk quietly in her ear. 'You okay?'

Her smile of reassurance was heavy with sadness. She gripped his hand and squeezed. 'I'm fine, Lachie. It's nice to hear people talk about your father with affection.'

'If you need a lie-down, just go. Everyone will understand.'

She reached high to touch his cheek. 'You're such a good boy.' She looked over to where Nick had his arm slung proprietarily around his fiancée Gaby's shoulders. 'You both are. He looks so happy.'

'Yes,' said Lachie, determined to keep his voice neutral. Each time he looked at Nick, jealousy sent his heart plunging. Nick and Gaby had announced their engagement four days ago, only a few hours before Harry died. Neither Nick nor Lachie was sure their dad had heard or understood, but their mum had assured them he had and was thrilled by the news. How she could tell, Lachie couldn't fathom. Harry's wakeful moments were rare and brief, his gaze seemingly unfocused, but Lachie supposed thirty-plus years of marriage taught you to read the small signs, and he believed her.

Minette gave his hand another squeeze. 'Don't worry. Your turn will come.'

'Haven't had much luck so far.' Kissing his mother's cheek, he stepped out of the way and let another well-wisher pass by.

Delamere's backyard milled with people, many of whom he recognised, but quite a few he didn't. He'd been away too long, chasing his own ideals. He grabbed a beer from an ice-filled esky and moved to the side to observe. Ever since his arrival home he'd suffered that same strange sense of unbelonging, as if he was no longer accepted here. Nick, in contrast, fitted perfectly—but so he should. Until he'd gone to uni a year ago he'd never left the place.

Lachie watched Nick with Gaby. He'd been genuinely pleased at their announcement, shaking his brother's hand with pride, kissing Gaby with delight. That the couple adored each other, no one doubted. The way Nick looked at Gaby with that sort of half dreamy, half I-can't-believe-my-luck expression said more than any declaration of love. And Gaby wasn't much better, with her huge smiles and tender touches. But as they'd outlined their wedding plans over a bottle of red wine at Delamere's kitchen table, Lachie's insides had turned colder and colder, his despair deeper, and his yearning for Brooke a constant strum on his heartstrings.

He fingered his phone again. Stuff it. He needed to hear her voice.

After glancing quickly over to his mother to check on her wellbeing, Lachie ducked around the side of the house and headed for the front verandah.

Billy raised his head from his paws, in a deep fug after being tied up in the shade under the house for the day, while delicious barbecue aromas tormented his twitching nostrils. Lachie paused to scratch his head. He should have remembered to bring a sausage, but given the amount of food his mother's friends had laid on for the wake, Billy wouldn't be short of leftovers to scoff.

Leaving Billy, he moved to the verandah and sat down on the top step and placed the beer beside him, thinking of how, not so long ago, he'd done the same at Kingston Downs. Only then Brooke had shared his perch, her hands jammed in to her body as though to protect herself from the news of his departure.

He jiggled the phone in his hand, wondering what the hell he was thinking. It was over. *Over*. His place was here now, managing Delamere, like he'd always wanted.

'You going to ring her or just sit there moping?' said Nick from the corner of the house.

Lachie eyed his brother, looking past him for his shadow, Gaby.

'She's with Mum,' said Nick, reading his mind. 'Thought you and I needed a chat.'

'Not a great day for chats.'

'No day's great for you at the moment.' He took the space next to Lachie, long legs stretching out, his carefully buffed boots now dusty. 'Bear with a sore head doesn't begin to describe you.'

'Funny, I didn't realise watching your father die was meant to put you in a party frame of mind.'

'I'm not talking about that. I'm talking about her.' He pointed to the phone. 'So are you going to call her?'

'Not with you here.'

'Fair enough.'

Lachie waited, expecting his brother to take the hint and leave. Instead, Nick remained seated, picking at non-existent loose threads in his trousers.

'Well?'

Nick straightened and angled his body to face him. 'I'm not going back to uni next year.'

'Don't be a dickhead. You only have two years to go.'

'Two years too long. I've had enough.' He gave Lachie a steady look, one Lachie recognised from childhood. A set-jawed, narrow-eyed expression that dared Lachie to try to change his mind. 'I never even wanted to go in the first place.'

Lachie swapped his phone for his beer. He had a feeling he was going to need it. A ripple of laughter filtered from the backyard. People enjoying themselves as they celebrated Harry Cambridge's life. What he and Nick should be doing too.

Lachie took a slug of beer. 'I buried my father this morning. I'm not in the mood for this.'

'He was my father too, Lachie, and I knew him a shitload better than you did.'

'All right,' he said, rising and placing his beer next to his phone. 'Let's get this over with. I know you've never forgiven me for walking out. Do what you have to do and then leave me alone.'

'Don't be such a fucking drama queen. I never resented you for walking out. Either time. I was happy you did. At least then Mum and I didn't have to put up with you and Dad arguing all the time. But you can't just waltz back in here and expect to take over as though you own the place. You don't. Mum and I are partners in this too.' Palms out, he stood and took a pace toward Lachie. 'Look, I've wanted to tell you for months. I'm sorry it has to be now that you hear it, but I'm not going back to uni. That was always your dream for me, not mine. I was happy to stay here being a dumb-fuck farmer like my old man, but you kept at me and then even Dad thought it might be a good idea.'

'Dad?' Lachie puffed out air in disbelief. 'Bullshit.'

'Yes, Dad. He knew the place was run-down, that he hadn't done the best, and he knew that if things became really bad it'd be helpful to have another means of bringing in money. And teaching pays well. So I agreed. But I'm not agreeing any more. As soon as Gaby's organ-ised she's moving in with me here. Mum says she's happy to move into Gran's old place in town to give us some privacy, so that just leaves you to sort out.'

Lachie's heart pounded. This was all too much. 'You want me off Delamere.'

'No, I don't. I'd love to work with you, bring this place up to scratch. But you need to decide what you want. And I don't think it's this. Maybe once it was. Maybe it was what drove you, but it doesn't any more.' He pointed towards the step and Lachie's phone. 'She does.'

'Her name's Brooke. Brooke Kingston, and it's over.'

Over before it even started. But not in his heart.

'Yeah, you keep telling yourself that, bro. I've seen you. Standing out here looking north-east. Daydreaming about Brooke. You think I don't know? You think I don't understand? Course I do. Takes a man in love to recognise another.'

Lachie glared at Nick, brain working over ways to tell him where to shove it, but fuming at the truth was as pointless as the hours he spent longing for Brooke. He *did* think about her. Sometimes he could go an hour without doing it. Once, over these dragging, painful weeks, when the farm's ancient tractor gave him grief and his dad had taken a turn, he managed an entire half-day without her name appearing in his head. But she was always there, at the back of his mind, smiling her sweet clear-eyed smile at him.

'My home's here,' he said stubbornly, refusing to give up on the ambition that had ruled his life for so long.

Yet all the while a little voice in the back of his mind kept reminding him of the time when he'd planned to forsake Delamere for Pitcorthie. When he'd decided to take the biggest chance of his life and tell Brooke that his dreams had changed. That he wanted a life with her.

But that was before his father had collapsed, before the world lurched and threw him off balance.

Nick smiled. 'You sure about that?' He nodded toward Lachie's phone. 'Go make your call. Then have a good think about how you feel when you hear her voice. Might help you realise what you really want.'

But Lachie didn't need to call. By the time Nick sauntered back around the end of the house, he'd already decided.

TWENTY-TWO

BROOKE SLID in behind the wheel of the LandCruiser and took several deep breaths, focusing on the cognitive techniques her counsellor had provided to combat her anxiety. The hydra swirled, whispering its terrible doubts, but she defeated each hissing head with logic and the well of gut-deep determination she'd discovered within herself. She could do this. She'd done it before. Two horses in the float were no different to one.

Chloe cupped her hand over the window edge, fingernails glittery with metallic pink polish. 'Are you okay?'

'Fine,' said Brooke, fists closing around the wheel as she ran through her checklist of reassurances. Robert and Sod were safe and calm. The road to the Pony Club grounds easy to navigate, the November day bright, visibility perfect, the LandCruiser and float in excellent condition. Chloe would follow behind. There was nothing to worry about. 'I'm fine,' she repeated, this time with more conviction.

Chloe cocked her head. 'You sure?'

Tight-lipped, Brooke nodded. Although she'd managed to tow horses around Kingston Downs without a problem, this was only her second trip out on the road alone. The week before, she'd taken Sod to the local dressage club's unofficial competition day at Muswellbrook showgrounds, and though she'd arrived covered in sweat and exhausted, she'd done it. And to her great pride, so had Sod. The confidence Lachie had instilled in him remained, and together they managed to overcome their fears. If nothing else, she would be forever grateful to Lachie for that.

Lachie. God, she had to stop thinking about him. Life moved on. No point wallowing in regrets and fear. She'd done enough of that to last a lifetime.

She smiled at Chloe. 'Absolutely positively fine. So let's get this show on the road.'

Chloe patted her arm and grinned. 'Attagirl.'

Brooke put on her seatbelt and started the ignition, concentrating on keeping the hydra at bay, but the monster was already settling, as though it recognised an entity tougher than itself. Brooke's mouth curled as her confidence surged. Yeah, she could do this, all right. She could do anything. Maybe today she and Robert could even put the Chiang-man in his place.

For a moment, worry for her two friends distracted Brooke from her pattering pulse. In the weeks since Chloe's revelation, Brooke had definitely sensed a certain electricity between Andrew and Chloe. Chloe tried to act her usual cheery self, but Brooke understood the emotional fragility and fear lurking behind her mask. Brooke fretted that, despite her best efforts, their friendship wouldn't survive another crisis.

She shook her anxiety off, killing it with reasoning. They were mature adults, not children. They'd survive this as they'd survived the last. After all, no matter what their dramas, life just kept moving on.

Life. Moved. On.

If she kept telling herself that enough she'd end up believing it.

She checked her mirror. Chloe waited patiently behind in her Nissan. Brooke hung her right arm out the window and waved to reassure her, then, with a deep breath, put the car into gear, slowly released the clutch and chugged across the yard towards the drive and the road.

Brooke drove with deliberate care, mind fixed firmly on her task. She couldn't afford to let it wander. Once a panic attack snatched her, it could be impossible to stop. Knowing the journey would be slow, she'd allowed extra time. No hurry. Just an easy six-kilometre trip to Pitcorthie Pony Club for a showjumping training day. A day among friends with a bit of friendly competition thrown in.

Although when it came to beating Andrew, there'd be nothing friendly about it. His endless brags about Marchment's incredible progress and talent had ignited her professional fire. Darling Robert might not have Marchment's imperious breeding and looks, but he possessed more talent in one hoof than Andrew's sleek black colt would ever own. Come competition time, she'd prove it.

She flicked the indicator and wheeled the float through the wide, white-painted double gates of the Pony Club grounds, sweat-covered hands slipping slightly on the wheel. Only when she straightened and trundled left past the ageing timber-clad clubhouse towards the tree-sheltered parking area did she realise how rapidly her heart was beating. Halting alongside Andrew's red and gold float, she let out a long breath and pressed her forehead against the steering wheel.

A thump sounded on the window, jerking her up.

Andrew opened the door, handsome as always in a red, designer-logoed polo shirt, a pair of beige breeches, brown short boots and suede half chaps. 'Cheer up. You made it.'

Brooke grinned as elation burst past the last ragged edges of her tension. 'So I did!' She tumbled out of the car, alive and bubbling with accomplishment, and stretched her fisted hands skywards. 'Yes! God, I'm in a mood now.' She poked a finger at Andrew. 'You better be on your mark, Chiang-man, because I'm going to whup your butt.'

'Want a bet?'

She froze as the hydra writhed and slithered painful memories into her mind.

Andrew gripped her shoulder in apology. 'Shit, Brooke, I'm sorry.'

Brooke forced a smile, determined to maintain her good mood. She'd made it to the grounds, with the horses and herself in one piece. No filth-spouting monster was going to ruin what she'd achieved.

'Don't worry about it.' A bang sounded from the float. Sod reminding her of his presence. He probably thought he was competing, but she'd packed him simply for the ride. Practice, after all, made perfect. For both of them. 'Come on, help me get this lot sorted.'

Despite her initial rough moment, Brooke settled into the morning. The nerves that had rattled her insides since waking faded as she immersed herself in what she loved best—delighting in the outdoors, riding and chattering about horses and life with friends, threading herself into Pitcorthie's tight community fabric. She instructed a class of juniors for an hour, running their ponies through training drills over poles and low-set cavaletti, yelling encouragement as they bounced cutely around, little legs and hands pumping, grins huge.

They reminded Brooke of herself at that age, when fortnightly Pony Club rallies were the highlight of her life. She'd scramble out of bed at dawn, waking Nan and Pop with her clatter, and belt out to the paddock to fetch her Connemara pony, Rascal. She'd spend the early morning grooming his dense, unruly coat, trimming the shaggy hairs around his fetlocks that seemed to grow longer and thicker no matter how many times she cut them back, and combing his mane and tail into temporary submission. By the time her grandparents loaded Rascal onto the float, her insides would be fizzing like a shaken-up Coke can.

Brooke smiled to herself as she watched a spectacularly freckled little girl with long blonde plaits coax her fat been-there-done-that pony over the last jump. Funny how the world turned in circles. This morning she'd felt the same as she had as a child, although for different reasons. And just as when she was young, bright sunshine, fun and laughter burned her nerves away and life continued, a little bit hollow without Lachie, but filled with hope and joy.

At lunchtime she joined Andrew and Chloe in the clubhouse, munching sauce-smeared steak sandwiches, chatting to riders and parents, before heading out to help set up the junior showjumping courses for the afternoon's competitions. The senior course was already built. She and Andrew had walked it earlier, goading each other as they measured strides, and Brooke remained confident that Robert had the jump on Marchment. She'd watched Andrew on the arrogant show-off earlier, and while the colt demonstrated undoubtable talent, Andrew had yet to harness it. The horse only trusted himself, not his rider.

After tacking up Robert, she spent a few moments with Sod, who kept casting her confused, sulky looks, not understanding why he wasn't being booted and saddled when he was, after all, the yard's resident superstar.

'Your day will come,' she said, kissing the tip of his nose. Although not until autumn when the local show season ratcheted into action. A nice relaxing summer growing fat was Sod's reward for enduring a difficult year. In fact, a holiday was what she planned for all the horses, and, bar haymaking, for herself. She'd earned a break. They all had. And when the new year rolled round, with it would come a new outlook, a new life.

Another lifetime.

She sighed and patted Sod's cheek, and moved around the float to Robert. Another lifetime was a dream. This one was real and she had every intention of making the most of it, with or without Lachie.

She rode out to the warm-up area on a loose rein, letting Robert peer around. As expected, the horse remained unperturbed by the activity—one of the advantages of picking up a horse with experience of Pony Club and shows. After several minutes' warm-up, she popped him over the small practice jumps provided, revelling in the immediate change in his demeanour. Robert reminded her so much of Poddy. They both shared the thrill of the jump, were supremely confident in their ability and, more importantly, trusting of their rider.

'Ready for a butt-whupping, Chiang-Man?' she taunted as she cantered past Marchment. The black horse skittered sideways, nostrils flaring, glossy coat rippling like satin. Only Andrew's strength and gluelike seat kept the colt in check.

'You don't stand a chance on that big dope.'

'Oh, yeah?'

'Yeah.'

She cantered back to his side. 'Then put your money where your mouth is.'

He shook his head. 'Don't, Brooke.'

'It's okay.' And to her delight she found it was. 'One bet. Come on, what have you got to lose?'

His eyes narrowed. 'I don't know yet, do I?'

Brooke indicated the clubhouse, where Chloe sat on the top rail of its surrounding fence, licking an ice-cream and laughing at some joke of the club secretary's. Her bright-pink top stretched tight over her ample bosom, its glittery silver motif matching the sparkle of her fingernails. A tightly woven French braid kept her hair from her face, exposing her delicate profile and creamy skin. Expertly applied makeup highlighted her sapphire eyes, matched by navy capri pants that clung to her long slender legs. She looked happy and gorgeous, a woman to make any man proud.

Brooked fixed her challenging gaze on Andrew. 'I win, you kiss her.'

'If I recall correctly, last bet I made like that turned pear-shaped.'

'Maybe this one will too. But then maybe it won't. You're the gambler. Play the odds. Anyway,' she said, gathering up Robert's reins as she dug home. 'I thought you said Robert and I had no chance?'

Grinning, she urged Robert into a canter and rode off. If that didn't get Andrew's competitive juices flowing, nothing would.

With fewer than a dozen competitors, Brooke didn't have to wait long for her round. Andrew drew second position, and as he passed her on the way into the ring he tossed her a 'You're on', leaving

Brooke smiling smugly. Someone had to poke her friends in the right direction, and it may as well be her.

In their attempts to act normal in each other's presence, Chloe and Andrew had become a pair of robots. The teasing, confident banter that had once marked their friendship had been replaced with shyness and uncertainty. But there was something there, a quiet wondering of what might ensue should one of them make a move, and Brooke sensed it as surely as she sensed Robert's rippling eagerness.

A win, and she'd force Andrew to do something about it.

Marchment's untidy but clear round put him into the jump-off, quickly followed by Robert, whose flawless performance pitched Brooke's morale skywards. She shot out of the gate slapping Robert's neck, whooping inside as she poked her tongue out at Andrew, who responded with, 'The carthorse just got lucky!'

Three other clears meant five horses made it through to the final round. Chloe wandered ringside to watch and hold the horses while Brooke and Andrew walked the jump-off course.

'You're toast,' said Brooke as she stood in front of a tall yellow and black upright, looking back at the line. The course designer had cleverly cut the course so that one of the out-of-play fences blocked a turn. Competitors could either ride on its outside and approach the upright square on, which was safe but time-consuming, or cut inside and take the fence at an angle, saving valuable seconds.

'In your dreams,' replied Andrew, tapping his whip against the side of his half chap as he contemplated the same move. 'Marchie will skid round that. Your carthorse doesn't have the turn.'

'Maybe not, but one of his strides is worth two of Marchie's delicate little skips.' And Robert did have the turn. He might be big, but he could spin on a twenty-cent piece. 'Face it, Chiang-man. You're beat.'

'One of the things I've always loved about you, Brooke, was your ability to delude yourself.'

They returned to the horses, Brooke observing closely as Andrew took Marchment's reins from Chloe. The moment their gazes met both looked away before furtively glancing back again; Chloe in her sexy, under-the-lashes manner guaranteed to twist even the most detached of men into knots. Even after Andrew vaulted into the saddle, the dance continued, hesitant and tense with confusion. A flirtation made clumsy by long-term friendship, but building in confidence with each smile, each touch.

Swamped with bittersweet emotion, Brooke mounted and rode away. She was happy for her friends, delighted, but watching them reminded of her of what she and Lachie had briefly enjoyed.

'Doesn't matter, does it, boy?' she whispered to Robert, swallowing the rough edge of her envy. She had more than enough. She had Kingston Downs, Sod, Robert, Elly and Venus. Friends, and a family who loved her. A rich life, one with more happiness than many enjoyed. So her heart was hollow, but it would fill again. One day.

The steward called her name. Brooke trotted to the ring, Chloe wishing her luck as she passed. She stroked her hand down Robert's neck as he broke into an impatient canter. The ground noise faded, overtaken by the sound of Robert's hoofbeats and snorts. She glanced at the course, tracing the jumps and the track in her mind, heart thumping as her excitement grew. Prepared, she saluted the judge and circled one last time.

She lined up the start flags. Immediately, Robert's head went up, his huge body coiling as he snatched at the bit in excitement. Hand on his mane, she leaned forward to whisper into his swivelling ears. 'Come on, Robert, my darling. Time to show everyone how brilliant you are.'

With an ease of her hands and a drop of her seat, he speared through the flags.

Clear over the first, a sharp turn to the left and three strides to the second oxer. Another slide left and a rustic gate. Robert took off and landed without a single check. As they thundered towards the double, such was the horse's power and enthusiasm that Brooke

could have sworn it was Poddy beneath her. Robert bounded over
the double without missing a beat, and when Brooke steered him
inside the jump that Andrew had scoffed she'd never make it
round, he spun as balanced as a ballerina, hurtling over the upright
at an angle so acute Brooke almost took out the wing with her
knee. The second last flew past and though his hind toe tapped the
final fence, they bolted through the finish flags with clear round
and a time flashing on the clock so low it left even Brooke
goggle-eyed.

She trotted back to the edge of the ring feeling like an Olympic
medallist. This was what she lived for. The thrill of competition, the
proof of all the hours she and the horses had put in at home. The roar
of blood as her heart pumped pure exhilaration.

'Carthorse, huh?' she yelled to Andrew in the warm-up area
before sliding off Robert and hugging the blowing horse hard. 'Champion, more like.'

'Holy shit, that was fast!' said Chloe, bounding over to take
Robert's reins and rub his face. 'And he didn't even look like dropping
a rail.'

'I know. He's awesome. And you, Missy, are going to be forever in
his debt for that round.'

'Why?'

She threw a smug look at Chloe. 'I made a bet with Andrew.'

Chloe's eyes widened in astonishment. 'What?'

'If I win he has to kiss you.'

A blush spread across Chloe's face, a secret smile playing around
her mouth as she hugged her arms to her chest. She nodded at the
ring, where Andrew now circled on Marchment. 'Watch.'

But Brooke didn't need to. The sound of the first rail falling was
enough. Andrew had thrown it. Though she rolled her eyes in mock
disgust nothing could stop her smile. The chance Chloe wanted so
desperately was hers, and Brooke couldn't be happier.

She gave her friend a nudge. 'This could be it.'

Chloe looked longingly towards the ring. 'I hope so.'

'Hey,' she said, hugging her. 'You're friends. That's most of the relationship done. The rest is icing.'

———————

Brooke threw a light rug over Robert's sponged and towelled-off body and fastened the buckles. Though she'd tried her hardest to cast it off, the same bittersweet emotion she'd experienced earlier kept swirling through her veins, keeping her fussing over Robert when it wasn't needed. She should be at the clubhouse, enjoying a cold drink and chatter about horses. Instead, she remained by the float, shielding herself from Chloe and Andrew's anticipation-laden glow.

Buckles secure, she patted Robert and wandered around to placate Sod and reward his good behaviour with a dose of attention. Leaning her shoulder against the float, she stroked his cheek and traced lines over his brow. Warmer weather had brought a tinge of gold to the outer edges of his coat, and at certain angles his normal dark colouring appeared an appealing deep bronze. Even the almost black tips of his ears were lighter.

'I'm so proud of you,' she whispered, running her finger down his face to caress the velvety hairs of his muzzle. 'You've been so good, and I bet you miss your friend Poddy, huh?'

As though in answer, Sod's ears began to swivel. Bunting her out of the way, he shuffled sideways, head up, nostrils flaring, ears pricked.

And then he whickered.

No. It couldn't be.

Brooke's stomach flapped and flipped like a silk flag in the wind. She didn't turn around. She *couldn't* turn around. Fear that this was imagination, a manifestation of her wishful thinking, held her rooted, breathless and trembling.

But Sod only whickered for one person.

'Hey, Brooke.'

And figments didn't talk with Lachie's deep gentle voice.

Her fingers fluttered to her mouth, eyes filling with joy and disbelief. Her entire being felt stretched, as though her body already reached for him. She turned, eyes widening as they devoured every magnificent, muscled centimetre of him. From the tips of his sun-lightened hair to the end of his shiny leather boots.

He stood, his hand on Sod's rump, in a pair of dark jeans and a crisp blue and white wide-striped shirt with the sleeves folded neatly up to expose tanned, golden-haired forearms. A hint of stubble flecked a jaw tense with nerves, while his hazel eyes, still surrounded by those gorgeously long lashes, were fixed intently on her.

Not even in her dreams had he appeared so handsome, so strong. So absolutely, perfectly *real*.

'Lachie.' It was the only word she could force past her choked-up throat.

Their gaze remained locked, neither able to break it. A gaze of yearning, of love, of hope.

Lachie slid his palm over Sod's rump and across his back as he moved closer, the horse curling under his touch like an arching cat, leaving Brooke with the irrational urge to push the horse aside and force her body in its place.

'How are you?' he asked.

'Good. And you?'

He smiled in a way that made her stomach somersault. 'Better for being here.' He took another step closer, hand gripping Sod's mane. 'I thought you might be interested to know I've been offered a job with Pitcorthie Rural as an agronomist.'

Brooke pressed her palm to her chest as her heart hiccupped. Pitcorthie. Here. Not Delamere.

'Nancy's offered me room at her place until I find somewhere permanent,' he continued. 'But I wanted to ask you if maybe I could rent the dairy.'

'No.'

His smile dropped. 'Oh.' He looked away.

'I mean, it's not possible. I'm still living there.'

'Why?'

'The cottage . . .' She uselessly raised her hand. 'Memories, you know.'

'Yeah, I know. That's why I'm here.' He dropped his hand from Sod and moved in, huge body shadowing hers, re-emerging smile tickling the edges of his mouth. 'You remember that other-lifetime thing we talked about?'

She nodded, insides singing as his earlier revelation began to sink in. Pitcorthie Rural. Renting the dairy. It was true. Oh God, it was actually true. *Lachie was coming back.*

'I decided I couldn't wait. So here I am.'

'But what about Delamere? Your home, your dream.'

'A wise man once told me that there's a lot to be said for knowing happiness is where your heart lies.' He stroked his knuckles down her cheek. 'And my heart—my everything—lies with you. I love you. I want a future wherever you are. This lifetime. Now. If you'll have me.'

Her eyes filled. 'Of course I'll have you. I love you. Kingston Downs hasn't been the same since you left.' Her arms wrapped around him, and she clung to him like he'd vanish if she let him go.

He buried his face in her neck, holding her with the same intensity as she held him. 'I missed you so much. Nothing seemed right. I kept replaying your phone messages just to hear your voice.'

'I did the same,' she admitted with a sob. 'I kept wandering around the cottage hoping to catch an echo of you. Not an hour passed when I didn't think of you. I thought I'd never recover.'

He cupped her face and kissed her. 'Now you don't have to.'

She sighed deeply, completely lovesick. 'You are the most amazing man, Lachie Cambridge.'

'Not sure about amazing, but I'm the luckiest for having found you.'

'No, I'm the lucky one. Can you kiss me again? I haven't had enough yet.'

'Me neither,' he said, bending his mouth to hers. 'I don't think I ever will.'

At the sound of a slow clap Brooke broke the kiss. Chloe stood near the end of the float grinning at them, Andrew by her side. Catching Brooke's eye, he smiled and gave a subtle nod. Years of friendship gave the gesture meaning. They'd navigated the rapids and survived. It'd be all right.

Chloe ceased her clapping and stepped forward, tears turning her blue eyes even bluer. 'That was so romantic.'

'You watched?'

'Not all of it. We did give you some privacy. But we had to see if Lachie's plan worked out.'

Brooke glanced at Lachie.

'I had to find out from someone where you'd be,' he said with a shrug.

Chloe rubbed Brooke's upper arm. 'I'm so pleased.' She smiled at Lachie. 'For both of you.' She glanced back at Andrew before returning her attention to Brooke. 'Andrew and I are going to head off now. Will you be all right getting home?'

'I'll be fine. You go.' She lowered her voice. 'And good luck.' She watched them saunter off, as Lachie stood with his arms wrapped around her from behind, hugging her protectively as he kissed the top of her head. Brooke sank into him, amazed at how the day had panned out.

'Should we go home, or is there other stuff you need to do?' he asked.

Home. She liked the way he said that.

She turned in his arms, smiling. 'There's plenty of stuff I need to do, but not here.'

'Oh, yeah? Like what?'

She fingered the buttons on his shirt. 'Like, I don't know. Remove all your clothes and kiss you from head to toe and all places in between.'

'I like the sound of all places in between.'

'So I can feel.'

'Okay,' said Lachie, removing his arms. 'We really need to get out of here.' He dug in his pockets for his keys and handed them over.

Brooke looked them, frowning. 'What are these for?'

'For the ute. I can't leave it here.'

'I realise that. But you can drive it.'

'And who's going to drive the float home?'

'Me.'

He blinked and then a delighted smile dawned. 'You can tow the float?'

She nodded, buoyant on a cloud of pride. 'I'm a bit slow and not fully confident yet, but I'm getting better.'

He cupped her face. 'You're amazing, you know that? Amazing, clever, beautiful and talented . . . and I am going to do really, really sexy things to you when we get home.'

'Is that a promise?'

'You bet it is.'

———

'I thought I'd find you here,' said Lachie, settling down next to Brooke in the space between Poddy's and Oddy's graves.

She smiled and leaned her head against his shoulder. Three days Lachie had been back and she still found it hard to believe he was here, that he'd chosen her and Kingston Downs over Delamere. She kept waking in the night, staring at his sleeping form in the darkness, listening to his steady even breaths while her heart raced.

With the cottage closed up, they'd been sleeping in the dairy. Brooke would have been happy to sleep anywhere as long as Lachie was with her, but she'd woken that morning with a nagging feeling of impermanence in her chest. Kingston Downs was meant to be home. It was time they made it one.

He draped an arm across her back. 'Everything okay?'

'Perfect. I just wanted to talk to Poddy.'

He said nothing for a moment and she knew he was digesting her answer in that careful way he had, probably wondering what she needed to discuss with a dead horse. 'You still miss him.'

'Always, but it's not as bad as it was.' She turned her face to Lachie's. 'So is Sam happy now you've made it all official?'

'Seems to be. Although I suspect half of it is because he conned me into signing up for the cricket team. He said I could start Monday if I wanted but I said the following week was fine.' He gave her a squeeze. 'It'll give me more time with you.'

'I'm worn out.'

'No, you're not.' He pressed his lips to her hair. 'Are you sure everything's okay?'

'Positive.'

'So what did you need to talk to Poddy about?'

'You.'

He stiffened. 'Have I done something wrong?'

'Not a single thing. Except . . .'

He shifted to his knees, facing her, searching her face for an answer. 'What?'

Brooke fingered Poddy's grave. Though still young, a few of the white ground roses she'd planted were already in flower.

'What, Brooke?'

She took a deep breath. She thought she knew what his reaction would be, but it was still a gamble. Life was about chances, though. Taking risks was how you made the most of it.

'Move into the cottage with me. Permanently, I mean. I want this to be home for you, for us. Can you do that? Make this real?'

His relieved grin glowed like human sunshine. 'Remember you asked me once if there was anything I couldn't do?'

'Yes. And you replied that you couldn't sing.'

'Still can't.' He moved closer, tilting his head in preparation to kiss her, hand sneaking up her thigh. 'And there are plenty of other things I can add to that list, but believe me, making this real, making you happy, will never be one of them.' His beautiful eyes sparkled with love and the suggestion of good things to come. 'Prepare your-self, Brooke. Because this is forever.'

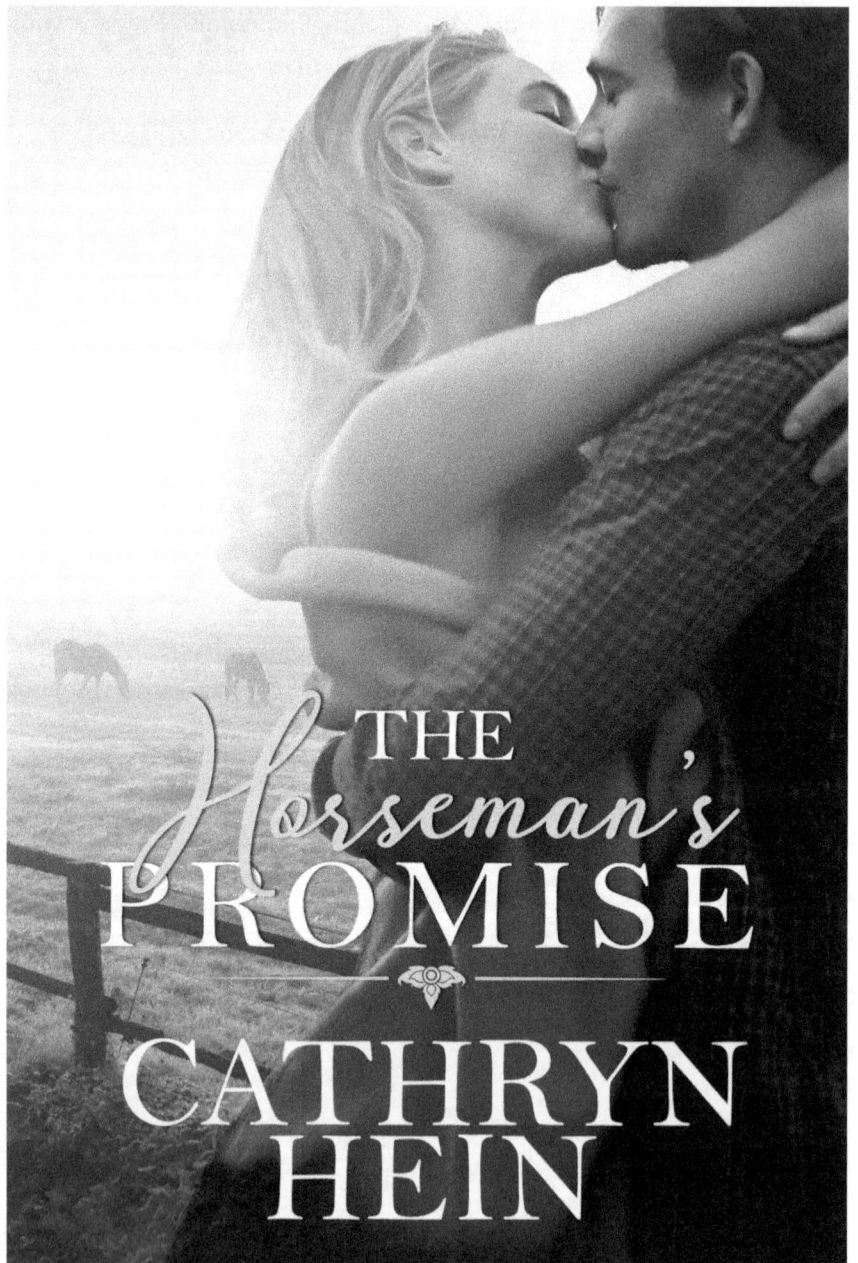

THE Horseman's PROMISE
CATHRYN HEIN

A father with something to hide, a jockey with a taste for blackmail, a man with an agonising secret . . . and a young woman in love, defying them all.

Sophie Dixon is determined to leave her tragic past behind and forge a bright future on her beloved farm. While looking to buy a new horse, she is drawn into her neighbour Aaron's Laidlaw's orbit, despite the bad blood between their families.

As the racing season unfolds, Sophie and Aaron's feelings for each other deepen. But Aaron is torn, haunted by a dark secret he fears can never be forgiven – especially by Sophie.

Sophie believes herself strong, but the truth behind her mother's death will test her strength, and her love, to the limit. She's been broken once. No one wants to see her broken again. Least of all the man who has grown to love her.

An emotional small-town romance about love, loyalty and forgiveness.

Order your copy in ebook or paperback from your favourite retailer today.

DEAR READER

Thank you so much for reading *Heart of the Valley*. I hope you enjoyed Brooke and Lachie's journey to love and happiness. If you did, and you have a few moments, I'd be very grateful if you could leave a rating or few words in review to help others discover my books.

If you'd like to know when my next release comes available plus gain access to exclusive content, news and giveaways, please subscribe to my newsletter via my website.

More information about me and my books, including the inspiration behind *Heart of the Valley*, along with plenty of other fun stuff, can be found at cathrynhein.com.

Web: cathrynhein.com
Facebook: facebook.com/cathrynhein
Twitter: @CathrynHein